"Utilizing his God-given talent
Dr. Nelson exposes Moses' heart t
which is true to the biblical record."

MW01488311

Reverend George W. Robertson, Ph.D.
Senior Minister
Second Presbyterian Church, (PCA), Memphis, TN

"With supreme reverence for the Biblical text and the God to whom it witnesses, Dr. Roger Nelson has retold the story of Moses in an eminently accessible and compelling manner. Utilizing the relatively bare threads of the Biblical narrative, Nelson has carefully and creatively woven them into a rich and engaging tapestry which invites his readers to return to the Bible itself with renewed and deepened appreciation for its human characters and their struggles, as well as for the character of God."

Dr. J. Clint McCann, Evangelical Professor of Biblical Interpretation
Eden Theological Seminary, St. Louis, MO

This book is an effort to convey the Moses of the Old Testament as a unique but very human conveyor of God's message of love and direction for his people. It is deeply researched, carefully referenced. The author makes understandable and clever recalculations of the numbers of Israelites. The scholarship appears impeccable and the text well-written and edited. It is a rewarding read.

Shirley K. Baker
Dean of Washington University Libraries and
Vice Chancellor for Scholarly Resources, (ret.)

This is a beautifully written retelling of the scripture story which fleshes out the day-to-day interaction of God with Moses and the Israelites. It includes some imaginative dialogues between the people as they strive to understand how to follow this inscrutable God. By "bringing to life" the Biblical people and their culture, the author helps the reader feel like YOU ARE THERE.

Bernadette McCarver Snyder
Internationally acclaimed author of
Bible and spiritual books for all ages

A HARROWING JOURNEY

A Historical Novel

J. ROGER NELSON, M.D.

FOX RIDGE PUBLISHING

A Harrowing Journey
J. Roger Nelson, M.D.
Fox Ridge Publishing. LLC

Published by Fox Ridge Publishing. LC, St. Louis, MO
Copyright ©2022 J. Roger Nelson, M.D.
All rights reserved.

Cover and Interior design: Davis Creative Publishing Partners, CreativePublishingPartners.com

Library of Congress Cataloging-in-Publication Data (Provided by Cassidy Cataloguing Services, Inc.)

Names: Nelson, J. Roger, author.
Title: A harrowing journey : a biblical novel / J. Roger Nelson, M.D.
Description: St. Louis, MO : Fox Ridge Publishing. LLC, [2022]
Identifiers: ISBN: 979-8-9858033-0-3 (paperback) I 979-8-9858033-1-0 (hardback) I
    979-8-9858033-2-7 (ebook) I LCCN: 2022906920
Subjects: LCSH: Moses (Biblical leader)--Fiction. I Pilgrims and pilgrimages--Fiction. I Slaves-
    -Egypt--Fiction. I Jews--Fiction. I God (Christianity)--Fiction. I LCGFT: Christian fiction. I
    Historical fiction. I BISAC: FICTION / Christian / Biblical. I RELIGION / General. I FICTION
    / Historical / General.
Classification: LCC: PS3614.E44569 H37 2022 I DDC: 813/.6--dc23
    2022

ATTENTION CORPORATIONS, UNIVERSITIES, COLLEGES AND PROFESSIONAL ORGANIZATIONS: Quantity discounts are available on bulk purchases of this book for educational, gift purposes, or as premiums for increasing magazine subscriptions or renewals. Special books or book excerpts can also be created to fit specific needs. For information, please contact Fox Ridge Publishing, jrogern@sbcglobal.net.

CONTENTS

ACKNOWLEDGMENTS

My heartfelt thanks go to those who helped with the first book, *The God Whom Moses Knew*, and this revision: to Sharon Miller and Carol Shaffer for their seemingly endless typing of the manuscripts; to Catherine Rankovic, Judy Bauer, Dayle Ferguson, and to Kimberly Fletcher for their thorough, painstaking, and surgeon-like editing; to Arthur Harter, Jr., the late Reverend Lewis Thomas, Mrs. Dale Griffin, my daughter Julie Manuele, Ned Durham, Dr. Dan Doriani, and Dr. Bernhard Asen for reading the manuscripts and for their encouragement; to Dr. Clint McCann, Dr. George Robertson, and Bernadette Snyder for their welcome encouragement and gracious endorsements; to Dr. Robertson for his vital, helpful, theological input; and to my dear wife Jan for her valuable corrections and suggestions, and for graciously allowing me the time to write. My thanks also go to Randy Elliott for his friendship. Thanks also to Tibor Nagy, Don Curran, and Steve O'Neal for the patient (and repeated) revisions of our illustrations.

I have deep gratitude to God, my co-author, Who opened the book of Numbers to me, then patiently, over many years, supplied me with an endless stream of surprising, unbidden, pertinent ideas and insights, day and night, to guide the writing of what is, in fact, His book (Psalm 139:4).

A Harrowing Journey

Introduction

Believing there is great drama in the early pages of the Bible, I have taken a moderate portion of the revered text and added appropriate fictionalized dialogue to explore the situations and the actions, the minds, and motives of many of the biblical individuals who lived during those difficult, troublesome days. I have been careful not to alter the facts of Scripture.

In this book, we walk with Moses as he is propelled by a God who is— at first—new and strange to him. But God perseveres, strengthening Moses' vacillating, and often tried, trust in Him. As Moses leads the Israelites from Egypt to Canaan, he encounters challenges from the pharaoh, his own family, his aides and tribal leaders, and conflicts with enemy armies, while battling his own emotions and enticements. He deals with the Israelites (Hebrews) in patient, firm, forbearing ways as he confronts their recurrent fears, doubts, skepticism, and reluctance.

There is frequent speculation among the Hebrews as they try to deal with the unique demands of, and surprising revelations from, this God who is suddenly in their midst. God is determined to establish Himself above all other gods and commands the undivided devotion of His people as He prepares them for short-term goals of Canaanite priesthood and long-term ones as they await the promised Messiah (Deut. 18:15-19).

As the story of Moses unfolds in Scripture, God discloses more of Himself to us, providing stirring, valuable, and, possibly, life-changing insights into His Being.

Although this study is about the Israelites (Hebrews), the apostle Paul wrote of the mystery that God revealed to him, that "the Gentiles are fellow heirs (together with Israel), and fellow members of the body" (Eph. 3:6). "A partial hardening has happened to Israel until the fullness of the Gentiles has come in" (Rom. 11:25). The Exodus trials and lessons, therefore, belong to Christians also. That is good news and bad news. The good: all the experiences with God plus His incredible promises to the Israelites apply to Christians today. But, the bad: all of the responsibilities, all of the commands given to them, all of God's desires for them fall equally on Christians' shoulders.

When gaps are present in Scripture, I have tried to fill them in with considered reasonableness. For example, when Moses kills the foreman of the Hebrew slave gang and the Bible says of the event, he "looked this way and that" (Ex. 2:12) before doing it, an explanation for his premeditated action and its consequences is offered. As another example, in describing the thirty-eight years wandering in the wilderness, I have taken what few facts are present in the Bible and tried to construct a credible, though largely fictitious, account of those years. I have given Moses a military role as suggested by the historian Josephus.[1] That occupation, although not so stated in the Bible, seems appropriate to his life. I have also speculated how Moses discovered he was an Israelite (Hebrew).

Two biblical quotations deserve special mention:

In Deuteronomy 4:2, Moses said, "You shall not add to the word which I am commanding you, nor take away from it, that you may keep the commandments of the LORD your God which I command you."

Proverbs 30:5–6: "Every word of God is tested.... Do not add to His words lest He reprove you and you be proved a liar."

It is not my purpose to add, replace, or write new Scripture, but rather, to offer you a narrative that will engage and re-acquaint you with the vibrant details of this portion of the Bible, and to try to connect some dots. You may wish to return to the original Scriptures with fresh interest and insights, more familiar with the individuals and their roles in unfolding this trying but divinely influenced journey.

Although I have tried otherwise, some ideas gleaned from books read over the years may have been inadvertently incorporated without referencing them. To those authors, I apologize and offer my sincere appreciation for their fine works.

Please note several topics that will help you understand the content and context of this book:

Culture

The time period and locales featured in this book were riddled with idolatry, sexual promiscuity, slavery, and the debasing of women. Although I do not support or condone these practices, I attempted to create scenes and dialogue from Biblical examples that accurately represent the historical context of the time.

Character Profiles
The brief profiles of the leaders and of Balaam are fictional.

The Israelite Travelers
There are a few facts dealing with the numbers of marchers on the long trek from Egypt to Canaan, the Exodus, that cause confusion. The Bible states that there were 603,550 men,[2] or approximately 1,600,000 persons on the march. (603,550 men, approximately 600,000 women, and some 400,000 under twenty years of age. With such a large number, walking in close array, how could they deal with refuse, procreation (thousands were born along the way), birthing, camping, bodily waste, and adequate food and water? If 1.6 million persons walked even 50 abreast, they would stretch back over 30 miles: (1,600,000/50 = 32,000 rows x 5 feet per row = 160,000 feet/5280 [feet/mile] = 30.3 miles). Exodus 14:9 states that Pharaoh and his army "overtook [the Israelites] camping by the [Red] sea." Instead, Pharaoh would have encountered them 30 miles before the sea.

If there were 1.6 million people, it would have taken at least two to three days for the last of the Israelites and animals to reach the sea and cross it, not just one night (Ex. 14:21–24).

Perhaps, as some believe, there was a mistranslation in the numbers of people. In some other evaluations, the estimated revised numbers range from 20-30,000[3] to as low as 6,000.[4] I will use 40,000, although with some reservations, because it seems to fit best with the many events of the journey and also "makes sense of the wonderful works of God on behalf of such a small group."[5] Regardless of the population numbers, the story is still the same.

When large numbers are given in the Bible, I have divided them by 40, i.e., 1,600,000 persons/40,000 persons = 40.

Topography
One more consideration: We must presume that the topography of the Sinai Peninsula was different 3,500 years ago than it is today. The Israelites were able to drive herds of animals across the land with adequate supplies of water to drink, and perhaps grass to eat—a difficult feat, considering my

understanding of today's terrain. The Bible mentions passing through "the great and terrible wilderness, with its fiery serpents and scorpions" (Deut. 8:15) and through "wilderness, through a land of deserts and pits … a land of … deep darkness … a land that no one crossed" (Jer. 2:6). I utilize such descriptions in this book.

On the journey, forests with adequate wood to build dwellings were found at several sites. Since then, God may have destroyed the fruitfulness of the peninsula as He did in the Jordan River Valley, Sodom, and Gomorrah, and as He threatened to do elsewhere if the people remained rebellious.

The exact site of many locations (i.e., Mount Sinai) is unknown, but is approximated in the book.

Language

In what language did God write the Ten Commandments and in what language did Moses write? No one is certain. Hebrew was not a written language until about 1000 BC, long after the Exodus.[6] Written languages before the Exodus were Akkadian, written in dagger-like symbols (2300 BC), Egyptian hieroglyphs (3000 BC), and Proto-Canaanite, the probable precursor of Hebrew.[7] Throughout the book I will refer to "Hebrew language," accepting that it may refer to Akkadian or Pro-Canaanite or some other that only God knows.

The book is fully referenced so the reader can easily find and confirm the described events. Most references are to the *New American Standard Bible* (Reuben Olson, ed., La Habra, California: Foundation Press Publications, publisher for the Lockman Foundation, 1971) as found in the *Ryrie Study Bible, New American Standard Translation,* Charles Caldwell Ryrie, Th.D., Ph.D., Dallas Theological Seminary. Moody Press, Chicago, 1977. A few biblical references are from other translations, and these are noted in the text.

Scripture and Endnote References

Conversations directly quoted from the Bible or closely paraphrased are noted by superscript letters; italics indicate words spoken directly by God. All Scripture citations are listed in the appendix. Superscript numbers identify words or phrases referenced in each chapter's endnotes.

Endnotes

1. Josephus, Flavius. *The Antiquities of the Jews*, translated by William Whiston, A. M., 1987, book 2, chapter 10.

2. "603,550," Num. 2:32.

3. "20-30,000." (*Numbers; The Daily Study Bible Series*. Walter Riggins. The Westminster Press, Philadelphia, 1983, pg.12-14). The word for "one thousand" might just be translated "one battalion" instead.

4. *How many came out of the exodus of Egypt*, Jeff Benner, Ancient Hebrew Research Center. Internet.

5. "small group," "Numbers", Daily Study Bible Series; Walter. Riggins. The Westminster Press, Philadelphia, 1983, pg. 14.

6. A History of the Hebrew Language, Angel Saenz-Badillos, Cambridge University Press, New York, 1996, p. 16-17. Also "How the Hebrew Language Grew", Edward Horowitz, M.A., DRE, Jewish Educational Committee Press, New York, 1960, pp. 12ff.

7. "precursor of Hebrew," The World Book Encyclopedia, World Book Inc. 1990, Chicago. "Sargon."

Tribe	Leader	Profiles
Asher	Pagiel (painter)	Page 117
Benjamin	Abidan (historian)	Page 79
Dan	Ahiezer	N/A
Ephraim	Elishama (archer)	Page 109
Gad	Eliasaph (stone mason)	Page 37
Issachar	Nethanel (bricklayer)	Page 60
Judah	Nahshon (jeweler)	Page 103
Levi	Aaron	N/A
Manasseh	Gamaliel (bricklayer)	Page 36
Naphtali	Ahira (soldier)	Page 155
Reuben	Elizur	N/A
Simeon	Shelumiel (carpenter)	Page 86
Zebulun	Eliab	N/A
		GOD (Page 144)
		Bezalel (Page 206)
		Balaam (Page 277)

From Book of Numbers, Chapter 1

The Israelites (Hebrews—Jews)

Adam and Eve

Cain   Abel   Seth
                    ⋮
            Methuselah (900 years)
                    ⋮
            Noah (120 years)
                    ⋮
            Abram (Abraham) Sara (Sarah)
                    ↓
            Isaac

Esau   **Jacob→ (Israel) 12 sons (the 12 tribes of Israel)**

Reuban   Simeon   Levi   Judah   Joseph   Benjamin   (and Dinah)
                            ↓   **Ephraim   Manasseh**
                            ↓
              Miriam   Aaron   Moses (Zipporah)

Section I
Egypt—Circa 1560 BC to 1480 BC

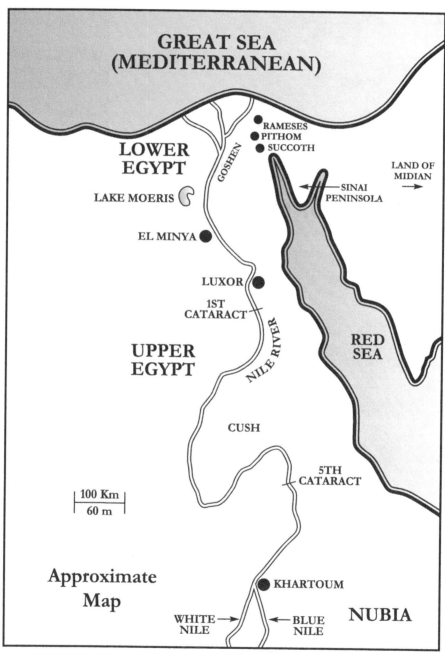

GREAT SEA
(MEDITERRANEAN)

LOWER
EGYPT

GOSHEN

● RAMESES
● PITHOM
● SUCCOTH

LAND OF
MIDIAN

LAKE MOERIS

←SINAI
PENINSOLA→

EL MINYA ●

LUXOR ●

1ST
CATARACT

UPPER
EGYPT

NILE RIVER

RED
SEA

CUSH

5TH
CATARACT

100 Km
60 m

Approximate
Map

● KHARTOUM

WHITE→
NILE

←BLUE
NILE

NUBIA

Chapter 1

A Prince of Egypt Dethroned

The annual torrential summer rains relentlessly battered the tropical forests, swamps, and grasslands high up in southern Nubia (Sudan). In rivulets growing into racing streams, they gouged up large chunks, even small islands, of the vulnerable, sodden jungle soil, carrying it down to deposit it into broadening streams that emptied into the White Nile River. These larcenous waters bore their nutritious booty north where they joined the Blue Nile River flowing up from the southeast, itself swollen by snow-melt from the mountains and by heavy rainstorms of summer and fall—at the mysterious city of Khartoum. From there the conjoined rampaging rivers cascaded over five cataracts, pulverizing its cargo as it tore its way north down into the lowlands where, as the Nile River, it overflowed its banks, flooding the lower valley for several miles on either side of the river to a depth of ten to fifteen feet from August to October. The rich clay of the land bonded with the abundant water-borne nutrients producing Egypt's extravagant fertility. When the waters receded, lush grasses awaited animal grazing, and elsewhere, seeds planted grew luxuriously, producing huge crops and great wealth for Egypt. Mud dams and levees allowed people to live in cities on the eastern edges of the Delta. As the prosperous agricultural giant of the world, she was the envy of her neighbors, some of whom sought to rule her. One was the ambitious king of Nubia.

Two years earlier his army had conquered and held the upper lands of Egypt and a portion of the more northern lower lands, including the city of El Minya, making its capital in the city of Luxor. At this time, the king sought to annex more of the lowlands, so he launched his forces northward. They were met by the Egyptian army, and an intense battle ensued.

From a sandy hillock, Moses, Commander of the Egyptian Army,[1] and his aides surveyed the weaving battle lines of hundreds of soldiers locked in hand-to-hand fighting. There were chariots on both the Nubian and Egyptian sides of the battle line west of the Nile River. Some were stationary with archers skillfully dispatching arrows toward enemies, others ferried men from place to place, and a few carried wounded officers to safety. Moses was occupied with sending couriers with orders by chariot or on foot to various parts of the line as needed.

*****

By midday, the Egyptian army, being outnumbered, began to yield, and in two hours their soldiers were retreating. Suddenly, a soldier rode up to Moses on horseback and, trying to control himself, called out, "O Supreme Commander, I was fighting on our left flank and commander Arthus has been killed by an arrow, and his troops are falling back even faster than the rest of our soldiers. The Nubians are overwhelming us, sir."

"Make ready my chariot," Moses ordered an aide.

"What are you going to do?" asked the soldier.

"Stop this rout!"

He mounted the two-horse, two-man chariot with the driver before him. Then he motioned two archers with their chariots to ride on either side of him. "To the left flank!" he shouted as his chariot rolled down the hill, leaping ahead of the other two and past the first of the retreating soldiers while Moses shouted to the soldiers, "Steady, men! For Egypt! For the gods!"

As he swung left along the battle line, he drifted into a group of retreating men—a company of slave-soldiers—and their attackers. A Nubian spotted Moses' chariot and threw a spear, which struck the unprotected neck of his right horse, severing its carotid artery. It faltered just as the left wheel of the chariot rolled up over a crumpled body, overturning the vehicle and throwing the two men out. Moses landed on his head, slightly dazing him, while his driver was thrown upon him. Four Nubians, noting the royal chariot, seized the opportunity and raced toward Moses, brandishing drawn swords. An enemy charioteer also swung his vehicle around and joined in the attack, shooting an arrow toward the two fallen men. It struck and killed the driver. Three Hebrew slave-soldiers quickly ran to intercept them, one leaping onto the chariot to skewer the charioteer just before being stabbed in the back by one of the attackers.

Yelling and wide-eyed, the two slaves fought as if possessed, skillfully wielding sword and axe. They killed two of the attackers as Moses recovered, rose to his knees, unsheathed his battle-axe from his waist band, and hurled it at short range. It split the skull of the third Nubian fighter. One of the Hebrews received a penetrating chest wound but managed to fall upon the last Nubian and, with one stroke, hacked him to death. As the slave fought vainly for breath, he caught the eye of Moses nearby and tried feebly to raise a hand in salute before dying.

Two Egyptian charioteers rode up to right Moses' chariot and cut the dead horse loose. Moses retrieved his axe and mounted one of the chariots to return to his command post.

The event was witnessed by many, and word spread quickly along the Egyptian line of the heroism of the slaves. Their courage spurred the men to not only stabilize the line but to begin to drive the Nubians back. The Egyptians on the right outflanked the enemy, netting a large number of captives.

Within hours, the Egyptian forces had driven the enemy back into their own land. Darkness stopped their advance, barely within sight of the city of El Minya. In the morning, the reinforced Egyptian army stormed and conquered that city.

Both sides suffered significant losses and Moses had no taste to go further. After several days of organizing and assigning the army to control the area, a small force was ordered to follow Moses back north to the capital city of Rameses.

*****

On the march north, Moses rode in his repaired chariot with a fresh horse and with a Commander of One Thousand who rode with him.

"Did you see the scrape I was in?" Moses asked.

"No, but I heard about it."

"I realize that it is what they are trained for, to give their lives for an officer in battle. All of our men fight well, but I have never seen anything quite like the zeal of those slave-soldiers. Such passion, such fury. They saved my life. See that they are commended, even those posthumously."

"Yes, sir."

*****

As they rode on, Moses' thoughts dwelled on the large number of Hebrew slaves that Egypt commanded. He had never given much thought to slaves in general, believing that, with exceptions, they were merely low-class objects meant to perform the menial tasks for the pharaoh—except for those in the military. Those relatively few men had undergone far harsher training than his regular soldiers. They had either been conscripted or had chosen to risk their lives in battle rather than suffer at the hands of their own foremen and the Egyptian guards. They had always accounted themselves well.

As they approached Rameses, he could not rid himself of the gaze of that dying soldier; it was one of reverence. Moses' eyes squinted. He knew gratitude, but such devotion—and by a slave. He felt awkwardly humbled.

Concern for the coming reception by Pharaoh interrupted his thoughts.

*****

"Here he comes," a tall peasant shouted from the midst of the throng lining the street in the city of Rameses as the commander led his victorious army up toward the palace.[1] Two forty-year-old men stood in the crowd. One leaned on a crutch, supporting his only leg. The other stared through his disfigured countenance; a scar slashed his face from nose to ear under an empty eye socket. They both grimaced as Moses proudly passed by on his large, black horse, riding erect, wearing a purple robe thrown over his uniform. Following him in procession were his own chariot, bedecked with orange and black streamers and flags, then six rows of paired flag-only decorated chariots of his Royal Guard, then ten rows of streamers-only paired chariots of his chosen officers. A charioteer manned each vehicle drawn by a muscular, black Syrian horse. Finally, there was a marching detachment of Egyptian troops and a selected platoon of slave-soldiers. The wounded, carried in chariots or on handheld stretchers, had already been delivered to their own homes.

"Look at him! Pompous as ever. Not a scratch on him," grunted the one-eyed man. "The gods look favorably on him. I hope one day he'll get what he deserves."

"He's no different from the other officers who expect so much," said his companion, both members of the trusted few, army slaves with proven loyalty who were permitted to observe the victory march. "They were harder on us Israelite troops. I'll never forget those long, hot marches Moses ordered to 'toughen us up.'"

"He was simply mean to us," the first man sneered. "I have seen Moses whip a poor slave-soldier himself, for a minor infraction. Granted, if we deserted or fought with hesitancy or fear, we deserved to be punished."

An old man kneeling next to them chimed in, "But men, give him credit. He usually wins the battles. Once, when I fought with unusual courage, my family received several pieces of furniture for our small home and my brother was given three days off from work."

"A small recompense, old man, and one that I never saw," said the one-legged man. "He has a smoldering contempt for us former shepherds."

As Moses came to the palace gates, he halted his troops. They stood at attention, receiving the adulation of the mixed crowd of Egyptian and segregated slave families, while women showered the soldiers with fragrant flowers. Many ran up to foot soldiers and fed handfuls of freshly-baked pastries into their hungry mouths, at times embracing the men.

Moses permitted this display for a while, basking in his commanding position. He reveled in the moment. The soldiers fought well, following his orders and maneuvers, but the victory belonged to him. Then he left his troops and approached a large group of women who had been corralled by his officers. Some were sobbing. Moses addressed them somberly from his horse. "Your sons fought and died valiantly under my leadership. They are honored by me and by the gods of war." He made a small salute to them and returned to his position at the head of the column.

He led this representative force through the palace gates into the spacious arena to the accompaniment of a seated band playing victorious Egyptian marches on lyre, castanets, drums, trumpets, and flutes. He wheeled his horse before the waiting dignitaries gathered in Pharaoh's reviewing stand. Despite moderate cheering, this reception was more reserved. Pharaoh—accustomed to success in the victories that expanded the borders of Egypt, or maintained them, and in the skirmishes that quelled riots against his harsh rule—was nevertheless elated over this latest victory over Nubia. He stood and congratulated Moses and the soldiers on their valor, loyalty, and skill.

After the brief speech, Moses dismounted, climbed the steps toward Pharaoh, and bowed. With set jaw, he grimly gave a tally of the land conquered, the slaves captured, and of his own troops lost. Two of the ladies seated near Pharaoh eyed him flirtatiously. Moses bowed once more to Pharaoh, mounted his horse, and led his troops out through the palace gates before dismissing them. He chose to ride to his own home.

*****

In the solitude of his large sleeping quarters, Moses' suppressed anger erupted. He threw off his outer garments and stormed into his study. Although Pharaoh and a few of his priests were the chief communicators with their gods, Moses, in his position, had a few of his own. Wheeling around to the small array of statues lining one wall, he strode to the two-foot-high image of Re,[2] the sun god, picked it up, and hurled it across the room. It shattered against the wall into several pieces. "You have failed me!" His eyes scanned his other idols, lifeless representations of gods, some of wood, others of ceramic or bronze. Picking up the lion-headed Anuke,[2] the goddess of war, in both hands, he raised it over his head and then fell to his knees. The bronze figure slipped from his grasp as he dropped his head into his hands. "You, Anuke, are capricious, allowing them to die. Arthius and Rexor, one a Commander of Thousands and one a Commander of Two Hundred and Fifty, my friends from my youth. We rose in the ranks together, fighting side by side. We drank together, boasting of our conquests. We knew each other's souls. And you let them be killed in one battle, by the shafts of two cruelly aimed arrows. What a waste! And now you leave me to live in sorrow."

Many minutes passed before he arose and looked at his collection of graven images. "Was Nubia—the land of vicious warriors—worth such a price?" he wondered. Exhausted, he fell into his bed and slept until early evening.

A familiar set of knocks on the door of his living quarters roused him. "Come in," he said, looking at the disarrayed statues with no remorse.

His twelve-year-old aide, Mateo, entered to dress his master for the banquet honoring him that night. Without a word, Mateo returned Anuke and carefully collected the broken pieces of Re.

*****

While Moses walked to the feast provided by Pharaoh, he felt his energy return as he recalled the public display and the homage paid him that day. Entering the Great Hall, he acknowledged many greetings, some exultant, some more reserved, before seating himself to the left of Pharaoh, knowing that his younger cousin would sit to the pharaoh's right. It was a table of palace dignitaries and his high-ranking officers.

Moses looked out over the gathered assemblage, smugly savoring his self-importance, enhanced by his latest victory. He did indeed live a charmed life. He had been raised as an only child and enjoyed all of the privileges of the palace with his cousins. His education had been supervised by his mother. Always obedient and conscientious, he surpassed all others in learning, including mastering mathematics, astronomy, science, literature, the arts, and the martial disciplines. He became proficient in interpreting both the older hieroglyphics and the newer hieratic writings. He excelled in physical games and became an accomplished equestrian. In his teens, he showed his mettle in battle and became commander of a regiment at sixteen and of the entire army by twenty-five. And now, fourteen years later, as he surveyed the revelers, he knew that the glory and accolades afforded him were well-deserved.

As the meal began, several of the officers at Moses' table offered toasts to him. "To our mighty Moses." "To our courageous leader." "To the man whose strategy won the hard-fought victory." A Captain of the Troop, quietly seeking to replace one of the fallen commanders, walked up from another table and said, "Commander, I owe my life and the lives of my men to your deployment of us. By it we secured the right flank as we defeated the Nubians."

Moses said courteously, "It was a well-conceived plan and you executed your part well. Thank you, Captain." With that he turned to continue eating.

The meal was heavy with succulent beef and lamb, flavorful fish, many of the vegetables grown in this bread basket of the world, and luscious desserts. Endless pitchers of beer and wine were poured to overflow repeatedly empty glasses.

Other friends and officials dropped by Moses' table to express their congratulations on the victory and condolences for the loss of his two close friends. Moses accepted their comments, warmly to some with bits of conversation, others with a nod and a handshake.

Midway through the party, the guests were entertained first by six energetic male tumblers, then by four scantily clad, female dancers who performed their sensual moves to the accompaniment of musicians playing enthusiastically on drums, lyre, and pipes.

As the evening progressed, more and more of the men were sharing their drinks with willing ladies and singing rollicking military and Egyptian songs. Some were dancing, the more boisterous ones bouncing across the floor with a partner. Some fell asleep in their chairs while others wound upstairs with their ladies, arm in arm, to one of many rooms made available to them.

Moses denied the advances of a beautiful, young Egyptian woman who could not hide her disappointment at his rebuff. He was not in a celebratory mood, still grieving his friends. He had never married, being unable to find a woman to challenge his ever-active mind.

One time, Pharaoh engaged Moses and his cousin in conversation. Pharaoh said, "You know my concern about the burgeoning number of the Israelite slaves and their potential threat to us. Should an enemy attack our northern cities, they might join themselves to those who hate us and fight against us and depart from the land."[a]

His cousin answered, "We assure that they are well-fed. We manage to keep the men under control, employing them in shepherding our herds and flocks, in the menial tasks of brickmaking, building, and such. Working them in the heat tires them and keeps them occupied. The labor culls out the weaker and the old."

Pharaoh asked, "What is their attrition rate?"

"Fourteen of them died working last month."

Moses said, "Are they not easily replaced? Besides, don't we have too many anyway?"

"Yes," said Pharaoh. "Of greater concern to me are the numbers of those slaves serving in your army, Moses. How are they performing, and do you still think that it is wise to use them?"

"They are valuable, tenacious, well-disciplined fighters," said Moses. "We have carefully selected those whom we trust, and they have sworn allegiance to you. Our officers keep a close eye on them, since they are housed in separate barracks. They are only issued weapons just before a battle, and they must return them afterwards."

"Are you sure we do not lose weapons to them?"

"Indeed, some are killed in battle so that the accounting is less than perfect, but our supply officers are very careful."

"See that they are."

Moses felt unusually tired. Before most of the people left the party, he excused himself and walked across the grounds to his home. As he entered, Mateo met him at the door. "Good evening, Master."

Moses had a special fondness for the boy, having plucked him from among the slaves. During a parade, Mateo had burst out of the viewing crowd and run up to Moses' chariot, just for the excitement of touching it. Instead of dispatching him, Moses, impressed by his courage and impulsiveness, grabbed him and pulled him into his chariot. He held him in front of him, looked into his eyes, and liking what he saw, kept him thereafter as his manservant, much to the delight of the young boy.

The lad assisted his master to prepare him for his evening rest. Soon after, Moses sank down into his bed and was overcome by sleep.

*****

That night, in a small, one-room adobe hut in the Hebrew enclave, two figures sat by candlelight facing each other, heads bent forward in intimate conversation. "I am old and frail, my son" confided the once robust woman, Jochebed. "The sufferings of our people have become intolerable. Remember that our God promised father Abraham that we would be freed after living in Egypt for four hundred years,[b] but a prophetess changed that to four hundred and thirty years,[c] the last number of years in slavery. I am told that we have been here over three hundred and ninety years. The time, either ten or forty years, is not far off. We must begin to make preparations.

"When Moses was a baby, I was told that the princess would keep his true identity hidden. And out here only our small family knows. I have believed all along that Moses' authority was somehow given by God, and that he will have something to do with our release from slavery. Since I may not live another year, it is time to begin to woo him to our side. We can do it through a series of messages. It may take a while for him to get used to being Hebrew. Aaron, you must begin to get notes to him."

"If we do, we must be secretive," said Aaron. "If it becomes known that Pharaoh has permitted one of us to rise to such power, Moses' safety might be jeopardized."

"How can we get it to him? Who in the palace is most trusted and loyal to Moses?"

"It is his servant boy, Mateo," said Aaron. After thinking for a moment, he added, "I have learned that he enters the marketplace every week or two, the midweek morning, to buy special pastries that Moses likes."

"Confront him there," she said.

*****

After working all the next day, Aaron began his task. He had taught himself to read and write the Egyptian script. He wrote on one of two stolen, palm-sized, flat pieces of papyrus, "All Hebrew males are circumcised. Your brother." He then clasped them together as hands in prayer and sealed them with two drops of hot wax, one to the top and one to the bottom. "For Moses," he inscribed on the front.

*****

Moses slept soundly but awoke puzzling over why his mind should be concerned about the Israelites slaves—but it was. His thoughts picked up where they had left him when nearing Rameses. Slaves from other countries were simply the booty of victory. But how did the Israelites become slaves? Until now he had no concern for the masses of them since their care was the responsibility of others.

While growing up he had read voraciously of history, but there had been nothing written about the Israelites—nothing. He had taken it for granted that they were an inferior class of people and let it go at that. But where did they come from?

*****

After breakfast, he donned his regal attire and walked with Mateo to the large chapel off of the sanctuary to host a small service honoring his two fallen comrades. He entered and was ushered down the aisle between rows of seated army officers and the families of the deceased. Moses seated himself with several members of his own family in the front row. One empty, symbolic casket was on the floor on each side of the rostrum in front of him.

At this time, the bodies of the two officers were in the seventy-day process of being mummified by skilled morticians, a procedure reserved for distinguished persons.[3] When completed, the bodies would be interred into sarcophagi located in the periphery of the sanctuary where three other fallen officers of similar rank had been laid out. That would be a grander memorial service officiated by the priest who, during the ceremony, would utter a spell, then touch the sarcophagus with a blade, symbolically opening it, which ensured that the mummy would be able to breathe and speak in the afterlife.[4] That ceremony would be attended by those gathered, plus the pharaoh, other dignitaries, and most of the officers.

During the present service, one priest representing the god of war spoke from the rostrum, followed by Moses, who eulogized each in a prepared speech. The priest of the god of the heavens finished the service, and then the mourners filed out.

After the service, Moses had lunch with the guests in Pharaoh's dining room. He tolerated conversations filled with small talk before returning home.

*****

Through Mateo, Moses arranged to meet with an old Hebrew man—a man that had been Moses' mentor when he wanted information about the Israelite slaves. The man had also taught Moses the verbal Hebrew language, a skill that proved a distinct advantage when dealing with the slaves who served in his army. How easily he had learned Hebrew!

Mateo guided the bearded old man with one half-closed eye and a deep, vertical crease between his eyebrows into Moses' library, then withdrew. At Moses' invitation, the man hobbled over and took a chair opposite him.

Moses put him at ease immediately. "You have been a reliable mentor to me regarding issues that have to deal with the Israelite slaves, and the information you have given me has always been helpful. Now I have a few questions for you. In a recent battle, several Hebrew soldiers saved my life, two even died for me.

"Is it true that your people came voluntarily into bondage with us?"

"No."

"Then how did it occur?"

"It is a long story, but I will give you the highlights, Master. Jacob, father Abraham's grandson, sired eleven sons and a daughter. He loved the eleventh, Joseph, more than the rest, the twelfth had not been born yet. While living in Canaan, Jacob foolishly gave Joseph a beautiful coat, one of many colors. His brothers grew jealous of him and sold him to a traveling caravan headed for Egypt. They, in turn, sold him to a captain of the Egyptian guards. Soon he was imprisoned on a trumped-up charge leveled by the captain's wife. There he discovered after a number of years that God had gifted him with the ability to interpret dreams.[d] When Pharaoh had a series of troubling dreams, Joseph was the only one who could interpret them. From the dreams, he was able to forecast seven years of plenty followed by seven years of drought. Pharaoh appointed Joseph to deal with the situation. As things progressed, the pharaoh later appointed Joseph to be his Prime Minister. It is said that Joseph even had his own chariot, riding just behind the pharaoh's."[5]

Moses interrupted, "Chariots in Egypt that early?"

"There is evidence that chariots may have been here centuries before that.

"Joseph stored up grain and food during the plenty years, then, during the years of drought, sold it to his people, then other nations—first for money, then for land, then for men indentured into slavery for their food. Egypt became a very wealthy, powerful nation. When his family of shepherds, seventy in all, came to Egypt seeking food during the drought, about three hundred and ninety years ago, Joseph graciously reconciled with them, and Pharaoh treated them well. He settled them and their animals in the lush grazing land of Goshen, in the eastern Nile delta.

"After Joseph died, a new pharaoh ascended the throne. That pharaoh, perhaps being of foreign extraction, did not know Joseph. He was fearful that the huge numbers of Israelites might rebel against him, so he began to harass them. Over the years, he had them registered separately and made them wear identifying necklaces; then he increased their taxes, confiscated some of their best animals, made Egyptian the mandatory language of the land, and rallied his people to persecute them. Another pharaoh succeeded him and continued the harassment. The next pharaoh became so fearful of them that he appointed taskmasters over them to afflict them with hard labor and finally enslaved them, as they are today."

"How do you think they are treated?"

"Their shepherds and artisans, fairly well. The rest of us are forced to work very hard, very long hours in the sun, but we are well-fed. We have our own humble dwellings and can raise our own families. If one of us becomes rebellious, he is beaten by foremen, but that is not too often," he lied, fearing further punishment if he dared utter how frequently they were struck. "A repeat offender might … disappear," he added softly.

"Your counsel is appreciated," said Moses, ignoring his last words. "I have one more question. We have idols to our gods, to Horus, to Osiris, to Anuket, and Hapi. What does the idol to their god look like?"

"Our God prohibits the making of idols."

"Why?"

"He is an active Spirit, so magnificent, so powerful, yet so loving that it would be blasphemous to consider that any idol could represent Him."

"So, he is to remain … invisible?"

"Yes."

"That will be all."

The mentor stood and departed.

*****

During the next week, Moses provided detailed reports and accountings to Pharaoh and his staff, visited wounded officers, accepted the final tally of his own casualties, interrogated several of his prized captives, and attended another banquet in his honor, while low-level officers relegated captives to various slave gangs.

*****

Meanwhile, Aaron proceeded with his plan, utilizing a privilege offered to very few men. The descendants of the twelve sons of Abraham's grandson, Jacob (Israel), the twelve tribes of Israel, each proudly carried the name of their forefathers: "I am a Levite, I am a Judahite," or a "Reubenite," and so forth. Each tribe elected a man to represent them in rare meetings with the Egyptian masters and in clandestine meetings among themselves. Aaron was the representative of the tribe of Levi, Jacob's third son.

The twelve men, as well as the Egyptian-appointed master foremen of the sons of Israel, were paid a paltry sum each month, as long as they remained obedient to the Egyptian government, maintained order among the slaves, satisfied quotas, and carried out their mandates.

In a further attempt to encourage cooperation, their Egyptian masters rewarded each tribal leader and master foreman with the privilege of going to the Egyptian market once each month to purchase desired items.

Aaron chose the first midday morning of the next week to go to the market.

*****

Early that morning, Mateo and a guard took his chariot to the marketplace to buy a few personal items for Moses and items for his library. They were moving toward a booth with his leather pouch when Aaron, his face and hair shrouded with rags except for his eyes, quickly stepped out from behind a small crowd and stood before Mateo, thrusting the pages into the boy's hands. Aaron said, "Pardon me, I have a confidential message for your master." He quickly turned and was lost in the crowd.

The boy stared at the papers in damped surprise since anonymous requests for leniency toward a slave had been slipped to him before. The guard who accompanied Mateo made a delayed move toward the bold messenger, but Aaron had disappeared.

They walked to their usual booths, purchased the required items, returned to the chariot, and rode to one of the entrances that led into the large slave quarters, west of the city.

*****

Extending far to the north and south and west of a road paralleling the Nile were many hundreds of small houses, adobe huts, and tents of the Israelite slaves with guard towers dotted at intervals. Companies of guards roamed the paths winding through these enclaves. Escape attempts by the slaves were rare since they would provoke vicious retribution on family members and tribes by the Egyptian soldiers.

This was the fertile Land of Goshen where the Hebrew shepherds, with their cattle, sheep, and goats, had been peacefully settled when they arrived from Canaan centuries earlier. As years went by, they multiplied greatly and were at first hired by Pharaoh as shepherds of his large herds and flocks. When the Israelites were finally enslaved, many of them were assigned to continue that work in Goshen, while most were used elsewhere as laborers.

The two men dismounted, walked through a gate and past a knowing guard, then continued some thirty paces to a small hut before which an old woman was seated on the ground. A small sample of the halvah candy that she made from a special recipe was lying before her on a cloth as an advertisement, candy that Moses craved. She would trade small bags of it for any item she could get, such as a colored cloth for her hair, a spool of thread, a leather thong for her shoes, or a rare item of food for her family.

Mateo liked the old woman who made the candy, so he always went in person to her hut every other week for Moses. "O Mateo, you are so handsome today. How is your master?" she would always say.

When Mateo arrived, she arose, took his leather pouch, went inside where it was cooler and where the candy was kept, placed a bag of it in the pouch, and exited. Mateo, as was his custom, gave her a small coin, took the bag, thanked her, and left.

*****

They returned to the palace grounds and Moses' home where they found Moses in his library. The boy knocked, was invited in, entered with a short bow, and told of his encounter in the market. He laid the filled pouch on a table next to Moses and handed him the sealed sheets. Moses studied the cover—perfect script. It must have been written by an older man since the last two pharaohs had outlawed formal schooling for Hebrew children. "How old would you say the man was?" he asked.

"About your age, sir."

He walked to a table where a small candle burned, held the edges carefully over it, melting the sealing wax, and separated the pages. He read the note to himself and frowned.

"They are all circumcised. So what? It must be a religious rite. But why tell me?" he wondered. "Egyptians rarely are. Or does he know something about me? How could he know that I was circumcised unless he saw me when we were children? I had occasionally considered that about myself. As boys, swimming nude in the Nile, only a few had the same mark. They explained that their parents had it performed to decrease their sexual lusts. My mother said I had abundant foreskin, that was all. But 'ALL Hebrews are circumcised.' What does this message mean? Am I to doubt my mother's word? Is the man trying to tell me that I am Hebrew? Nonsense." He sat down in his chair.

"No, I am Egyptian, the princess' son, born and raised in the palace. Raised, anyway. I don't know where I was born; I remember nothing of those first few years. And he signed it 'Brother.' I have no brother … that I know of.

"What did the man look like who gave this to you?" Moses asked.

"He was a bit shorter and thinner than you, and agile. His face was partly covered," replied Mateo.

"Did he have an accent?"

"Slight. I have had little contact with them, but I wondered if he could be … Hebrew?"

"Hebrew!" Moses exclaimed.

"I—I'm not sure."

"Nothing more?"

"No, sir."

Moses realized that it would be fruitless to go to the market and look for him. "Tell me if you remember anything more about him. If you see him again, invite him to see me. But do not let him get away. Now go."

Moses reread the message. "Circumcision—Hebrew—accent—brother." Is the man delivering a message about an Egyptian brother or is he implying that he, a Hebrew, is my brother?"

He paced the floor, turning thoughts over in his mind. Then he sat by a window and stared blankly outside. He wished to dismiss the note as nothing but a prank, but was unable to. "Someone is playing a harsh game with me. He wants me to doubt who I am, to wonder, 'Could I possibly have come from a Hebrew family?' Or did my father have a child—me—by a Hebrew mistress? Ridiculous."

*****

Dinner that night in the palace was with Pharaoh, his mother and aunt, two of his cousins, several of Pharaoh's staff, and a few of Pharaoh's friends. The meal was sumptuous, but a nagging concern about the note undermined his concentration.

During the dinner, a cousin asked, "Moses, tell us about the Nubian campaign."

"The battles were intense," Moses said, "yes, and our soldiers fought valiantly. The Nubian forces were well organized, as usual."

"How many days did it take?"

"The war lasted eight days."

"They had invaded our southern border, isn't that correct?"

"That is right."

"Were you able to drive them out?"

"Yes, and we continued to occupy their land, even conquering El Minya."

Conversation was halting. Previously, Moses would have included all of these questions in a flowing description of the engagements, possibly the tactics and the most successful regiments. He would have explained the factors leading up to the death of his commanders. Some of those details only surfaced after more questions that night.

When the evening was through, he returned home and retired. As he lay in bed, he determined to find out what he could about his alleged brother. He slept a deep sleep that night and awakened refreshed.

*****

Life was busy for Moses during the next ten days, being absorbed in routine military matters, staying in touch with the welcomed calm along Egypt's southern border, writing reports to the pharaoh, reviewing his troops, keeping up his physical workouts and skills, and enjoying well-prepared meals while eschewing the lasciviousness of the palace. He was often disturbed as he thought of the written message, yet was uncertain of his next move.

*****

At his hut two days later, Aaron wrote another message on a scrap of papyrus, "Moses, you are Hebrew—as we are. May our God guide you. Your brother." He walked silently to the small house of a Hebrew artisan, assigned to the Egyptian woodworking shop, who had secretly cobbled together a small, wooden box and a lid for him. He put the new message into the box along with a thumb-sized wooden turtle that featured a few flecks of broken, colored glass for its eyes. His father Amram had carved duplicate pieces for Moses and him when Moses lived with them. "Did Moses still have his?" he wondered. "I pray that he does," as the artisan sealed the lid with pitch.

*****

Two days later, Mateo and the guard finished their purchases at the market and chose to ride their chariot to pick up the halvah pastries. They parked, passed by the guard, and walked toward the familiar hut.

Jochebed had been waiting hopefully, out of sight near the gate, and was delighted when she saw them enter.

Mateo walked to the candy woman's hut where she greeted them. She went inside, inserted the candy into his pouch, and walked out. Mateo gave her a coin and left.

As Mateo and the guard were approaching the gate, Jochebed, sitting on the ground facing away from them, slowly rose and bowed to Mateo. "O Most Honorable Servant, my grandson serves in the army under your master Moses. I am so proud. In appreciation, my husband has made a small gift for your master," as she handed him the box.

"Who are you?" Mateo asked, accepting the box.

"My name is Jo," she said. "I am of no account and have no right being this close to you. Forgive me," as she turned.

"Wait. What is in the box?"

"Only a small carving my husband made. For Moses' eyes only." She began to shuffle away.

"Shall I stop her?" the guard asked.

"No," said Mateo, placing the box in his pouch. "This is but a simple, harmless gift from a kind, old woman." He was not overly surprised at the box. Such gifts were rare but well-meant while he was in the slave quarters.

They returned to Moses' home and to the library door. A knock was followed by an "Enter." Mateo placed the pouch on a table. Then as Moses began to empty it, he told of the encounter with the woman near the gate.

Moses picked up the box and shook it, causing a faint rattle. "Take it to the carpenter to open, then come back."

The carpenter loosened the lid of the hand-sized box with a few taps of a hammer. He remarked as he looked inside, "There is a message inside and a carved turtle, a very nice one." Mateo glanced at them then replaced the lid loosely and returned to Moses' library, handing him the box.

"How … how could anyone have stolen my turtle?" Moses exclaimed as he opened the box and picked up the carving. Then he saw the scrap of papyrus, picked it up, and read the message. Stunned by both, he placed them on a table, walked to an open bookcase in the corner of the room, and reached up to retrieve a dark, squat, wide-mouthed ornamental vase from the top shelf. He was surprised as he reached in and felt *his* turtle! He drew it out and returned to the table. He took one in each hand and turned them over, looking intently at them. The new one was an exact replica of his—both hand-carved with a tiny fleck of colored glass imbedded in each eye socket! He had never seen another like it before. Where had this mate come from? And where had he gotten his as a child?

"Maybe this is not a trick. The turtle is real, and no one knows I have it except mother. She couldn't be involved. Did my 'brother' or could 'our father' have carved them both? A Hebrew father? No!"

26

He looked at the message again. "Their god? But what god? Guide me? As if their god speaks to them!" For most of his life he had spoken to and prayed to his array of Egyptian gods for things he wanted. He needed rain, he prayed to the rain god who gave him rain—with some exceptions. Before battle, he prayed for victory to the god of war and was given it—with exceptions. The goddess of love satisfied him—also with exceptions.

But never had a god imparted any message to him or tried to influence him. Had he ever heard of a god speaking to a person? Then he remembered that during one of their sessions, the mentor had said that one of their gods had spoken to their patriarch, Abraham, once. Moses had brushed that off as a fable then. But was it? He must know.

"This alleged brother of mine is disturbing me. If he is a bastard Egyptian son of the pharaoh, he could safely confront me in person. Not so if he is Hebrew; if the members of the palace knew, we might both be in danger. If he is my brother, is the old woman—my mother?! What do they want from me? I must find her … and him."

He suddenly remembered that Mateo was still in the room.

"Tell me about the woman," he said.

"Old, I'd say she was about seventy, with a prominent nose. Surely, she is Hebrew."

"Go back immediately and see if you can locate her. If you can, bring her here. If you cannot, find out everything you can about her," he said to Mateo.

*****

Mateo and the guard rode back to the gate, dismounted, and entered. He questioned the guard, several other women nearby, even the halvah woman. Those who admitted they had seen her all agreed that they did not know her, that she must have come from a different section of the compound. Mateo offered a sizable reward for any information, but no one accepted.

*****

When Moses heard the news, he was distraught, dismissing Mateo with the order to return to the market the next day and interrogate people again. And to call the mentor back.

*****

The next day Mateo's visit to the market produced no further information about the woman.

* * * * *

Two afternoons later, the mentor arrived, and Mateo brought him into the library.

Moses, seated at his desk, said, "Thank you for coming on such short notice," and offered him a chair next to his.

"It must be urgent," the mentor said.

"On your last visit, you explained how the Israelites became slaves. Mentor, I am a man with many responsibilities, as you know. I therefore must utilize any piece of information regardless of the source. I am loyal to my gods, who grant us blessings in response to our gifts or prayers. But never has a god guided me. Now I hear of an Israelite god who takes the initiative of guiding them. Is that true?"

The mentor said, "He not only guides us but makes verbal promises to some others and rewards obedience. Many examples have been passed down through the ages. Shall I elaborate?"

"Yes."

"He told Noah to build an ark before a great flood and rewarded him by saving the animal kingdom. He told wealthy Abraham to leave his farm in the land of Ur, in Mesopotamia, and go west to an unknown destination. Without question, Abraham packed up immediately and headed west. Only then did God give him his precise destination, which was Canaan."

Moses asked, "How does this god communicate?"

"Visions or dreams or spoken words. Sometimes our tradition leaves that unknown."

"Go on."

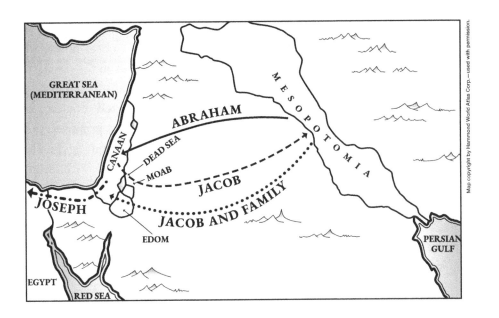

"He told Abraham to sacrifice his son, Isaac, as a test, stopping his hand at the last moment when he proved obedient. God rewarded him for his faith with great promises, telling him, *'I will greatly bless you … because you have obeyed My voice'*—that he would have a multitude of descendants even though his wife, Sarah, was well past the childbearing age. Nations that blessed the Israelites would be blessed, those who cursed them would be cursed; Abraham's descendants would be enslaved in Egypt for four centuries before God brought them out. He told Joseph …"

"Wait. God is going to free the slaves?"

"Yes, that is what He promised long ago as He spoke to Abraham."

"I'd like to see that! What a grandiose idea!" Moses quipped. "I wonder if the pharaoh knows that. Just what did he say?"

"All part of His plan, though we do not understand the whys of it all. He said that we Israelites will be in Egypt for four hundred and thirty years and be harassed for four hundred of those years, most of that time as slaves; then we will be freed somehow."

"And how long have they been here?"

"It is about three hundred and ninety years. Since God's promises are true, something should be stirring soon. Would you like to hear how God spoke to Abraham's son, grandson, and even his great-grandson?"

"Perhaps another time. Thank you for coming." And he dismissed him.

After the old man left, Moses thought, "Their idol-free god promises to free the slaves? Preposterous! Yet he has delivered on his past promises: the flood, a child born from a barren woman, four hundred years in Egypt. He seems more reliable, more alive, more involved with them than any of mine are with me. Truly, I have become skeptical of my gods anyway." He began to consider the possibilities.

"To have a god who actually speaks to me! And one who would reward me for obedience. And to know bits of the future. I would covet that; I would look for such a reward."[f]

*****

The next morning, he took a walk by himself, carrying his turtle, as he confronted his changing loyalties. "Could it be that I am a Hebrew living in the palace? A Hebrew leading the army! Not the princess' son. Just a slave by blood!

"Then who are my true parents? I must have been born into a Hebrew family and given to Pharaoh when very young, and he allowed me to live. But why? I know that he had decreed that all Israelite male babies be drowned in the Nile. Or was I Pharaoh's child secretly by an Israelite woman? I remember nothing of my first three to four years. And who knows about me in the palace? Certainly, Pharaoh and the princess. Who else? I must know."

He decided to speak to Pharaoh.

*****

Two days later, after breakfast, Moses knocked on the door of the palace study. Since the pharaoh regarded many gods highly, Moses would approach him through them. He entered after hearing a familiar response from within. Looking up from behind a desk was a stately, seasoned man with military posture whose eyes darted at Moses. Only the wrinkled skin of his neck and hands betrayed his years.

"Grandfather, I must speak with you," Moses said.

"Yes, what is it, Moses?"

"I have had several disturbing dreams lately," he lied. "I actually have one recurring dream from the supernatural that has bound my thoughts like a tightening net. A god has called to me persistently over the last two weeks, telling me to stop harassing the slaves."

"You have had dreams before."

"Yes, but never ones like this. A fierce flaming god accosts me with threatening words. He laughs and shouts to me that I am, in reality, not Egyptian."

Pharaoh stood, taking a few steps toward Moses, and calmly asked, "And which god is it that has visited you at night? Some are not to be trusted, making up tales to draw us away from competing gods."

"I do not know his name, but he speaks with authority. The dreams torment me with questions of who I am. They suggest that I am not born of royalty, but that my true parents were ... Israelites."

"Nonsense! Look at you, Moses. You are my grandson, my finest grandson, born to my daughter forty years ago. There can be no doubt about your lineage. You are a prince, a commander. Perhaps your next dream will suggest that I, too, am Hebrew. Ha! You are wise enough to know that no one can interpret dreams. Let us talk about the Philistine threat on our eastern border."

"Sir, this god will not let me go. I must know who I am. Perhaps I have been leading a false life all of these years. The weight of that possibility wearies me." Moses walked to the far side of the room and turned. "You have explained away my lack of resemblance to anyone in the family, telling me that I looked like my great-grandfather whom I never knew, just as mother has rationalized my circumcision. I, alone, in our family? But I wonder. Please, sir, if you give me confirmation, I will not have to confront mother."

"Has someone talked to you about this?"

"No one. The facts are adding up. I must quit the army until I can be sure, one way or another."

Pharaoh drew himself to his full height, looked into Moses' intense eyes, and sighed deeply. "Moses, Moses, must we do this? I have prayed that this day would never come, but your resolve tears at me. The gods must be doing something in you that I cannot deny and I respect them. It will not hurt for you to know now. You force me to break a pledge of many years." Sinking onto a nearby chair, he continued, "My daughter found you floating in a basket in the Nile and had pity and love for you. She sent you back to a Hebrew wetnurse to wean and raise you. When she presented you to me at age four or five, you greatly impressed me and I permitted you to live."

"Grandfather, why did you allow me—a Hebrew—to live?" Moses interrupted.

"When you were finally brought to me by the princess at age four, she explained the happening at the Nile, her pity for you, and her desire to keep you since she herself was childless. 'Please, father,' she implored, 'may I keep him as my son?' She whispered to me, 'He believes that he is one of us, an Egyptian, and that I am his mother.'

"Boy, speak," I said. "You stood tall, Moses, appearing strong for your age, with alert eyes. You bowed humbly before me and spoke in crisp Egyptian saying, 'I hope that I please you, my King.' I was taken by your appearance and courtesy. I reached to a table nearby, took up a piece of papyrus with hieratic writing on it and handed it to you. 'Can you read this?' I asked.

"You looked at it carefully, 'I cannot read it all, but isn't it a request for someone to visit you?'

"Satisfied, I said 'Yes, you may keep him.' I also said 'yes' out of pity for my barren daughter who had been widowed a year earlier when her husband was killed in an accident. I thought that I may have use for you later since I had only mediocre aides in my palace. One Hebrew could not hurt. 'What do you call him?' I asked."

"Since I drew him out of the water, I call him 'Moses,'" she answered.

"Through the years," continued Pharaoh, "I began to think of you as a potential embarrassment to me should others find out you were Hebrew. Many times I thought of destroying you. Several times when you were young and in the army, I even ordered that you be placed at the head of our charging army, but you seemed to be protected by a god of war. You proved to be a tenacious fighter, a great leader, and you have the courage of six men. I have grown to respect you and to love you as my own."

Moses was disturbed, yet relieved, by this final confirmation. "Then I am Hebrew, set adrift by my Israelite parents, at a time ..." He paused. "I know this must be as difficult for you as it is for me. Do you know my real parents?"

"I do not know them. That was forty years ago. They are probably dead by now."

Moses' heart leapt within. "They may be alive!" he thought. "Grandfather, I must search for them somehow."

"Consider carefully any action you may take, and let me know of it beforehand," Pharaoh advised. "You must not allow this revelation to become public—that I have knowingly, willingly raised an Israelite as my grandson these many years. It would be too great an embarrassment."

"Thank you, thank you for your honesty," said Moses. "I will be careful."

As he left the room, he thought, "A Hebrew for sure. That finally explains why grandfather arbitrarily appointed my younger cousin to be the crown prince, a source of great resentment to me then. I was to lead the army, he to follow his father as the next pharaoh."

Walking down a hallway, a Hebrew charwoman bowed to him. "Straighten up," he commanded as he walked past the surprised woman. He was not Pharaoh's daughter's son anymore!

*****

The sweltering midmorning sun assaulted the small blacksmith's shop in the rear of the palace grounds. The perspiring, dark-skinned smith stood over the hot furnace, his prominent neck muscles blending with those of his upper chest and bulging, granite-like arms. He ran a calloused fingertip along the edge of the battle-axe in his hands.

"Would that I owned this one," he said to Mateo. "I'd venture that Moses took it off a dead Philistine in the war."

"It seems that you have ground the edge well, for my master had dulled it by frequent practice," answered Mateo.

"I have done only as instructed. I would give ten of our bronze axes for this. See the width of the blade, larger than that of our bronze ones, the setting of the handle into its eye, the balanced weight of it. On the rare times I can work such iron, I see it respond to the furnace and feel its soothing warmth.

It gives me even greater pleasure than the breasts of a harlot. Mateo, you are wise. Who, besides the Philistines, has an implement to match it?"

"I have heard that the tall king of Bashan has a very long, iron bedstead,[8] his prize possession," recalled Mateo.

The smith shuffled tongs that rested on an anvil and then stared at the boy. "Mateo, what is going on with your master? He came to me with a set face, complaining that the edge was not sharp enough." The smith looked away briefly. "I have heard that he is caustic with his younger cousin. Ha! That man is pampered, but Moses—"

"Careful with your tongue, smithy, we are only Hebrew slaves."

"You know better than I the tales surrounding Moses. He doesn't resemble his family. Who was his father?"

"Why, the princess' husband."

"The husband was able to sire but one child before he died, eh?"

"Give me the blade that I may take it to my master," Mateo said curtly.

*****

The heavy wooden door of Moses' study echoed with the firm, measured knocks. Mateo entered, carrying the axe, cradled in a twice-folded, thick, red muslin cloth. He bowed and presented the weapon to his master. Moses' finger gently touched the honed edge and found it to his liking. Turning the weapon over, he shifted it from hand to hand, checking its balance, again satisfied. He dismissed his aide absently.

*****

That afternoon he spent two hours exercising and battle-axe throwing, a skill at which he was proficient, to exhaust his growing tension. It was a weapon he was seldom without.

*****

In the evening Moses attended a large palace banquet at the pharaoh's pleasure. His conversations were subdued as he was self-engrossed. Unobserved, he briefly searched each face, wondering who knew about him. If they did … he caught himself. Those thoughts were quickly replaced by a feeling of indifference. He deserved to be where he was. He had earned his position, his honors, his privileges, all aside from his lineage. Yet … how much of what he possessed derived from the advantages of being Pharaoh's grandson? It had probably helped some. But he was wiser than any one of them. They were fortunate to have him. He basked in his talents. Observing the many guests, he granted that Pharaoh's family was powerful, insightful, and wealthy; but the luxuriousness and carnality of social life, the passing pleasures of sin,[h] held no attraction for Moses. Against this facade were his officers, true fighting men, and he was proud of them.

The pharaoh's eyes caught and held his for a brief moment, then winked. Moses smiled. He loved the old man.

Once, his cousin, younger than he, asked, "Moses, are you all right?"

"Yes, of course."

After a reasonable time, when the musicians and dancing girls came in, he excused himself, again showing no interest in those activities. He crossed the grounds to his home and retired with Mateo's assistance. But his thoughts did not rest.

"How can I find my parents and brother? Who could help me? Some Hebrew? I know the names of only two or three of them, ones I have heard at the semiannual conference that is held with the selected Hebrew elders, one from each of the twelve tribes." Moses knew that the session's purpose was to distribute information, issue new orders, and remind attendees of the severe punishments for insubordination and failing to meet quotas. He had always belittled the other reasons for having them—to assuage the Israelite elders, to keep them under control, to listen to any of their complaints. The meetings were usually a sham, and both sides knew it; little was ever accomplished. Moses' cousin, along with several judges, took charge of these meetings, meetings that Moses occasionally attended out of curiosity when otherwise unoccupied. He remembered two elders who had represented their tribes well through the years. Their names were Gamaliel and Eliasaph. And, oh yes, a third man called Aaron.

"Once I recall the man called Eliasaph argued, saying something like this: 'O Great Venerable One, the good food you provide for us is appreciated. Our men accept wallowing in the brick pits making bricks for your lustrous buildings. We appreciate the special care you give to our talented people—the seamstresses, the sculptors, the leather workers. But this we request. Few of our men ever reach the age of seventy-five years, and most of those who do cannot keep up with their quotas. We all suffer as a result. We request that you lower the age at which a man no longer must work the pits from seventy-five to seventy. Thank you.'

"At another time, the man Aaron, known as an eloquent speaker, made a reasonable request that was eventually fulfilled. He said, 'Venerable One, we appreciate that you have water piped from the Nile by the shaduf pumps to the laboring areas. Would you consider increasing the number of spigots the men drink from? I believe that you could get more work from them if their thirsts were quenched.'

"I remember those three, yet I cannot approach them directly to question them concerning my new identity. I must first learn more about the slaves themselves, their ways and beliefs, and the only way to do so will be to visit their neighborhoods, something I never would have thought of doing."

As he considered the possibility, he decided to do so the next day.

*****

Gamaliel

Gamaliel, an elder of the tribe of Manasseh, was a brawny, handsome man, half-a-head taller than average, with sloping shoulders, a light complexion, intense eyes, and a boxlike jaw housing ample lips. A deep voice commanded attention. His stamina, physical strength, and perseverance promoted an unassuming self-assurance.

Behind his roughness, this idealistic man had a woman's intuition that, blended with a compassionate nature, afforded him the ability to discover unique solutions to difficult inter- and intra-tribal disputes. "Gamaliel the wise bull," he was called.

In his teens, he was assigned a role as a bricklayer, rising to foreman in four years and master foreman in another four years. Now, at twenty-five years of age, his belief in the Hebrew God afforded him a beacon that, some believed, was the true basis for his confidence. He was, along with Eliasaph of Gad, a spiritual leader among the tribes.

He and his wife, a woman of unusual worth, had three children; he was truly his family's shepherd.

*****

Eliasaph

Gad's Eliasaph was four years older than Gamaliel, heavyset and a little shorter than his friend. He was more deliberate in his thoughts and actions. Cautiousness of mind contrasted with the quick movements of his large, calloused hands and heavy wrists as they moved quickly in molding smooth walls with odd-shaped stones—a Class 4 stonemason— as well as in settling occasional disputes.

As a boy, with the secret help of a scholarly Hebrew priest, he taught himself to decipher Accadian, the hieroglyphs, and some of the newer straight-line writings, the hieratics. He occasionally stole a word-filled papyrus sheet from an Egyptian teacher, always secretly returning it after reading.

Eliasaph was a quiet yet sincere worrier, believing in some measure that his worrying prevented some tragedies. He worried also about his wife, who was frail and of a complaining nature. Her frequent illnesses had spared her the task of bearing children. As she gradually adopted the status of an invalid, Eliasaph assumed her household chores; at first, with a helpful, almost prideful attitude. But as the years passed, a smoldering resentment clouded his love for her.

Coupled with knowledge gained from his voracious reading, he became a natural elder of his tribe. Because of his faith, he often led group prayers to Abraham's God but also secretly carried a small amulet of the god Rompha in his pocket.

*****

The mothers of each of these two men believed in the God of Abraham, beliefs borne from answered prayers. They instilled that faith into their sons, with His name, El.[6] It was a rare thing, but neither would allow even one idol to an Egyptian god in their homes—to their knowledge. As their sons became acquainted with each other, the mothers too became fast friends.

*****

Moses and Mateo arrived in two separate chariots at a section of the slave quarters. One of two guards opened the gate. Moses brought one of the drivers along for their safety and one of the guards as a guide. The four walked into the slave quarters on dirt paths, passing huts and small wooden houses on either side. Of the few occupants present, some stared at them in disbelief, others turned their backs to them as being royal reminders of their enforced servitude. Moses noticed the physical weakness of many people—some old, with prominent cheekbones and sunken eyes.

An old man sitting by the side of the path, a sturdy stick by his side and a torn shirt on his lap, was humming a lilting tune, clapping his hands slowly. The song sounded strangely familiar to Moses and caused him to stop. Unconsciously, he hummed a little of it softly. A shiver went through him. How did he know that?

Mateo was quietly surprised.

As they continued, Moses saw the shabby dress of several crippled peddlers, several missing a limb, and many old women and men who were selling to guards or, more likely, trading among themselves. The offered items included pastries, threadbare yet colored clothing, pieces of pottery, healing balms and potions, and drinks of some liquids served from a wineskin. Many were barefoot, while some wore sandals made of a flat, thin strip of wood or, occasionally, made of leather. The sandals were secured with a lace thong over the foot. Walking sticks were simply stripped tree branches. Moses had looked at these wretches before but had never really seen them. An unfamiliar feeling of pity touched him.

He searched the faces of many men, but none were of his age; the brickyards required most of them.

A blood-stained whipping post stood at the junction of three paths. Moses turned to the guard. "I want to be notified if anyone is to be beaten."

The surprised guard replied, "Yes, my lord," as they turned and walked back toward the gate. His visit had produced no clues concerning his brother.

On the way back to the palace Moses questioned his driver: "I selected you as my driver, but before that, weren't you a guard over the Israelite slaves?"

"Yes sir, for nine years."

"If they are harshly treated, how do they manage to survive?"

"They are a strange lot, Master. May I be frank with you?"

"Yes, tell me what you know."

"The Israelites, even though their bodies are subjected to the whims of the Egyptians and they humble themselves before their masters, secretly consider themselves superior to the Egyptians, largely through their heritage and the promises of their God. They are *the* Israelites, they are *the* chosen. They have their own counsels in which they elect ten elders from each tribe."

Moses said, "They survive on pride?"

"Largely, and good food, sir."

*****

When Moses reached the palace grounds, he went to his library. He sat alone and allowed his mind to reflect on the events of the recent weeks. To him, the non-military slaves had once just been faceless peasants to be used; then he learned that they had not been nobly acquired in defeat, but simply harassed. And finally, they were swallowed up in slavery by the pharaohs, partly because of their cliquish bonding and prideful arrogance at being a chosen, religious people. They believed that this was all planned by their god, a god who speaks, promises, and rewards.

"Now I see faces of the poor, the toughness of the overworked. Is it pity I feel for those wretches … rather, those courageous ones? And I belong there! How can I be loyal both to the palace and to them—and to their alive, vibrant god? A god I am being reluctantly drawn to?"

*****

When word reached the palace of his foray into the slave section, it was received with shock, considered by a few as dangerous but, by most, disgraceful. To Pharaoh it was more than unsettling.

He spoke to the crown prince, "Was Moses only searching for his parents, or is there another motive? He must be watched closely."

*****

Lunch the next day was shared with the pharaoh and the crown prince. Conversation included updates on the Nubian front and on Moses' recent venture.

The crown prince asked Moses, "I hear that you have been in the slave quarters. I have never been there. Your servant, Mateo, goes there for you occasionally, I understand. Is it safe? What is the attraction there?"

Moses parried, "Some Hebrew ladies have a baking talent far beyond the abilities of our chefs and produce tasty foods that I like with their minimal equipment. Some men can weave marvelous figures out of old pieces of leather. I go to eat and admire, perhaps buy."

"Go there often?"

"Only rarely."

After the meal was finished and Moses was alone with Pharaoh, he confided, "Sir, in all honesty, I went there looking for any sort of a sign ... to find out if my parents are still alive."

"Did you discover anything?"

"No, nothing," he said, withholding the growing respect he had for them.

*****

The next afternoon Moses, Mateo, and the charioteer set out on a pleasure ride to the Nile.

*****

In a small house on the outskirts of the city, Mannel, an Egyptian guard, pulled his smock over his head, tightened his leggings, and tied on his sandals. He brushed the black hair back from his tanned forehead. Sturdy arms, with a bronze bracelet encircling each bicep and wrist, easily lifted the club decorated with a carving of Isis on its small end. He turned to his wife, Rovann, as she rinsed the pottery dishes, a whiff of garlic in the air. "I am assigned to those slimy Israelite slaves again today. By the god Amon, what a duty! They work well, but so many are scrawny and tire easily."

"Are they a worry to you, Mannel?" she asked.

"They are as numerous as we Egyptians here in Rameses," he answered, tucking a whip into his belt at his back. "I'll take my cudgel with me, just in case."

"Some saw Moses walking near the brickyards yesterday. They say that he has recently shown an interest in the Hebrew slaves. Beware of him."

"Don't worry. I will be home for dinner."

*****

During the hot morning, Mannel joined another guard to oversee his slaves. They whipped an occasional indolent one and shackled two contrary ones together, laughing as they fell while treading in the brick vats. But the afternoon did not go well for Mannel.

"You, Mannel!" shouted the head man. "Your Hebrews are working today as if it were a holiday! They are short of their quota again. Make it up."

Mannel's whip encouraged action as all picked up their pace except for an old man who swore softly to himself and glanced bitterly at the guard. Near day's end, Mannel's cudgel to his mid-back sent the elderly slave sprawling to the ground. Another blow to the side of his hip evoked a scream. "Now, by the gods, you will work faster," growled Mannel.

Moses observed the action from a small hill overlooking the brickyards where he and Mateo had paused on their ride to the Nile. Moses watched with newfound compassion. Mateo pointed out Mannel. "I am told that he is the guard most hated; 'Mannel the asp' he is called. He is said to smile whenever he beats a slave, and often gives his bloodstained rod to the slave to wash with his own saliva. If it is not returned to him spotless, others are punished."

Moses saw the man struggle to his feet and hobble away from Mannel. "That is his habit? Discipline is all right. Even striking a slave has its place. But that is brutal ... cowardly!" spat Moses. His frustration and anger intensified as he observed Mannel's continued ruthlessness on another.

Moses dismounted. "Stay here," he ordered.

He slowly walked toward the brickyards, not sure of his next move. When the guard left his post and walked to a secluded bank overlooking a dry creek bed, Moses followed, skirting around the slaves. As Mannel began to relieve himself, Moses looked this way and that, and when he saw that there was no one around,[i] he crept up to within twelve paces of the guard who, when he finished voiding, turned around. At that moment, Moses hurled his axe. The weapon split open Mannel's upper sternum and shattered his trachea, propelling the unconscious man backward over the sandy bank. Moses leaped over the edge to the body and, bracing his foot on his chest, pried out the axe. A second chop killed the dying man. He quickly pulled a linen cloth from his belt to soak up the spurting blood. Some had splattered on Moses' left arm and soiled his tunic sleeve.

He had killed others before in battle, but never, as he stared at the body, had he felt such a sense of satisfaction; a justified death. He had anonymously helped the Hebrews by erasing one of their prime offenders.

Moses scooped out a hollow in the bank, put the bloody cloth with the body, and hid him in the sand.[j] Then he rubbed the blood off the axe and his arm with sand and scaled the bank. He returned to Mateo and his chariot and, taking a back route, encountered no one on the one-mile ride back to the palace. There, he slipped past the guards, hiding his bloodstained sleeve. In the secrecy of his room, he washed the blood from his garment.

*****

The next morning, Mannel's wife reported her husband's absence and soldiers were dispatched to the brickyard. Two Hebrew slaves remembered the direction he had taken when last seen, and one thought he saw Moses follow him. By noon, Mannel's body was discovered, and reports of the incident reached the palace.

*****

In the late morning, the war minister informed the eighty-four-year-old Pharaoh of Mannel's death and of the growing suspicion by Hebrews and guards that Moses was the murderer. The pharaoh walked to the window in silence and looked out. His worst fear had been realized. He turned to the minister. "It appears that it is my grandson who committed this crime, not simply against a guard, but against the throne." He drew himself up. "Although I have loved him and treated him with great respect, I believe he has become a threat to us, an insurrectionist. Kill Moses[k] before he stirs up a revolt."

The shocked, but secretly pleased, minister hastily summoned the captain of the guards, who dispatched twenty men from the palace guard to find Moses and then sent runners to the city gates to prevent his escape.

*****

The news spread rapidly among the slaves. Although they did not understand why the powerful Moses, esteemed by the palace, was being hunted down simply for killing a lowly guard, many were eager to see him captured and executed. To them, Moses was not the hero he had hoped to be, but simply one of the despised powers behind their prolonged suffering.

*****

Earlier that morning, Moses had ridden his horse into town alone, drawing no more attention than usual. Being curious, he rode out toward the brickyards after a small meal and, on the way, saw two Hebrews fighting.

When he dismounted to break up the quarrel, the two slaves stopped fighting and glared.

"Who made you a prince or a judge over us?" one snarled. "Are you intending to kill me as you killed the Egyptian?"[l]

Breathing heavily, the other warned him. "Soldiers are after you, Moses. Run!"

Moses was startled! He thought, "I visited them in their village; I killed for them. Don't these men, my brothers, understand that their God might want me to help them?"

Moses said nothing but, knowing his crime had been discovered, mounted his horse. "Pharaoh would not stalk me for killing a guard; I have such authority," he told himself. "He knows that I have defected. I am an embarrassment to him, his alleged grandson, a loathsome Hebrew. I must leave. If I am dead, I can do no one any good." An unexpected peace filled him as he mounted his horse, not fearing the wrath of the king.[m]

*****

Realizing that he could not return to the palace to exchange his muscular war horse for one better suited for the desert, he trotted toward the city gates, stopping briefly at a market to buy a large skin of water, bags of seeds, nuts, fruit, a leg of mutton, and a large bag of oats. As he rode past a small crowd of people huddled over a body, someone yelled, "The king's messenger was running and has fallen and broken his leg! He seems in much pain!"

Sensing that the messenger was sent to stop him, Moses spurred his horse on, wondering, "Could this be their god's work?"

At the eastern city gates, he questioned the guard, who recognized him. "Has a caravan left here recently?"

"Yes, a day and a half ago, the southern route," the surprised guard replied. "But, sir, you are alone?"

"Others will follow soon. I must retrieve one of their members."

The guard waved him through as Moses exhaled in relief.

*****

As he rode he wondered, "I am giving up all that I have enjoyed and worked for these forty years: the honor and prestige of being the Commander of the Army, a prince of Egypt; the freedom to live my life as I please; the power to give orders and have my slightest demands met; the chance to enjoy the infinite pleasures of the palace." He considered each one carefully. "All lost by a single act." Then, "Will my Commanders of a Thousand be able to lead the army? They must."

*****

He rode east during the rest of the day, pausing once to bury his royal jacket. Late that evening the trade route divided, one branch to the north following the shore of the Great Sea; the southern one skirted the northern tip of the Red Sea. He read signs in the sand, including traces of camel dung, confirming that the caravan had taken the southern one leading toward the land of Midian; he chose that route. The next day he would overtake the caravan. Would they recognize him? Would they accept him? Would the pharaoh's men come after him? Would this new god help him? He would soon find out. That night he slept in the open.

*****

In the early morning, he spurred his horse and overtook the caravan. Making his way to a fat man under an umbrella, a man who was riding on the finest camel, Moses asked, "You, sir, are you the caravan master?"

The toothless man growled as he fingered the hilt of a saber hung from his belt. "What have you to do with me?" His breath smelled like that of his camels.

Turning his head slightly away, Moses said, "We are traveling the same route. My horse and I are hungry and wish to join you."

Sizing Moses up, he said in a guttural voice, "You are welcome to our protection and provisions. For a fee, of course."

"I can pay."

Two other armed caravanners with coarse, weathered features rode up on camels, flanking Moses.

"You ride a fine stallion. Stolen, I presume?" said the master to Moses.

"No, I am in the army."

"Your animal would ennoble me," he spit out. "You may ride on one of our camels—until you leave us."

"I can pay you …" countered Moses.

"The horse or nothing."

Although unafraid, Moses thought, "I cannot give him up. Not to that …
black-hearted fool."

"I will ride him until I leave you," Moses countered again.

"No!" the other barked. "You may steal away some night with my prize."

Moses knew that it was many days' journey to the first village, and he
could not make it alone. He was left without a choice. Resolutely, he buried his
face in the nape of the horse's neck, breathed in deeply of its scent, and stroked
the soft velvet of its muzzle. "Goodbye, dear companion." As he walked away,
he carelessly flicked a drop of moisture from his cheek.

He traveled with them five more days into the land of Midian where, far
to the south, he could see "the Horeb mountain range, with Sinai as its highest
peak," according to the caravanner. In two more days, they entered a village
where the caravan resupplied. Moses withdrew and walked on alone until,
tired and thirsty, he rested by a well.

*****

Seven girls, ranging in age from four to fifteen, came with ten of their
father's flock of sheep to draw water.[7] As they approached the well, three
blustery, young shepherds appeared from bushes nearby and tauntingly
laughed as they blocked the girls' way. One knocked a water bag from the
youngest. "G'afternoon, young ladies. Here for some water, eh? Be nice and
we'll just take the three oldest with us."

Moses, taller than they, approached from the other side of the well, his
axe in hand. "Lay a hand on one and you'll soon be one-armed. Now, go!" he
barked as he strode toward them.

One raised his hand. "All right, all right, we meant no harm," as they
walked away.

"Thank you, sir," said the oldest daughter. They watered the sheep, filled
their bags, and left with the animals.

*****

When they returned home, the girls told their father, Jethro, a Midianite
priest, of the man who had come to their aid. To the two oldest he said, "Find
him and invite him to dine with us."

The sun was still up when they found him. Moses gladly followed them home.

"I am deeply appreciative to you for protecting my daughters today," said Jethro, bowing a balding head atop his plump body to the tall stranger. "You are most welcome in my house. May I ask your name?"

"I am Moses," he stated respectfully to the priest, with a slight head nod.

"Moses, the Egyptian commander?"

"Yes," said Moses, looking into Jethro's placid eyes. "But I come as a refugee, not as a leader." To discourage further questions, Moses quickly added, "Have you work that I may perform in order to find a temporary haven with you?"

Respecting the obvious diversion, Jethro sighed. "I am overburdened, having only seven young daughters to help me. My eldest is only now developing a measure of strength. I notice that your hands are not those of a laborer, but that is all I have for you to do. You may stay if you do not shy away from hard work and some danger."

"I am used to danger," said Moses. "I will do my best."

The next day, Jethro took Moses to his sheep pen. "My shepherd was killed two weeks ago, and I have no one to herd my sheep. I know you are of high position, but if you stay, that must be your duty. I will hire an experienced herder to teach you."

Moses had to strain to hide his disgust as he looked at the large number of animals before him and inhaled the rank odor of a wet woolen sweater he once owned. He was repulsed by the assignment, because all Egyptians had been raised to believe that every shepherd is loathsome,[n] the lowest of all occupations. But the priest and his daughters were hospitable, and he had nowhere else to go. He detested the job—how far the commander of the Egyptian army had fallen! But with determination he persevered. He felt safe, in an obscure job and separated by oceans of sand from Egypt. Besides, Pharaoh was probably glad to be rid of him.

*****

One night, having proven himself to be conscientious and reliable, Moses spoke to Jethro. "As you have guessed, I am a fugitive from Egypt," he confessed. "I was raised and educated in her courts. However, I committed a crime that cost me my position."

"And what was that?" asked Jethro.

"I murdered a man."

Jethro looked him in the eyes. "Should we be worried for our safety?"

"No, it was a singular act of passion. I killed a guard who was harassing Hebrew slaves."

"And why should that have been a concern of yours?"

"Who understands motivation? Was it compassion or pity? Perhaps I was finally driven to it because of the guard's brutal treatment of them, far beyond acceptable levels. I lashed out at one of the worst."

"An occasional slave who escapes to us confirms the harsh treatment they receive," said Jethro. "We still wish you to stay with us."

*****

Moses was gone for a month, pasturing the flock on distant hills. When he returned, he enjoyed dinner with Jethro's family and the attention paid to him by the seven daughters. He was a delightful novelty.

"I have developed the greatest respect for you and admire the way you and your wife raise your fine daughters," Moses said to Jethro after the meal. "However, a question has arisen in my mind. Some shepherds I have befriended speak somewhat warily of you and your priesthood. I notice that few men come to seek your counsel. Why is that?"

"Many do not approve of me," answered Jethro. "Along with our other gods, I also worship the God of Abraham, Isaac, and Jacob because twice I have seen His hand in my own life. Most other priests have rejected Him, being loyal only to Midianite gods."

Moses was surprised. "This god of Abraham has caused my trouble. But I thought he was the god of the Israelites? How can you know him?"

"We revere Abraham, but not through his wife, Sarah. After Sarah died, he took another woman into his tent, the younger Keturah,° who bore him six more sons, the fourth of whom was Midian. When strife arose in the family in Abraham's old age, over five hundred years ago, he dispatched Keturah and her sons eastward with many gifts.ᵖ The sons had grown up with the passionate faith of their father, and after Midian settled into this area, he and some of his descendants carried his beliefs down to us."

Moses spread his hands and said, "If your god has use for me, he must tell me."

"Perhaps He will," said Jethro.

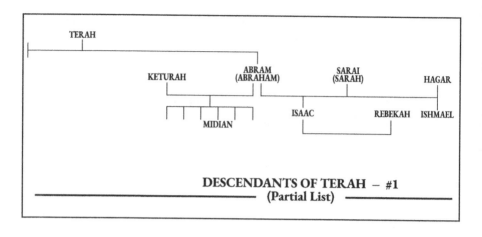

DESCENDANTS OF TERAH – #1
(Partial List)

* * * * *

Several weeks later, Moses returned home unexpectedly, his left forearm wrapped in an animal skin. "A wolf tore it open as I was fighting him." he said, as Zipporah, one of Jethro's daughters, began to gently remove the covering. The gash was moderately deep and would require repeated bathing, rewrapping with fresh sheepskin, and then binding with leather thongs. As Moses lay on a table, he spoke to Zipporah and Jethro. "You have welcomed me into your home, yet I have not been honest with you. You deserve to know the truth. I am neither an Egyptian nor Pharaoh's grandson."

"You are not Pharaoh's grandson?" repeated the worldly-wise Jethro, eyebrows raised.

"No, as I recently discovered, I am Hebrew, merely a slave who has masqueraded as a prince. I never knew my true parents—Israelites who set me adrift in the Nile as a baby to be found by Pharaoh's daughter. I have been wrestling with that revelation for many weeks, a predicament involving your god of Abraham. I must know more about him. Will he speak to you?"

"No, He speaks when He wishes, and then, only rarely," replied Jethro. "If you wish to learn more of Him, I suggest you pray to Him for guidance."

"I will."

"What do you know about Him?" asked Jethro.

"Little about him or the Hebrews. I am aware that their slavery had somehow been predicted by their god. They must circumcise their sons for some reason. And there is another curious claim they make. Their god gives them protection from many of the diseases[q] the Egyptians suffer. If their god were truly benevolent, they wouldn't have been in slavery in the first place, would they?"

"You are searching, aren't you? God will reveal Himself to you in time," assured Jethro.

*****

Moses had learned from others that Jethro had always yearned for a son. However, his wife produced only four daughters. In frustration, Jethro took another wife, a woman from the Cush area of Nubia whom he had wooed away from a caravan traveling from Nubia to Syria. She was beautiful, but birthed only three more daughters, to Jethro's distress. The next to youngest, Zipporah, had seemed to Moses to be the most attractive.

*****

A number of years passed and Moses, his hair now graying, approached Zipporah as she sat outside on a stool, spinning wool.

"Zipporah," said Moses as he stood uneasily before her.

"Yes, Moses?" She paused to tighten a loose sandal strap. She was tall for a woman, and her skin was smooth, the color of burnt umber. A blanket of long, wavy black hair cascaded over her white, full-length gown to the middle of her back.

"I am but your father's shepherd," Moses began. "I have shared many hours with him and we know each other well. I have waited patiently for you to grow up."

Zipporah seemed somewhat confused. "You have been with us fifteen years and I greatly respect you. But, what do you mean … you have waited for me to grow up? This I do not understand."

Moses' heart was full of affection. "Zipporah, you are the finest of the daughters, and I have great love for you."

She gasped, catching the full impact of what he was suggesting. "Moses, we have had many good conversations together, but would not one of my older sisters be more suitable for you? Besides, as you know, I do not share your faith in the Hebrew god."

"Jethro has given me permission to marry you," he persisted.

She looked away in silence. Finally she said, "Well, if you are sure and father agrees with it, then yes, Moses, I will … marry you."

Moses and Zipporah lived in a house next to Jethro and his family, a family finally blessed with a son, Hobab. Zipporah ran an efficient home, while Moses continued shepherding Jethro's growing flock. After a time, Moses' hopes for a child began to wane, until one day he joyfully learned that his wife was pregnant. The pregnancy went well, and on the second day after their son was born, Moses entered their sleeping quarters.

"After all these years," said Zipporah, "we finally have a child, Moses. But why must you call him Gershom, which you say in Hebrew means 'a stranger here?'"[7]

"I am made to feel welcome in your home," he replied, "but yet I feel like a foreigner. My people, my true family, are in Egypt."

"But he is such a handsome boy, and he looks like you. Perhaps he will become a priest, like father," she said.

"As he wishes, but his name is Gershom," pronounced Moses.

*****

A week later, holding the crying baby, Zipporah confronted Moses. "You have circumcised him, Moses! I did not agree."

"It is the law of the god I am trying to serve, and I will obey what little I know of him. Perhaps he will bless us with another son."

"It is *your* law!" she retorted angrily.

*****

The couple shared the joy of watching Gershom grow. Although wishing otherwise, Zipporah had not become pregnant again. Many years passed before she announced their long-awaited news. "I am again with child; perhaps a brother for twelve-year-old Gershom!"

"Zipporah, we are indeed fortunate."

"We are," she smiled.

"If it is a boy," Moses said, "he'll be called Eliezer. It means, in Hebrew, 'the God of my father was my help.'"[8]

"Still your god," Zipporah hurled back. And then sighed shortly after, "All right, but he will not be circumcised!"

*****

For four decades, Moses and his family lived near Jethro. Fit and healthy at the age of eighty, Moses knew every sheep path, every hill, every valley, wadi, and oasis over the wilderness to the east and to the west, even beyond Mount Sinai. Many were the days he subsisted on biscuits and water, always with an ear listening at night for a sick sheep or a marauder threatening the flock. Having to occasionally carry a wayward two-hundred-pound sheep over his shoulders made him strong. His arms were scarred from battles with predators and his palms calloused from brandishing his rod. He had grown to love these odoriferous beasts.

He surprised Semitic merchants traveling in caravans to and from the northeast with his knowledge of Hebrew. For hundreds of years, Hebrew had only been a spoken language, but from the merchants of the caravans, he learned to read and write the newly developed Hebrew alphabet[8] that had arisen in the countries east of the Great Sea. The knowledge and wisdom accumulated over his first forty years lay useless. His life was as if a king's lead horse had been relegated to the plow. He often regretted that murdering the Egyptian had deprived him of his chance to help the Israelites; if they were ever to be helped, their god would have to appoint another.

Although he increasingly included the Hebrew god among those he prayed to, his knowledge of that god remained rudimentary, and Jethro was of little help. Was it their god or was it just time that had molded him from an often arrogant commander into a humble man, more humble than any other?[t] As he surveyed his flock at the first glow of sunrise, he felt at last content to live out his life in Midian.

*****

Endnotes.

1. Josephus, Flavius. *The Antiquities of the Jews*, translated by William Whiston, A. M., 1987, book 2, chapter 10.
2. "Anuke, Re" *Gods and Mythology of Ancient Egypt.* http://tourgegypt.net/godsofegypt.
3. *Mummification in Ancient Egypt*, Joshua J. Mark, Ancient History Encyclopedia, 14 Feb. 2017.
4. *Ancient Egyptian funerary practices*, Wikipedia.
5. "chariots," *Chariotry in Ancient Egypt*, Wikipedia.

6. "naming them with His name, El," Edersheim, "The Exodus," *Bible History: Old Testament,* 1949, page 30.
7. Jethro story from Ex. 2:16f.
8. "Hebrew Alphabet," A History of the Hebrew Language, Angel Saenz-Badillos, Cambridge University Press, New York, 1996, p. 16-17. Also "How the Hebrew Language Grew", Edward Horowitz, M.A., DRE, Jewish Educational Committee Press, New York, 1960, pp. 12ff.

Chapter 2
Turmoil in the Grain Storage Cities

The sun rose over the horizon in the cloudless sky, slowly illuminating the thriving city, progressively coalescing the generic darkness beyond into identifiable shadows of the many public buildings, the treasure house, and the fort. The city was Pithom,[1] five miles east of the Nile, twenty miles south of Rameses, and fifty-five miles south of the Great Sea. A six-foot wall surrounding the city briefly shaded the non-Hebrew slave community on the eastern edge of town. Four timbered guard posts overlooked its large collections of adobe huts and small houses.

The fort was at attention that early morning. Shiny weapons intermittently caught and reflected the rays of the sun into Pharaoh's eyes as he made his official inspection of the three groups of military personnel arrayed in front of him. The first set was a line of forty men facing him, with nine parallel lines of men behind. Each soldier in the first six rows held a two-foot sword or battle axe against his left chest as he stood at attention. Soldiers in the four rear rows held longer spears.

The tanned and slender thirty-three-year-old pharaoh slowly walked in front of the soldiers, hands clasped behind his back. He wore the official black, shoulder-length headdress, a white robe over an orange and black knee-length skirt, leather sandals, and three gold bracelets encircling his left wrist. The only softness about him was the crop that dangled loosely from his right hand. By his side was the proud, self-assured company commander, and to the rear strode the paunchy vizier of Lower Egypt.

Pharaoh's focused, discerning eyes missed nothing. Occasionally he would rivet his gaze on a soldier, like a hawk on a mouse. Woe to he who met his stare.

The second group, seven rows of archers, separated from the first by three spear lengths, maintained a kneeling position, shoulders back, left arms thrust forward, their hands firmly gripping polished composite bows. A quiver with twelve arrows was strapped to the back of each archer by a single thong that encircled the chest, attached at the left waistband, and arched over the base of the right side of the neck. None moved in this military tableau.

As Pharaoh walked, he turned slightly toward the commander and spoke in clipped tones. "I see some slaves sprinkled among your soldiers. How do they serve you?"

"The blacks that we have brought up from Nubia are compliant and know their place," the commander replied. "The exceptions are the few that come from Cush in northern Nubia. They are the better educated but weaker, often arrogant, and occasionally unruly. We deal with them appropriately."

"The Israelites?" asked Pharaoh.

"The ones we have in the military make adequate fighters, but they tend to be an independent, surly lot—and argumentative. When properly dealt with, they can be controlled," said the commander, confident in his knowledge of these details. "I know little about the slaves who work the pits or who are shepherds."

"They proliferate like rabbits, you know," said Pharaoh. "My great-grandfather once commanded that all of their male babies be cast into the Nile.[a] The Israelites created such a commotion that he eventually rescinded the order. Someday, I may have to reinstate it."

The last contingent was of thirty-eight war chariots, each pulled by two brown horses harnessed together, their manes adorned with orange and black ribbons. Each chariot had two bronze-rimmed wooden wheels and a three-foot-high, orange-painted oval carriage with an open back. A charioteer stood on the platform of each, reins in one hand and a composite-bow in the other, an arrow-filled quiver over his shoulder. An almost imperceptible nod of Pharaoh's head signaled approval.

As he approached the middle of this line, Pharaoh paused and spoke again to the commander. "I am informed of the recent war exercises of the Philistines[2] on our eastern border. God Re, we lost many good men when they drove us out of the Sinai four years ago with their blasted iron chariots. My father died shortly afterwards, you know, I believe partly from sorrow. But I hear that, for the present, they seem to have no further designs on Egypt, wanting to complete their conquest of Canaan, a land I covet. But with the Philistine army interposed over the northern route, those chances seem slim. We will bide our time. Besides, Canaan is becoming a power in her own right under the coalition rule of the six kings. Perhaps the Philistines represent a welcome buffer after all. Our division is battle-ready, and I am satisfied that your garrison is also."

"Of course," responded the commander.

Pharaoh finished the review, the final item on the agenda of his annual four-day visit. During that time, his aides met with the local governor and his cabinet. They reviewed the need for greater taxation, further measures to control the slave horde, the accounting of the year's grain harvest, and plans for enlarging the irrigation canals.

"This inspection went well. You seem to have your troops ready. I will confer with my aides and send a report to you within two weeks," said the pharaoh.

Pharaoh mounted his waiting chariot. He half-smiled as he inhaled the rich, warm, earthy smell of the two black Syrian stallions that drew it, each bedecked with a black blanket interwoven with splashes of orange, the color of glowing coals. Their manes were adorned with a long row of tightly-tied orange ribbons. Pharaoh sat on the cushioned bench in the back of the black, four-wheeled chariot. His rod-straight charioteer flicked the horses with his whip and the chariot sprang forward, swirling dust. Pharaoh preferred to be near the front of his caravan, following the king's guard of horsemen. The chariots of the vizier and Pharaoh's fellow dignitaries wheeled in behind as they rolled out of the low-walled compound, followed closely by six warrior-manned chariots.

*****

As they approached the city gates, Pharaoh observed masons building a brick watchtower near the left gate. Ten paces before the tower, he heard the *thwap, thwap* of the guard's whip striking a lighter-skinned slave on his knees, blood seeping down into his left eye. Nearby, his hod lay on the ground, its brick load scattered, two of the bricks broken. "Clumsy Hebrew," Pharaoh muttered with disgust.

Beyond the gates, Pharaoh turned to view Pithom. How proud his father would have been of him for his dogged perseverance in enlarging and prospering that city. Egypt was rightfully his!

They turned onto the double-lane dirt road that led north through the eastern portion of the Land of Goshen.[b] Immediately Pharaoh passed by guards patrolling a line of men marching in lockstep as they headed from the Hebrew slave quarters on the west to the brickyards of Pithom, their shackles clanking.

The chariots proceeded and, in a few minutes, Pharaoh looked to the east and saw the vague outlines of the city of Succoth above the horizon on the road to the highly productive copper mines.

The road wound to the northwest and elevated ground overlooked the low floodplains that extended to the Nile. It was mid-autumn, the flood waters had receded, and slaves were plowing and planting the lower fields of Goshen, or mucking out the accumulated silt from the labyrinth of irrigation ditches. Some of the workers were adequately paid Egyptian laborers, but the wealthy landowners were mainly dependent on the Israelite slaves.

Five miles north of Pithom, a road branched off to the right to one of the area's large limestone quarries. Limestone was found in abundance in the hills of the east bank of the Nile, but only a few sites yielded stone of construction quality. The majestic, thousand-year-old pyramids to the south, many built with native limestone, had weathered the desert winds well.

Scattered potholes irritated Pharaoh, and the thick cushion helped little to ease his plight when he grew tired of standing.

About halfway to Rameses, the caravan entered a village and halted in front of a small, one-story brick building. Pharaoh and his leaders climbed down from their chariots, entered, and reclined at the tables, grateful for the respite. Two barefoot young girls in white dresses brought in trays holding several pottery-mugs of beer and fresh, sweet pastries.

"We have had two consecutive subnormal harvests," the pharaoh said to his minister of waters and agriculture. "You are my authority on such matters. What is the cause of this?"

The hunchbacked minister nervously stroked his swept-back black hair. He answered defensively, "Some years, the god of the Nile, Hapi,[3] gives us good crop yields, and in some years, they are less, depending, as you know, O Pharaoh, on the depth of our annual flooding. The river has been unpredictably miserly lately. We know nothing about what the gods do in the hills and mountains of the lands farther south."

"Have you any suggestions?" asked Pharaoh.

"Perhaps, mighty Pharaoh," stammered the minister, "we should sacrifice more animals to Hapi and his goddess, Anuket."[3]

"I'll consider it," snapped Pharaoh.

More mugs of beer were quaffed before the troupe's thirst was slaked, and they continued on their journey.

* * * * *

The city of Rameses, where his grandfather had relocated the capital fifty years earlier, renaming it after himself, lay south of the Great Sea, near the easternmost branch of the Nile. As the caravan approached the city, Pharaoh caught glimpses of ships to his left between the clumps of palm trees lining the river banks. Small pleasure boats with pointed ends and brightly painted sails scudded past barges carrying exports of grain, vegetables, limestone, gold, copper, and papyrus northward. Others were bound for Nubia to exchange their cargos for spices, ivory, slaves, and well-bred cattle; some were cruising into port with Syrian horses and cedar logs from Lebanon.

The chariots rumbled on, past a string of oxen-pulled carts that had moved aside to allow the entourage to pass. They carried high-quality clay, a bane to the Israelite slaves who were forced to dig it up day after day and transport it under the broiling sun to the nearby brickyards.

A short distance beyond, Pharaoh observed a flurry of activity at the brickyard, a yard several times larger than the one at Pithom. Under the prodding of Egyptian guards, a myriad of slaves shuttled their burdens in weaving lines between mountains of straw, great heaps of clay, and the large trenches of water where the two were mixed to make bricks. The tons of straw—dried stems of wheat, rye, and barley—had been gleaned from the fields, mainly by hired Egyptian laborers. Masses of milling, sunburned men hoed or churned the viscid, gummy, maroon mixture in the trenches with their bare feet. Other slaves shoveled the final mixture into molds of different sizes to be sun-dried or baked in bronze ovens to satisfy Pharaoh's expansive plans to enlarge his cities. The smaller, finished bricks were loaded onto wooden troughs carried on men's shoulders, while the larger ones were piled onto wooden-wheeled carts to be rolled to construction sites. Most of these slaves were Hebrews, with fewer darker-skinned ones, the booty from southern conquests.

Pharaoh smiled when he saw Egyptian guards strutting on the periphery of the lines, punishing laggards with whips and rods. When the pace of a worker flagged, harsh words punctuated by the sting or cut of a whip temporarily revived fatigued muscles. The perspiring workers moaned long, spontaneous, singsong chants while an infrequent tree cast a morsel of shade toward them.

Pharaoh's royal cohort approached the bridge over the stagnant moat guarding one of the three entrances into the walled city of Rameses. Two guards on horseback galloped through the city gates and clattered toward the procession over the wide, wooden bridge. They saluted Pharaoh, who briefly raised a hand, and then turned to escort the caravan into the bustling fortress city. Two larger-than-life sculpted granite tigers flanked the city gates. The company crossed over the bridge and down a street with buildings on either side. Most of the larger ones were of limestone, the smaller of brick, many adorned with columns and ornate facades of carved animals.

Pharaoh prized this city. As a heavily-manned fortress, with large numbers of chariots, it supplied the means to protect Egypt from enemy forces coming overland from the east. The royal navy, moored to the south where the Nile branched, was positioned to repel forces coming up the Nile.

As they rode through the streets toward the palace, wealthy and poor alike fell to their knees in worship because the pharaoh was more than a king; like all pharaohs before him, he was believed to be the embodiment of the god Horus,[3] king of the gods of the earth.

The horses pulled the chariots through an archway and into the courtyard of the palace. Servants brought wine and sweet cakes, and court magicians and priests greeted Pharaoh with deep bows as he entered his royal home.

The calm of Pharaoh and his court was, however, superficial. Moral decadence simmered beneath the peaceful surface of the land, and its insidious influence was increasing. Though the Egyptians worshipped and sacrificed to their many gods, diseases spread and the number of graves multiplied. Even the wealth of this mighty country could not buy cures from her ill-equipped physicians, magicians, and soothsayers.

*****

The masses of the tyrannized Israelite slaves, living in the city's western slave quarters in Goshen, were bowed to the breaking point, full of anger and revulsion. Generations had known nothing but poverty and fear. Year after year they worked for the cruel powers of the empire, and then as slaves. Men, women, and children were nothing but human beasts of burden to be used and discarded, always at the whim of their masters. Others, conscripted as soldiers, died valiantly in the wars of the Egyptians. Even those who herded the pharaoh's and their own animals were treated with disdain. Since the ascension of the new pharaoh, their lot was even worse.

Occasionally, a talented artisan slave would be recognized and become employed in a semiskilled or skilled position. These more fortunate ones were treated moderately well and were less enthusiastic when they occasionally joined in the prayers for freedom. But the great majority had ceased outward resistance and desperately cried out for relief from a supernatural power. Some prayed to the Egyptian gods, but growing numbers turned to Abraham's familiar God Most High, Possessor of Heaven and Earth,[c] even though such prayers over the centuries had produced only occasional visions through His few prophets and prophetesses.

*****

Six slaves sat at the far end of a large wooden table and finished their brief lunch at the brickyards in the city of Rameses.

One spoke softly, "My friend, the historian Abidan, calculated that it won't be many more years until the year Abraham said we would somehow be freed."

Nethanel answered, "Freedom, not too far off … ha! I never want to hear the name 'Abraham' again. Why did he agree to follow that god, knowing that it would cost us over four centuries of persecution, much in back-breaking slavery—and here in Egypt? He told Abraham that all the families of the world will be blessed through him, but what about us? I hope that his god is satisfied."

"You speak for many of us," said another. "Were it not for Abraham, all of us would be living in peace and prosperity in the land of Ur now. Free. Not driven day by day building monuments for that pompous pharaoh. We follow laws, commands, all set by him. I swear by Moloch, if I ever get out of here, it's 'do as I please' from now on. No more laws, no more orders."

The first said, "Some say that Abraham's God predicted our long-suffering through observing our attitudes, but I say it was a contrived plan on his part. It's bad enough to become enslaved by a tyrant or a victor, but to have it arranged by a god is inhuman. He owes us. We are 'the chosen.' Maybe to make up for it he will break our chains."

Nethanel said, "The only way God could free us is to cause the death of their leaders, or maybe a foreign army could conquer Egypt and set us free."

Gamaliel, a stocky man, whispered, "From God's point of view, our enforced slavery must have been a great gamble, a great risk for Him. To keep our trust through these tough years? I wonder if He can regain the allegiance of our people? Many of us still do pray to Him for release."

"You dream," said Nethanel. "I'll stay with my Egyptian gods."

*****

Nethanel

Nethanel was the youngest of the tribal elders at thirty-two years of age. Easy, inviting eyes contrasted with a measure of acquired arrogance that covered his shame, living with a pock-marked face from a childhood disease. Although he applied himself, the basic schooling lessons taught by his rather simple, but canny, mother escaped him.

He strove to excel in every physical endeavor, trying to please a father who regretted his unplanned birth and wore his resentment like a medal. Continually rebuffed, Nethanel found acceptance in three male friends who shared his passion for novelty. He was the first to try beer, to ride a "borrowed" horse, and to seduce a girl, Nara, one night behind the remote tannery. The hot, tangy smell of leather always reminded him of her.

He developed a taste for beer and fighting. When he was fifteen, his father, believing him to be incorrigible, enlisted him in the army as a foot soldier. As the new recruit in a barracks stocked with hostile, testing veterans, his defiant attitude brought many bloody defeats. In six months he had grown and strengthened, winning fights and respect.

During his second campaign, to the east, Nethanel and three other young soldiers drank too much date wine and, by stealth at night, captured an outpost manned by a dozen enemy soldiers. When his senior officer tried to discipline him for disobedience rather than praise him, Nethanel struck him. He was punished, discharged from the army, and put on permanent brickmaking duty.

Nara remained his one true female friend, slowly tempering his impulsive, confrontational nature. She encouraged his trustworthiness and boldness. They were married when he was twenty, and she bore him a son and a daughter, whom they cherished.

Though shunned by the Egyptians, he gained approval from his tribe of Issachar for his unwavering courage to stand for justice in word and deed and for an uncommon honesty. Eventually, he rose to become an elder at the age of twenty-six.

Endnotes

1. "Pithom" and "Rameses," Nicholas Reeves, *Ancient Egypt: The Great Discoveries,* 2000, pp. 189, 198. See also David Daiches, *Moses: Man and His Vision.* 1975, p. 84.

2. "Philistines," Avnr Raban and Tobert R. Stieglitz, "The Sea Peoples and Their Contributions to Civilization." *Biblical Archeology Review,* Nov.-Dec. 1991, pp. 40–42.

3. "Hapi" "Anuket" "Horus": *Gods and Mythology of Ancient Egypt.* http://www.touregypt.net/godsofegypt/ page 1.

Chapter 3

A Sheepherder to Lead?

For four centuries, God had minimally intervened while the Egyptians oppressed the Israelites, and the Israelites, likewise, had distanced themselves from Him. When, at last, greater numbers of them cried out to the God of Abraham, He finally responded, initiating the surprising, wrenching process of liberating them.

His first need was for a leader, a trained man who sought Him and was willing to learn obedience. Such a suitable captain was not to be found in Egypt. Although most of the Hebrew elders believed in God, their leadership qualities had been suppressed by the subjugation of slavery and intimidation from their masters. However, just as God had allowed Joseph to stew in prison until his time to lead arrived, so also God had sequestered His chosen one—a spry, eighty-year-old Israelite refugee.

*****

One day, while Moses was out pasturing Jethro's flock near Mount Sinai, he saw before him a lone bush with flames leaping from it.[1] He drew closer to investigate, stunned that its leaves, and even its fruit, were not even singed. As he approached, the bush spoke to him.

"Moses ... Moses ..."[a]

He stepped back in wonderment. Then, mystified by who might be behind the bush, he answered, "Here I am."[b]

But walking toward the flaming shrub, it rebuked him. *"Do not come near here; remove your sandals from your feet, for the place on which you are standing is holy ground."*[c] The bush demanded obeisance! He took his sandals off and moved three steps to the side. There was no one behind the bush. The voice had come from the fire!

Moses was apprehensive. "Who is here commanding me?"

At that, the voice identified itself. *"I am the God of your father, the God of Abraham, the God of Isaac, and the God of Jacob."*[d]

"This is their god!" he stunned, "right here—before me—and he is actually speaking to me—their god—the god of my father who commands me!" Moses hid his face in his cupped hands.

"*I have surely seen the affliction of My people ...*" said God, "*and have given heed to their cry.... I have come down to deliver them from the power of the Egyptians, and to bring them ... to a land flowing with milk and honey, to the place of the Canaanite.*"[e]

"*His* people, the Hebrew slaves? He does plan to free them, as He promised! Have they been treated so poorly that he must come to their rescue? But why does He tell *me* this?" wondered Moses.

"*Therefore, come now,*" God said, expecting immediate compliance, "*and I will send you to Pharaoh, so that you may bring My people, the sons of Israel, out of Egypt.*"[f]

"Wait a minute god," he thought. "You are asking too much. This must be some sort of trick or an illusion. I don't care that much for the slaves in the first place. But to get that horde to follow me? Impossible. Who am I that I should go to Pharaoh and bring your people out of Egypt?"[g] he asked. "Would I even know the new pharaoh? Maybe I could have influenced a pharaoh forty years ago, but now I am too old."

Besides, what was Egypt to him but remorse, disillusionment, buried hope, and worst of all, his arrest and probable execution? If he agreed, how many of the Hebrews would actually come with him, and where would they go? Free the people? Lead them? All he led was sheep.

"*Certainly I will be with you, and this shall be the sign to you that it is I who have sent you,*" God said. "*When you have brought the people out of Egypt, you shall worship God at this mountain.*"[h]

"God seems to assume that I—that *He* and I could succeed in this wild plan," thought Moses. "In reality, I am just one of the Hebrews. I would be turning against the palace, the crown, my friends who respected me—forty years ago. Who of them is still alive?

"Even if I did get to Egypt and explained to the Israelites that their god had appeared to me, would they not surely doubt me and ask, 'What is His name?' What shall I say to them?"

"I AM WHO I AM," God responded. *"Thus you shall say to the sons of Israel, 'I AM has sent me to you.'"*

"I AM? Names had specific meanings, but this god must be beyond definition, His qualities too great to be captured by a name. How would that name convince the people?"

"Go and gather the elders of Israel together, and say to them, the LORD, the God of your fathers, the God of Abraham, Isaac, and Jacob, has appeared to me, saying, 'I am indeed concerned about you…. I will bring you up out of the affliction of Egypt to the land of the Canaanite.'"

Moses had been thrown into this; his mind struggled with thoughts. "The elders? I know of Gamaliel, Eliasaph, and Aaron only. But to get an audience with their fellow elders? And if I can, what a message I would bring!"

God added, *"Say to [Pharaoh] 'the LORD, the God of the Hebrews, has met with us. So now, please, let us go a three day's journey into the wilderness, that we may sacrifice to the LORD our God.'"*

The god of the Hebrews—all right, Pharaoh would know the Hebrews. Then he thought, "If we are bound for Canaan, what good would a three-day pass to make a sacrifice do? Pharaoh would never allow that."

Sure enough, God confirmed this, admitting to Moses that Pharaoh would not allow them to leave. But since he would not, God would *strike Egypt with all [His] miracles which [He] shall do in the midst of it; and after that [Pharaoh] will let you go.* But God told Moses that the Israelites would find sudden favor in the sight of the Egyptians before they left; the Egyptians would give them of their wealth. *Thus you will plunder the Egyptians.* God clearly proclaimed His authority over, and his stored-up righteous wrath against, the Egyptians while revealing the framework of His plan as its Master Strategist. The slaves would walk out of Egypt to freedom with newfound wealth!

"What miracles? To harm the Egyptians?" Moses, now a meek man after forty years of sheepherding, did not despise Egypt and shunned being the go-between for this god whose anger was apparent. "We were mean to the slaves, but the latest pharaoh must be utterly cruel," he thought.

Moses remained unconvinced for some time. "What if they will not believe that the God of Abraham actually appeared to me, an eighty-year-old fugitive, a sheepherder?" he asked. "'Ha!' they'll laugh, 'Prove it to us.'"

"*Throw* [your staff] *on the ground,*"[n] God demanded.

As he did so, it became a serpent that slithered away.

"*Grasp it by its tail,*"[o] commanded God.

As Moses tentatively approached and grabbed the snake, the staff's hard texture returned. "It's a staff again, but now," he squirmed, "leprosy, like snow,[p] consumes my other hand!"

"*Now, put your hand into your bosom,*"[q] said God.

In fear, Moses again obeyed and, withdrawing it, exclaimed, "It is restored like the rest of my flesh!"

"*If they will not believe even these two signs … take some water from the Nile and pour it on the dry ground; and … [it] will become blood on the dry ground.*"[r]

"The miracles have begun!" Moses recognized he was relatively sure that these three miracles would convince the elders. But he pushed God's patience to the limit. "I have never been eloquent … but slow of speech … and tongue."[s]

"*Who has made man's mouth? … Is it not I, the LORD?*" Then He added, "*I will … teach you what you are to say.*"[t]

Moses crumbled. "Please, LORD, now send the message by some other person, anyone but me," he begged.

God became angry. "*Is there not your brother Aaron, the Levite? I know that he speaks fluently. And moreover, behold, he is coming out to meet you … I will be with your mouth and his mouth, and I will teach you what you are to do. Moreover, he shall speak for you to the people.*"[u] God also reminded Moses to take with him his staff with which to perform the signs. As the bush fire subsided, Moses felt God's insistence.

"So, Aaron is my brother! My real brother! The eloquent Hebrew slave. And I am one of the tribe of Levi," Moses acknowledged. "Aren't the Levites some sort of a religious sect? He will be able to assemble the elders. He will speak for me, and I will not be alone before them. I will learn about my family from him.

"And it was he who sent the messages to me," Moses' mind tumbled.

"God has imposed on him to come out here to help me. How he must resent my favored life." Then he realized, "I must treat him with the greatest respect."

Alone, bewildered, and unsure of himself, Moses herded the sheep toward home, preoccupied with his mysterious encounter, but resigned to obey. He knew that it would be a difficult task, a long and trying mission, so he sought support, deciding to bring his family along with him. Doubting that Jethro would permit that, when he arrived home he presented a harmless plan to his father-in-law, veiling its true purpose with a lie. "Please let me go that I may return to my brethren who are in Egypt and see if they are still alive."[v]

To Moses' surprise, Jethro considered the benign journey and said simply, "Go in peace."[w]

With that permission, Moses described to Zipporah the excitement of his encounter with God at the burning bush and of God's commission for him.

"Go to Egypt?" she blurted out. "Are you not afraid to return to your people?" Then, anxiously, she added, "And for me, forty-seven years I have lived in one place. Now, I am to be suddenly uprooted with our children?" Despite her apprehension, Zipporah regained her composure, touched his arm, and said, "Moses, if you must go, our sons and I will go with you."

*****

Later that day, while organizing his few selected goods, Moses was startled when the voice of God spoke to him again, telling him that the Egyptian leaders who had sought his death had all since died. He also warned Moses that, in spite of the three miracles Moses would perform, Pharaoh would not let the Hebrews go. Then God said a strange thing: "*I will* [even] *harden* [Pharaoh's] *heart so that he will not let the people go. Then you shall say to Pharaoh … 'Israel is My son, My first-born … Let My son go, that he may serve me; but you have refused to let him go. Behold, I will kill your son, your first-born*.'"[x] And with that, God departed, giving no further information.

Moses sat on his bed, shoulders slack, as he struggled to make sense of God's puzzling, conflicting revelations. Inexplicably, God would harden Pharaoh's heart, purposely making him unyielding, and thereby denying the success of Moses' first assignment—the release of the Israelites. Was this God totally on his side or was he testing him by making his task almost impossible? Moses wanted counsel, but who could he ask? The burden must be his alone, he acknowledged, as he finished preparing for the trip.

After bidding goodbye to Jethro's family, Moses, staff in hand, walked westward with Zipporah and their two sons, Gershom, twenty-one years old, and Eliezer, eight, mounted on a donkey.[2] Grassy plains gave way to desert as they traveled, finding wadi along the caravan route. As they prepared to go to bed in their tent on the third night, Moses said to his wife, "God must have great love for us. He won me over by—"

"*Moses!*" God angrily called out, interrupting Moses' reflection.

Zipporah, jumping up in terror, could see light through the wall of the tent. "Is that *your* god, Moses? He has come back here!" she cried.

God roared that He would put Moses *to death.*[y]

Zipporah grabbed Moses' arm. "What does he want?"

Moses understood. "The circumcision," he said slowly.

"No!"

"We must or he will kill me," Moses said, leading Eliezer out of the tent.

Shaken by concern for her husband, Zipporah grabbed a sharp piece of flint, bolted out ahead of the two, saying, "I will do it."

"Lie down," she told her son. She raised Eliezer's robe and straddled his legs. To the sound of his muffled cries, she cut off his foreskin and threw it at Moses' feet. "Because of the circumcision," she hissed, "you are not a husband of love, but a bridegroom of blood to me."[z]

Moses stood still, staring at the piece of flesh that had been a chronic source of marital conflict.

"Zipporah," said Moses, "my love for you is boundless, but our sin covered us with filth. By removing it, you saved us from this God who demands total obedience." Then God left them alone; the light contracted and disappeared.

*****

Later that night, Moses confided to his wife, "Zipporah, the enormous task of convincing the Israelites to leave Egypt with me may be made more difficult if you are with me. They have laws against intermarriage. It is best if you and our sons return to your father's home for the present."

"If we are more of a hindrance than a help," said Zipporah, relieved but acting resigned, "then we shall go. Your trust in this god far exceeds mine. I shall be greatly concerned for your safety, my dear Moses," she said, and kissed him. "Come back soon."

The family journey, launched with a lie to Jethro, had run aground. The next morning, Moses assigned Gershom to lead them back to Jethro while he proceeded on foot toward Egypt.

And toward his older brother.

*****

One morning in Rameses, a week earlier, as Aaron came in for a morning meal, his wife remarked, "Aaron, I hope that look is not for me. You seem troubled."

"I am. God spoke to me this morning—oh, it was not a dream, but clear words, and He gave me a mission."

She stared in disbelief. "God actually spoke to you?"

"Yes."

"And what did He tell you?"

"He wants me to go to my brother, meet Moses in the wilderness,[aa] and accompany him back here. He promised to lead me to him." He paused. "Moses has been selected to help us all gain our freedom."

"Moses?" she asked. "We have not heard from him or spoken his name in almost forty years." She thought a few moments. "If God has finally decided to act on our behalf, couldn't He find a leader from among us? How about you, you who are a spokesman in the council? You have stayed here in bondage while your brother ran away."

"Elisheba, it is God's choice, not mine."

"Will you go?"

"I must."

"And free us! How did God say that He would free us?" she asked.

"He didn't say, only that I should go. It's not that I want to go; I certainly do not know the desert."

"What will people think when they learn where you have gone? To Moses? Only your sister Miriam, father, you, and I know that you and Moses are brothers."

"Do not tell the people that I am gone," Aaron warned. "Tell them that I am sick with a possibly contagious illness. Our guard is friendly toward us and will accept that."

"Aaron," she asked, "how do you feel toward your brother?"

"In truth," he replied, "I still harbor some resentment. What privileges were his in his acquired life while we had such a meager existence! All four of our sons, and even our two daughters, work hard, and for what? For food, clothing, and a small house. Our roles could have been reversed but by the fate of birth. You could have been my queen."

"You wouldn't have met me."

Ignoring her comment, Aaron added, "These last forty years he probably has been enjoying himself sumptuously in his freedom while we labor under arrogant masters."

"How right you are. But Aaron, how will you escape?"

"I will find a way. Before that, I must explain to our sons. I hope to return within ten days."

*****

Aaron knew that to travel on foot in the torrid sun with only the little food or water he could carry would be difficult. Since slaves had not been permitted outside of the city for generations, the only information about the surrounding areas was that which trickled down from caravanners. There were a few villages on the eastern caravan routes where Aaron must travel to meet Moses, but they were at some distances, and Aaron had no transportation.

Asking about, he discovered that a caravan was heading eastward in four days and that the caravan master, Husani, was a man for whom he had done a favor several years earlier. He had hidden his brother, sought by the Egyptians for striking a guard, in the slave quarters for a week until he was able to escape in a caravan.

Aaron sent a message to the master through an older Egyptian guard who had grown to respect Aaron through the years. In their brief encounters, Aaron's comments to the guard had always been cogent, sometimes surprising, but always helpful. The message was that Aaron had to meet his brother out on the desert. The dark-skinned Husani granted his request, and two nights later, Aaron, disguised, secured his escape to the east as a hired hand in the caravan. He endured long days of travel but was convinced that if God had called him, He would find Moses.

*****

The caravan encountered Philistine scouts as the route passed by the northern edge of the Red Sea. The guards gave them free passage. Under God's direction, Aaron left the caravan two days later when it turned north, and continued toward the southeast. In the afternoon of the second day, he came upon a man in shepherd's clothes, walking toward him. He approached cautiously and thought he recognized him. "I am Aaron. Are you Moses?"

"Aaron!" Moses exclaimed. "So you are my brother?" They embraced and kissed. Moses looked into his face. "You would come all the way out here to meet me!"

"I was sent," Aaron answered.

"You look hearty. Has your journey been difficult?"

"I would not wish to do this often," he answered.

They shared a drink of water and two biscuits from Moses' pouch. Moses noticed that Aaron was a head shorter than he, with prominent ears, curly white hair, and a trim beard. Aaron entwined his long, slender fingers uneasily as they spoke. As they resumed walking, Moses asked, "It was you who sent me those messages?"

"Yes, but to little avail. Our relationship had been guarded by a pledge until mother decided to … bend it."

"I am grateful to her," Moses said softly. "We wouldn't be here without the messages. You know, Aaron, I do remember you. On several occasions, I heard you plead the case for the Israelites. With your logical arguments, you marshaled support for your causes. Now, God has told me that you are to be instrumental in accomplishing His task for us."

"I will help as He sees fit," said Aaron.

As they walked on, Moses asked, "Aaron, how did you get the turtle?"

"Our father was a skilled carpenter, though his talents were little used in Egypt. He made the pair of turtles with stolen wood, and since you liked to play with them as a child, he sent one back to the palace with you."

"And you kept the other?"

"Yes. We sent it thinking that it would cause you to believe more in the messages."

"It did. Now, my brother, listen to what God has done here." Moses detailed the events of the past weeks. When he told Aaron of the three miracles, Aaron gave his interpretation. "Moses, first, I believe that you are to overcome the snake that is the national symbol of Egypt with your shepherd's staff. I suppose that God will heal the Israelites, leprous in His eyes through their worship of other gods. As for the third, God will also control, perhaps destroy, the life-giving, sacred Nile."[3]

"You are as wise as God has said," reflected Moses. "Once I accepted his persistent offer, He revealed his plan, disciplined my wife Zipporah and me, and now He has sent you to me. He overlooks nothing."

Aaron fought back the lingering pride of the older brother and responded hoarsely. "Had I talked with you years ago, I could have taught you Hebrew cunning and wisdom; you could have been patient, harnessed your efforts, formed alliances, tested waters, and saved us then. But instead, you impulsively struck and did us no good. I hope that you have cooled down in forty years."

Moses returned his gaze. "I have matured as a protector of sheep as I never would have as a ruler of persons. And now, I must depend on you. I know few in Egypt but, as God implied, you are highly respected. Will you be able to obtain an audience with our people?"

"I can," Aaron answered. "Now, let's be on our way. It is a long journey."

*****

There was little conversation as the brothers proceeded during the heat of the day, retracing the route they had taken out of Egypt. Refreshed by the cooler evening and a meal of rationed food and water, talk came more easily.

"Aaron," said Moses, "I have told you what God did with me. Now, tell me what has happened in your life."

"I have a devoted wife, Elisheba, and four strong sons. Nadab, the oldest, was conscripted to become a soldier, and Abihu, the second boy, who idolizes Nadab, serves as an oarsman on a naval ship. The two younger boys, Eleazar and Ithamar, are brickmakers. Nadab and Abihu have always been high-spirited, but the younger ones are quieter, more thoughtful boys. I have two daughters who are both talented with their hands. One cards and spins wool, and the other is a seamstress."

Moses smiled. "And you seem strong yourself."

"After I'd been digging clay for five years, the potter's assistant became ill one day. Being nearby and respected by the guards, I was thrust into that position. I developed a skill at that trade, and in two years, began to produce vases that were appreciated. I learned to paint bright, variegated birds and fish on them, and have done that ever since."

"Had I known sooner who I was, I could have spared you and your sons," said Moses.

"And risked exposure—maybe death? No, you were safe only as an Egyptian grandson to the king. What has your life been like, Moses?"

"I married in Midian and have two fine sons, twenty-one and eight years old. My family started out with me on this journey, but at my request, returned home. I have a kind father-in-law who is a priest to his people. Life has been as peaceful as a shepherd can have."

"We followed your successful military exploits," Aaron said. "But what of your years growing up? It must have been an easy life."

"My clearest memories are those after the age of about six. I did enjoy the many luxuries of the palace, where I received a broad education and mastered the Hebrew language without difficulty, though that should not surprise you. In the military, I must have accounted myself well because I became commander when I was twenty-five."

"I quietly took some pride in your victories."

*****

Two nights later, Moses asked, "Who rules Egypt now?"

Aaron said, "In the forty years you have been gone, the old Pharaoh and his son—he would have been your alleged uncle—both died. You uncle's son, your 'cousin,' who would have been about your age, died of an illness eight years ago."

"That cousin was always jealous of me."

"His son, your nephew, now reigns."

Moses: "That boy was not born yet when I left. How old is he?"

Aaron: "I would guess about thirty-five."

Moses: "And how does he treat you?"

"He is more vicious than all of the rest. We are often in chains, and the beatings have multiplied. But he has bonded us together in our hate of him, a revulsion that overcomes our resentfulness of the God of Abraham putting us into this slavery. We have become far more united in including God in our prayers, even our cries for His mercy and freedom."

"We are to meet with my nephew. Will that be possible?"

"I am well-respected as spokesman for our tribe and if he knows your reputation, I believe that we will."

*****

During the long journey, they passed through Philistine territory unheeded. One night Moses and Aaron sat talking. "I know the story of my parents placing me in the basket in the Nile to save me and of the princess finding me," said Moses. "But I have often wondered who my—our—parents were."

"Our father is still alive, and he is one hundred and five years old. Our mother, Jochabed, died eight years ago. She was a fine woman who provided well for us with what she had. She tried to instill into us her unwavering faith in our God with endless stories of our ancestors. She made us swear we would never reveal that you were a member of our family, an oath we kept."

"I am in great debt to her and to our father."

*****

As they approached Rameses, Moses said, "Aaron, were you ever jealous or angry of my good fortune?"

"No, I was glad that you lived and that your life had been favored," he feigned.

"I'm not sure I would have been able to see it that way."

"It is just maturity," said Aaron.

*****

The brothers skirted the northern reaches of Rameses at night, reaching the entrance to the slave quarters, manned by a friendly guard. They entered and walked toward Aaron's home.

*****

Elisheba had finished her job mending soldiers' uniforms and returned to their home where she was preparing dinner for herself. She had thought of Moses that day more than usual. Long-standing resentments for his fortunate station in life blended with a slight physical attraction born of two chance glimpses of him. He should arrive in a few days, and she would try to be courteous to him and show warmth.

*****

After a short time, she was surprised by a knock on the door; the brothers entered. Aaron began, "Elisheba, I want you to meet my brother, Moses." Here he was before her—tall, still handsome at his age. The resentment she carried waned. She bowed her head slightly and said, "Welcome, Moses, you have weathered well the years of your absence. It is a pleasure to meet you. Our home is yours, as our children live elsewhere."

Her elegance, overshadowing slightly frayed clothes, put him at ease. He answered, "Aaron has spoken well of you, Elisheba, and of your family. I am honored to meet you and to be in your home." He knew that he would not be welcome in the palace, so he added, "I appreciate your hospitality, and I accept your offer. Aaron and I may have much business together soon."

"Elisheba, I would like to take Moses next door," said Aaron.

"Of course. It will be quite a surprise, for both."

At the house next door, they were met by a tall, pleasantly stout, head-erect woman with dark eyes and long braided hair of the same hue. "Moses, this is your sister, Miriam," said Aaron.

"Miriam! My sister!" as he looked into her eyes.

Miriam moved toward Moses with the grace of a young dancer, belying the wrinkles of her forehead and corners of her eyes, and briefly embraced him. "My brother, I heard that you were coming with Aaron. It has been many years since you were in my presence. I am glad that you returned. Elisheba says that you have a mission."

"Yes, but later."

"Come," she said.

She took Moses to an old man seated in a shadow in the corner of the room. "Moses, this is your father, Amram." As Moses reached out to touch his shoulder, he saw a faint smile cross the deep lines of a face sculpted by affliction. Drooping lids draped dark eyes. Moses leaned toward him, "Father."

"He has difficulty hearing," Miriam said.

"Father," he repeated louder, "it is so good to finally meet you."

His answer came in a hoarse whisper. "To be able—see and talk to you, my son—" Tears formed in his eyes, as he reached out a withered hand, "and to touch you."

Moses knelt before his father. "I am profoundly indebted to you for my life. It must have been agonizing for mother and you to watch me live as I did and not to be able to communicate with me."

"It was. But those—buried years now—you are back. *You* saved me—I was—chief prey for—animal Mannel—the guard hated my insolence—beat me. Weeks after you killed—Mannel, I became ill—was—relieved. I recovered, but never had—return to pits. I—grateful for your act."

"Could he be the same man I saw?" thought Moses. "I am so sorry, my father, that we were such heartless rulers. But thank God that you are still alive."

"I have lived—this moment," Amram said with a dry throat, as Moses leaned forward and kissed him on both cheeks.

Moses turned toward his sister. "Miriam, this is not the time but, if you will, I look forward to learning from you some details of my infancy. How did our mother feel toward me?"

"She saw that you were special and reveled as that prediction came true. How happy and proud she would be today."

"Some of her stories must still be in my mind. An outstanding woman," said Moses.

"She was," replied Miriam. "Now, you must be tired. Elisheba and I will prepare a meal for you, and we will share the past. Will your stay be long?"

"I do not know. I am on a mission ordered by the same God who communed with you."

"He still does," corrected Miriam.

*****

The five sat on stools around the small, unpainted wooden table and ate the last few bites of their meal.

"Miriam, your purple tunic came from the east," observed Moses.

"A gift from an emir whose caravan was saved from highwaymen by my vision. But tell us, Moses, how will you proceed with your ambitious task?"

Moses began slowly. "Aaron and I are to go to Pharaoh and plead for the release of the slaves. God has miracles with which He will strike Egypt so that they will finally drive us out. The details are His."

Miriam pondered a moment. "God has revealed nothing of your mission to me. As Aaron may have told you, I have a moderate following among our people as a prophetess.[bb] What role shall I play in this venture?"

"I know no more. He asks for our blind trust."

"Of course," Miriam said, but she looked disappointed.

*****

Twenty-two Hebrew men, elders from the tribes, assembled at Aaron's invitation in the large, secret room dug beneath the house of an Israelite. Most squatted, some were seated on the ground, and a number stood. In the front of the room, four white candles burned on a waist-high, wooden table, painting shadows of the standing men on the opposite wall. Aaron introduced Moses, and many greeted his presence with surprise. Filmy threads of his past had been preserved and handed down by venerable elders, including tales of his royal upbringing and of his flight from Pharaoh many years before. Caravan travelers had added to the mystery, bringing occasional rumors of his residence as a shepherd in the east. Yet here he was standing before them, but not as Aaron's brother. Fear of Moses' fugitive status had convinced Aaron not to reveal their kinship yet. There would be time for that later. The midwife and Jochabed had carried the secret to their graves.

*****

One of the older leaders, Gamaliel, addressed Aaron. "You are a trusted, proven one among us. Why have you brought this Moses into our midst?"

"God sent me to bring him to you and sent Moses to obtain our freedom," Aaron replied.

"Our freedom?!" Gamaliel wondered in disbelief.

"And what a nice idea," Nethanel sneered. "I have nothing to do with any god. But how does this god of yours plan to do that?"

"The details have not yet been revealed," said Aaron.

"You are serious, are you not?" asked Gamaliel.

"Yes."

The elders mumbled among themselves. Finally, Shelumiel, the carpenter, asked, "What is the name of this god of ours, Moses?"

With apprehension, mixed with a sense of his mission, Moses rose and spoke, "The God of your fathers, the God who identified Himself with two names: one simply '*I AM*' and the other, '*The God of Abraham, the God of Isaac, and the God of Jacob.*'[cc] He told me of His keen concern for your plight, and He supplied me with proof of His powers."

"And what proof is that, Moses?" Shelumiel asked.

"Look," said Moses.

He tentatively dropped his staff before them and watched as God transformed it into a snake and back. Then Moses demonstrated the healing of his suddenly leprous hand. At that, he picked up a pitcher of water, drawn from the Nile, and it poured out as blood. The amazed elders became silent and, one by one, briefly bowed their heads in respect for God.

Moses looked at them and thought, "God has delivered on His promises. But the miracles were *His* feats. Somehow I must gain their trust—convince them that I am also personally concerned for them."

"What more can you tell us about how you will do that?" asked another.

"All I know is that your God will perform a series of acts to accomplish it. I know no more today," answered Moses.

"We shall await further word from you, Moses," said Gamaliel, as the meeting disbanded.

*****

On the evening of the new moon, three of the Israelite elders gathered in the small house of Abidan, of the tribe of Benjamin, sharing a skin of pilfered beer.

Nethanel began, "If we are to believe these two old men, one a stranger to me, then the God of Abraham is finally acting for us. It was he who got us into slavery in the first place, or was it only a coincidence that our ancestors migrated here from Canaan? But," he asked the age-old question, "why has He waited so long to help us?"

Eliasaph, from Gad, spoke deliberately. "Nethanel, perhaps God has kept us here to mature, to become less contentious, since we come from a quarrelsome and jealous stock. You know the stories as well as I: Cain killed Abel out of jealousy; Hagar, the maid, when she bore Abraham's son, was banished to the desert by his envious barren wife, Sarah. Abraham's grandson, Jacob, coveted his older brother Esau's birthright and stole it. Then he cheated his uncle out of a large number of cattle. Even Joseph's brothers sold him out of jealousy. Perhaps God hoped that the poverty of slavery would overcome our jealousies. After all, doesn't envy dissolve when there is little to envy? As for this Moses, I will tentatively support him."

"If God truly orchestrated all of this," offered Abidan, massaging one of his deformed knuckles, "He might have seen a way to use this evil to help us stay together and multiply. Left to our own, our people would have scattered as chaff blown by the winds. Look again at our history. Abraham and his nephew Lot were nomads, and when strife arose between them, they split up and lived separately. Jacob ran off to Mesopotamia to escape his angry brother, and where he sired twelve sons and a daughter. And even Esau, when he married outside of our tribes, moved south to the land of Edom. Joseph was shipped to Egypt by his jealous brothers. And now God has wisely kept us together in the midst of this awful servitude." He paused and then continued slowly, "As for me, I too believe that Moses carries God's credentials."

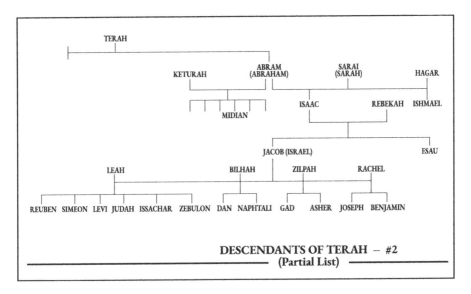

DESCENDANTS OF TERAH – #2
(Partial List)

Nethanel said, "Slavery could produce either humble people, willing to follow this god, or angry, resentful ones. With Moses here, we may find out soon which our people are; I suspect the latter for most."

Eliasaph, rubbing his calloused hands together, replied thoughtfully, "Perhaps we have relied too long on our many gods. It seems that Abraham's God has waited for our allegiance."

"Our task is to quietly begin to disseminate some of this freedom information to our tribes," said Abidan, "without raising their hopes too high."

* * * * *

Abidan

Because of diffuse, teenaged-onset arthritis, the Benjaminite, Abidan, had been excused from brickmaking. The sun provided him with some relief from his joint pains, and long hours outside had deeply darkened his skin. In his mid-thirties, the inflammation and pain gradually subsided, leaving him misshapen hands with prominent, deformed knuckles, deviated fingers, bulbous knees, and gnarled toes. He eventually walked without pain, but his gait was slow and choppy. Years of pain had produced puckered eyebrows and pinched eyelids.

His mind dwarfed his misshapen body. Early in life, he had been very inquisitive, pestering any and all for disparate pieces of information. He pieced together most of the oral Israelite history. With his physical limitations, he was assigned to work in the library, where he learned to read, gratifying his zeal while memorizing large portions of the written Egyptian history.

His intellect gained him eldership in his tribe.

His disabilities developed in him a tenderhearted empathy; he rejoiced with the fortunate as easily as he succored the grieving. The community saw him as a totally selfless person but, in truth, an intense need for approval drove his life. As he matured, his actions remained the same, but a growing self-confidence changed his motives, and his kindness to others became more genuine. He was beloved by most. Fortunately, his fun-loving wife kept the atmosphere light at home. She was physically suited to perform the heavy work of a household while rearing their three sons.

*****

Endnotes

1. The recounting of Moses' meeting with God is told in chapters 3 and 4 of Exodus.
2. "donkey," Ex. 4:20.
3. "Snake, leprous hand, Nile," Alfred Edersheim, *Bible History: Old Testament*, "The Exodus." 1949, pp. 50, 51.

Chapter 4

The Day of Reckoning

Aaron was a reliable and diligent worker. When he requested intermittent relief from his job because of meetings with the pharaoh, his foreman was impressed. "Take what time you need, but keep me informed," the foreman allowed.

Armed with the support of the elders, yet harboring concerns of Pharaoh's rejection, Moses and Aaron approached the palace gate.

"Who goes there and for what purpose?" challenged the guard, wearing the familiar orange and black.

Aaron responded boldly. "I am Aaron, spokesman for the Hebrew tribe of Levi. I bring with me Moses, a man from Midian, with news from the east for the highly esteemed pharaoh."

"Wait here," the guard ordered. He walked through the palace doorway into a large atrium, down a short hallway to the pharaoh's study.

Pharaoh sat at a desk peering over several parchments near the right wall of the room. He was puzzled at the news.[1] "I have heard once of the eloquent Aaron, one of the Israelites. But Moses? Many years ago there was a Moses in my grandfather's court, I believe. Is he an old man?"

"Yes, but lively," said the guard. "He says he has come from Midian and promises important news for you from that land."

"Bring them in—and remain with us." The guard bowed and departed.

The brothers followed the guard through the courtyard and into the palace atrium. On the modestly-decorated walls of forty years ago now hung a dozen large, rich, colorful paintings of sinister-appearing gods—some winged—and four exquisite but dark, dangerous landscapes. One painting was of torture instruments. Four limestone pedestals bearing busts of more gods and warriors were evenly spaced about the periphery of the hall. A slender female attendant, decked with gold and copper bracelets, anklets, and necklaces, poured liquid into a purple vase near the door to the study. Moses halted momentarily as memories washed over him. As a youth, regal surroundings had seemed important to him, but in the intervening years, his simple lifestyle and the dominant importance of his family had eroded their value. Still, they were magnificent.

Moses was familiar with the hall but not its furnishings. "Who produces this artwork?" he asked the guard.

"Most is by our Egyptian craftsmen," he answered. "But selected Hebrew slaves have also been trained to make them."

Moses remembered the few favored slaves of his time but was anxious for current information. "What skills have the slaves acquired?" he asked.

"Some of the more talented ones have learned to do all sorts of work as carpenters, potters, stonemasons, metalsmiths, artists, and jewelers. Some even design the patterns. Pharaoh uses them well."

Moses wondered if indeed all slaves yearned for freedom. "Are the craftsmen treated better than the slaves?" he asked.

The guard laughed. "Pharaoh is wise; he has a soft hand toward the artisans. Come, Pharaoh waits."

He led them down the hall toward the study. Moses paused again. Apprehensively, silently, he wondered, "Will I be welcome? Was the murder truly forgotten? God, prove Yourself again!"

After an answered knock, the guard led them into the study. A faint smell of incense greeted them. An exquisite Eastern rug covered most of a highly-polished, dark wooden floor. Pharaoh had moved to a black velvet throne at the far end of the carpet. A large tapestry of men in battle hung behind the throne. As they approached, Moses glanced at the ornate fabric coverings on two walls and the dark wooden shelves filled with scrolls on the third. Light streamed through windows on the fourth side of the room.

"O great Pharaoh, I present to you Aaron and Moses," the guard announced.

The brothers came forward and dropped to their knees.[1]

"You may stand," said Pharaoh. "Moses, I have heard of you—occasional whispers, rumors when I was young. You would have known my father, my grandparents, and great grandfather, the pharaoh of your youth. For years, it was forbidden to speak your name within these walls after you left. I myself bear you no ill will and have no interest in pursuing the reasons for your departure." Then, curtly, "Now, what news do you bring? I am quite busy."

Moses bowed again and spoke self-consciously. "I have been sent to speak on behalf of the Israelite slaves. This is what the LORD, the God of Israel, says, *'Let My people go that they may celebrate a feast to Me in the wilderness.'*[a]

"What kind of strange news is that?" parried a surprised Pharaoh. "Who is this lord that I should obey his voice and let Israel go?[b] I do not know him. And let the slaves go anywhere? Ha!" he laughed. "You fools have bizarre ideas." Then slowly, scornfully, he said, "Who are you to bother me with such a request?"

"The God of the Hebrews has met with us!" Moses replied. He paused, but Pharaoh was unmoved. Then Moses pleaded, "Please, let us go a three days' journey into the wilderness that we may sacrifice to the LORD our God—" he hesitated, "lest He fall upon us all with pestilence or with the sword."[c]

"Who do you think you are to threaten us, old man? If I halfway believed this 'meeting with a god' tale, I would still not consider getting by without the slaves for even one day. Now leave! Guard!" barked Pharaoh.

The brief encounter was over. They were hurried out.

*****

Word of Moses' intervention spread among the Israelites. "Freedom is imminent; forget the bricks," the Hebrew slaves joyously said to one another. But a different order came from the enraged Pharaoh: "Maintain your quotas, but—get your own straw!" Moses' visit with Pharaoh had worsened their plight. Having to forage for their own straw doubled the slaves' work and, as the production of bricks diminished, the Israelite foremen were beaten.

Those men angrily confronted Moses and Aaron. "May the LORD look upon you and judge you, for Pharaoh will put a sword in the foremen's hands to kill us."[d]

As the dispirited brothers retreated toward Aaron's home, Moses raised his eyes heavenward and cried out, "God, why didst Thou ever send me? I've only brought suffering and Thou hast not delivered Thy people at all."[e]

"Now you shall see what I will do to Pharaoh," answered the voice of God, *"for under compulsion he shall let them go, and ... shall drive them out of his land."*[f] Sensing Moses' discouragement, God stayed with him, reminding him that He had steadfastly been the God of Abraham and of his descendants, even while they suffered in Egypt. Moses' flagging spirits gradually lifted.

"*I will deliver* [the sons of Israel] *from their bondage*," God reconfirmed. "*I will also redeem* [them] *with an outstretched arm and with great judgments … I will be* [their] *God … I will bring* [them] *to the land which I swore to give to Abraham, Isaac, and Jacob, and I will give it to* [them] *for a possession*." And then for emphasis, "*I am the* Lord."[g]

Moses listened carefully, later relaying this conversation to the disillusioned foremen who scowled, "Get away from us, Moses; we do not listen to you anymore."

*****

Three days later, God reappeared to Moses, telling him to plead again with Pharaoh for his people. Moses replied dejectedly, "Behold, the sons of Israel have not listened to me; how then will Pharaoh listen to me, for I am unskilled in speech."[h]

God encouraged him: "*See, I make you as* [a god] *to Pharaoh, and your brother Aaron shall be your prophet.*"[i] God explained that He would prevent Pharaoh from releasing the Hebrews so "*that I may multiply My signs and My wonders in the land of Egypt…. And the Egyptians shall know that I am the* Lord."[j]

*****

With renewed spirit, Moses and Aaron followed the guard again into Pharaoh's study. He grudgingly heard them, this time in the presence of four regal council members and two magicians. The brothers again requested release of the slaves. "If your God is so powerful, show me a miracle," laughed the pharaoh.

At God's instruction, Aaron cast down his staff and it became a serpent. Not to be outdone, the court magicians threw down their staffs next to Aaron's and they were also transformed into serpents. Aaron watched in astonishment as his serpent swallowed up their staffs.[k] Aaron picked up his reformed wooden staff.

"I am not impressed. You take up our time with your little game. Out!" said Pharaoh with a sneer. His attendants quickly hustled the brothers out of the palace.

*****

Perplexed, Aaron said, "Could Pharaoh not see that the powers of our Hebrew God far exceed the black powers of his court magicians? What will it take?"

"We must wait for God's next move," said Moses.

God soon disclosed to the brothers the next piece of his plan. Neither by war nor insurrection would He pry His people out of Egypt, but through a series of plagues—predicted, precise disasters—that would also show the Egyptians that the One True, Sovereign God was alive and at work in their midst.

*****

It was late summer and time for the first plague. God gave instructions to Moses and Aaron.

Pharaoh made the brothers wait another week before again admitting them to his chambers. "What is it that you want this time? I don't know why I keep allowing you in here," he said.

When permitted to speak, Moses said to Pharaoh, "God tells you to let His people go, or He will turn all water in the land into blood."

"Are you trying to intimidate me?" Pharaoh retorted. "We are accustomed to seeing red-brown Nile waters every summer with the floods without consequence. So what?"

"At sunrise tomorrow morning," asked Moses, "will you come to the Nile and see a miracle happen?"

"A miracle?" scoffed the pharaoh. "I will enjoy your embarrassment."

*****

The flooded waters of the Nile were receding as Aaron approached their edge the next morning. "Oh, God, help your servant to succeed," he said as he raised his staff over the river's edge before the small, gathered royal crowd and Moses. Then, when he obediently struck the Nile, all water above ground in Egypt—wide rivers, small streams, and pools—was changed suddenly into viscous blood.

The court magicians at the pharaoh's side, by trickery or by the sorcerous power manifest in them, also changed some water they had brought with them into what looked like blood.[1] The relieved Pharaoh mounted his chariot. "I have no concern for this inconvenience. Magicians, bring water into the palace," he said as he departed.

*****

Gamaliel and Abidan stood, small shovels in hand, at the edge of a branch of the Nile that ran through the slave quarters, when Shelumiel walked up.

"Even the water I was drinking at breakfast suddenly tasted briny. I poured some out and it was like blood!" said Shelumiel. "Now look at the river! It is covered with floating dead fish who soon will begin to smell. And I am thirsty."

Gamaliel said, "Moses said that we could dig down near the water's edge to find potable water."

"So this is what Moses warned Pharaoh about," said Abidan, "plagues against the Egyptians until they free us."

Shelumiel looked at Abidan. "Here, Abidan," he said, "you cannot shovel with your deformed hands. Let me dig for you."

As they worked, Abidan said, "This God is in competition with other gods for the Egyptian's minds—and ours too. This miracle seems to give our God an edge."

"Abidan," Shelumiel said, striking water, "fill up your wineskin and take it home. Who knows how long this will last?"

After three days, God cleansed the waters.

*****

Shelumiel

Shelumiel, the carpenter, an elder of the tribe of Simeon, had shiny black hair, thick, black eyebrows, and a slender body as hard as the handle of his hammer. He wore sleeveless shirts that displayed taut muscles and a balled-up left biceps, like an egg in the midst of a rope. He was strong, meticulous, and skilled, able to create perfect, free-hand mitered joints. Raised with four siblings, he was devastated as a child by the deaths of the sister who was closest to him and his mother, victims of the "blooded pneumonia." He retreated into a lifelong emotional shell to protect himself from further hurt but remained a keen listener. He was pragmatic and reserved in speech, though given to issuing occasional frank and sometimes caustic opinions.

Perfection was his goal, and he expected no less from others. With the perseverance of a tiger, he gained great respect from his peers but, eschewing personal involvement with others, made few friends.

He repeatedly resisted the normal infatuations with women until, at age thirty-three, he fell under the spell of a soft-spoken, bright, attractive, nurturing woman of twenty-two. Just being in her presence brought him great satisfaction, and—although searching for flaws, as was his custom—he found no reason to avoid her. After one year they were wed, a relationship he was to guard with an uncommon jealousy.

*****

When another twelve days had passed, God sent a further message for Pharaoh through the brothers. They received an audience with him and said, "God warns that another plague will descend upon you and your people, one of filling the land with frogs, if you still refuse to let the slaves go."

"Ha!" said Pharaoh. "We are used to frogs, as they come up out of the Nile after the rains. Besides, they are representations of the gods to us."

"When God sends them, they will engulf you and you will suffer," said Moses.

"Leave!" ordered the impatient Pharaoh.

Once again, the next day, Aaron was chosen by God, and when he lifted his staff over the waters of the Nile, invading armies of slimy, green frogs rose up from them and inundated the cities—each home, each living area, leaping seas of them everywhere. The court magicians showed off their black powers to Pharaoh by duplicating the feat on a smaller scale.[m]

*****

After several days of trying to avoid the leaping amphibians, Pharaoh called for Moses. "Entreat the LORD that He remove the frogs from me ... and I will let the people go, that they may sacrifice to the LORD."[n]

Noting that twice the pharaoh referred to God as LORD, Moses smiled: "The honor is yours to tell me when the frogs shall be destroyed."[o]

"Tomorrow!"

"It will be, so that you may know that there is no one like the LORD," and, Moses added, "our God."[p]

The next day, Moses cried out to God, and the frogs died. They were shoveled out, piled in heaps, and the land became foul.[q] But Pharaoh again revoked his promise to Moses.

*****

All was quiet for several weeks. One night Moses asked Miriam to take a walk with him. He had found an old bench several houses away that was unoccupied. They sat down and he asked, "Miriam, you are older than I and must have been living with our parents when I was born. Will you tell me how I ended up in the basket, how you managed to help me? I know that the pharaoh, fearing that the growing numbers of Hebrew slaves might rise up some day and threaten his empire or side with an invading army, decreed that all Hebrew newborn males be drowned in the Nile, and hundreds were being killed that way. But how did I avoid that fate?"

"Jochabed, our mother, once told me of a conversation she had with our father," said Miriam. "One day she said to our father, 'Amram, I have tried to avoid becoming pregnant but ... well, I am. Let us pray that it is a girl. I would never be able to drown a male baby.'

"He said, 'We will pray often and our God will provide.' They believed in our God of Abraham devoutly. The pregnancy went well, and since mother was a seamstress, she could work from home the last three months. When she went into labor, a midwife came unobserved and stayed until the delivery. She returned on the eighth day, again secretly, to perform the circumcision. Many families ignored the procedure, but since mother and father thought you might be sacrificed in the river soon, they wanted to be sure that God would approve of you."

"Could the midwives be trusted?" asked Moses.

"While an occasional traitor, even a rare Hebrew, divulged names of new parents to the Egyptians for money, a midwife would never do that. And God greatly blessed them.

"Our parents soon realized that you were an unusually beautiful child[r] and somehow felt that you were lovely in the sight of God,[s] so they hid you at home for three months. They knew that the pharaoh's legions would soon find you, so they had to act. Mother had a premonition that someday you might grow up to be of help to the slaves. Therefore, trusting in God, she risked your life by floating you in the river in a basket made waterproof with pitch, right into the reeds along Pharaoh's shoreline, into the very mouth of the lion. She hoped you might be picked up and raised in the palace, later to do God's bidding, whatever that would be."

"They must have agonized over that decision," said Moses. "How fortunate for me."

"The princess went to the Nile to bathe with her two maidens, saw the basket among the reeds, heard you crying and sent her maid to retrieve it. She recognized that you were Hebrew."

Miriam continued. "I had followed the basket, wading near the shore and carrying a few wet, men's clothes in my hand. When I saw the princess, I waded up to her. I told her I had been washing the clothes of my master and saw the basket some distance down the river. I was naturally concerned, so I followed it. Before I could reach it, it lodged in these reeds. I apologized for intruding into her private waters.

"She forgave me and said that she wanted to keep 'the boy' but could not nurse you.

"'I am also Hebrew and perhaps I can find a mother to nurse you,' I said.

"She was appreciative and offered to pay the woman well for nursing you as long as I could be sure you were well taken care of.

"I assured her that I would.

"She told me that I must keep your existence secret but that I must bring you back to the palace for a visit every four to six months to see her, telling no one that you were hers.

"'My father must not know,' she said.

"I agreed. Then I told her that, being a male baby, your life may be in danger in the slave quarters.

"'I will get you a royal card signed by me that you may show to any inquiring soldiers,' she said.

"The two maidens and I were sworn to secrecy.

"After receiving the card, I took you back to our mother. She took you in and raised you until the age of four, bringing you to the princess secretly every six months. You thrived at home. You were very smart and learned quickly. Mother was careful to refer to herself as a maid and to the princess as your mother, saying, 'Better alive to acquire the benefits and position of the palace. We can always inform him later of us.' You learned both Hebrew and Egyptian and soon became wise enough to speak Egyptian in the palace, Hebrew at home. Speaking Hebrew was forbidden in the palace. Mother taught you to read whatever texts she could obtain from the princess.

"The princess, barren after three years of marriage, realized that if you were later to be acknowledged as her own, she must leave for three to four months, the time to deliver 'her baby,' should anyone later doubt her motherhood. Your existence would remain a secret until you would be brought to her when you were four or five years of age. Therefore, she and her husband 'vacationed' to a secluded chateau up the Nile, 'for a needed rest,' taking with them only the two maidens who were with her at the river."

"A wise idea," said Moses.

"That is all I know for sure," said Miriam. "Why the pharaoh allowed you to live and to stay with them, I do not know."

"Pharaoh filled in that part," said Moses.

"Once you were delivered to the pharaoh, mother was prohibited from ever visiting the palace again. You brought a small case of clothes and a few toys with you. I was allowed to see you only once more, to bring you a small gift on your fifth birthday. You confided to me then that once in your assigned room, being wary of the palace, you hid your favorite, thumb-sized turtle that your father had carved for you. On a shelf high up in the corner of the room was an ornamental vase along with a few dusty pieces of pottery. You guessed that they were largely ignored so, being agile, you put your feet on lower shelves, climbed up, and dropped your turtle into it."

Moses interrupted, "Other toys came and went, but the turtle remained. As years passed, I still enjoyed occasional times to handle it but soon forgot its origin—and my real mother. I accepted that I was the princess' son. Thank you for telling me this—and for helping me then."

"It was just my duty," said Miriam.

*****

Several weeks passed before God said to Aaron, *"Stretch out your staff and strike the dust of the earth."*

As he did so, dust particles throughout Egypt were transformed into tiny gnats, the air a heavy fog of them, flying into eyes, crawling into ears, nostrils, and mouths of men and beasts, swarming on the skin, taxing the sanity of all.

"This is the finger of God!"[u] conceded the frustrated magicians, unable to vivify even a single grain of dirt.

"Hmmmph," responded Pharaoh, trying to ignore these transient afflictions.

Three days later, God dispelled the gnats, the third plague.

*****

Pharaoh and his eleven-year-old son, Anubis, were finishing a midday meal of mutton, leeks, and cucumbers when his son said, "My nose is raw from blowing those blasted bugs out. Can we do anything to prevent more of these mysterious, awful inconveniences?"

Pharaoh answered, "He expects me to free the slaves. Ha! Our best workforce. How many do we have?"

Anubis answered, "There are about 23,000 here at and near Rameses and 12,000 further south at Pithom. There are another 5,000 artisans—craftsmen and such—who live in the two cities, most in the compounds. Some women domestics live with their masters. Many men are housed near their owners or groups of owners. We need them all."

The pharaoh said, "So does this powerful, alive god who warns and punishes us—precisely on time. But why should he punish me? I provide well for my family, conscript a strong army, and have stabilized our empire. I feed the slaves well and if only they worked harder, they would not have to be disciplined. Why doesn't this god honor me as a god and consult with me directly rather than through these underlings?"

"He should, with both of us," said the boy.

*****

Nethanel returned from a long day's work to see his friend, Abidan, sitting outside soaking up the last of the sun's rays.

Nethanel moaned, "Work was difficult these last three days with those gnats. The bricks even felt good today. Abidan, you believe in gods. Could this One's power really cause these scourges?"

"I don't know. We silently do our jobs daily but with a measure of anxiety," said Abidan. "What will God cast on us next? Will our families be at risk? We shall see."

"I have had enough," Nethanel sighed.

*****

A month later, when the LORD next sent Moses and Aaron to Pharaoh, they bowed low, declining the kneel, and then confronted him. Moses began, "God has said to us, *'Let My people go, that they may serve Me. [If not], I will send swarms of insects on you and on your servants and on your people.... But ... I will set apart the land of Goshen, where My people are living, so that no swarms of insects will be there, in order that you may know that I, the LORD, am in the midst of the land.'"ᵛ*

"I cannot understand why I remain curious about and receptive to your visits," said Pharaoh. "Havoc is your ever-present companion, and Aaron's staff is my bane. No, the Hebrews must stay!"

* * * * *

The next day, God acted without using Aaron's staff. He sent great swarms of fly-like, biting, chewing insects that invaded the houses of the Egyptians and despoiled the land. But this time, He completely spared the Israelites. Moses was summoned to Pharaoh, who spat out his orders. "Go, you and your people, and sacrifice to your god. But do not leave Rameses."

"If we sacrifice animals here, the Egyptians—who consider them sacred—will attack us," said Moses. "We must go a three-day journey into the wilderness and sacrifice to the LORD our God as He commands us."ʷ

"All right, if you can manage to dispel these horrible insects. But do not go far away."

Obtaining the promise he sought, when Moses left Pharaoh's, he fell to his knees for the first time and prayed to God. A great wind blew the insects away. But once again, the crafty pharaoh revoked his promise.

* * * * *

That night, Gamaliel met Nahshon, Nethanel, and the carpenter, Shumeliel, outside the latter's hut.

"Finally," said the carpenter, "after all of these years, He protects us!"

"It is a gift, Shelumiel, we see another side of Him." said Gamaliel. "We had to suffer first to appreciate it as He tries to free us ..."

"... to go to Canaan, Moses says. And how would we get there? I hear that there is only hot sand and mountains between here and there," said Nethanel.

"A thousand camels?" opined Shelumiel. "Or maybe Pharaoh will give us chariot rides."

"You can be sure I am not walking," said Nethanel.

"You'll stay here?" jabbed Gamaliel. "For now, we will see if He still favors us should these plagues continue."

*****

Soon the Egyptians began their planting season of barley and wheat.

Days broiled on and the Israelites continued to struggle under their task-masters. After three more weeks had passed, Moses, with increasing trust in God, boldly carried a new communication into Pharaoh's library one morning. He warned him that God would send a fifth plague, this one of death that would attack every animal left out in the field if the Hebrews were not freed. Pharaoh was irritated by the message but not enough to make him yield. Except for the fish kill, the plagues had been mainly nuisances. His attendants, however, spread the warning quickly to the populace.

On the following day, every Egyptian cow, horse, donkey, camel, sheep, and goat that was left outside of barns and stalls, unprotected by their doubting owners, developed rigors, sapping fevers, seizures, and breathlessness. They then collapsed to the ground and died while the Hebrew animals grazed in safety.

*****

Gamaliel and Eliasaph stood observing the fields next to theirs where workers were hauling away the many animal carcasses strewn across it.

"God is venting His anger—but not on us. We have done nothing to deserve such favor," said Gamaliel.

"The severity of the plagues escalates—now with killing. This God is not to be played with. Would He kill people?" asked Eliasaph. "I am beginning to feel a little pity for the Egyptians. When will Pharaoh yield?"

"Soon, I hope. Our shepherds are angry. Pharaoh is confiscating many of our herds to partially supplement the lost meat and milk needs of his people," said Gamaliel.

"We did not get off free this time, did we?"

*****

Pharaoh lamented the slaughter but became worried that even worse lay ahead. Therefore, he decided to allow the Hebrews to leave. However, God sensed this change and would have none of it, as He hardened Pharaoh's heart[x] against the Hebrews, preventing their release. All of the plagues must play out to achieve God's determined goal.

*****

"Pharaoh, my God has more agony in store for you if you remain stubborn. Let the people go," warned Moses several weeks later, as he and Aaron stood before Pharaoh again, omitting the bow.

"I loathe you and the mounting burdens our nation must bear because of you and your insane requests," Pharaoh fumed from his throne. "If you have any control over this vexatious god, stop him! You are gradually destroying us. But greater disaster would occur if I release the slaves. My answer is still *no!*"

On this occasion, God chose Moses to initiate the plague. He invited Pharaoh outside, and then walked to a kiln, gathered handfuls of soot, and threw them into the air. Painful, pus-filled boils broke out on all of the Egyptian people and their animals throughout the land, the innocent as well as the flagrant persecutors—but the Israelites were again spared.

"My magicians! Where are my magicians?" called Pharaoh. "You and your ruthless god have damaged the health of my people. Have you no pity?" His magicians gave no answer, for they tended to their own sores.

*****

Many days later, long after the sores of the last plague had healed, God prompted Moses to rise up early and meet Pharaoh and his aides at the river where the pharaoh bathed.

Moses said to Pharaoh, "God has told me that He could have easily killed all Egyptians with pestilence, but He has allowed them to live to witness that there is no power like His in all the earth, so that His name may be proclaimed everywhere. Can't you understand?" Moses pleaded, touched with pity, "He wants you to know Him, Pharaoh. Abandon the gods you worship, your fertility gods, the gods of the skies, nature, war, and more, so that all people may worship Him as the only God. If you do not heed Him, a greater disaster for your people is imminent."

"Give up my gods?" Pharaoh shouted. "You suggest that I turn my back on the ancient gods who give us life, who sustain us, who provide wealth and power? It is you who must give up your god. Do you dare think that I—a god by birth, a god by reputation, experience, and by my own wisdom—should give credence to this ... this evil power? Your mind deserts you, Moses. And these plagues you bring in have become lethal weapons cast wantonly from your staffs. Don't you think you have afflicted us enough?"

"Were it but mine to control," said Moses solemnly. "Now behold, tomorrow He sends another plague—of hail. All people must seek shelter, along with their remaining livestock. Those who do not will die."

"Leave!" commanded Pharaoh.

Moses grieved in frustration, regretting his impotent role as but a harbinger of harrowing hail. The announced ordeals were inevitable, and his pleadings with Pharaoh were worthless by divine decree. What could he do for the innocent? In anguish, Moses briskly walked the roads all day and into the night, spreading the warning, shouting to those who would listen, "Every man and beast, inside! Seek shelter! Death is on the way!" The Hebrew shepherds, tending a section of the pharaoh's animals and their own, moved quickly to herd what animals they could into barns and stalls. But some of their Egyptian counterparts, who received their instructions from the palace, taunted the Hebrews and ignored the warnings.

In the morning light, Moses stumbled home.

✶✶✶✶✶

The sky blackened and winds roared through the land, vanguards of a great storm. The people leaned into it, running for cover.

"Stay inside!" wailed the fortunate.

In a few moments, bolts of lightning and fire exploded out of heaven; large hailstones struck all that was in the field in the land of Egypt, both man and beast. The hail also struck plants and shattered every tree of the field.^{y} All who were exposed, and their innocent animals, were killed while the storm parted around the Israelite dwellings and fields. After two hours, the winds calmed and the sky lightened.

Pharaoh was unmoved.

✶✶✶✶✶

During a time of quiet in Egypt, Pharaoh was deeply embroiled in the consequences of these disasters. His dwindling grain stores could barely satisfy a restless nation hungry from loss of the vegetable and barley harvests, all destroyed by the hailstorm. Desperately, Pharaoh promised relief to his people since a bumper crop of wheat would ripen in five weeks.

* * * * *

Meanwhile, Moses continued his facade as a stranger befriended by Aaron and Miriam with whom he freely shared his conversations with God. One afternoon, God's voice came clearly to Moses. It was time to visit the pharaoh again. "Yes, God, and the message?" Moses asked.

God told him to go to Pharaoh and tell him to, "*Let My people go, that they may serve Me. For if you refuse … behold, tomorrow I will bring locusts into your territory. And they shall cover the surface of the land … [to] eat the rest of what has escaped … from the hail.… Then your houses shall be filled, and the houses of all your servants … something which neither your fathers nor your grandfathers have seen … until this day.*"[z]

* * * * *

Moses and Aaron were ushered into the study.

"I had not heard from you for quite a while," Pharaoh began. His hard-soled sandal heels clicked on the floor as he paced beside the throne. "I was hoping that perhaps the hail had brought an end to your visits and, with good fortune, your lives as well. What do you want now?"

When Moses advised him curtly of God's threat that locusts would destroy anything green, including the late-ripening wheat, Pharaoh's advisors pleaded with him, "Let the slaves go; do you not realize that Egypt is destroyed?"[aa]

"All right, go," said Pharaoh to Moses, "but, who are the ones that are going?"

"All go, young and old, and our flocks and our herds," insisted Moses.

"The young must stay," said Pharaoh through his hardened heart.

"All or none," said Moses resolutely. "Otherwise, we shall all stay to observe what God will do next to you and your people."

"Who are you to threaten my empire? Get out of my courts! Guards, throw them into the street!"

* * * * *

"*Moses, stretch out your hand over the land of Egypt,*"[bb] God commanded. As he did so, an east wind blew in carrying clouds of voracious locusts and grasshoppers, covering the land, and filling all Egyptian houses. Soon, nothing green was left. The entire anticipated, life-preserving wheat crop was decimated, except in the spared Hebrew fields.

"I have sinned against the LORD your God and you," admitted Pharaoh two days later. "Please forgive my sin … and make supplication to the LORD your God, that He would only remove this death from me."[cc]

Moved by his remorse, Moses agreed, went outside, and raised his staff again. For many hours, a strong west wind took up the locusts and drove them into the Red Sea.

Then Pharaoh sent word to Moses: "The slaves stay!"

*****

Nahshon, dressed in his hallmark white robe, was walking at night with Shelumiel and Eliasaph. Nahshon looked at Shelumiel and said, "I wonder if the pharaoh is becoming humbled or angered by the plagues—and with us, the cause of his troubles. He cannot destroy God, but if he becomes desperate, could our lives be in danger? His great-grandfather slaughtered all of those babies out of fear of us."

Shelumiel responded, "Could happen. Many see us as evil omens. And yet some guards are easing up on us, even talking to us, asking about our God, worrying about their own safety should Pharaoh fall."

Eliasaph offered, "One guard asked me if he should discard his idols. One even asked me to pray for him, a guard who has whipped me. No, Nahshon, I doubt the pharaoh could garner enough willing forces to kill us all."

*****

The ninth plague arrived unannounced. *"Moses, stretch out your hand toward the sky,"*[dd] said God. Complete and terrifying darkness covered the land for seventy-two hours, a darkness that may be felt.[ee] No Egyptian stirred from his house, while God graciously provided light for the Israelite dwellings in Goshen. As light gradually returned to the Egyptians, Pharaoh, agitated at his slipping command over his exploited empire, ordered Moses to court.

"Moses," the pharaoh announced, "I must have some kind of accord with this vengeful God of yours. He manipulates not just water, earth, and the heavens, but also dispatches the creatures of the water, earth, and the air to inflict his plagues as he wills. Yet, how he protects the slaves!" He took a step toward Moses. "If I permit them to go, will he leave us alone?"

Moses was silent.

"Well, go, but since our animals have been slaughtered, leave your flocks and herds behind."

Moses countered confidently, "Not a hoof will be left behind, for we shall take some of them to serve the LORD our God.... We ourselves do not know with what we shall serve the LORD,[ff] until we get out into the wilderness. We are like a feather in His wind."

"Then stay!" Pharaoh said. "Now, get away from me! Be sure that I do not see your face again or you will die."

*****

It was late spring, marking more than ten months of the intermittent plagues.[2] Moses sat down to eat the morning meal with Aaron. "Brother, God spoke to me again last night," said an intent Moses.

"Whenever He does, I know that trouble is coming," observed Aaron with a shake of his head.

"Yes. But after that, God has said, Pharaoh will not just let us go but will surely drive us out of Egypt completely." Each visit from God seemed to energize Moses.

"What will He do?" Aaron asked.

"I don't know yet, but we will not leave empty-handed. It may sound absurd, but we are to tell each Israelite to ask his or her Egyptian master, owner, even neighbors, for articles of silver and of gold and of clothing[gg] as a free gift. I can't imagine that they will comply, but seemingly, God can bring about anything He wishes."

"Would He transform me into the pharaoh?" mused Aaron.

*****

The Hebrews hesitantly, but obediently, solicited their neighbors and were surprised because, once again, God changed the hearts of those who oppressed His people. The Egyptians looked with favor on their slaves and gave generously of their riches, including gold and silver jewelry, dishes, and bowls. Even Moses, the perpetual deliverer of bad news and the archenemy of Pharaoh, had risen to be greatly esteemed in the land of Egypt.[hh]

Surprisingly, many accepted the gifts reluctantly. "We need no handouts; we have not worked for these."

*****

God's voice came to the brothers that same day with details about the coming plague—death to all Egyptian firstborn males.

In a flash of illumination, Moses understood what God had told him at the burning bush: *"Because Pharaoh would not let my first-born go,"* referring to the Israelites, *"I will kill his first-born."*[xi]

But first, God added, a feast must be celebrated. The Israelites must mark that day as the first day of the first month of the year henceforth and, on the tenth day of that month, each family—or two families together if they are poor—must select an unblemished lamb or goat and care for it. Then on the morning of the fourteenth, every home must be cleansed of all leaven. At twilight on that fourteenth day, they were to slaughter their lambs by bleeding, being careful not to break any of their bones, and were to collect the blood and paint some of it on their doorposts and lintels. God said that He, Himself, would descend on the land with wrath later that night and the blood would signal Him to pass over their homes. They would then roast the lamb and eat it, garnished with bitter herbs;[jj] whatever meat was left over must be incinerated by the next morning. They must do this while dressed and prepared for travel, with loins girded, wearing sandals, and with staffs in hand.

Also, without leaven, all bread made during the following week would thus be unraised, unleavened; and the week should be celebrated as the Feast of Unleavened Bread because God said, *"On this very day, I brought your hosts out of the land of Egypt."*[kk] Anyone who eats anything leavened during that week shall be cut off from Israel.[ll]

*****

Moses summoned a few of the elders and informed them of God's bold and terrifying plan.

"We will hold a feast to celebrate the coming of a plague, indeed the worst one?" asked Shelumiel. "We have never done that before. Are we so crass?"

"We are to celebrate God's protective and liberating power over us," replied Moses. "It is a dangerous plan, but He seems assured of its success. God says that Pharaoh will finally give up."

Nethanel said, "So, this is it! We are really going to move out, leave Egypt? And on foot! I don't relish that. God had better have provisions ready for us. None of us has many belongings to pack."

"We must notify our people, including the shepherds," said Eliasaph. "I will see to it that the tribe of Gad will be ready."

"This will be disastrous to observe—and frightening," said Nahshon. "Do you think all Israelites will go?"

"I believe so," said Moses. "Your responsibility, Nahshon, is your own tribe, the Judahites."

*****

On the morning of the fourteenth day of the month, Moses and Aaron arrived at the palace. The chief servant met them and guided them in. "Oh, great Moses," he cried, "bring no more sadness to our master. He is no longer himself. We cringe at his anger. Sometimes he speaks in riddles. Dinner trays return hardly touched. Some days, he scarcely moves from his room, yet his sandals scuff the marble halls in the depths of night."

"I grieve for you all," said Moses, "but greater sorrow comes tonight, this time in the form of a death that you cannot escape. Now, please let me see him."

With wide, red eyes, a rumpled cloak over his unbuttoned shirt, and only a single sandal, Pharaoh met Moses in his study.

"Bring me good news. How can I despise you, yet," Pharaoh said, voicing God's implanted perception, "respect you as you burden us with evil? Haven't you something better to do than to plead for the lowly, mindless slaves?"

"No, Pharaoh, I haven't," Moses paused, his faith in God now strong. "But now, your time has arrived. There will be no more frogs, insects, darkness, disease, or hail to do God's work. Tonight at midnight, He Himself will come to kill all of the firstborn in all of Egypt. There shall be a loud cry in all the land of Egypt such as there has not been heard before and such as shall never be again.[mm] Your precious gods will also be destroyed." As Moses repeated God's threats, the horror of such a plague filled his own mind. His voice rose as he said, "And yet, O Pharaoh, against any of the sons of Israel, a dog shall not even bark.[nn] Then your servants will call to us and insist that we leave." Trying to control himself, Moses added, "Pharaoh, O Pharaoh, what a great calamity you have brought upon Egypt!"

"Get out, get out! I'll decide—tomorrow," said Pharaoh.

"It's too late! God help you for what you and your people have done!" Moses stormed out of the palace and walked down the street, filled with the same uncontrollable anger as on the day he had murdered the Egyptian guard forty years earlier.

*****

As evening approached, the fearfully apprehensive Israelites reasoned among themselves. "Moses' predictions have been accurate, so we must do what he says. The stakes are enormous. Smear plenty of blood on the doorposts so that God, if He does come, will be sure to see it."

They roasted their lambs, and later that night, obediently dressed for travel, and ate the meat and herbs while waiting—anxiously waiting. At midnight, God struck, accompanied by a band of destroying angels^{oo} spreading their terror house by house, field by field. Death sucked the breath from her selected Egyptian victims as every firstborn died, from the house of Pharaoh to the smelly dungeons, including the firstborn of all animals. There was no home where there was not someone dead.^{pp}

God executed His vengeance against all the gods of Egypt,^{qq} pulverizing every one of their statues and idols and destroying their places of worship.

"There is only one God," the devastation cried out, one God whose long-standing chastening of the Egyptians abruptly escalated that black night. But on that night, even His consuming wrath was overshadowed by His pure, protective love for the unscathed Israelites. "Remember this Passover, remember."

*****

An hour before dawn, Pharaoh hastily summoned Moses and Aaron. As they walked toward the palace, cries from the sobbing Egyptians filled their ears. "Go quickly," one called to them, "before we are all killed."

The brothers were brought into the study where a barefooted Pharaoh sat on the floor, leaning against his chair, defeated yet tearless as his son, Anubis, lay dead on the rug near his feet. His sleepless eyes stared through Moses as he said, "Moses, you have brought this disaster upon us. I, too, would have died save for an older brother who died in infancy. Now, rise up, get out from among my people, both you and the sons of Israel, and go, worship the LORD as you have said. Take both your flocks and your herds as you have said and go." Then Pharaoh pitiably held out his hands and begged, "Bless me also,"[rr] but received no answer.

* * * * *

Moses and Aaron hurried into the night and to their homes, collected Elisheba and Miriam, and alerted Aaron's sons. They gathered their small sacks of belongings and bags of food before hastening toward the city gates. News of Pharaoh's order spread rapidly, shouted from house to house, and thousands of Israelites streamed out of their city and slave quarters, and fell in behind Moses and Aaron. Even the hesitant departed. Most of them, reveling in their release from slavery, strode pridefully and defiantly[ss] in victory, contemptuous of the state of their stricken, heartbroken masters.

They drove their healthy herds down roads of despair, past barns and fields littered with carcasses of less fortunate animals, as they left the city and headed east. They carried with them all of their recently acquired silver and gold, expensive bowls and cloths, tools, as well as swords, bows, and arrows. Another promise of God to Abraham had come to fruition: that when His people left the foreign land, they would come out with many possessions.[tt] The time that the sons of Israel lived in Egypt was four hundred and thirty years—to the very day.[uu]

* * * * *

Accompanying the Israelites was a mixed multitude[vv] of non-Israelites from Lower Egypt, some disenchanted, others disenfranchised, and a number who chose to leave their homes to follow this new, powerful God.

* * * * *

As the suddenly emancipated masses jubilantly surged forward, many singing and chanting familiar ballads of long-desired freedom and shouting to Moses words of praise and thanksgiving, two men accosted Moses.

The first to speak was Javell, of the tribe of Dan, a talented lyre player in Pharaoh's court. His cold eyes looked at Moses accusingly from behind long lashes.

"Moses, I swear by the gods that you will regret what you have done to our families, you and your foolish mission! We are being disgorged, the vomit of the Egyptians, dispatched as refugees. The home that I built was not luxurious, but it was decent. My family lived an adequate life with plenty of good food. We were safe. And now you have driven us out toward the desert with only what we can strap onto our cow. I would not want to be in your shoes if anything goes wrong."

His fellow tribesman, the large-chested Hasor, panted from walking briskly to catch up. "You have greatly troubled us, Moses," he huffed. "The gold and silver given us by our neighbors do not make up for what we left behind. I am a metalsmith. What is to build out here? Man, do you know what you are doing?"

Nahshon was walking near Moses and overheard the remarks. "Moses, you warned us that to be free we must travel to the land of Canaan, which you described as a near-paradise. Surely, we welcome freedom, but I am hesitant to go there. I know from the stories our historian, Abidan, relates that Noah angrily swore that his faulted grandson, Canaan, would live under a curse. Later, father Abraham forbade his son Isaac from marrying a Canaanite woman. Isaac barred his sons Jacob and Esau from similar entanglements. Abidan hints that the Canaanites have become a highly contaminated, poisonous people."

Surprised by their attitudes, Moses said, "God says that Canaan is a good place for us, the land and its fruits, if not its people. They will be His problem. I realize that, for some of you, this departure represents a difficult change, but see what miracles have already occurred. They give us trust that He will take us there safely, and that the land and our new freedom will be worth the trip."

Javell grumbled. "We seem to have no choice now but to go with you. Don't you and your God let us down."

"Canaan may prove too great a task even for your God," said Nahshon as he lagged back from the striding Moses.

*****

Nahshon

Nashon, the thirty-five-year-old jeweler, was born into the tribe of Judah. His father, a soldier, had been killed in battle when the boy was eight years old. Nahshon was soon put to work gathering straw for the brickyards. One day, at age eleven, while on an errand for his foreman, he walked past the jewelry shop just outside the slave compound. When he looked into the shop window, he was dazzled by the colors of the lapis lazuli and jasper stones he saw there. He hesitantly spoke with the benevolent jeweler and was soon invited to observe his skills. On Nahshon's once-a-month days off, he was permitted to visit the shop and his new friend. Allowed to assist, he showed great dexterity in fashioning simple rings.

Soon the jeweler invited him to become his assistant. The foreman of the straw gatherers grudgingly approved. When the jeweler died after fourteen years, Nahshon, though still a slave, was appointed chief jeweler of that shop with a smidgen of a salary.

He stood tall and spear-straight, an anomaly among the brow-beaten slaves, a posture that gave him a regal bearing and radiated self-assurance. His external confidence, however, hid an inchoate anxiety that plagued him with bouts of insomnia and periodic insatiable gluttony. His insecurity was tempered by a modest cache of cuttings and stone chips pilfered from the shop over the years.

During meetings he would often sit back, hands on his knees, with squinty eyes as if daring others to question him. An innate shrewdness in his wily dealings with fellow Israelites and with Egyptian customers gained him respect and eventual election as an elder of the tribe of Judah.

He wore a long white robe with a white, square, flat headpiece while at work. A wise wife kept him pleasantly subdued at home. His faith was confined to himself; gods were for others.

In truth, he was more tin than bronze.

*****

When word of Pharaoh's decision reached the similarly devastated city of Pithom, their Israelite slaves were also freed. The throngs from the cities met and made their first camp southeast at the town of Succoth. Celebration was blended with apprehension as they set up their tents. Sleep was fretful for many. The next morning Moses called a meeting of the elders outside of the camp. He had become acquainted with those from Rameses, but a new group from Pithom was present. Among them were Ahira, the soldier of Naphtali; Pagiel, the painter of Asher; and Elishama, the brick foreman of Ephraim. Moses welcomed them. "I have heard of you all and we are honored to have you join us. I have a brief message, then you may all get to know one another. Please be seated."

They seated themselves on the sand facing him.

"God has spoken to me with several messages. Your people endured Passover well, but He was disappointed with the triumphant, haughty attitude of many as they walked away from its devastation. He decreed that a Passover feast must be observed every year in remembrance of His liberation, and it must be celebrated with pious and humble thanksgiving.

"Also, because your firstborn had been spared during the Passover, in the future, all Hebrews must sanctify to God every new firstborn if it is a male, both of man and beast, for they belong to Him.[ww] For the firstborn male animals, two turtledoves must be sacrificed[xx] on an altar; each firstborn son of Israel must serve God and his life be redeemed for four shekels.

"God has also permitted two other groups of men to celebrate Passover: first, the Hebrews' male slaves who are indentured for unpaid debts, after being circumcised, and the second, the non-Hebrew sojourners who travel continually with us. In order to celebrate Passover, a sojourner first must convince all male members of his family to be circumcised with him.

"You may discuss these things and get to know one another. I will leave you for a while."

After he left, Nethanel said, "I will bet that there will not be many foreign celebrants."

"It does separate true believers," said Shelumiel.

Elishama complained, "More new rules! I was afraid of that. Freedom lasted a day or two. This god didn't like my attitude! He hadn't been in slavery for many years."

Nethanel asked, "Why sacrifice birds and pay money just for the birth of a male? He didn't bring them into being—or sire them."

"We are learning about this God and His demands," said Eliasaph. "Perhaps He has a hand even in successful procreation," he smiled, "and we owe him. He *did* protect our firstborn mightily at Passover."

The new group intermingled with the others, exchanging opinions, stories of their families and work, and wonder at the recent events.

*****

Three women of the tribe of Benjamin were baking bread in a small oven on that first morning at Succoth.

"All bread that leaves these fires today is flat," observed Ruth, the heavyset eldest, a mother of three. "The dough must have bounced too much to rise on the journey last night."

Chaletra, fondling her recently acquired dangling gold earrings, said, "God is clever. He said that if we ate raised bread this week, we would be cut off. We will eat unraised bread today, but not because we were obedient. My husband warned me that leaven represents imperfection to this God."

"Ha!" chimed in Shum, the young, dark wife of a laborer. "This God expected us to rid our homes of all leaven yesterday morning. What a waste. Last week, I sold some of it for a nice profit. But Moses insists that we are to burn it or to crumble it and throw it to the wind.[3] How will I replace it?"

"You could buy some from a Gentile or just leave the dough outside and wait for the gods to seed it," said Chaletra.

Shum smiled, "Leaven may be bad, but last night was good. I am rid of that vicious mistress of mine. Always 'Come here, you!' And she worked me hard. Well, she got hers last night when her oldest son and husband both died," she gloated. "Thought she could buy me off two days ago when she began to fear what this God might do to her because of us; gave me silks, gold and silver dishes, jewelry."

Ruth said: "We all received such gifts. They were either afraid or else this God worked on their minds."

Chaletra remarked, "So many Egyptians died for our freedom. God must have a great mission for us."

*****

Endnotes

1. The encounters with Pharaoh are told in Exodus, chapters 5 to 11.
2. "ten months," Alfred Edersheim, *Bible History: Old Testament*, "The Exodus." 1949, p. 70.
3. "burn leaven or crumble it," Jacob Neuser, *The Mishnah, A New Translation*. "Pesahin 2:1, 2, 3," 1988, p. 232.

Chapter 5

Slaughtering Their Enemies, Gaining Their Trust

After three days of rest at Succoth, the mission continued as Moses and Aaron began to lead the horde of people, numerous as the stars of heaven,[a] in their march.[1] They were assisted by the elders of the thirteen tribes, who quickly organized their people into a marching order, preventing a confused flight. Safely in the midst of the crowd were two honored Israelites, selected by Moses, to carry a purple-draped chest. It contained the bones of Joseph, satisfying a pledge made by his sons to have his remains returned to his homeland for proper burial when at last they migrated to Canaan.

*****

After they had walked only a short distance, suddenly a moving, whirling, white pillar of cloud[b] appeared before Moses. Hearing God's voice from the cloud, Moses was startled, realizing that God had materialized, wrapping Himself in that vapor and changing His purely verbal captaincy into a visible one. The cloud was one more marvel to the people who followed as it led them southeast all day. There was a pause for dinner, but instead of camping as night fell, a fire appeared in the cloud,[c] producing a light that mimicked daylight, allowing them to proceed another two hours before setting up camp.

Several elders met as they filled bags with water at a nearby wadi.

"Another impressive miracle," said Nahshon flatly. "The supernatural intrudes—in person—as a cloud."

"Maybe He doesn't trust Moses to lead or us to follow," said Ahira.

Gamaliel offered, "Oh, if the Egyptians could only see this."

"I cannot believe that a God would condescend to come to earth, particularly out here. He seems more like a man than a god. I can worship an ethereal god but—this live one?" quipped Ahira.

Gamaliel, "God is here because He is committed to you. Trust Him."

"Better be," said Nahshon as he walked back toward camp.

*****

In the morning, the throng broke camp and the cloud, having replaced the fire, led them farther south. Occasional songs were heard, but the mood was more subdued following God's scolding.

It was midafternoon when the procession rested. Three of the elders sat down on the sand surrounding Moses, who was resting on a large rock. Young Nethanel, seated next to Moses, asked, "Moses, why are you not leading us toward the early sun? We know now that Canaan lies there."

"True, but there is a tenuous truce between Egypt and the Philistines, whose troops are stationed at Egypt's northeastern border," said Moses. "Our people might want to go back to Egypt if threatened by the Philistines. The southern route is safer."

Elishama, of the tribe of Ephraim, in his early forties, as were most of the elders, interjected, "I fought in the southern campaigns as a young archer but know little of the Philistines and the weapons of iron that we hear they possess. You are experienced in the east, Moses. Tell us of them."

"Stories blow like the sands of the Sinai," said Moses. "Many have I heard in the land of Midian where I lived, and their reliability may be no better than the camel drivers themselves. I have learned that the Philistines originally lived in the islands of Caphtor[2] and Cyprus in the Great Sea. They developed a highly trained but restless army. Twenty years ago, they sailed northward to attack the armies of the Hittite empire,[3] an empire that encompassed the land extending far beyond the northern shores of the Great Sea, a land rich in iron ore. The Hittites had developed a method of extracting the iron[4] and forging it into tools, weapons, and chariots, far stronger and more durable than the bronze ones of Egypt.

"Last year, equipped with iron weapons, the Philistines invaded the Egyptian mainland,[5] driving back the army of Pharaoh's father, and occupying part of Egypt and some land to the east. A truce now exists. We will skirt around that area on our way to Canaan."

"We may avoid the Philistines, but if we invade Canaan, we should have a relatively easy victory," said Abidan, emphasizing his point with a raised crooked index finger. "Remember the curse that the Canaanites live under?"

"What curse?" asked Elishama.

"I'll tell you as I remember it," said Abidan, proud of his knowledge. "Long ago, after Noah finally landed on dry ground, he planted a vineyard.[d] Later, he drank excessively of the nectar of the grapes, lay down naked in his tent, and fell asleep. One of his three sons, Ham, came upon him, stared at him with contempt, then brought his own son, Canaan, to similarly look at him with disrespect. Ham sought out his brothers to ridicule Noah. The brothers, however, were dismayed, went to their sleeping father, and covered him with a blanket. When Noah awoke and learned what Ham had done, he was filled with disgust. He swore a curse on Canaan, that his descendants would eventually become servants to his brothers. They have become a nation of vile, evil people."

Abidan laughed as he reached down to rub a sore knee. "Perhaps we can bring that curse to fruition and make them our slaves also, eh?"

"That is not our charge," Moses sternly reminded them. "We are to organize an army and defeat the nation of Canaan and to occupy their land. Fortunately, the Philistines have not moved into that area. With God's help, we shall be victorious."

*****

Elishama

Elishama was chosen as an elder of the descendants of Ephraim, one of Joseph's two sons and Manasseh's brother. When Elishama was an infant, his father was cudgeled to death after accidentally spilling muddy water on a guard. He and a brother were raised by a loving, doting mother who had, he felt, slovenly habits. Overreacting, he became obsessively tidy and organized.

At age eight, he was sent to the fields daily to gather hay and stubble for brickmaking. He and other children were transported in wagons and were required to fill them by sunset or receive the bite of a whip. At twelve, he became a hod carrier. At eighteen, he begged a friendly Egyptian archer for a chance to try his bow. His innate skill surprised the archer, and he was soon trained and served well in the army in many battles until his left leg was torn by a Nubian arrow. Prolonged infections scarred and deformed the limb, producing a permanent limp. Retrained as a stonemason, he soon became foreman, a promotion that brought out the disciplinarian in him. He commanded subordinates to obey their Egyptian masters' orders and to refrain from swearing. His zeal for organization and his commanding presence brought him great tribal respect.

He kept his skill well-honed with his retained bow and a few arrows stolen from the armory.

A teasing girl nicknamed him "Barley" because of his long, narrow face and neatly groomed, short-cropped, wiry hair. That same girl later became his wife, managing to keep the house of their three sons and two daughters in tolerable order under his close scrutiny.

*****

The troupe of 40,000 continued their southern march, traveling three days before setting up a camp at Etham. From there, another three days brought them to a campsite past the village of Baal-zephon. There was a dour mood throughout the camp: the drudgery of the shepherds in their unfamiliar role of herding their plodding cattle and sheep along through the heat of the day while they tolerated the beasts' slop and smell; the smoldering anxieties and regrets, primarily of the older ones, of having abandoned their accustomed life of slavery to follow God onto this unfamiliar desert; the fatigue of the women, particularly of those pregnant; and the stress of trying to keep the children occupied. Displeasure increased when Moses informed them that by following the cloud and continuing south, they had bypassed the last land route to the east. Conversations grew rebellious as increasing numbers lobbied to return to Egypt. Concerns were also heightened when one of Pharaoh's sentries was occasionally spotted observing them in the distance.

*****

Their negative attitudes were being observed by a disappointed God who had failed to win them over by sparing them from the sufferings of the plagues. And He must win their trust for this mission to succeed. He refrained from altering their minds as He had with the Egyptians when they parted with their wealth. They must come to Him by their own choice. He decided that another miracle was necessary to deepen their confidence in Him.

The next morning the cloud moved eastward, and the people followed. In the middle of the day, when the tired troupe looked to the distance, they saw an arm of the Red Sea stretching as far as they could see to the north and to the south—and they were heading straight toward it.

God's directed voice came to Moses from the cloud telling him that they were to double back and camp at Baal-zephon so that Pharaoh would think

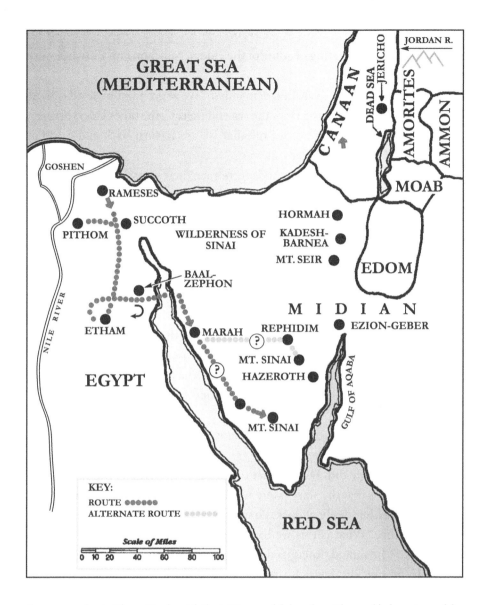

they were lost. Then God said that He would *harden Pharaoh's heart, and he will chase after them; and I will be honored through Pharaoh and all his army, and the Egyptians will know that I am the LORD.*[f]

"How would the recapture of these people convince the Egyptians?" Moses wondered quietly.

*****

Moses called a meeting of some of the elders. Nahshon and Eliasaph were the first to reach Moses.

"Now what, Moses?" Nahshon demanded. "We've got a watery dead end. At the sea, are we to turn south? Does the sea end there?" The other elders arrived.

"Do not worry. God has told me that we are to turn back and camp at Baal-zephon,"[g] Moses told them all.

"Turn back? Get these thousands to retrace their steps?! That is doubling back a three-hour journey. And for what?" Shelumiel said, with rising irritation. "Was God as surprised as we were to find the sea blocking us? I thought that He was supposed to know everything."

The people, watching the cloud, saw it disappear then reappear just beyond them in the west.

"We must just trust Him," said Moses as he walked through the crowds, encouraging them to follow the newly directed cloud.

The elders informed their surprised tribes. The confused people were relieved to leave the sea, but trust in God and Moses was fading.

The cattlemen yelled to the disgruntled masses retracing their steps, "Watch where you put your feet!" The troupe returned to Baal-zephon to make camp.

Meanwhile, God set out to prick Pharaoh's soul.

*****

And prick it He did. During that morning, the pharaoh received reports from his sentries that the slaves were wandering aimlessly in the desert about fifty miles away. Suddenly, at dusk, Pharaoh was overwhelmed by the enormity of his decision. "What is this we have done, that we have let Israel go from serving us?"[h] he ranted. Energized out of his lethargy by this God-generated agitation, he quickly devised a plan. Leaving small forces to maintain the truces to the east and south, Pharaoh dispatched the remainder of his army toward Baal-zephon that night. "Bring them back!" he shouted and ordered all of the chariots in Lower Egypt to report to Rameses.

Within thirty-six hours the chariots were assembled, and in the next morning, they and his horsemen were following after the army, with Pharaoh in the lead vehicle. Later that afternoon, they joined forces with the soldiers five miles from the Red Sea.

*****

That same morning, as the Israelites broke camp and were ready to leave, confusion reigned and some shouts of anger arose from the bewildered Israelites when they saw the pillar of cloud back in the east. Several puzzled elders sought Moses who was packing up his tent.

Abidan spoke first. "Moses, this god has changed his mind or he is playing dire games with us. I have studied maps in Egypt and there is no end to the sea to the south. Who does he—"

Moses interrupted tersely, "I believe that God knows exactly what He is doing. Let us follow the cloud."

The people complied but grumbled bitterly. Late in the day, as they began to make camp near the sea, they looked back to the west where they saw a tower of dust and sand far in the distance. As they watched, stunned, they realized that the sand was being churned up by many chariots that were charging toward them.

"It's the pharaoh and his army!" shouted one. Terror swept quickly through the camp. They were trapped; behind them was the pharaoh and in front of them was a choppy sea, with no boats or barges in sight. "We'll be slaughtered like animals or taken captive again and marched back—beaten and humiliated."

Moses was standing next to the tribe of Asher and one of its elders, the goatee-bearing Pagiel. The panicky people cried out almost in unison, "God help us! God save us!" Nothing happened as the chariots drew nearer.

Pagiel led the others as they turned on Moses. He stammered, "Is it because there were n-n-n-o graves in Egypt that you have taken us away to die in the w-w-w-wilderness? Why have you d-d-d-dealt with us in this way, bringing us out of Egypt?"[i]

Many felt betrayed. Was Moses in league with Pharaoh? With mounting anger Nahshon rebuked Moses, "Is this not the word we spoke to you in Egypt, saying, 'Leave us alone that we may serve the Egyptians? For it would have been better than to die in the wilderness.'"[j]

"Better in Egypt! Hmm!" thought Moses who, piqued by the chiding Israelites, shot back, "Do not fear. Stand by and see the salvation of the LORD, which He will accomplish for you today. He will fight for you while you keep silent. The Egyptians whom you have seen today, you will never see again forever."[k]

"How did I know about their soldiers?" Moses questioned himself. "Words just given to me?" He lowered his voice as the grumbling of the crowd lessened and said, "We will somehow be victorious in this battle. The word will reach Egypt and, therefore, as God has said, *'the Egyptians will know that I am the LORD when I am honored.'*"[l]

Gad's Eliasaph confronted Moses, "Is this why we pulled back? Did God tell you that it was to lure Pharaoh to come after us?"

"Yes," admitted Moses. "If I had told you, you would have resented it and might have refused to go."

"We are not just His chosen wards, are we?" asked Eliasaph. "Freed from slavery, but not for our benefit! Our whole nation is being used merely as a decoy, as cast-out bait, for His purposes."

Moses replied, "In this instance, you are right. And God may use you in other ways later to accomplish His plans. Now, see how God will fight for you!"

*****

Pharaoh's legions drew near to the camp. At that, the angel of God suddenly withdrew the cloud pillar and settled it in front of them, expanding and blanketing the Egyptians in heavy darkness. Pharaoh, riding in the lead chariot, ordered his legions to halt. Although he was becoming resigned to God's series of antagonistic miracles, he was perplexed by the sudden intrusion of the night and commanded his forces to simply light torches and make camp. The troops hastily set up their tents and settled in.

*****

Moses, enjoying continued sunlight, separated himself from the crowd. He had spoken confidently, but his own faith was faltering. He said to God, who had returned, "How can we possibly win this battle? The odds are overwhelming against us."

God scolded him, *"Why are you crying out to Me? Tell the sons of Israel to go forward. And as for you, lift up your staff and stretch out your hand over the sea and divide it, and the sons of Israel shall go through the midst of the sea on dry land.*"[m]

"Divide the sea?" thought an incredulous Moses. "So that is the way He will save us; there is to be no battle at all. But what will happen to their army?"

Holding it firmly, he obediently thrust his staff out over the sea, not sure what to expect. He saw the waters quickly retreat on each side of a wide channel as if it were gravel drawn back by a pair of mighty hands. Wild winds from the east wedged through the channel, drying the sea's sodden floor as the people braced their backs against the blowing force. Moses slumped to his knees into the gale and bowed his head to look at the staff in his hands, humbled and overcome by what he had just done.

When the winds subsided, the Israelites and their livestock cautiously followed Moses and Aaron onto the sea floor. The threat of the pent-up water, restrained by unseen dams, seemed less to them than that of Pharaoh's legions. While the Egyptians slept, the Hebrews cautiously descended the gradually sloping floor to the center of the sea, a depth of two hundred feet, and then began climbing up the far side.

*****

The cloud pulled the darkness away from the Egyptians at dawn as Pharaoh arose from a fitful sleep. After a brief meal, he mounted his manned-chariot and led his army over a hill and down to the Red Sea shore, where they halted in astonishment. In the distance, the Israelites were walking up the slope to the shores between the parted waters! Driven into a rage by frustration, Pharaoh shouted to his commanders, "Follow them! Destroy them all! Don't let them get away! Our gods will protect you." He grabbed the whip from his charioteer and struck his horses, who reared up then bolted ahead toward the water. He paused at the shore and looked around to watch his thundering phalanx of chariots lead the marching troops obediently onto the wide expanse of the sea bed.

Once the entire army was committed, God released rivulets of water that moistened the sea floor, and their chariot wheels became clogged in a sodden, gooey mass. Horses' hooves pawed into the muck and, too late, the Egyptians discerned God's hand.

*****

When the last Israelite was safely on the opposite shore, God told Moses, *"Stretch out your hand over the sea so that the waters may come back over the Egyptians, over their chariots and their horsemen."*[n]

Moses looked at the cloud gravely. "God, wilt Thou do it?" he whispered. He wanted safety for the Israelites, but a profound honor tore at his mind. He had once commanded a similar army of fine men, men who trusted him and even, he remembered, gave their lives for him. And now he was to be their executioner. Why not just send them back home? He caught himself, remembering that he now served under a wise Commander, One who expected obedience. "I must obey."

Hesitatingly, but with confidence in God, he raised his staff again up over the waters and the invisible dams that held them back were removed. The released waters roiled and crashed down, drowning the screaming army and their wide-eyed, struggling horses. Not even one of them survived.[o] Moses watched in awe. His thought to drop to one knee to honor the dead soldiers was quickly suppressed; he knew that would show contempt for God's command. So instead, he began to walk away.

*****

Gamaliel and Eliasaph were observing Moses from a distance.

Gamaliel said, "That man has cast his lot inexorably with God."

"I have great compassion for him" said Eliasaph. "He didn't do that easily."

"This should secure the people's trust in him," said Gamaliel.

Eliasaph answered, "We will see."

*****

A number of Israelites lined the shores, awed by the sight of corpses as they bobbed to the surface of the restored, white-capped waters. Many men helped Moses gather up the weapons that washed up on the shore by current and wind.[6] Women sobbed from a mixture of terror and relief; men stood in stunned silence; many of the adults embraced children. However, at a distance farther inland, sounds of dancing and joy were heard.

*****

As they walked away from the sea, Pagiel, fingering his goatee, and Ahira approached Moses "This God deals d-d-death freely when necessary—as

Noah learned—for which we are g-g-grateful—but warned," said Pagiel. "The first-born killed and now a whole army—to p-p-protect us."

"Retribution for the many babies his great-grandfather drowned in the Nile?" questioned Ahira.

"Perhaps," said Pagiel. "Moses, when we entered the sea, were you aware that the army would d-d-d drown?"

"No. I only knew that God would somehow be honored through these events and that Egypt would recognize that He, alone, is LORD over everything."

Ahira asked, "Why is it so important to God that Egypt believe in Him?"

"I do not know. God doesn't waste His words. It seems that a restored Egypt will be important to Him someday,"[p] Moses replied. "Now that their forces are decimated and the pharaoh presumed dead, I wonder what God has in store for Egypt?"

✶✶✶✶✶

Pagiel

"Pagiel the peculiar." His early playmates taunted him because of his stuttering and protruding eyes. Long nights of crying slowly grew a determination to not only be accepted but liked and respected. He learned to speak with assurance, stumbling doggedly through occasional difficult sentences without embarrassment. His stuttering riveted listeners' attention while the end of a sentence often brought belly laughs or admiration for his uncanny wisdom. With passing years, his affliction lessened and was bothersome only when he became angry, tired, or deeply frustrated. He wore a constant half-smile, looking like he alone knew where the treasure was hidden.

He was thrifty, keeping frequent and accurate account of the few coins that passed into his hands. His stinginess may have contributed to his remaining a bachelor.

The Egyptians disliked his insightful, cutting humor, and he never rose above being a house painter for them. However, he was immensely popular among his tribe of Asher. His sharp-witted, ad lib satires of Egyptian royalty, and even of the caustic guards—enhanced by his black goatee—provided laughter and temporary relief from drudgery for his fellow slaves. He could effortlessly sway audiences to his wise ways of thinking, a skill that led to his appointment as an elder.

*****

The three, Pagiel, Ahira, and Moses, continued walking and came upon a great number of people in a festive mood, who reveled at their rescue. After seeing the great power that the LORD used against the Egyptians, the people feared and believed in the LORD and in his servant Moses.[q] They knew that God would carry them, His special children, safely to Canaan. All they had to do was to watch Him perform His miracles.

"Moses, we need a song to sing. Write one for us," they pleaded.

Aroused from his sadness by their passion, Moses took Pagiel and Ahira a distance away and, with a papyrus sheet, they composed a song of salvation, one of thanksgiving;

*****

The Song (paraphrased):
I will sing to the LORD for He is highly exalted.
The horse and its rider He has hurled into the sea.
The LORD is my strength and song,
And He has become my salvation;
This is my God and I will praise Him; My father's God and I will extol Him.
The LORD is a warrior.

Pharaoh's chariots and his army He has cast into the sea;
And the choicest of his officers are drowned in the Red Sea.

Thou doest send forth Thy burning anger, and it consumes them as chaff.
And at the blast of Thy nostrils, the waters were piled up.

The enemy said, "I will pursue, I will overtake, I will divide the spoil;
"My desire shall be gratified against them."
Thou didst blow with Thy wind, the sea covered them;
They sank like lead in the mighty waters.

Who is like Thee, majestic in holiness,
Awesome in praises, working wonders?

In Thy lovingkindness You have led the people whom Thou hast redeemed;
In Thy strength Thou hast guided them to Thy holy habitation.
The peoples have heard, they tremble;
Anguish has gripped the inhabitants of Philistia.
Then the chiefs of Edom will be dismayed;
The leaders of Moab, trembling grips them;
All the inhabitants of Canaan have melted away.
Terror and dread fall upon them;
By the greatness of Thine arm they are motionless as stone;
Until the people pass over whom You have purchased.
Thou wilt bring them and plant them in the mountain of Thine inheritance,

The sanctuary, O LORD, which Thy hands have established.
The LORD will reign forever and ever.[7]

*****

As he composed, helped by the many words of prophecy that God gave to him, Moses felt some relief because he realized that, "LORD, Thou didst blow with Thy wind; the sea covered them."[r] He did not kill but simply raised his staff, requesting God's action. "The enemy whom You destroyed were not just innocent soldiers under orders but greedy men who wanted to divide the spoil[s] of the silver and gold given to the Hebrews." Moses solemnly declared that God had now become his strength, his song, his salvation, and his God, as well as his father's God, and he would extol Him.[t]

But as Moses examined the song's words again, he was puzzled. "Why did God include the countries of Edom and Moab? Those lands were not on the route to Canaan."

*****

And the people sang the song.

Miriam picked up a tambourine, waved it vigorously, and began to dance in a high-stepping march, calling on all to join her. A throng of women, buoyed by her enthusiasm, fell in behind, slapping other tambourines and singing.

When she looked back at them, a welcome pride filled her. She climbed up on the bed of a small cart and led them as they repeated the words, "Sing to the LORD, for He is highly exalted; the horse and the rider He has hurled into the sea."[u]

Observing the singing, Abidan said to Eliasaph, "The evidence points to this God as the most powerful of all gods, but not, however, the only god to be worshipped. Other gods have also previously produced such events as drought, rain in its season, and the quieting of storms. Yet, the attraction of this God is compelling. I think the people will trust Him now!"

"Really?" wondered Eliasaph, as they made camp.

✻✻✻✻✻

Endnotes

1. The story of the trip from Egypt to Mount Sinai is told in chapters 12 through 19 of Exodus.
2. "The Philistines came from the Islands of Caphtor." See Exodus 13:17, Jeremiah 47:4, and *Interpreter's Dictionary of the Bible, Supplementary Volume*, "Philistines," Keith Crim, ed., 1991, pp. 666ff.
3. "the armies of the Hittite empire," See *Interpreter's Dictionary*, ibid. p. 412.
4. "The Hittites developed a method of extracting the iron": See Dr. Werner Keller, *The Bible as History: A Confirmation of the Book of Books*. Translated by Dr. William Neil, 1964, p. 83.
5. "the Philistines came south and invaded the Egyptian mainland": See Exodus 13:17 and Bryant G. Wood, "The Philistines Enter Canaan: Were They Egyptian Lackeys or Invading conquerors?" *Biblical Archaelogy Review*, Nov.-Dec. 1991, pp. 44–52. See also Immanuel Velikovsky, *Ages in Chaos*, Vol. I., 1952, pp. 59–90.
6. "current and wind," *Josephus, Antiquities of the Jews*, William P. Nimmo, Scotland, 1867. Book II, Chapter 16, vs. 6.
7. Moses' song consists of selected phrases from Exodus 15:1–18. Lyrics adapted from the New American Standard Bible. ©Copyright 1960, 1962, 1963, 1968, 1971, 1972, 1973, 1975, 1977 by The Lockman Foundation. Used by permission. (www.Lockman.org)

Chapter 6

Tried Trust

Two days later, the cloud floated southeastward, tracking the Red Sea down the coastal lowlands of the Sinai Peninsula. The Israelites followed day after day, resting only at night. One morning, the cloud ascended and turned east. The people, with their livestock, climbed up the seven-hundred-foot slope that led onto a vast limestone and granite plateau with mountains in the distance. When Aaron, in the forefront with Moses, surveyed the expanse, he asked his brother, "Are you familiar with this area? Are we likely to encounter settlements along the way?"

Moses said, "Probably. I know of small villages and towns, some near the copper and tin mines."

"The area looks too dry for all of us to survive."

"I have been here twice, once even during a rare rainstorm. The water pours off this limestone and is carried away into long, sandy-bottomed wadis, some shallow, others quite deep, holding water even in dry seasons. We will probably pass by many of them. There are also natural springs scattered along the way that provide oases with grass for the animals."

"I hope God knows where He is going," complained Aaron.

"I believe He does."

*****

Midway through the first day on the plateau, they came to a large, deep, rock-walled wadi with abundant water. Plants, green and blue flowers, and vines grew through the cracks in the side wall. After a welcome refreshment, the caravan departed with bags full of water.

The cloud continued eastward. A loose rectangle of marchers and animals followed, advancing across a long front up to ten to fifteen people abreast and extending two to three miles to the rear. They traveled with unaccustomed freedom, expecting no major problems as God's chosen, protected people. Memory of the Red Sea victory blurred their preceding panic. To determine if the Red Sea miracle had produced any improvement in their attitudes, God devised three tests for them, two of thirst and one of hunger.

Four days after leaving the wadi, the travelers' water stores ran out, and they began to thirst. Finding another wadi, they eagerly knelt to drink, but instantly spat the water out.

"Moses, we are parched in this heat and now this water is foul-tasting," Elishama grumbled on behalf of his people. "Have camels been here first?"

Others grumbled, "O Moses, what shall we drink?"[a]

The carpenter, Shelumiel, shouldered his way through to the water, knelt, cupped his hands, and drank without showing his distress. "Though it is bitter, it at least quenches my thirst," he muttered. "Boil some, you who are so spoiled."

A number of people near Moses, disgusted by the taste, wailed, "Why have you led us here to suffer so?"

Moses shuddered when he too sipped the water. He arose and walked away from the crowd. "They are complaining of thirst and the water is bitter," he cried out to the cloud.

God indicated to Moses a particular tree that would sweeten the waters. Moses instructed two of the complainers to put an axe to the allotted tree, and as it toppled into the wadi, the water immediately became sweet and fresh. They drank their fill, convinced that they deserved it.

"Another miracle. How God loves us," Abidan was heard to say. "We complain and He acts."

Moses was dismayed at their response to the bitter water. "Do not displease God further with your complaining," Moses told them. "We have all personally witnessed His terrible anger while in Egypt. Let it not fall on us."

In truth, God was sorely disappointed with them and their grumbling. Had four hundred years of bondage produced a band of whiners rather than the trial-hardened, committed company He sought? The next day, He sternly warned them again through Moses. *"If you will give earnest heed to the voice of the LORD your God, and do what is right in His sight, and give ear to His commandments ... I will put none of the diseases on you which I have put on the Egyptians; for I, the LORD, am your healer."*[b]

✳✳✳✳✳

Elishama limped over to where Abidan, leaning on his cane, was deep in thought. "Hey, Abidan, what do you think of the latest miracle?"

"Amazing. Do you think He fouled the water to see our response? We did not do well. But I am thinking about His last words."

"You mean about the diseases?" asked Elishama. "A bit humbling."

"Yes," said Abidan. "We always thought proudly that we had a special immunity that protected us as Hebrews. Not so. God just blessed us—again."

"Or was it protection from the diseases of the plagues?[1] He warns us that our protection now is dependent on our following His commandments," said Elishama.

"What commandments?" asked Abidan. "We have those concerning circumcision and Passover. Are there more to come?"

"We shall see. I see that the cloud is moving."

The people named the place Marah, meaning "bitter water."

*****

After God's exhortation, the cloud led them a half-day's journey to another large oasis called Elim. The people rejoiced, set up camp, and drank luxuriously from the cool, clear, fresh waters of twelve bubbling springs. Nearby was a stand of seventy tall, stately date palms, their high fronds forming a canopy overhead to shade them from the hot sun. Young boys easily scaled the trees and returned with arms full of fruit savored by the travelers.

*****

After resting overnight, the caravan left Elim and continued southeastward. Physically refreshed, their stores of water replenished, many of the people were enthusiastic, embarking with lighthearted joy. Others advanced with caution, realizing that God's blessings had become conditional.

Sixty days after leaving Rameses, and twenty-two days after leaving Elim, another problem arose. They had encountered no other travelers to trade with and their food supplies were exhausted. Three tribal elders confronted Moses and Aaron on the people's behalf: the jeweler Nahshon, Ahira of the tribe of Naphtali, and Shelumiel.

Shelumiel spoke up first. "We are starving, Moses. We have rationed our food for several days, and now it is gone. The people are hungry and angry."

Nahshon, one hand in the pocket of his robe, spoke for the whole congregation, which grumbled against Moses, "Would that we had died by the LORD's hand in the land of Egypt, when we sat by the pots of meat and ate bread to the full;

for you have brought us out into this wilderness to kill this whole assembly with hunger."[t]

Ahira, the military man, considered their stand and then interposed, "Moses, I believe I can see to it that the tribe of Naphtali will not complain."

Moses had gone without food himself for five days, so he empathized with them. "Ahira, this is a problem we all share. I believe that God will not abandon us, although He has been silent. Perhaps we are being tested again. Let me go away a distance and see if He will provide some food."

"You must do that," Shelumiel said. "By tomorrow, the people may begin to slaughter their own animals, the stock we may need later."

As Moses and Aaron separated themselves from the others, God gave them a message for the people.

*****

The next morning, when the congregation had assembled, Moses stood before them. "The LORD told us that He is wearied by your continued complaining. Because of that, however, He has taken us into His confidence again, telling us of another great, surprising gift to satisfy your need. He says that He will *rain bread from heaven for you.*"[u]

Even as Moses spoke, the attention of all was drawn to the desert where they saw the familiar cloud rapidly approaching. But this time, its appearance was different. From its center shone a white light of such brilliance, they had to look away.

God called to Moses from the cloud and spoke to him: "*I have heard the grumblings of the sons of Israel; speak to them, saying, 'At twilight, you shall eat meat, and in the morning you shall be filled with bread; and you shall know that I am the LORD your God.'*"[x] The glory of the LORD faded as swiftly as it had come.

Moses thought, "Of course, You are God, but this congregation is still not convinced. Where will You find bread and meat for this crowd?"

Moses relayed this new message to the people, adding God's order to "*Gather a day's portion every day, that I may test them, whether or not they will walk in My instruction. And it will come about on the sixth day, when they prepare what they bring in, it will be twice as much as they gather daily.*"[x]

Shelumiel allowed himself a doubting chuckle as he considered this unlikely feast.

*****

Early the next morning, Lashinar, a herdsman from the tribe of Manasseh, arose full of expectation. Departing his tent, he met fellow tribesman Sorin, the weaver.

Lashinar said, as his sandals kicked at the moist ground, "Moses promised us food, but I see only heavy dew."

"Another ruse to keep us quiet," answered Sorin as they walked about, puzzled and discouraged. Others joined them in their fruitless hunt for the promised bread. They were about to give up their search, but as the dew evaporated in the warming sun, they noticed it left an unfamiliar residue. Lashinar bent over, scooped up a handful of it, and sniffed it. He gingerly put a little into his mouth.

Startled, he said, "Try some, Sorin! This white, odorless grain is not bad; it is somewhat tasty, almost like wafers with honey."

"Yes, and the ground is thick with it," said Sorin, sharing Lashinar's excitement. "Get a bag and we will fill it."

Returning from their tents, they began to scoop it up. "Why such a large bag, Lashinar? We were told to gather only one day's worth each morning."

"Foolish Sorin! How sure are you that this will be here tomorrow? I will gather plenty for my family."

"My friend, you refuse again to comply. Testing God?" challenged Sorin. "I have all I need. I will see you again tomorrow—if you are still here."

Lashinar reached down for the final few handfuls and then brought the bag into the cool of his tent.

"What have you there?" asked Coresha, his wife.

"Food from the sky, I suppose. We had to gather it from the ground," said Lashinar, as he poured a portion out into a large bowl.

Coresha allowed some to run through her fingers and then licked them. "Lashinar, what a surprise. It is fine and flaky and even tastes good raw. I will grind it and bake some into cakes and boil another part of it. We shall have enough for a week for us and our daughter."

When she opened her bin the next morning, she reached for a cake then dropped it quickly. "Holy Moloch, it is crawling with slimy worms. Where did they come from? I baked it well."

"It is God's doing," said Lashinar, and he carried the bin to the door and threw the remainder outside. But, looking down, there was a thick field of new white flakes as far as he could see. "Give me my bag, Coresha. I'll collect some before the heat of the day. And to avoid God's slimy crawlers, only today's portion."

"Tomorrow is the Sabbath, and you are not to gather then. Should you not collect enough for two days?" she asked.

"One day at a time," he insisted.

*****

There were some men, however, like Sorin, who were learning to trust God. On the Sabbath, they refrained from searching for their food, their *manna* they called it, a word meaning "what" or "what is it?"[2] The one-day's portion, collected and baked the previous day, miraculously doubled in size, providing enough for the Sabbath—and it did not become wormy.

*****

That same Sabbath morning, Lashinar and many others arrogantly defied God and carried their bags out to collect but found only grass on the ground. "Why does He inconvenience us so?" Lashinar said to others.

God saw them searching about, and His growing frustration mounted. He challenged Moses. *"How long* [will these people] *refuse to keep My commandments and My instructions?"* As a penalty, He added, *"Let no man go out of his place on the* [Sabbath]*."*[h]

*****

Sorin approached Lashinar the next day. "I hope you are satisfied. Because of men like you, we must spend every seventh day cooped up in our tents with our energetic children! There will be no gathering from there! God is so wise."

"A small inconvenience, Sorin. Now people will get to know their children better," said Lashinar.

God also told Moses to keep a portion of the manna in a sealed jar to show to the coming generations the bread He fed them in the wilderness.

As usual, after a punishment, God provided for them, keeping another promise. That evening, many quail flew over, dropped into the camp, and were captured, providing a welcome dinner.

*****

Moses knew of various tribes who inhabited the lands through which they would travel and suspected that some would be protective of their individual domains. They had accepted him as a lone shepherd, but he was uncertain of their response to this traveling throng of foreigners. To prepare for possible hostilities, he sought a leader to organize the people into, at least, a rag-tag military unit. After consulting with some of his ex-soldiers, Moses chose Joshua, son of Nun, a bright, athletic nineteen-year-old, who had served in Pharaoh's army, having been promoted twice. Battle turned this humble, allegiant, God-respecting man into a canny and vicious fighter. However, the meekness returned after each engagement when the fire within him would temporarily subside. He had a crooked, battle-damaged nose, long, red hair that was often windblown, and soft eyes that had an inner passion.

Joshua felt honored by the appointment. He quickly assembled a skeleton staff of would-be officers to lead groups of ex-soldiers and others. Every man over the age of twenty would be enlisted and supplied with some form of weaponry from the many brought out of Egypt.

Joshua was assigned to walk next to Moses and Aaron in the lead when the cloud moved off to the east. After an uneventful week of walking, in the third month after leaving Egypt, a series of mountains became visible beyond the plateau. As they progressed closer, they could see some very high, barren peaks that blended with lower mountain ranges and stretched north to south as far as they could see, territory familiar to Moses.

"The Horeb Range," Moses pointed out to Joshua, "and the highest is Mount Sinai. The closest mountain is Rephidim. We shall make camp at its base; there is a large oasis nearby."

Joshua squinted his eyes. "We should reach it in about two days," he calculated. "It will be welcome because our water stores have about run out."

*****

That night Moses visited Miriam in her tent. After some casual conversation, Moses asked, "Miriam, did you ever observe a drowning?" Moses asked.

"No, but during the months they hid you, mother told me she walked to the river several times to see if any babies were being spared. None were; there were always armed soldiers present to assure the drowning. She saw a father, with his wife at his side, wade out into the water, cradling his trusting baby in one arm. Glances were exchanged between the parents before the father drowned the baby. She saw a woman wrap a thin, worn, woolen shawl around a baby sucking at her breast and walk out into the water, her legs struggling against the current. The baby sucked as its head disappeared beneath the water, then, choosing to share the watery grave, the mother exhaled and walked on, her head silently disappearing beneath the surface.

"Mother said it happened every day. Some babies were pushed out into that river on blankets or fragile rafts, or simply laid on cherished cloths to struggle and sink."

"And I was to have the same end?" asked Moses.

"Yes, until I helped to procure your survival."

"I owe you a debt I cannot repay," said Moses

"Perhaps someday you may be able to," she frowned.

"I will look forward to that opportunity," said Moses.

*****

After a night's rest, the mass of people traveled toward the mountains. The morning sun bore down on them. Lashinar groaned, "Yesterday, my daughter suffered bites on her leg from a stinging scorpion. Today, the wounds look angry and red. I despise this infernal trip to—only God knows where."

"I am sorry about your Zessa, but if she is no worse than you say, she should recover. But don't complain," said Sorin. "You are not stomping in clay pits today, are you? And this god does not carry a cudgel in that cloud of his. Today, my feet carry me in my own honor, buoyed along by a god who provides all I need: food, water, and shelter for my family."

Lashinar answered wryly. "Come now, my martyr friend, tell me you do not miss that tasty food of Egypt, the vegetables, and occasional fish! Do you prefer your own home, or the one you must carry on your back?"

"Lashinar," said Sorin, "the air is sweeter on this side of the sea, the ground softer, and the sun that sapped our strength in Egypt nourishes my soul now. Even the cattle seem joyous. I'll trade fish and fruits for freedom any day."

"I don't know about you, Sorin, but our family ran out of water yesterday."

"Here, I have a few spoonfuls in my canteen. Look ahead, we are but a day or two from the mountain. Moses tells us that there is an oasis there."

* * * * *

While the desiccated troupe approached Rephidim three mornings later, Joshua dispatched four men to go ahead and see if the oasis was unoccupied. They returned as Moses and Aaron reached the mountain with the news that the oasis was dry and, after scouting around for a distance in each direction, they found no water.

This news spread quickly. Then, with parched throats and urged on by their complaining tribes and crying children, ten of the elders approached Moses.

Nethanel said, "Well, Moses! We speak on behalf of our tribes. There is no water at all anywhere around!"

Elishama snapped, "Why, now, have you brought us up from Egypt, to kill us and our children and our livestock with thirst?"[i]

Pagiel, the painter, staring bug-eyed, demanded, "Give us water that we may drink!"[j]

Moses surveyed them carefully. "You have all come, except Gamaliel and Eliasaph. Where are they?"

"Those older men thirst in silence," said Shelumiel. "They try to remind us that God has provided in the past and will do so again. That bit of rhetoric doesn't moisten our lips."

"Why do you quarrel with me? Why do you test the LORD?[k] The cloud brought us here. Trust Him if you can, but do not complain," snapped Moses through cracked lips.

Abidan shook a gnarled hand at Moses and taunted, "Is the LORD among us or not?"[l]

Some men nearby, pushed to the limit by their thirst and feeling hopeless, glared at the brothers. They looked around and gathered palm-sized chunks of limestone in their callused hands and took a few steps toward them. A number of the elders raced in front of them, attempting to hold them back.

Moses stood still, feet apart, his eyes darting from one scowl to another. Sensing their resolve, he cried out, "God, what shall I do with these people? A little more and they will stone me."[m]

God, observing them, responded with unexpected patience. He softly answered him, *"Pass before the people and take with you some of the elders of Israel; and take in your hand your staff with which you struck the Nile, and go. Behold, I will stand before you there on the rock at Horeb; and you shall strike the rock, and water will come out of it, that the people may drink."*[n]

*****

"A rock: to the men, a missile;
to Him, a fountain?" thought Moses.

*****

The cloud-pillar appeared, then hovered over a huge boulder at the base of the mountain, some distance away. While Moses and Aaron quickly walked away from the crowd toward the cloud, Joshua motioned to the elders to follow. They followed him across a large field and gathered around the cloud-topped boulder. Moses raised his rod and with growing confidence, struck the rock. To the surprise of the elders, the rock split open at a seam, and cool, clear water gushed from it. The larger body of the Israelites, unable to see Moses' stroke, saw the gurgling stream and rushed headlong to it, gulping the fresh water to satisfy their thirst. When they discovered its origin, they stared at Moses, dumbfounded; many offered praise in recognition of his supernatural power. One man claimed that Moses learned this trick from Pharaoh's magicians. All quenched their thirst and filled their water bags before watering their livestock.

*****

The spindly Javell spoke excitedly to his friend and fellow tribesman. "Hasor, I know that your breathing prevents you from walking distances, but I searched all about that giant boulder Moses struck—even around the hill behind it. There was no water on any side of it."

"It's a miracle, all right," said Hasor, "but why does this God repeatedly wait until we are suffering before He satisfies us? Wouldn't it be much easier if He would anticipate our needs?"

"Maybe this is all part of the testing that Moses told us to expect," said Javell.

"Well, we got our water—and this time without any reprimands," grumbled Hasor.

"Not so," answered Javell. "I heard that Moses must rename this site 'Meribah' meaning '*The people strived with God*.'[3] Because of our continued quarreling with God and asking 'Is the LORD among us or not?' all future travelers or nations will know that we treated God with contempt here. That is worse than worms."

They traveled several miles farther before those in the lead began to set up camp near the mount of Rephidim.

*****

End notes

1. "...of the plagues"; idea from *Tabletalk* magazine, May 2022, page 63.
2. "manna; a word meaning 'what' or 'what is it?'" according to the footnote for Exodus 16:15 in the *Ryrie Study Bible*.
3. "Meribah,' from the Hebrew word meaning 'to strive,'" according to the footnote for Numbers 20:13 in the Ryrie Study Bible.

Chapter 7

The Raid

Suddenly, a host of men with horses and chariots, brandishing swords and battle-axes, swooped down on those in the rear in a vicious attack, quickly overwhelming the few armed sentries. With unintelligible whoops and shrieks, they killed many Hebrews, gathered up the possessions from those who fled, and took many captives. A large band of armed Hebrew men hastily gathered and confronted the attackers who fought briefly before retreating over the hills. One of the attacker's horses stumbled, throwing its rider to the ground. Joshua and ten of his men brought their injured prisoner to Moses.

"Who are you?" Moses demanded.

"A member of the army of Amalek,"[1] he answered defiantly in broken Egyptian.

"Do you live here, and if not, where have you come from?"

"We have come from the land of Arabia, to the south and east of here," he said, appearing unafraid.

"Why are you here now?"

"We were powerful at home and ruled the country for many years. However, strange illnesses have weakened us, and the Assyrian army attacked us and drove us out. We traveled north and west with our herds and flocks for four months and settled but a short distance away. Our lookouts have been observing you for days."

"Why have you attacked us?" asked Moses.

"Our leaders were threatened by your huge throng marching toward our best lands. We see also that you have many fine possessions that we shall have soon."

"What will your army do now?"

"You will see. Tomorrow you will be annihilated!" the captive said. "We are part of a powerful army, and you look to be but a motley band of refugees."

"Do we?" asked Moses. He ordered two of Joshua's men to remove and guard the prisoner. Then he addressed the remainder. "We lost over one hundred travelers when they swept in as a whirlwind. They scooped us up like sand. The number of men in their full army is probably several times our force. Their arms are superior, and they drive swift chariots. They will surely return tomorrow.

"Joshua, notify your men tonight and prepare to defend our company. I am too old to fight, but I will climb to the top of that hill over there with the staff of God in my hand and entreat Him to help us."

"Moses, my master," replied Joshua, "God has protected us since we left Rameses. If He is really in charge, why did He allow this attack? Has our repeated complaining angered Him?"

Moses placed his hand on Joshua's shoulder. "You have the understanding that escapes many. God's blessings please us, but we must learn from His discipline."

*****

The next morning, before sunrise, Moses took his wonder-working staff and, with Aaron and Hur[2]—Miriam's husband and a highly respected elder of the tribe of Judah—ascended to the top of the hill overlooking the valley of the Hebrews; all while Joshua organized his resistance force on the field below. The Israelites had no choice; resentments put aside, they had to fight in an organized fashion behind Joshua or die. No complaints were heard. Joshua positioned his armed, hand-picked men in a frontal array across the valley, some of whom had been trained foot soldiers in Egypt. Two other rows of recruits stood behind them. Former military archers and novices held the left flank, partially obscured by some small mounds and bushes. Elishama joined the archers while the soldier, Ahira, commanded the right flank.

Joshua's faith and outrageous courage sustained the motley band as they waited, some fervently praying that the enemy would not appear. As the sun rose in the eastern sky, just as the captive had predicted, the entire well-equipped Amalekite army charged at the Hebrews from over a distant hill. Joshua, with flowing hair, bravely led the outnumbered Israelites into battle.

As the armies clashed, Moses impulsively raised his staff toward heaven. The Hebrews contended well, suffering few casualties as they drove their foe backward. After a time, Moses lowered his staff, his aching shoulders crying for rest. The tide of battle turned instantly, and the Hebrew line of soldiers gave way. Perceiving the bloody rout inevitable, Moses raised his hands and the staff again, beseeching God's help. To his utter surprise, the retreat ceased, the Hebrews held, and they soon went on the offensive again.

"It is the staff, held up to God, which brings success," Moses realized. After another hour, fatigued, he said, "God honors me, but my strength fails. I cannot hold my hands up any longer." As he lowered them, the Amalekites surged forward.

Aaron and Hur, observing the tides of battle, rallied to his side. "Sit down; we'll hold them up for you." As Moses sat on a rock, they stood beside him, each cradling one of his outstretched arms in theirs. The clang of metal against metal, the occasional shrieks of impaled men, and the snorting of horses rose above the battle lines. The tiring Hebrews, stumbling over dying horses and around overturned chariots, routed their foes under the late afternoon sun, the survivors retreating beyond the hills.

A grateful Moses turned to Aaron and Hur. "This God rewards our worship. Our men fought hard, but the outcome of the battle was His."

"All we did was to hold up your hands," admitted Aaron.

"I could not have done it without you two," answered Moses.

As the three descended the hill, the victors gathered up their plunder amid the stench of blood and entrails. The surviving horses were corralled. A tired but jubilant Joshua surveyed the battlefield where they had fought. His unaccustomed pride quickly faded when Moses told how the course of battle had followed his raised staff. Joshua accepted the explanation, and his respect for Moses and his faith in God grew.

Moses directed a stone altar to be built in profound gratitude for God's victory and named it, The LORD Is My Banner.[a]

*****

Meanwhile, over the hills, the bloodied camp of the Amalekites bound up the wounded and buried their dead. "We have been humiliated by a band of ex-serfs!" growled Medor, their king. "Spread the word and warn the caravans. There was something almost supernatural in their fighting. We were defeated today, but I vow that we shall yet have our day with them."

*****

As if in response to Medor's vow of retaliation, God promised His retribution for the cowardly attack on His people the previous day. "*Write this in a book as a memorial,"* He told Moses, *"and recite it to Joshua, that I will utterly blot out the memory of Amalek from under heaven."* Despite the promise, the obliteration would be long delayed, as God added, *"The* LORD *will have war against Amalek from generation to generation."*[b]

Moses dutifully recorded God's promise on his papyrus pages, writing in the Semitic alphabet he had learned in Midian. He read God's message to Joshua, who spoke Hebrew, but although tutored by Moses, was not yet able to read it.

End notes

1. "Amalek": See Immanuel Velikovsky, *Ages in Chaos,* Vol. I., 1952, pp. 59–90. Also, following story from Exodus 17:8f. See also George Rawlinson, *Moses, His Life and Times,* p. 136.
2. Story from Ex. 17:8f and *Josephus,* Kregel Publications, Grand Rapids, MI, Book III, Chap. 2, p. 68.

Section II
Indoctrination at Sinai

Chapter 8

Listen! It is God!

Five days after their victory, following the cloud, Moses led the Hebrews from Rephidim to the mountain named Sinai in the southeastern part of the Sinai Peninsula, one hundred and fifty miles from Rameses. As they approached, the travelers were surprised to see the lushness of the area and the small forests to the east and south.

"In this whole valley," exclaimed Miriam to Moses, "the grass is so tall and green that my feet hide in it![1] The trees are laden with fruit. There must be many oases nearby and higher rainfall than anywhere we have been since leaving Egypt. Are these God's fields?"

"Perhaps, but it is always this way," said Moses. "I have pastured sheep here occasionally, though I do not remember so many nearby trees. By bringing us here, God has kept yet another promise to me. He says that we are to make a more permanent camp and stay for a while, probably to be prepared for Canaan, though that land is still about two weeks' journey away."[a]

"I will be in no hurry to leave this garden spot. God has led us here," she hesitated and then added, "through you. He speaks to you so much more often than to Aaron and—" she looked down at her feet, "never to me anymore, since you arrived in Rameses."

"He loves you just as He loves Aaron and me," Moses said gently. "I just happen to be His appointed leader."

"Yes, I suppose that is so," she conceded.

*****

God's plan, only partially revealed to Moses, was to park them all at Sinai for a year. Because of the difficult times that lay ahead of them, He would tutor them and try to mold them into a well-organized, cohesive community with a steadfast trust in Him. He would then guide them into Canaan, overpower the inhabitants, and establish a principled nation there.

*****

The next morning, God called Moses to the mountain that towered two thousand feet over their camp and told him to come up. "Climb up to God

Himself?" It was a daunting proposition. Moses felt a wave of peaceful assurance flow over him as he walked to its base, passing by the pillar cloud and assuming that God had left one of His angels in it. Moses began ascending the rocky slope, seeking worn paths, wondering why God wanted him on the mountain. He had never had any difficulty hearing God's word from thin air or from the cloud or fire before.

Halfway up, God spoke to him from the summit. *"Thus you shall say to* [the people], *'You yourselves have seen what I did to the Egyptians, and how I bore you on eagles' wings and brought you to Myself. Now then, if you will indeed obey My voice and keep My covenant, then you shall be My own possession among all the peoples, for all the earth is Mine; and you shall be to me a kingdom of priests and a holy nation."*[b]

Moses sat down, trying to understand the enormity of His new message. "This then is God's goal," he thought. "It is not just to enable us to conquer and enjoy Canaan. No, much more. We are to become an entire holy nation, a whole kingdom of priests, like Jethro, whose life is dedicated to working and praying for others. But pray for whom? Neighbors? The world? Maybe Gamaliel could become a priest. But with the elders we have and their persistent lack of trust in You, I sometimes doubt that we will even make it to Canaan. God, I know that you are powerful but ...

"And I am to facilitate it? Their obedience to the few laws we have is shaky at best, and more laws may be on the way. 'God, You must help me,' he cried out. 'Make them willing!'"

With doubts, he descended the mountain.

*****

That night God spoke to Moses and told him that He had selected the Israelite elder from each tribe who was best qualified to be their tribal leader—their prince. Those chosen were Pagiel, the painter of Asher; Abidan, the arthritic of Benjamin; Ahiezer, a shepherd of Dan; Elishama, the stonemason of Ephraim; Eliasaph, the stonemason of Gad; Nethanel, the feisty bricklayer of Issachar; Nahshon, the jeweler of Judah; Gamaliel, the bricklayer of Manasseh; Ahira, the soldier of Naphtali; Elizur, a cattleman of Reuben; Shelumiel, the carpenter of Simeon; and Eliab, a shepherd of Zebulun.

Moses sent word out that a meeting of the elders was called for the next day's afternoon.

*****

Almost a hundred men met together on the outskirts of the village as the sun was setting. Moses first told them which of them God had appointed to be the new tribal leaders, one from each tribe, the select group of twelve. Some responded joyfully, others with disappointment, and for a few, relief. Reserved head nodding and some smiles were interchanged. Then Moses conveyed God's message to them. "Consider carefully and fully God's offer. If acceptable, you must take it to your people. I will leave you to your discussions." Moses walked away.

Elishama, "Barley," stood to speak. "I am uncertain. This God insists that we follow Him who knows where and do whatever He may demand of us in the future. Are we making too great a commitment to Him if we recommend that our people accept this?"

"In effect," said Abidan, "He wants us to yield our wills to Him, becoming servants with Him—priests to serve, pray for, and intercede for others—and to ignore our other gods."

"I think," replied Eliasaph, "that is what Abraham was told, that 'all of the families of the earth will be blessed through us.' He asks much of us, but consider what He has already done! The plagues, the division of the Red Sea, the manna, the victory at Rephidim, water from a rock. Fellow travelers, He has my vote."

"I am not interested. I live for myself and my family," said Shelumiel. "I'll establish my own carpentry shop in Canaan and that should keep me busy."

"I'm not all that keen on devoting my life to this God and strangers," said Ahira. "Maybe as a part-time priest."

"If we refuse, might He just leave us out here to fend for ourselves?" worried Nethanel.

Gamaliel said. "That is unlikely. He seems to desire the best for us. I believe that He will ask no more than we can give. As for me, I'll side with Eliasaph. Hasn't He already answered the prayers of more than the last four generations? Let us accept. We have much to gain!"

"Nahshon, Shelumiel, and others, listen. Moses' father-in-law is a priest. He has his own family, his animals. Priesting does not have to be a full-time job," pleaded Eliasaph.

There was a contemplative silence before Shelumiel said, "All right, I won't keep this from going to the people,"

"I, too, at least for now," said Nahshon, grudgingly.

After another short silence, Eliasaph inquired, "Are there other dissenting views?"

"I have but one question," asked Elishama. "When we present these offers to our people, will the foreigners have a vote in this?"

"No," said Eliasaph. "This is God's offer only to the Israelites. We are all in one accord then?" he asked.

Their answers, "Yes," were staggered and soft. Nahshon, Shelumiel, and Ahira simply nodded their heads.

*****

The tribal leaders took God's proposition to the people. After many questions—many similar to those asked by the leaders—and long discussions, all of the people responded together: "All that the LORD has spoken, we will do!"[t]

Moses climbed back up the mountain with his staff to give God the good news, hopefully setting God's special plan afoot. God accepted that but told him, *"Go to the people and consecrate them today and tomorrow and let them wash their garments ... For on the third day the LORD will come down on Mount Sinai in the sight of all the people."*[d] Moses was instructed to set stakes around the mountain so that neither man nor beast would climb up or even touch the border of the mountain. Those who dared to would die. *"When the ram's horn sounds a long blast, they shall come up to the mountain,"*[e] God said.

The people prepared as commanded and were told to refrain from sexual intercourse for those three days.

Everyone arose on the third morning to barrages of thunder and shattering flashes of lightning that illuminated a thick, black cloud covering Mount Sinai. The stentorian blare of a ram's-horn trumpet, heard even above the claps of thunder and the lightning, cowed the people until Moses alone stepped forward. "Follow me!" he shouted, and beckoning to them, led the frightened people toward the foot of the mountain.

What had appeared at a distance to be a dark cloud was now clearly seen to be an intense fire discharging smoke as from a furnace. God had descended onto Mount Sinai. As if the atmosphere were not terrifying enough, the entire mountain and the very earth on which they stood shook violently, scattering the people.

Assuming a cloak of bravery, Moses raised his staff. "Come, trust in God!" he commanded.

When the quaking ceased, calm returned to them. As the sounds of the trumpet grew louder, Moses called out to God, who answered him with further peals of thunder and an invitation to climb the mountain, this time all the way to the top.

"Climb into that smoke and fire! Will He protect me?" Then, with mounting trust and affection, he realized, "I now believe that I am ready to give my life for Him if He wishes."

*****

Buoyed by his own words, Moses left the assembly and ascended, disappearing into the rolling smoke and toward the fire. After more than an hour, he reached the top of the mountain unharmed.

Again, God's voice came to him. *"Go down, warn the people, lest they break through to the* Lord *to gaze, and many of them perish."*

After his long climb, Moses had to turn around and go back down to simply repeat a warning he had been given previously. Up the mountain, down the mountain, up, down, up, down. How was Moses responding to his training as an eighty-year-old errand boy? Not a whimper, not an argument, no "Why again, Lord?" was recorded; Moses' maturing meekness was confirmed.

Before descending, Moses assured God that the people would obey; the mountain, God's mountain, would be untouched. Then God told Moses that when he returned to the people, He would deliver His message to them. Afterward, He wanted Moses to return to the mountain, this time accompanied to its base by Aaron.

When Moses rejoined the people, the thunder, the lightning, and the trumpet sounds all ceased. A portentous silence followed. No one dared move beyond the appointed boundaries at the foot of the mountain. Many wondered what God would say. Would He pronounce a dreadful sentence on them for their lack of trust, their lack of obedience to Him? Trembling, they listened attentively; all was quiet.

*****

GOD

God created humans for fellowship with Him, placing them into a perfect environment that they might enjoy it fully. However, when He allowed Adam and Eve to be tested, they succumbed, falling from that ideal state.

They multiplied and, generations later, their descendants had become so evil that God decided to destroy the world with a flood, sparing only faithful Noah's family. At the same time, He reduced man's lifespan from the previous eight to nine hundred years to a paltry one hundred and twenty years. Sadly, God's hope that man would follow Him and His precepts was short-lived, as man descended again into lustful self-centeredness.

Eventually, God—still intent to have fellowship with his creation—implemented another strategy: He would create a nation of priests to minister to the world and to save it. He began with another man who listened and obeyed—Abraham. God guided Abraham's progeny, the thousands of his descendants, for more than five hundred years, finally bringing them to this very mountain. What would He say to them, in these, His first words to such a multitude, having spoken only to individuals through the ages before? How could He convey to them the glorious, totally satisfying, joy-filled, and successful lives that He desired for them with all His Being—lives of service born of His love for them? Only He knew the true path that they must walk, the path that wound safely through the jungle of distracting obstacles and worldly temptations. Here, at Mount Sinai, He had gathered His people to tell them.

*****

Breaking the stillness, God's voice boomed out clearly through the surging smoke into the valley below, pausing between each commandment to allow thought for the people.

*****

"I am the Lord *your God, who brought you out of the land of Egypt, out of the house of slavery."*⁵ Let there be no doubt that it was their powerful God, who knew their past suffering, who was speaking.

"You shall have no other gods before Me." "Do I, don't we—still?" Moses mused.

"You shall not make for yourself an idol, or any likeness of what is in heaven above or on the earth beneath or in the water under the earth. You shall not worship them or serve them"—His imageless Spirit would, must, satisfy—*"for I, the* Lord *your God, am a jealous God, visiting the iniquity of the fathers on the children, on the third and fourth generations of those who hate Me, but showing lovingkindness to thousands, to those who love Me and keep My commandments."* The people's descendants would either continue to suffer for their rebelliousness or would revel in the fruits of their obedience. "Discard the idols!" thought Moses.

"You shall not take the name of the Lord *your God in vain, for the* Lord *will not leave him unpunished who takes His name in vain."* Revere His name—or else.

"Remember the Sabbath day, to keep it holy. Six days you shall labor and do all your work, but the seventh day is a Sabbath of the Lord *your God; in it you shall not do any work…. For in six days the* Lord *made the heavens and the earth … and rested on the seventh day."* "The seventh day is entirely Yours, God," acknowledged Moses.

"Honor your father and mother that your days may be prolonged in the land which the Lord *your God gives you."* A command with a valuable reward.

"You shall not murder. Moses winced.

"You shall not commit adultery.

"You shall not steal.

"You shall not bear false witness against your neighbor.

*"You shall not covet your neighbor's house; you shall not covet your neighbor's wife or his male servant or his female servant or his ox or his donkey or anything that belongs to your neighbor."*⁶ Moses understood, "The most important matter—that which dealt not with actions, but with the mind, not with the tinder, but the spark—was left for last. The transient desires of each individual must be subordinated to the well-being of the community if it is to survive and have vitality. I must remind them again and again."

*****

After the Ten Commandments were issued, thunder, lightning, and the wail of heavenly trumpets burst forth again. God's first words to the people had not been greetings or promises, but a stern message. "God has come in order to test you," Moses shouted to the people, "that the fear of Him may remain with you, so that you may not sin."[h]

Tradition told the frightened people that they would all die if God persisted in instructing them directly.

Abidan shouted at Moses, "Go forth and communicate with Him alone on our behalf. We will withdraw." And they did.

As Moses approached the mountain base alone, God told him to remind the people that although the fire and smoke were on the mountaintop, His message was from heaven and carried that authority.

*****

The Israelites had been released from the crushing burdens imposed by harsh Egyptian laws, but God knew that the absence of law would breed tumult. Therefore, He now began to issue His own new set of commandments, laws that defined the behaviors of individuals and by which Moses could judge the people; laws regarding personal injury; the care of indentured servants, widows, orphans and animals; the sabbath; the first-born; theft; interest on loans and many more. God would give the people the option to accept or reject His laws. If they accepted them, Moses was to build a large altar and sacrifice sheep and oxen to God in burnt and peace offerings, ceremonies already familiar to the Israelites, rituals engaged in since the time of Cain and Abel. When all of this was accomplished, then God would bless His people.

God continued His other laws to Moses by repeating the second commandment, *"You shall not make other gods besides Me; gods of silver or gods of gold, you shall not make for yourselves."*[i] "Why did He emphasize this prohibition—this ban on making gods of gold?" Moses wondered.

Next, God reconfirmed two things that he had told Abraham: His people would receive great blessings in all that they did if they believed and remained obedient to His commandments. The condition was equally clear, however, that if His chosen people broke His laws, God would punish them just as harshly as He would their enemies.

God said that they must also allow their fields to lie fallow every sabbatical (or seventh) year, because rest for the soil was important. God would triple the yield from the year prior to the Sabbath year to feed them through the fallow year without spoilage.[j]

"Three times a year, all your males shall appear before the LORD God,"[k] He said, at a place to be specified by Him—at the Feast of Unleavened Bread, and at the feasts of the celebration of the first and of the last day of the year's harvest. And when you go to appear, God said, *"No man shall covet your land."*[l]

God promised to play a powerful role in the inevitable battles they would have on their way to Canaan. He would send an angel who would guard them along the way and bring them safely to Canaan and destroy their enemies there. God would *be an enemy to* [their] *enemies and an adversary to* [their] *adversaries.*[m] However, God warned: if His people continued to disobey, the promise would not hold.

*****

After his long audience with God, Moses called the leaders to a meeting at a large central tent that evening.

Moses began, "The people have considered and agreed to obey God. Now we and they must also consider the details of God's proposed, new covenant."

With that, Moses, given perfect memory by God, relayed the commandments to them.

Gamaliel was the first to speak. "Now that Moses has told us of God's many laws and of the great protection and the provisions He offers—only if we obey—shall we respond any differently? God has given us the opportunity to reconsider our acceptance."

"The new laws seem practical enough and not too difficult to follow," said Shelumiel.

Ahira said, "What do you think of punishments to the third and fourth generation for what wrongs I might commit?"

Gamaliel responded, "Each person is individually responsible for and suffers for his own wrongs,[n] although the unsavory environment of the wrongdoer may taint subsequent generations. However, as I see it, His loving kindness—kept for thousands of generations for those who love him—so far overwhelms His judgment on three or four generations who hate him that it stupefies."[2]

"Were you amazed," asked Abidan, "when He promised that our neighbors will not covet our lands, wives, or animals while we leave our homes to go up to worship Him later in Canaan? He will get inside their minds to change their thinking for us just as He accomplished with the Egyptians when they gave us their valuable possessions. How He blesses us!"

The carpenter Shelumiel said, "He changes others' minds but He gives us no power to obey—and so far we are not doing very well. Maybe the priests will give us reminders."

"Gentlemen, we have important business before us," interrupted Gamaliel. "Consider the advantages God promises us: no more sickness, no miscarriages, and no barrenness. In battle, He will send His own terror into the enemy ranks. What do you say, Nahshon? You are the representative of the lead tribe of Judah. Three months ago, you were outspoken against this journey."

Nahshon, smoothing his white robe, rose deliberately. "I came out of Egypt objecting and doubting, as did some of you. But now, our newfound freedom goes down well into my soul and I like it. That freedom may become bound by these new laws, some of which seem strange to me, and invade my privacy. However, His promises carry the day for me. It seems proper to accept His offer again."

"I don't think that our people are going to like s-s-some of the laws, but their adherence to them will be our responsibility. I, too, le-le-le-left Egypt reluctantly, but I believe Him," said Pagiel, siding with Nahshon.

Eliasaph added, "How privileged we are. God's laws address even the smallest details of our lives. No other nation has these."

"You speak wisdom," said Gamaliel. "This will not be easy, but don't we seem to be together? Is there anyone who disagrees?"

After a silence, Nahshon said, "No. Let us recommend to our people that they accept His offer."

*****

When the leaders had circulated details of Moses' new message among the people, the congregation reiterated, "All that the LORD has spoken, we will do." Moses painstakingly penned all of the words of these laws and promises of the LORD into his papyrus scroll, calling it the Book of the Covenant.[o]

Early the next morning, Moses assigned eight young men to construct an altar with twelve pillars at the foot of Mount Sinai, each pillar representing one of the original tribes of Israel. He gathered the people there to celebrate the ratification of this covenant. Selected young men brought several young bulls to the altar to be bled and sacrificed. Profoundly aware of the magnitude of this occasion, Moses took half of the blood and poured it on the altar, signifying God's dedication to the people and to the covenant. One more time, he read God's words from the Book of the Covenant for all to hear.

The people chanted once again, "All that the LORD has spoken we will do," and this time added, "and we will be obedient!"[p]

Hearing those words, Moses walked slowly among them, sprinkling the remainder of the blood randomly on them, saying, "Behold the blood of the covenant, which the LORD has made with you in accordance with all these words."[q]

*****

The tribal leaders were seated in two rows in the front of the congregation as Moses passed them. "Three times God has asked, three times we accepted," said the puzzled Ahira. "Then an altar, commanded animal sacrifices, and blood doused on the altar and on us. This is no ordinary covenant. God has forged a strong bond with us."

"This ceremony was a moving one; I shivered when the blood splashed on me," said Shelumiel. "It seems to me we have become enrolled as willing vassals to a beneficent master."

"You interpret it as if we've become slaves?" offered Abidan, looking quizzically at Shelumiel. "Do you think that He would celebrate our entry into bondage? It seems more like being adopted as His children."

"Such a ceremony Moses enacts at God's bidding! Almost like being married," said the slender Elishama.

"Certainly, we must not consider ourselves His equals," cautioned Ahira.

"When Moses sealed our acceptance with blood, did we know that our commitment would be as words engraved into stone?" asked Shelumiel. "We must take seriously this sacred agreement."

Gamaliel said, "I believe this to be another step in His plan to make of us *His holy nation, a kingdom of priests.*"[r]

*****

Following the ceremony, Moses invited chosen men of the Israelites—Joshua, Aaron, Aaron's older two sons, Nadab and Abihu, and seventy of the elders, including Hur—to accompany him to the foot of the mountain as God had commanded. As they were walking toward the mountain, their new, personal God, now Master/Father/Husband, materialized before them, not in the form of a cloud, but this time as a Man whose only discernible features were His feet. The rest of Him was covered, and under His feet there appeared to be a pavement of sapphire, as clear as the sky itself.[s]

Startled at this unexpected manifestation of God, they feared greatly for their lives. But they were not harmed. Instead, a surprising peace filled them, accompanied by a thirst and hunger that were satisfied as they drank water and ate portions of the recently sacrificed bulls placed before them. Suddenly, He was not a God just to fear and obey, but they recognized Him as a God of love, One who enjoyed their fellowship and radiated a calming peace. These were His qualities the men would carry back to share with the assemblage.

Endnotes

1. "the grass is so thick" Edward Henry Palmer, *Desert of the Exodus,* Vol. I, 1872, page 117.
2. "His loving kindness kept … stupefies." Quotation from written letter from the Reverend George W. Robertson, Ph.D., senior minister, First Presbyterian Church (PCA), Augusta, Georgia.

Chapter 9

The Panic of Abandonment

The people were encouraged by their report confirming the warmth and caring of God.

He then singled Moses out of the group and said, *"Come up to Me on the mountain and remain there, and I will give you the stone tablets with the law and the commandment which I have written for their instruction."*[a]

Moses' previous ascents to hear God's messages had been trips lasting half a day. This time, although he was simply to go up for the tablets, he had been told to remain there, indicating a stay of at least several days.

Moses spoke to his brother privately. "While I am gone, it is most important that you act as God's leader in my stead, handling disputes with Hur's help. Will you do it?"

"Of course," said Aaron. "Will you be back in a few days?"

"I hope so," said Moses as he prepared to leave.

Joshua accompanied Moses as far as the base of the mountain while the others returned to the camp. Moses climbed alone but soon was stopped by a heavy cloud cover as the glory of the LORD rested on Mount Sinai. To the people below, it appeared that Moses was ascending into a raging fire and would die soon.

Moses stayed where he was for six days, unable to move in the obscuring darkness. The eerie silence was unbroken. Deprived of most sensory cues, Moses felt an initial uneasiness and apprehension that was soon washed away in an all-pervading tranquility in which physical hunger and thirst were nonexistent. On the seventh day, God's voice called out to him, the darkness lessened, and he climbed upward until he reached the summit, where he fell asleep.

The next morning, he was awakened under a light haze by a familiar voice. God informed Moses that for His creation to achieve its greatest joy, peace, and satisfaction, He must be the primary object of their worship, and in the performance of the worship services, there must be a sacred place, a sacred person, and a sacred time.

First, the *place*. God gave long, precise instructions for the building of a tabernacle in which He would reside and be worshipped: its size; its rooms; the composition of its walls, roof, and doorway; its furniture; and even the size and makeup of the surrounding courtyard. He constructed a scale model for Moses with exact measurements.[b]

The days stretched into weeks as God continued His instructions. He had decided to appoint a high priest as the *person* to provide the worship on behalf of the people, and He chose Aaron for that consecrated position. Moses was to anoint him and his four sons as assistant priests in a special ceremony.

*****

(Day 7) Back at the camp, the people kept themselves busy, engaging in their usual daily chores the first week. However, the cool nights were becoming disquieting. Moses was still absent, perhaps dead, and no word had been received from God.

(Day 14) The second week brought growing doubts. Although the manna continued and fresh water was available, restlessness was setting in. Why had they not heard from God? Had He abandoned them?

(Day 21) At the end of the third week, Abidan, Pagiel, and Gamaliel called for a meeting of the council leaders.

Pagiel began, "We had put our hopes in that man who b-b-b-brought us up out of Egypt. It has been twenty silent days since he entered the mountain fire. He may be dead, for all we know, or else he has abandoned us …"

Ahira added, "… to his brother and sister. Before he left for the mountain, he told us that Aaron was his brother and Miriam, the prophetess, was his sister. Many of us knew Miriam for her talents; others knew Aaron, although he was a stranger to me."

Ahira tapped his fingers nervously on his thigh. "The persistent absence of those two reeks of a concocted scheme. Our family is growing leery of Moses, and my people wonder if all of this was just some ruse to get us out of Egypt—to die here."

"I understand your concerns," interrupted Gamaliel. "We are all uneasy in this remote land, but I call for patience. God and Moses have both been true to their goals for us in the past. Let us give them another two weeks, and then we shall reconvene."

They conversed awhile longer. "All right, fourteen days," concluded Ahira.

*****

Ahira

Ahira, a soldier, had a prominent brow that shaded deep-set, challenging eyes between which his long, hooked nose seemed to peer into a small mouth, a mouth surrounded by his unkempt beard. Fidgety fingers constantly tugged at the bushy growth.

At nine years of age, he was conscripted by the Egyptians to carry water to their soldiers, often bivouacked near the front lines. During military withdrawals, he occasionally became embroiled in the battle scene. Amazingly, he survived battle after battle, whether by God's providence, by the pity of opposing soldiers when they encountered his unarmed, skinny frame, or by his agility as he wove between charging chariots or ducked under a slashing sword.

At fourteen he was promoted to foot soldier and accounted himself well in battle, with his bronze axe and a captured sword. At eighteen he was made a Leader of Twenty, developing a reputation as a man of great bravery—although secretly, he remained intensely fearful before each battle. He was admired by his men, being sensitive to their needs.

He was often resourceful. One time, when the Philistine war was going badly, Ahira led twenty Egyptian soldiers as they crept within bowshot range of a group of Philistine chariots and began to rain arrows on them. They felled a horse and wounded a charioteer, and then escaped, leading their Philistine pursuers into a lethal ambush.

On another occasion, with his regiment surrounded, Ahira and two others entered the enemy camp at night and kidnapped a senior officer. He was coerced to reveal the Philistines' most vulnerable point. Ahira's entire force was able to attack it at dawn and battle through to safety.

As a long-standing member of Naphtali's council, he was tapped by God to lead, earning the pride of his wife and three children.

*****

When Aaron was left in charge of the assembly by Moses, he enjoyed the new position. He settled the issues of many who came to him. His was the last word in leaders' disputes. He walked with a newfound, confident air. However, he often lamented, "This was some of the authority God has denied me. Before the plagues, God charged Moses and me *to bring the sons of Israel out of the land of Egypt.*[c] I thought Moses and I would be equal partners. However, except for one or two instances, God speaks only to Moses, and that freely. He only communicates to me through Moses: 'Tell Aaron to do this or tell him to do that—to throw my staff down to become a serpent, to stretch my hand over the rivers, to strike the dust with my staff, to save some manna in a jar, or to hold up his hands.'

"I have obeyed God. I even left Egypt to enter the wilderness to bring Moses back to Rameses. I have done all that has been asked of me. Yet, God ignores me directly. I am but my younger brother's servant.

"Even now, he is off with God—alone. Why not me?"

*****

On the mountain, God again put special emphasis on the fourth commandment, the Sabbath day, the *time* for worship. Its observance as a mandatory day of rest was to be more than just a day for refreshment; it was to act as a *sign … that you may know that I am the* LORD *who sanctifies you* [and whoever profanes the Sabbath]... *shall surely be put to death,*[d] said God. He seldom decreed death as a penalty and that only for egregious errors. The Sabbath was to be holy.

Then He gave Moses the two promised stone tablets that were engraved on both sides by the finger of God.[e]

*****

Four Sabbaths dragged by for those waiting in the Israelite camp. Anxiety had penetrated their wavering commitment. They had put their faith in a God who seemed to ignore them, though that strange, nonconsuming fire continued to burn on the mountain.

(Day 32) As the fifth Sabbath approached, the council met.

Nethanel was the first to speak. "Where is this Moses? If he is not dead, he has run off with his God someplace—perhaps enjoying the luxury of His company on that smoky mountain. What do you wish to do?"

"I join with many of my people," said Shelumiel. "We'll never see Moses again, or God. We are ready to leave this place. But where should we go?"

Ahira absently picked at a scar on his cheek. "We could go on toward Canaan. It must be straight north and cannot be more than another week or two's march. Or we could return to Egypt—if we could find our way."

Elishama rose, his clothes now hanging loosely on his slender frame. "I have been secretly constructing maps of our journey at the end of each day, plotted by the position of the sun and the Dog Star. I believe I would be able to lead us back."

"But how would we be treated in Egypt?" asked Ahira. "Probably slaughtered after the trouble we caused. I wonder who rules, without Pharaoh or his army?"

Pagiel's quick speech had slowed markedly. "Who knows? What a ripe grape she must be for an outside power to pl-pl-pl-pluck. No matter, she is still home to me. I'm also r-r-ready to go, forward or back—even tonight, since I cannot s-s-s-sleep anyway."

Nethanel added, "I have lost interest, even in collecting the manna. And our people, they have turned to their trinket idols for worship."

"As I originally predicted, this march has failed," Nahshon said, "and now we are on our own."

Elishama nodded. "My people of Ephraim are grumbling that we should make a sacred god for the whole congregation's benefit, one that provided for us in the past before this one took over."

Aaron had been listening quietly, patiently, to the discussion. Finally he spoke up, "You speak from worried hearts. Remember what marvels He has already done for us. Nothing is beyond His reach. Besides, I believe my brother will return soon. Delay."

Gamaliel, working the muscles of his square jaw back and forth, stood up. "God has indeed proven His faithfulness repeatedly. Surely, He knows our plight. Besides, He specifically forbade idol worship. Ten more days; if He or Moses do not return, then we will encourage Aaron to make other plans."

Shelumiel concurred. "Our last ten days, then?"

*****

(Day 39) By well into the sixth week of Moses' absence, the gloom of hopeless abandonment swallowed the camp. The depressed sought isolation, some considering suicide; the fearful cringed; the defiant raged at their betrayal by God and Moses; and the contentious erupted in fistfights and stealing. Driven by ineffable anxieties, increasing numbers of the people clamored, "Aaron, make us a god who will go before us; as for this Moses, we do not know what has become of him."[f]

* * * * *

Aaron sensitively absorbed each pleading voice, adding to his growing agony as he stood with Hur.

"They have all given up on our God," Aaron said. "I have been able to hold them off for almost six weeks, but they desperately need something to worship, to give them hope. I share some of those feelings myself. Don't you?"

"I am not proud of it, but I do," admitted Hur.

"Don't they realize that I cannot make a god for them?"

"Many strong men are not just fearful but are angry with you. I have heard threats. I am concerned for your safety," warned Hur.

"If only God and Moses would come back—today. What should we do?" asked Aaron.

"Your call," Hur dodged.

"Of course," as Aaron walked away. But the crushing pressure of the people's demands was outweighing God's commandment.

* * * * *

(Day 40) Early the next afternoon, leaving the murmurings outside, Miriam stalked into Aaron's large tent where Elisheba sat at a table with two of her sons. Aaron slowly paced before them. He paused, and after exchanging pleasantries, offered her a stool, which she refused.

Miriam addressed them all. "This camp is about to boil over. Moses must be dead or else he has deserted us again. Our prayers to God and our other gods go unanswered. Something must be done. God prohibited the making of an idol—but He has quit us, and so has our exalted brother. Besides, God will never know what we do."

Aaron's son Abihu interjected, "Father, I will back whatever you do."

Nadab added, "We are only human, father. God will understand. After all, His absence caused this dissension."

Elisheba looked at her husband. "You are sensitive, Aaron, and courageous, but now we are all of one mind."

Looking at Elisheba, he took a deep breath and slowly nodded his head. He put his hands behind him, walked to the tent opening and as he stepped out, Miriam prodded, "Make it of gold."

His eyes searched the base of the mountain for only the third time that day. He walked about slowly, aimlessly, rehearsing his plan. He had considered making a clay idol. But now "gold!" "The congregation would like that. I don't dare tap the gold that is stored in the holy room; that would anger God. Where else is gold found? Our women and children! They have never had golden jewelry before now. They will resist giving it up. If the men forcibly remove it from them, that will involve them." Then he decided, "The decision is mine." He thought a moment. "A bull calf, powerful like God!"

He walked out among the crowds and shouted, "Tear off the gold rings that are in the ears of your wives, your sons, and your daughters, and bring them to me!"[g]

"Finally!" the mob cried, as they ripped the jewelry off and rushed it to Aaron in blood-tinged hands.

Aaron took the accumulated metal, melted it in a cauldron, and using a graving tool, fashioned it into what, to him, was a natural representation of this powerful God—a small bull calf. Unveiling it to roars of approval, he shouted, "This is your God, O Israel, who brought you up from the land of Egypt!"[h]

The shiny yellow beast so filled Aaron with pride that he had an altar built before it and proclaimed, "Tomorrow shall be a feast to the LORD!"[i]

The next morning the people gathered about the calf and, in thanksgiving, sacrificed some of their animals to it. In a burst of relief, the people exploded into celebration and dancing—merriment that soon slid into wild drinking, debauchery, and even sexual immorality.[j]

*****

God was watching. He ordered a surprised Moses, *"Go down at once, for your people, whom you brought up from the land of Egypt, have corrupted themselves. They have quickly turned aside from the way to which I commanded them. They have made for themselves a molten calf, and have worshipped it, and have sacrificed to it, and said, 'This is your God, O Israel, who brought you up from the land of Egypt!'*[k]

"Now, then, let Me alone, that My anger may burn against them … [a stiff-necked people] … and that I may destroy them; and I will make of you [Moses] a great nation."[1]

Moses' shoulders drooped. "A calf! No! They wouldn't!" he sorrowed. "Twice they had heard God's specific command against just that." During the last forty days he had focused on God and His loving plans for the people and little on Aaron; what could have happened? He must return and see. But before that, God said that He will destroy them all, including His priest-elect, Aaron! Moses became so concerned with the people's safety that he ignored God's proposal that He would greatly promote Moses to *a great nation* at the expense of his wards. He would not allow himself to consider that offer.

Instead, with great respect, he began, "O Lord …" and then reminded Him that this idolatrous people were His, not Moses'. Then he said, "If Thou wilt kill them, the Egyptians will speak, saying, 'With evil intent, He brought them out to kill them in the mountains and to destroy them from the face of the earth.'[m] Turn from Thy burning anger and change Thy mind about doing harm to Thy people. Remember Abraham, Isaac, and Israel, Thy servants to whom Thou did swear, *'I will multiply your descendants as the stars of the heavens, and all this land of which I have spoken I will give to your descendants, and they shall inherit it forever.'"*[n]

God listened patiently to Moses' pleas and finally yielded, resolving not to destroy the entire contrary mob but to judge harshly only the most shameless of the people. Moses was humbly impressed that this powerful God could be persuaded to change His mind by just a sheepherder. Or was he being tested?

*****

He apprehensively descended Mount Sinai, carefully guarding the stone tablets, having been sustained for forty days without food or water. Near the base of the mountain, he came upon Joshua, who was relieved to see his beloved master. Joshua had been protecting the mountain against interlopers and also had been without food or water. As they approached the village, Joshua was alarmed as he heard shouting: "There is the sound of war in the camp."[b]

But Moses assured him, "It is not the cry of triumph, nor the cry of defeat, but the sound of singing I hear."[p]

As they came into view of the crowd, Moses was overwhelmed with disbelief and disgust as he saw the people gyrating around the knee-high, fat, glistening, metal figure. He was so filled with uncontrollable anger at their devilish reveling that he willfully raised the sacred tablets above his head. "You do not deserve these!" he shouted as he hurled them to the ground before the people, shattering them.

He peered at the crowd thinking, "God was going to destroy them all and I intervened. Was I wrong?"

Then Moses turned to Aaron—who had done nothing to stop the demonstration—demanding, "What did this people do to you that you have brought such great sin upon them?"[q]

Aaron retorted, "You know the people yourself. They are prone to evil. They said to me, 'Make a god for us who will go before us.' I said to them, 'Whoever has any gold, let him tear it off.' So they gave it to me, and I threw it into the fire, and out came this calf."[r]

Moses had witnessed many of God's miracles but doubted that this was one of them. He stared at Aaron suspiciously, realizing that in His wrath, God sought to kill his brother along with all of the people. Overcoming his own anger, Moses impulsively dropped to his knees and prayed that God would spare them. And God listened.[s]

Then he rose and turned to the crowd, many of whom were still wildly dancing.

He picked up the calf, flung it into the fire, scorching it, and then grabbed a nearby mallet and pounded it into powder. He scooped up handfuls of the gold dust, threw them into a nearby brook, and demanded of the people, "Go, drink of it!"[t]

But more was necessary. God does not leave the guilty unpunished.[u]

God's anger could only be appeased by the death of the most flagrant offenders. Moses shouted to the people, "Whoever is for the LORD, come to me.[v] Reuben, Simeon, Levi, Judah, Gad, Asher, Benjamin ..." All thirteen tribes were encouraged to come forth.

*****

Aged, stooped Zuriel, one of the elders of the tribe of Levi, quickly gathered a number of his younger tribesmen together and spoke to them. "Look! No one goes forth to answer Moses' call! If you Levites can have courage, this may be the opportunity for which we have waited five hundred years, years deprived of leadership because of Simeon and Levi's violent sin."

Hamal, a Levite soldier, said, "Simeon and Levi should not have been considered criminals, but heroes by God for avenging the rape of their sister, Dinah, by the king of Shechem.[1] And it was right that their father, Jacob, demanded that the king and all of his men be circumcised before he would allow the marriage of Dinah to the king, the marriage mandated by our law."

Zuriel said, "And in revenge, the brothers hacked to death King Shechem and his men the day after their circumcisions. You call that heroic? But now, perhaps we can atone for that and regain God's approval. Will you answer His summons?"

Hamal raised his sword and shouted, "For the tribe of Levi!" and walked toward Moses with many Levitical soldiers falling in behind him.

Moses had watched God seethe with an exterminatory anger that could only be appeased by the death of the flagrant offenders. So Moses shouted, "Thus says the LORD, the God of Israel, 'Go back and forth from gate to gate in the camp, and kill every reveling man, his brother, his friend, and his neighbor!'"[w]

How much easier their task would have been had Moses instead called the worshippers of the golden calf "heinous sinners." However, the Levites killed, in all, seventy-five[2] of the brazen offenders that day, including some members of their own tribe.

* * * * *

That evening, a tired, remorseful, and sober Zuriel sat and wrote in his diary:
> Brothers of slavery, kindred of mine,
> Dined at my table, drank of my wine.
> But raucous and drunk, you worshipped the calf,
> As you pierced God's heart, scribed your own epitaph.
> Executioner? Friend, we assume that façade,
> Strange to us, but ordered by God.
> I harvest you my neighbor like sun-ripened wheat,
> Scythe the blade from the beard, see—it bleeds!

* * * * *

The next day, Moses walked between two long rows of newly mounded graves. "Had I returned sooner, these might not have died," he thought. "Why was

I up there so long? To bolster my commitment to Him? That did happen. I used to speak to God as one person to another; now I want to bow before Him."

He knelt beside a grave. "Was it to test our people? If so, they failed, betraying God's trust. For that I was angry, the same anger I had toward Mannel and toward Pharaoh's hard-heartedness." When his mind calmed, he realized that he was angry, in part, because the people had flouted his leadership, breaking the rules he had brought to them from God: *You shall have no other gods before Me.*[x]

He cringed when he remembered that he had broken God's tablets in his rage, the most holy items he had ever held. His feelings of guilt widened as he admitted to himself that, early on, when the Levites began killing the offenders, he felt a certain satisfaction, a feeling that abated as the numbers of slain grew.

As he walked back to camp, the cloud joined him for a short while to comfort him. Then, God assigned him a new task, a more joyous one—to reward the obedient Levites.

* * * * *

Meanwhile, Miriam was seated while Aaron paced behind her in his tent. "Miriam," he said, "the punishment that God, or Moses on his own, dealt out was too great for their celebration. Seventy-five dead!"

"The people drove you to it," said Miriam. "Don't feel guilt, my brother."

"Who does Moses think he is, demanding such a penalty? And why should I have to be accountable to my own brother? He was up there, enjoying himself while I was reluctantly in charge here, to face those angry mobs. He would have done the same thing."

"Don't worry, Aaron, we will have our day."

* * * * *

The following day, Moses assembled the Levites with their bloodstained swords to give them God's message. Their leader, Aaron, was conspicuously absent.

"Dedicate yourselves today to the LORD,"[y] Moses exhorted them, "in order that He may bestow a blessing on you today. You Levites, because you alone stepped forward to execute God's judgment, you are designated by God to become the priestly tribe among all of the sons of Israel. After the high priest is ordained, you will assist him and his family in the religious and spiritual life of the community."

"That is supposed to be our reward," asked a Levite in puzzlement, "for being the only tribe to answer your call to obediently and methodically step forward and kill our brothers?"

"So God says," answered Moses.

"We are to put our weapons away to peacefully serve a priest? Who will be this high priest?" asked another.

"God has appointed your leader, and my brother, Aaron."

The crowd fell silent. Many shared glances of disbelief. Two of them had overheard Aaron try to explain the calf to Moses, and that information had passed quickly through the whole tribe. Aaron had lost their respect. It was not because he caved in and molded the calf, or that he entangled them in the forbidden deed, but because he lied to Moses. Had he manfully admitted that he molded it, he would have been punished, and probably severely. But perhaps those killed might have been spared.

One man in the crowd, Korah, blurted out, "Aaron lied to you about the calf!"

Moses responded, "If he did, he will have to live with it, and God will deal with him. I am under orders. Now I am going up to the LORD; perhaps I can make atonement for your sin."ᶻ

The crowd grumbled among themselves before finally slowly dispersing.

*****

Abidan, Elishama, and Ahira walked away together.

Abidan said, "So, Aaron is to be ordained as high priest—on orders from God, according to Moses."

Elishama said, "Something has happened to Aaron. In Egypt he was a well-respected leader with wise, clever, convincing speech. He was honest, even liked by the Egyptian rulers."

"But he never was in a position of authority," said Ahira. "The stress we put on him before the calf, even the threats from some, might have been too much for him—for anyone. He did hold out for six weeks."

Abidan said, "We'll see what kind of a priest he will be."

*****

Moses returned to the tablets, picked up a few pieces as his chosen symbols of repentance, and walked toward the mountain. He sighed. As he looked up, he saw that a large white cloud had replaced the smoking fire.

When Moses attained the barren summit, the brisk wind billowed his shirt while leaving the cloud overhead motionless. He spoke to the cloud, knowing that God would hear. He readily admitted the great sin that the people had committed and accepted God's punishment. "But now, if Thou wilt, forgive their sin," he begged. If God would not forgive their sin, he offered himself up to die saying, "then blot me out from Thy book which You have written."[3]

God did not forgive the people and rejected Moses' self-sacrificial offer. He simply told Moses to lead the people north and claim the land He had promised to them. *"I will send the angel before you and I will drive out the* [inhabitants of Canaan] *before you,"* said God. "[However,] *I will not go up in your midst because you are an obstinate people, lest I destroy you on the way."*[4]

*****

Moses descended the mountain again and gave the people God's command to take their *ornaments from you, that* [He] *may know what to do with* [you].[aa]

They took off their new idolatrous items of jewelry but stubbornly refused to budge. Accustomed to having the real presence of God in their midst, they found His angel an unsatisfactory substitute. Moses also realized that without God with them, he was powerless.

Moses returned to the foot of the mountain, carrying the despondent mood of the people. He climbed up and boldly said to God that the angel was inadequate for the people and beseeched, "If Thy presence does not go with us, do not lead us up from here."[bb]

God responded that because [Moses has] *found favor in My sight,*[cc] He would lead them Himself.

Buoyed by God's strong affirmation and by his own growing devotion, Moses brazenly asked to know God's character, His thoughts: "If I have found favor in Thy sight, let me know Thy ways that I might know Thee."[dd]

God did not immediately tell Moses of His ways, His character.

Pushing his advantage, Moses made a fourth request. Even knowing that to see God's face would bring instant death, he persevered, "I pray Thee, show me Thy glory."[ee]

God's love for this man was overflowing as He granted, "*I, Myself, will make all My goodness pass before you.*"[ff]

Moses was overjoyed. Yet humbly, he suddenly wondered, "God has never done anything like this for anyone before. *All* of His goodness! Could I withstand such a view? And why would He do this for me?"

God answered him by revealing a requested facet of His character, adding, "*I will be gracious to whom I will be gracious, and will show compassion on whom I will show compassion.*"[gg] God was free to make His own decisions; He was accountable to no one.

*****

Back on level ground, God set Moses in the cleft of a rock, placed His hand over his face, but removed His hand as His glory passed by. "*You shall see My back, but My face shall not be seen.*"[hh]

Moses never described what he observed during that moment of unparalleled intimacy. Was it too sacred? It belonged to him alone. Would God's spectacular condescension bind him to God in a permanent loyalty? Moses hoped so.

*****

After two days, God called Moses to return alone onto the mountain a fifth time. God was chafing because Moses had smashed His stone tablets. So, He told Moses to cut out two stone tablets himself and bring them up; then He would rewrite the Ten Commandments.

Moses was still deeply concerned that God might destroy the people because He had not formally forgiven their sins. Therefore, when Moses reached the sunlit mountain peak carrying the two tablets and his scroll, he prostrated himself in desperate submission for many days.[ii]

Finally, one day, God descended as a cloud and hovered near him. Moses was still unaccustomed to these manifestations, and rose only at God's invitation. Moses had asked to know God's ways, and God chose to answer him. "*... the* LORD *God, compassionate and gracious, slow to anger, and abounding in lovingkindness and truth; Who keeps lovingkindness for thousands, who forgives iniquity, transgression, and sin; yet He will by no means leave the guilty unpunished.*"[jj]

Moses bowed low to the earth. Of his four requests, three had been promptly granted. Only one request remained unanswered, perhaps the most difficult of all. God does forgive sins; but has He? Therefore, he called out to the LORD again, "Pardon our iniquity and our sin, and take us as Thine own possession."kk

God did not specifically forgive their sins, but responded, *"Behold, I am going to make a* [new] *covenant."*ll The covenant: *"Before all your people, I will perform miracles which have not been produced in all the earth, nor among any of the nations;… for it is a fearful thing that I am going to perform with you. Be sure to observe what I am commanding you this day: behold,"* God repeated, *"I am going to drive out* [the inhabitants of Canaan] *before you. Watch yourselves that you make no covenant with* [them] *… lest it become a snare in your midst. But rather, tear down their altars and smash their sacred pillars and cut down their Asherim* [worship symbols to the mother of their god, Baal] *for you shall not worship any other god, for the LORD, whose name is Jealous, is a jealous God."*mm

The covenant also emphasized a warning that their sons must not play the harlot with Canaanite gods or sacrifice to them. God reiterated a number of old laws and told Moses to record all of these words.nn Moses opened his lengthening papyrus scroll and did so.

Moses gathered these writings and the two rewritten stone tablets and descended the mountain. Growing hungry, he realized that God had sustained him without food or drink for a second forty days. As he reached the camp, he found that no significant disobedience had occurred in his absence. There was no golden calf. He placed the stone tablets into his tent for safekeeping.

*****

Moses entered Aaron's tent. Aaron said, "Moses, the skin of your face glows so brightly that I cannot look at you."oo

Hearing that, Moses realized that some of God's glory had been transferred to him while in God's presence, an appearance that would add credulity to the message he would deliver. "I shall put a veil over my face" After doing so, he asked, "Aaron, do you love our mother and obey her?"

"Yes," said Aaron.,

"Would you ever do anything to hurt her?"

"Of course not," Aaron said.

"Why not?"

"Because I know her and how much she loves me," replied Aaron, "her proven faithfulness to me; I know her feelings, what pleases her, what makes her angry, what worries her. She would do anything she could to make my life totally complete."

"That is the same with God," said Moses. "He has tried to gain our singular loyalty and commitment by the many miracles so far. Now, like our mother, He has told me His feelings and thoughts and facets of His character so that we can know Him and appreciate Him and His goals. I will tell the people about Him. Perhaps that will stop complaints; they might even come to respect Him more."

*****

When Moses, sans veil, summoned the leaders and several elders to the large tent to tell them about this God and to convey the terms of God's new covenant, they were shocked and were reluctant to approach him. Assured that they had all seen him, he replaced the veil and insisted that they come near to him.

Moses began, "On my way up the mountain, God met me and revealed His heart to me, telling me things about Himself that I had not learned the first time up the mountain, things about His own character. Listen, He wants you to know Him. He is total *truth*, His promises and love for us are rock-solid and forever; He is *compassionate*, full of sympathy and committed to our well-being; *gracious*, doing good for the undeserving; *patient* with our failures and, therefore, *slow to anger*; *He abounds in tender kindness and mercy because of His affection for us.*"[pp]

Moses continued, "Through the sacrifices, He readily *forgives iniquity, transgression, and sin,* but *He will by no means leave the guilty unpunished.*[qq] That is who He is."

"Thank you, Moses, that is helpful," said Ahira. "But did He tell you what sorts of things we should avoid so we do not provoke His anger?"

"As we have seen," Moses answered, "God becomes saddened, disappointed, when His people forget Him and complain against Him, scorn, or forsake Him.[rr] When we worship other gods or sacrifice to demons or gods, betraying Him, He becomes jealous, a powerful jealousy that He admits can become a consuming fire[ss] that will be kindled against us."[tt]

Eliasaph spoke up, "Listen and know Him. Is it not easier to sin, to rebel against a person or God for whom you have no personal feelings? Just a cold judge? Many see God that way. But it is not so. Now, brothers, tell your people these things so that they may know Him."

Moses read from his scroll all of the words of God's proposed covenant to them from the mountain, including a few old laws of the Sabbath, feasts, and tithes, plus a series of challenging new ones. Then Moses replaced the veil over his face, asked the leaders to consider the terms of this covenant, and left.

✳✳✳✳✳

Gamaliel hunched his broad shoulders forward and with an intent look was the first to speak. "God hates the symbols of Canaanite worship. In this covenant, He will perform terrifying miracles to help us drive them out. In doing so, we are to make no covenant with them—and keep their girls away from our boys."

Ahira sat on the other side of the circle, pulling a hair from his beard. He said, "I presume that God can supply us with superior weaponry and wise tactics before the battles. He even said that He would send swarms of hornets into the enemy ranks.ᵘᵘ Hornets? We'll see."

Nahshon said, "To assure that we worship no other gods, He wants us to tear down the Canaanite shrines that their gods occupy and smash and burn their sacred pillars. He destroyed the Egyptian gods at Passover, but now *we* have to do that. We must have the courage and conviction to believe that in wielding hammer and fire to the shrines of, admittedly, some of the gods we used to worship, we can rely on Him to protect us from their vicious retaliation. Quite a test for us. He leads us into temptation; can we believe He will deliver us?"

Shelumiel said, "We've seen the wrath of this God of Abraham; dare we antagonize other gods? No, my friends, it will take much more convincing before I'll put my axe to another god's shrine."

Elishama, hands around his bent, bowed leg, said, "The only way I could do that is if I were to fear our God more."

"This God certainly has the authority to order this demolition. And He does offer us a great promise," said Gamaliel, "if we can somehow keep our end of the covenant. Remember that He has chosen us out of all the peoples who are on the face of the earth to become the kingdom of priests, the holy nation that He desires."ᵛᵛ

"I am willing," said Abidan. "Why don't we agree to His offer now? When it comes time to act, maybe He will do the dirty work Himself."

"I'll accept that," said Shelumiel. "Any who disagree?" The silence of approval followed.

The meeting ended, and each sought his own home, a sometimes difficult task in the fields of tents. The leaders had tried to keep their own tribes together but with only marginal success because friends tended to congregate, often intermixing tribes. Lacking an overall housing plan, the Israelites lived with disorder.

*****

Disordered also described Shelumiel's mind as he addressed the six-member council of Simeon four days later. "The tribe of Levi was restored by their boldness while we still walk in disgrace. Had I acted, we too might have answered Moses' call and been honored. It is best that you replace me."

"I was told that it was old Zuriel," said one, "and not their tribal leader who challenged their young men while we all delayed. We're all to be blamed. Stay, Shelumiel, you serve us well."

Another man stood up. "I did not volunteer to kill because I had favored Aaron's golden calf, as did many of those hypocritical Levites. Remain, Shelumiel."

Others nodded in agreement.

"If you feel that way, I will stay, but with a burdened heart," Shelumiel said solemnly. "We must learn from this."

As he left the meeting, Shelumiel met his friend, Dathan, a council member of the tribe of Reuben. "Why so glum, Shelumiel? The burials are over. We must go on."

Shelumiel sighed. "The matter I discussed with you earlier has been settled. I have been retained as tribal leader."

"Your tribe was disgraced because of a slaughter, mine from Reuben's sexual lust," said Dathan. "Believe me, we will not miss another opportunity like this one."

"Agreed. Keep alert."

*****

As the glow of Moses' face began to decrease, he kept the veil on so that they could not see its diminution.[ww] However, whenever he went in to talk to God, he removed the veil, perhaps hoping to have the fading brightness replenished. In time, as the glow subsided, so did the people's awe for Moses, and the veil was soon discarded.

But Moses' commitment was not lessened. His six-week engrossment with God had transformed him. He would continue to speak, cry out, or pray to God as before but, when under intense stress, he would unhesitatingly fall on his face before God in public supplication.[xx]

Endnotes

1. Story of King Shechem, Gen. 34.
2. The Bible states that "3,000 were killed." However, using my number of marchers as 40,000 rather than the biblical 1.6 million, the number killed would be 1.6 million/40,000 = 40; then 3,000/40 = 75.
3. Moses' plea was one with two possible meanings: If Moses meant for God to destroy his earthly body, he would head the elite list of the courageous men who sacrificed themselves to save the lives of others, the shepherd giving his life for his sheep. But, more likely, if Moses offered to relinquish his life after death, his very soul, it would be the most astonishing gift anyone had ever offered.
4. Author's note: Might even God become unable to control His righteous anger or was He further testing Moses?

Chapter 10

His Sanctuary in Their Midst

One day, a traveler advised Moses that his father-in-law, Jethro, was bringing his family to join him.[1] So two days later, when Moses heard from the northern outpost that a party of four was approaching on donkeys, leading several sheep, he left his tent and broke into an easy trot to meet them on legs well-conditioned by the march.

"It is good that you have come. I have greatly missed you!" Moses exclaimed as he reached up to kiss Zipporah, who was riding the lead donkey. The smell of her unique perfume was not wasted. "My role with God and the people is more assured than a year ago, and I believe they will welcome you." Zipporah smiled back at him, still gently holding on to his offered hand.

"And you two, how good it is to see you," he said, turning to his sons, who were walking at her side. Dust puffed from their shirts as Moses embraced each briefly. "You look healthy," admired Moses. "We will find plenty for you to do to earn your keep. Gershom, you were always good with an axe. You and Eliezer might build a little home for us." They nodded absently, their eyes bewildered by the mass of people nearby.

Moses turned and bowed down before his father-in-law as he dismounted. Then Moses rose and kissed Jethro on both cheeks. "Tell me," Moses began, "how you have been during my absence. Have you missed your shepherd?"

"Your sons, my boy Hobab, and my other growing grandsons tended to your tasks," Jethro said. "Since you have returned to Sinai, I felt it proper to reunite your family. Moses, word fills the land of God's actions through you and of His deliverance of the Israelite slaves. I want to hear more."

"Come into my tent and rest and I will tell you." Moses signaled to a nearby attendant. "Show my wife and sons to a cool bath."

"It is our God's work," Moses began as they sat, and he detailed God's wonders over the last year.

Jethro listened carefully. "Now I know that the LORD is greater than all the gods,"[a] he said. "Come this evening, bring Aaron and the elders, and I will offer sacrifices of my sheep to Him. We will all share a meal."

That evening, there was a great feast and celebration. The months of separation brought a crowning reunion of Moses and Zipporah.

*****

Jethro remained ten days with them. He observed that Moses spent most of each day listening to and judging disputes, petty ones and grave ones, employing the recently revealed laws of God.

"Moses, if you keep this up, you will exhaust yourself," said Jethro. "You have other important matters to attend to. Let me give you some advice. Choose able men to judge the people and teach them God's laws to use. Every major dispute they will bring to you, but every minor dispute they themselves will judge. The judges must have three characteristics: they should fear God, be men of truth, and hate dishonest gain. If you do this thing, and if God so commands you, then you will be able to endure."[b]

Moses agreed and selected capable men to act as judges, some to judge over groups of ten people, others over fifty, some over hundreds, and the most capable men to judge over thousands, leaving him freer to serve God.

His task completed, Jethro departed to begin his solitary journey back home.

*****

That same evening, several leaders were eating a light meal together. "Moses has invited us to join him again tomorrow as he goes out a distance from the camp to set up his tent and to speak with the cloud a third time—I mean with God," said Abidan.

Eliasaph's eyes lit up. "What a unique opportunity! I took my spare small tent and went four days ago, and I'll go again tomorrow."

"It is handy now," said Nahshon. "I suppose that Moses finally proved his loyalty to God by all his trips up the mountain, so now God will meet with him here in a tent. I may join you tomorrow." Nahshon admitted to himself that it was purely curiosity that would draw him there.

Eliasaph said, "You other three, you should go. We pitch our tents a small distance from Moses' tent and stand in front of ours. Moses enters his tent and has chosen to bring Joshua along for this sacred visit. When they are both inside the tent of meeting, they call it, they leave the flap open, and the cloud suddenly appears. Moses stands there inside, the cloud outside, and they talk face-to-face, as I might talk to you."

Pagiel asked, "Can you hear what they talk about?"

Eliasaph said, "No, but when I am bowed down in front of my own tent, I know that God hears my prayer. Only later does Moses tell us about their conversation."

"It's eerie," interrupted Elishama, "how I feel tingly while the cloud is there. Then when it disappears, I feel normal again, as Moses leads us back to the camp."

"God is getting closer to us and I enjoy it," said Ahira. "Would He want to dine with us?"

"Wouldn't that be something?" said Eliasaph.

"How privileged Joshua must feel to be there. He stays in the tent all night long out of reverence to God and Moses, he says," said Gamaliel. "What an experience for him, rising from a simple Hebrew boy. Seems that he is being groomed for something."

"I'm not interested in going," said Nethanel.

"How about you, Pagiel, will you come with us?" asked Gamaliel.

"Yes, tomorrow," said Pagiel.

*****

Having given Moses the detailed plans for the construction of His tabernacle,[2] God also appointed the workers. Twenty-four-year-old Bezalel, compulsive and stubborn, had been one of Pharaoh's most respected artisans. He had designed the tigers at the entrance to Rameses. His wood carvings, placed on pedestals throughout the palace, uniformly drew acclaim from visiting dignitaries. His creative, precise works in gold, silver, and bronze ranged from heavy commercial items to delicate artworks. Pharaoh had appreciated this man.

God appointed him to supervise the construction of the tabernacle. He endowed him with the rare, precious gift of His own Holy Spirit, thereby magnifying his skills. God also gave special talents to the chief weaver and engraver, Oholiab and to all the workers for their appointed tasks.

Speaking through Moses, God asked for volunteers to contribute necessary items for His tabernacle and for Aaron's priestly garments. In spite of the persisting undercurrent of dissatisfaction with the journey and with Aaron, many of the people responded quickly, donating generously. Most items were those plundered from the Egyptians. Some soldiers, who had stripped the fallen Amalekites, also brought their stolen booty to Moses. More goods were received than were necessary.

The craftsmen and craftswomen diligently set to work, using the tools they had either brought with them or fashioned in the desert. The settlement was abuzz with activity. The woodsmen hewed the hardwood acacia trees from the nearby forest and shaped them to the needed sizes. The weavers made curtains. Carpenters cut boards, made poles, and built furniture. The seamstresses cut, spun, and wove goat's hair and made curtains of dyed porpoise and ram skins for the roof. Metalsmiths hammered and shaped intricate items of gold, silver, and bronze, and jewelers set them with precious stones. Small furnaces were built to cast bronze handles, bases, and tools; woodcarvers, embroiderers, and perfumers also worked tirelessly. In the middle of the ninth month at Sinai, the twelfth since leaving Egypt, the tabernacle was almost complete and the furniture installed—as God had commanded.

*****

Moses gathered two foremen outside the courtyard on the day of the final inspection. He led them around the perimeter of the rectangular 150 by 75-foot courtyard fence, composed of spaced vertical 7 1/2-foot-tall acacia pillars. Each pillar was anchored by two bronze sockets into long baseboards. As the men walked, they stepped carefully over bronze pegs driven into the ground to hold taut ropes attached to the tops of the pillars, securing them.

When they reached the east side, they entered into the courtyard, drawing aside a doorway curtain that was part of a continuous curtain made of tightly interwoven purple, blue, and scarlet linens that hung all around the inside of the fence. The curtain completely shielded the courtyard from outside view.

The most prominent structure in the courtyard was the tabernacle in the west central area. In front of it stood the 8 by 8-foot sacrificial altar, 5 feet high, made of acacia wood overlaid with bronze to withstand the heat of the fires within. Rising above each of its four corners was a wooden horn covered with bronze, to which the sacrificial carcasses could be secured. Pails, shovels, flesh hooks, and fire pans of bronze were kept on a large table placed between the bronze altar and the tabernacle.

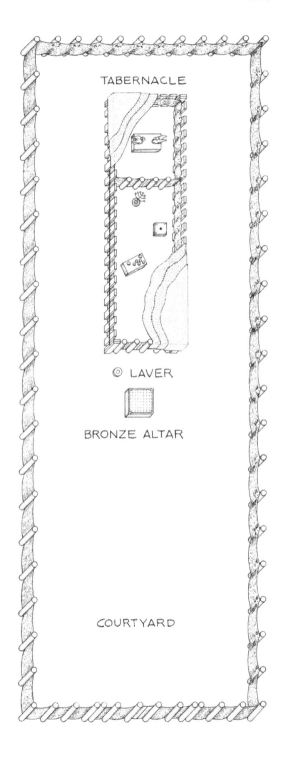

TABERNACLE

© LAVER

BRONZE ALTAR

COURTYARD

The inspectors then walked with Moses up to the boxlike, gabled tabernacle, 50 feet in length and 15 feet in width. The roof was composed of three layers: an inner one of woven goat's hair, a middle one of ram's skin, and a water-shedding outer layer of hand-sewn porpoise skins that overhung the sides of the tabernacle halfway down its 17-foot-high acacia walls. Below the covering, one could see the lower halves of the spaced vertical pillars that made up its four walls. Long horizontal poles of acacia passed through gold rings on the outer face of each board, connecting them all together and stabilizing the walls.

"Are we permitted to enter?" they asked apprehensively.

"Only this once, for the inspection," said Moses.

*****

Moses led them into the tabernacle by pushing aside a matching exquisite doorway curtain on the east that hung from silver hooks on the inside of the wall boards, hugging the entire inner wall of the tabernacle.

As Moses watched, two workmen finished installing the final item, a thick, tricolor curtain, two-thirds of the way toward the back of the room that divided the tabernacle into a larger front anteroom, or holy room, facing east, and a smaller back room, the holy of holies, facing west. The curtain, or veil, was suspended from hooks on four vertical acacia pillars.

Moses inspected the three items in the holy room: the waist-high golden altar of incense with two golden horns attached to opposite corners on the top; the slightly shorter table of holy bread with a top large enough to hold bread, dishes, bowls, and jars, to be used in ceremonies. Both of those pieces had rings attached to their sides and poles nearby for carrying.

The third item was a golden menorah-like lampstand with small golden lamps installed on the ends of each curved branch to hold oil that, when lighted, would illuminate the anteroom.

Moses parted the veil and entered the sacrosanct holy of holies alone—reserved for the high priest and Moses—the room of the ark of the covenant and the mercy seat. The ark, about the size of a large writing desk, was made of acacia wood and set on four cast-gold feet. Two rings were attached to each side of the ark, each pair holding a pole of acacia wood for carrying. Those poles were never to be removed from their rings, allowing for its immediate emergency transportation. The tablets containing the Ten Commandments and the jar with a portion of the manna were placed inside a drawer in the ark. Every exposed wood surface in the tabernacle was overlaid with gold, including the wall boards and poles.

A thick, flat, rectangular slab of pure gold lay on the top of the ark, of its same width and length. Affixed on top, at opposite ends, were two hammered-gold cherubim, angels with wings spread apart, facing one another. God called the structure the mercy seat,ᶜ on which He would appear as a cloud between the cherubim when He met with Moses.

As Moses returned through the veil, he paused before the golden altar. He touched the grainy, perfumed incense inside the golden cup and brought it to his nose, sniffed, and was satisfied. He picked up another cup, swirled the holy anointing oil within, and enjoyed its odor. The men exited through the curtain into the daylight.

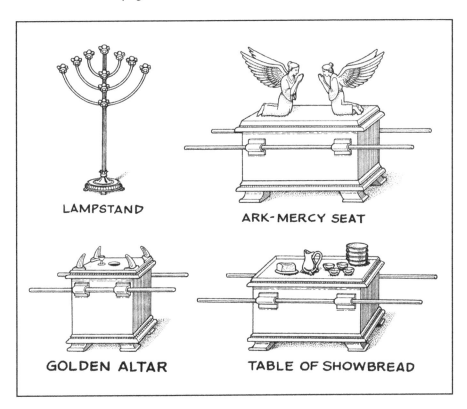

LAMPSTAND

ARK-MERCY SEAT

GOLDEN ALTAR

TABLE OF SHOWBREAD

*****

During the many months the workers were building the tabernacle, and the masses of people were trying to learn God's rules, a large group of garment makers, empowered by God, were making the clothes that Aaron would wear[d] when God said, *"he may minister as priest to Me."*[e] In spite of Aaron's demonstrated frailties, he was still God's designee. Given time and authority, his faith could grow.

"I went by the clothiers today," said Moses as he spoke to Aaron and Miriam in Aaron's tent, "and your garments are nearly complete; the inner tunic and the covering blue robe. The short, sleeveless outer smock, the ephod, is not finished but will be handsome. It is made of scarlet, purple, and blue twisted linen interwoven with threads cut from thinly hammered sheets of gold. Aaron, you will be honored above all other men as you honor God with them."

"Except for you," Aaron added.

"Mine is a different calling. Be gracious and humble in your new role," advised Moses.

"I am told that there are bells sewn into the hem of my robe that will jingle as I walk. What are they for?"

"God says that His ear is carefully attuned to their soft, tinkling sound, as a mother's ear to her baby's cry. He will hear and protect you whenever you enter or leave the holy of holies. If you try to enter that room without the bells on, or if an unauthorized person does, he will surely die."[f]

"By what means?" Aaron asked. "God cannot always be present at that veil. Even you see Him as a focused God who, as you said, 'rides the heavens to your help.'"[g]

"I'm not sure. Death seems automatic. There must be a lethal power guarding it, perhaps Death himself, or an angel, like the destroying ones at Passover. Warn your sons, who will wear no bells, that they are prohibited from ever entering that sacred room. Only I am permitted in there, when invited, without the bells."

"Will there be a reference to the tribes in Aaron's garments?" asked Miriam.

"Yes," said Aaron, "on the front of the ephod is a square plaque with a dozen precious stones attached, one for each tribe, and epaulets with an onyx stone on each with the names of the tribes inscribed."

"Lastly, a turban for Aaron and tunics, sashes, and caps for the four sons," said Moses, "and linen breeches were made for all five priests, to be worn when serving God."

"I'll be pleased to see it," said Miriam.

*****

God's desire to dwell among the Israelites was about to be satisfied. No longer would He hover as smoke on the nearby mountain or visit Moses' remote tent in the form of a cloud. His tabernacle was completed, and all was ready.

Early the next morning, Moses and Aaron entered the courtyard. Moses walked alone into the tabernacle, lighted the oil in the lamps, placed incense in the cup on the golden altar, and then exited as God had ordered. The tabernacle was to be vacant. As the two brothers waited expectantly, the bright cloud suddenly hovered over the tabernacle and indwelled it. Even the curtains surrounding the tabernacle glowed from the inner light; the glory of the LORD filled the tabernacle.[h]

*****

That first day of His residence was to be a busy one. It was imperative that the vacillating Israelites comply with God's first commandment—*You shall have no other gods before Me*[i]—or else their devotion would be milked away by the world's idolatrous enticements, destroying the perfect society that He sought for them.

Soon after the cloud had settled into the tabernacle, God called Moses into the holy of holies to inform him that the priest and people were to worship Him through sacrifices.

Those sacrifices must be the most highly prized animals that they had bred and raised—perfect, unblemished one-year-old males; sheep, goats, oxen, birds, and grains. Those would be true sacrifices. The lesser animals would continue to provide for the Israelites' needs as usual.

God told Moses of the specific rituals of worship, designating the name and occasion for each sacrifice and the items required. God named the first sacrifice a *burnt offering*.[j] If the people wished to show Him great respect, devoting themselves to the Lord, they must bring an animal to the priest, kill it, and burn it completely on the bronze altar.

If a person wished to thank God for a remarkable blessing, such as the unexpected healing of a child, restoring of a broken relationship, or answer to a prayer, a second type of sacrifice could be made, the *thanksgiving (peace) offering.*[k] In it, the priest retained a portion of this slain animal's meat for his own family to eat, showing God's acceptance of it, and then returned the remainder of it to the donor. This was the only time that a layperson could share in the consumption of a sacrifice. Since there would be a large amount of meat left over from a goat, lamb, or bull, the giver was encouraged to hold a banquet. Passover was this type of sacrifice.

If a man broke any of His laws, God—being absolutely holy and sinless— could not tolerate such sin, and the lawbreaker deserved to die. However, in mercy, God offered the man a surrogate, one of his own cherished animals, to die in his stead. This *sin sacrifice*[l] would satisfy God, who forgave[m] the sinner as long as the sinner was contrite.

God was eager to forgive the sins of a common man and He inhaled the smoke arising from his sacrifice as a "soothing, sweet odor." The meat of the sacrifice for the sins of more respected men, leaders, priests, congregation as a whole was considered vile by God who refused to "inhale its foul odor."

*****

Moses met with the leaders outside of the camp. He stood in the middle of the group while the leaders sat on a hillside under the late-afternoon sun. Aaron was treated politely, but coolly.

Nethanel said bluntly, "Moses, in Egypt, our councils and the Egyptians handled serious crimes. We raised our animals and never gave a thought to the idea of sacrificing them. Now we'll have to sacrifice them because none of us can keep all of the commandments, always. Why does He give us these laws?

Moses said, "The laws were given to convict us of our sinfulness. If sins are condoned, others might similarly sin, destroying God's goal of making us into a *holy nation, a kingdom of priests.* Through the sin sacrifice, we can be forgiven and gain His forgiveness.

Moses added, "I have told you how to treat the meat of the animals. Now let me tell you of Life, as God has directed me, that essential force that God exhales into the nostrils of every living being. Powerful and sacred, once inhaled, it resides in the recipient's blood.[n] Therefore, it is an abominable thing for any man to ingest any of another being's lifeblood. We must never imitate the practices of other peoples who consume the blood of specific animals to gain their capabilities, such as the deer for speed and the bull for strength."

"That's why all animals must be bled to death before being prepared for a meal or a sacrifice?" asked Shelumiel.

"Right," said Moses, "and that blood contains strong, sin-cleansing properties outside of the body, as it may also have within it. God has a special use for it.

"For example, if a man breaks a law," Moses explained, "that sin takes on a vitality of its own,[3] defiling the sinner with a pervasive guilt. That sin also pollutes God's holy items, sticking to them like scum; lesser sins befoul only the bronze altar, but the more serious ones invade the tabernacle.

"The blood collected from every sacrifice must be sprinkled about the bronze altar to symbolically soak up the sin that befouls it, like a sponge, cleansing the altar. However, only a portion of the blood collected from the animal sacrificed for the sin of a priest, or the congregation as a whole, whose meat has been rejected by God, should be spattered about the bronze altar. The remainder must be carried inside the tabernacle's holy room by the high priest and sprinkled before the golden altar to eradicate the sin that has invaded the tabernacle and to gain God's forgiveness."

"Moses," said Pagiel, leaning forward, "let's be honest. Some people will not confess a sin they committed in secret, perhaps unwittingly, like gossiping, or even one committed hau-hau-hau-haughtily—like a-a-a-adultery. What are we to do about those?"

Moses answered, "Those unconfessed sins accumulate at the altar and will eventually seep into the tabernacle, contaminating it so much that God might not enter it. To remove those sins, once a year, and only once a year, the high priest must carry some of a specific animal's blood into the holy of holies room and sprinkle it on the ark's mercy seat to cleanse it. That is the Day of Atonement. The three altars are therefore of graduated holiness: the bronze, then the golden, and most sacred, the mercy seat.[4]

"The Day of Atonement as well as our personal sin sacrifices offer us another great gift, freedom from our feelings of guilt, and most of us are familiar with those. Only when guilt is washed away by forgiveness can the opportunity for love return."

Nahshon asked, "Moses, the sinner must bring his animal into the courtyard, right up to the bronze altar, give it to the priest, press his hand on the animal's head, transferring his guilt to it, and slay the animal himself, with help, in a bloody ceremony. Why not have the priest do the killing?"

"God's laws, not mine, Nahshon. He wants us to realize the seriousness of sin," Moses said.

Gamaliel said, "These details are important. Sacrifices are the only way that we individuals can communicate with God now that Moses' tent of meeting has been discontinued. Only Moses speaks directly to Him and, I suppose, Aaron and his sons will also when they are ordained."

Shelumiel said, "Moses tells us that the priest will kill a lamb every morning, one every evening, and an additional one on the first of each week. Seems a waste just to satisfy this God."

Eliasaph wagged a cautionary finger. "A waste to you, perhaps, but consider we must show our trust that He is God and will provide for us—even if we give Him ALL of our animals."

Gamaliel said, "Don't forget that we are to also burn some of our grain every day—the *grain offering*—to acknowledge that all sustenance comes from Him."

"Gamaliel, will we not deplete our stores of grain by such daily sacrifices?" Ahira asked.

Moses answered, "Use only a portion of the grains you brought with you, Ahira, because God's manna will satisfy your hunger until we reach Canaan, where we will find fields ripe with grains."

As the meeting was drawing to a close, Moses said, "Another feature of the sacrifices: God stipulated that since leaven is considered to be a symbol of evil, it must never be offered on the altar."

Endnotes

1. The story of Jethro in this chapter is based on Exodus 18.
2. Chapters 25 to 31 of Exodus give details of God's plan for the tabernacle.
3. "that sin takes on a vitality of its own" *Interpreter's Dictionary of the Bible, Supplementary Volume,* "Atonement," Keith Crim, ed., 1991, p. 79.
4. "altars of graduated holiness" J.H. Kurtz, *Offerings, Sacrifices, and Worship in the Old Testament,* 1998, p. 49.

Chapter 11

God Means What He Says

Moses was fatigued from the day's activities and slept well that night, awakening near dawn for another appointment with God. God spoke from the cloud above the mercy seat and told him that it was time for him to ordain Aaron and his sons as priests.[1] Moses invited a number of congregants into the courtyard for the ceremony the following day.

*****

When the crowd gathered, Moses led Aaron and his four sons, clothed only in their breeches, to the doorway of the tabernacle. Ten strong Levites led two rams and a bull ox up to the altar.

As Moses helped Aaron to dress in his full priestly outfit, he said, "Today's ordination ceremony is instructed by God to elevate you to a sacred position closer to Him. All subsequent high priests will be descended from you."

Then Moses filled a small vase with anointing oil and anointed the head of Aaron and his sons as he dedicated them to the service of God.

Moses killed the three animals as surrogates after the three had placed their hands on them: the bull to wash away their sins, one ram as a burnt offering, and the second ram as a ram of ordination.

Moses piled the fatty organs of the second ram, a piece of unleavened bread, and some oil onto their opened hands as God gave them sole authority over His sacrifices. He removed the items and burned them on the bronze altar.

The five boiled the meat of the second ram and ate it along with some of the unleavened bread in front of the tabernacle before entering into its holy room. There they would stay for seven days for God to finish their ordination.[a] On each of those days, a bull must be sacrificed for them as a sin offering.[b]

As the crowd began to disperse, Moses detained the twelve tribal leaders. He said to them, "The tabernacle is reserved as the priests' private place of worship. The bronze altar, however, is for the people's worship. I dedicated the tabernacle, but it is you who must dedicate this altar.[c] Each tribe will be assigned one day in sequence to bring their offering. Even though tribes vary greatly in size, all will bring the same, so that none will expect greater blessings.

"Each leader on his appointed day will bring a large silver dish filled with flour and a bowl with oil as a grain sacrifice, and a smaller gold pan filled with incense to be put into the tabernacle. Also, bring twenty-one animals—three bulls, six rams, six goats, and six lambs—to be sacrificed as burnt, peace, and sin offerings because it is a sacred altar."

Whereas the smaller golden altar in the tabernacle was warmed only slightly by the oil that Aaron alone ignited in it twice a day, this larger bronze altar outside would be a busy place. There the fires would smolder continuously, to be stoked into blazing heat as necessary to incinerate the parts of the carcasses thrown upon it by the priests.

*****

God selected the tribe of Judah, Israel's (Jacob's) fourth son, to initiate the dedication of the bronze altar. In a society where the firstborn deserved all honor as the leader and a double portion of inheritance, God had rejected Judah's three older brothers: Reuben, the eldest, when Israel discovered him in bed with his concubine, Bilhah;[d] and Simeon and Levi for the vengeful slaughter of the Shechemites.[e]

The following morning, Moses stood before the tabernacle and received the portion of grain and the tableware acquired from the Egyptians from Judah's Nahshon who, with his many assistants, consummated the animal sacrifices. Then, each day, a different tribe brought their offerings.

On the eighth morning, after Gamaliel had paid his tribute for Manasseh, Moses went to the tabernacle door and called to Aaron and his sons. They emerged solemnly, keeping to themselves whatever insights they had gained in God's presence during their period of seclusion.

Moses said to them, "I want to emphasize one particular law to you priests: since the golden altar is sacred, never place any strange incense or burnt offering or wine on it.[f] Also, now that you are ordained, you must make the daily sacrifices for the congregation. Sacrifices such as the ones Jethro made, or that I have been making, will no longer be acceptable."

*****

Weary from assisting in the sacrifices, Nadab and Abihu, Aaron's sons, retired to Nadab's empty tent that evening. They flopped on a couch, passing a skin of stolen wine back and forth between them.[2]

Nadab began, "I've had enough. I am tired of being ordered around by father and his God. We spent most of our lives following the dictates of those Egyptians. And now, being free, no one is going to tell me what I can and cannot do. After all, we are ordained priests.

"How can this God tell us, after all His work we do," as the pitch of his voice rose, "that we cannot go into the holy of holies, where only our father can go once a year—and Moses for awhile. Ha! Father with all of His faults. Well, by Osiris, we're important too."

"God cannot get by without our services," added Abihu.

"Miriam tells us that our old friends, who we used to get together with after dark, taunt her whenever they see her, saying that we are no better than they," said Nadab.

As they drank more, Nadab said, "We'll show them. Let's do it. God won't be there at this time of night. Just in case, let's take our censers with us. I'll get some coals for them. But where can we get incense?"

"We can use some skin lotion. It won't make any difference. The smell is about the same," said Abihu.

They walked into the courtyard, swinging their smoking censers on cords, Nadab guzzling from his wine skin. They entered the tabernacle's holy room. Giggling, Nadab spilled some wine on the golden altar.

"All right, Abihu," said Nadab. "Let's see if God is in there or not."

"Bells or no bells …" Abihu began as they parted the curtain and walked into the holy of holies. Before a further word was spoken, a sword of fire shot out from the mercy seat and consumed their flesh.

*****

When Nadab and Abihu were reported missing, Moses, Aaron, and his other two sons set out to look for them. As they searched, they came upon a man who recalled seeing them walking toward the courtyard. The foursome hurried through the gate into the courtyard.

"Have you seen Nadab and Abihu?" Moses asked a Levite sitting on the ground near the fence. He pointed toward the tabernacle. As they entered the tabernacle, Moses held up his hand and ordered, "Stay here," and then parted the curtain and walked alone into the holy of holies. He stared in shock. Lying before him were the bodies of the two sons with charred skin covering their skulls and hand bones that protruded from their tunics. Aghast, he fell to one knee, gently touching the tunic of one.

Moses dragged their remains out through the veil, one at a time, and laid them down in front of Aaron, who buckled to his knees in grief and horror at the fearful sight of their blackened, featureless heads. Their brothers turned away, disgusted. Moses walked outside, called to the Levites, and told them to summon two of Aaron's male cousins.

When they arrived, Moses gave them a terse order: "Carry your relatives away from the front of the sanctuary to the outside of the camp."[g]

One asked, as the cousins viewed the bodies, "What happened?"

"God," was the only answer that Aaron could murmur.

"Their bodies are burned, but look, their tunics are intact," said one of the cousins as they picked up the bodies.

"God's aim is perfect," said the other.

Moses turned to Aaron, gently grasping his forearm. "God has said, *'By those who come near Me I will be treated as holy, and before all the people I will be honored.'*[h] No anointed one can expect sympathy when he willfully breaks God's laws. I know how you must sorrow, but you must not grieve and do not show your troubled faces to the people lest God become wrathful against all the congregation."[i]

Aaron, fighting back tears, stumbled silently into Eleazar's arms as Moses consoled him, "All of the other Israelites will grieve in your stead for Nadab and Abihu."

God's cloud appeared and warned Aaron, *"Do not drink wine or strong drink, neither you nor your sons with you when you come into the* [tabernacle], *so that you may not die."*[j]

As the cloud receded, Aaron said to Moses, "Could they have been drinking?"

Seeing the wineskin, Moses answered, "Perhaps. All I know is that God's word is reliable, either as a warning or promised blessings."

*****

Early the next morning, a haggard Aaron and his two sons faithfully dressed and entered through the courtyard gate to sacrifice the mandatory year-old lamb. After that, Abidan and a cadre of men from Benjamin brought their bronze altar sacrifices to Aaron into the courtyard. Moses also entered the courtyard to bring God's reminder to Aaron that it was the ninth day of the month. The Israelites had been so busy dedicating the altar, and the priests so preoccupied with their own ordination and then the tragedy, that all had forgotten to prepare for Passover, one year after leaving Egypt. *"Let the sons of Israel observe the Passover at its appointed time,"** said God. The next day, all families selected their lambs and prepared them.

Four days later, following the bronze altar sacrifices of Naphtali, the twelfth and final tribe, the entire company of people celebrated Passover. They stripped their houses of the last vestiges of leaven, killed the lambs at twilight, roasted them, and ate them quickly with unleavened bread and bitter herbs.[5]

"Why bitter herbs?" Elishama asked Nahshon.

The jeweler answered, "It was bitter living in Egypt. But it was also bitter, I'll wager, for God to kill all of those firstborn Egyptians. Perhaps we have some bitterness ahead of us. You decide."[1]

*****

God's sacred circle was now complete: the various sacrifices themselves, the fully ordained priests to administer them, and the dedication of the altar on which to proffer them.

Endnotes

1. Leviticus 8 describes the ordination ceremony.
2. Story of priests testing God told in Leviticus 10.

Chapter 12

God's Word: A Lamp Unto Their Feet (Ps. 119:105)

Passover was celebrated. The next day Moses arrived at his large tent where he had called another meeting with his leaders in the midafternoon. He seemed wearied as he greeted them. "I spent the morning with God in the tabernacle; He gave me many more laws for us to live by and by which judges may arrive at their decisions."

"Why more laws, Moses? Can't we make our own?" asked Shelumiel.

Moses answered, "If we are to become a successful nation in Canaan, He realizes that it is imperative for us to have a well-devised legal system to govern us. His laws are far better than ones we could devise. You will understand as you hear them."

*****

He began to read from his scrolls, laws showing God's intimate concerns for the issues of their lives, even the smallest ones; laws concerning diseases, appropriate sexual behavior, care of slaves, love for all neighbors, as well as the penalties for breaking them.

"The ownership of the land that sustains human existence was important to God. To guarantee that each family would always have their apportioned plot in Canaan, He established the Year of Jubilee, a time to be celebrated every fifty years, at which time all land deeds would revert back to their original owners at no cost. *"The land, moreover, shall not be sold permanently, for the land is Mine; for you are but aliens and sojourners with Me,"*[a] said God.

"That is a novel idea—but a g-g-good one," said Pagiel.

Moses continued, "In consideration of the poor, farmers should leave the ends of the crop rows unharvested, and the fallen grapes in the vineyard for them to gather so they would not have to steal."

He finished by saying that, partly for health reasons, God divided the animals into those that were edible and those that were not.

Ahira spoke up. "God's new laws add to the burden of the people who have little motivation to obey. Why should they? They have been conscripted into a hazardous mission with scant hope of a favorable outcome, what with the battles that lie ahead of us."

Elishama said, "We obey only out of fear."

Gamaliel: "Don't you do it out of respect for Him or gratitude for all that He has done for us?"

Elishama: "Gratitude? Fifty-seven dead? We are walking in this hot sun, on hot ground, day after day, driving cattle mile after mile. Our children find little time to play. Boring manna. And now, with these laws, I must worry about possible punishments."

Nahshon: "Many in our tribe are convinced that God hates us[b] and is sorry He brought us here and is out to destroy us."

Some others nodded in agreement.

Moses said grimly, "Nashon, God loves you deeply; He is totally committed to you. He hates only what you do when you rebel or complain against Him."

Eliasaph asked, "Moses, by giving us these laws, is God giving you all authority to govern us, without His stern and sometimes lethal intervention anymore?"

Moses answered, "No, God is not abdicating His authority. He continues to deal with attitudes and actions of the people, individually and at large."

*****

A few days later, Aaron and his properly attired sons were preparing to sacrifice the morning lamb for the congregation. While Ithamar held the lamb firmly, Aaron began cutting away the wool from the left side of its neck.

"Ithamar, the meal that your wife served us yesterday was fit for a pharaoh," said Aaron. "She is a magician in the kitchen."

"I'll thank her for you, father."

"She is a beautiful woman. And the little jewelry she wears is simple but elegant," said Aaron.

"She chooses well."

"Yet, her jacinth ring appears expensive." Aaron looked at his son sternly. Ithamar was silent.

Aaron continued, "It looks like the ring that Sorin gave to the treasury a month ago in thanksgiving for God having brought his son through the high fevers."

Ithamar silently tightened his grip on the shoulders of the animal.

Aaron stopped his cutting. "If that is true, how did you get the ring?"

Ithamar finally met Aaron's searching eyes. "Our treasury is well stocked from the census and other gifts. I told her of the ring once, and her mind settled on it."

"You stole it?" asked Aaron. "God has forbidden such a thing! You may bring down His anger on us all!"

"I am sorry, father." There was a pause before Ithamar continued, "Will I be burned as my brothers were?"

"No," answered Aaron. "But you must return the ring and offer a sacrifice. Ask the herdsman, Matalel, if you may have one of his bull calves."

"How can I pay for it?" asked Ithamar. "I have spent the little personal money I had."

"Good fortune is yours. In two weeks, the tribes must give their first tithe to the Levites, one tenth of their possessions, and they in turn must give to us priests a tenth of what they receive. You may barter with Matalel."

The two weeks passed and Ithamar received his share of the tithe, including two goats and four lambs that he traded for a bull calf. Matalel and his four helpers brought it to the perimeter of the Levite camp the next day, where Ithamar met him with his brother Eleazar.

"I will go with you," said Matalel, holding one of two ropes fastened around the animal's neck, "because this one has an element of trust in me." The animal had been fed a large portion of a tasty root that made it more compliant.

The seven men herded the animal down a wide path through the Levite grounds to the curtain around the courtyard. When they parted the curtain and walked through, the calf began to pull against its ropes. The perspiring men strained to wrestle the 220-pound animal up to the bronze altar.

"Tie its legs together, front to front and rear to rear," said Aaron. Two of the men shackled the limbs of the bull, allowing a hand's breadth distance between each leg pair, as the animal began to thrash. An additional rope was secured about its middle.

Ithamar knew the routine. He placed his hand briefly on the bull's bobbing head, identifying it as a substitute for himself.

"Now cut," commanded Aaron. Ithamar had never sacrificed a bull for himself. He quickly, nervously tested the edge of the knife blade and then, following his father's pointing finger, stuck the knife into the right side of the bull's neck. The animal jerked its head in pain, and Ithamar's moist hand dropped the knife.

"Plunge and slice!" yelled Aaron. Ithamar picked up the knife, drove it into the fettered bull's neck again, and pulled hard toward himself. The life-filled blood shot toward the ground in a steady, pulsating stream. Eleazar, bucket in hand, tried to catch it by moving in synchrony with the jerking victim. The bull's bulging eyes followed Ithamar as he raced around the men, steadied himself, and sliced into the left side of the animal's neck. Other helpers with buckets caught as much of the blood as possible, as puddles of red stained the earth. Then, on his knees, Ithamar stabbed into each groin. Blood issued from the right side only, into a waiting bucket. The bull began to sway. After several minutes, its eyes rolled back, its breathing became shallow, and it sagged, being pushed onto a waiting cart. Shaking, Ithamar looked away as Aaron took the knife from his hand.

"See that you sin no more," Aaron warned his humiliated son. "Being an anointed one of God, your deed contaminates not only the bronze altar, but also invades the very tabernacle itself."

Aaron took one of the pails of warm blood in his hand. With the other he prodded Ithamar to walk before him as they started toward the tabernacle's holy room.

Addressing the Levites, Aaron ordered, "Haul the carcass of the bullock out of the camp and burn it to ashes in a clean place. God will refuse to inhale its foul odor."

Section III
Preparation for Departure

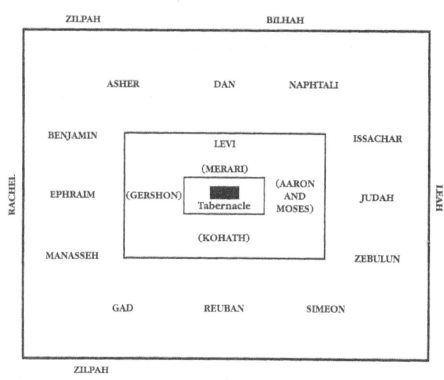

Camping Order

Chapter 13

Organizing

Ithamar's chastisement would not be forgotten. His love and respect for his wise father deepened as did his commitment to his obligations.

Soon, the first day of the second month of the second year since leaving Egypt arrived. Only God knew that in just four weeks, the Israelites would embark on the last leg of their journey to invade Canaan. Were they ready? Up to this point, the Hebrew's time was spent learning the ways in which God should be worshipped, ways that would enable them to spurn the licentiousness of Canaan's inhabitants. Several practical matters needed to be accomplished before their departure. How many people were at Sinai, how strong an army could they muster, and in what order would the mass of people camp?

God summoned Moses into the holy of holies one day and called for a census of the people.ᵃ God enlisted the help of Aaron and the twelve leaders to assist Moses in the census.

*****

The census concluded that the seventy persons of Jacob's family who had immigrated to Egypt had multiplied to 40,000* The census completed, God's next concern was the formulation of a housing plan.

During the months at Sinai, the village of the Israelites had consisted of a somewhat random—often confused—arrangement of families in their huts and tents. God, being a god of order, gave detailed instructions to Moses about the camping order of the Israelites. The tabernacle and the courtyard were always to be in the center of the encampment. The guardians and custodians of the tabernacle, the tribe of Levites, were divided into the three families descended from the three sons of the long-dead Levi—Gershon, Merari, and Kohath—and they camped on three sides of it. Moses and Aaron's families, also Kohathites, were to be located in the place of honor, on the east side. The descendants of the other twelve sons of Jacob—Joseph's two sons, Ephraim and Manasseh succeeding him—would be camped, tribe by tribe, in a rectangle

*Bible numbers were 603,550 men.

surrounding them, one step further from the tabernacle. Judah, the lead tribe, would be in the center on the east side.

The three tribes of Reuben, Gad, and Manasseh were camped together because they had large cattle holdings that could share grazing.

God told Moses that as each campsite was vacated, the tribes were to march in the same order as at the bronze altar dedication and at the camping sequence: Judah, Issachar, Zebulun, Reuben, and so on.

Chapter 14

Fidelity to God and Husbands

Judah's commanding position augmented Nahshon's self-assurance and pride. He was enjoying a walk the day after a heavy rain when he approached three friends who were inspecting a nearby flooded wadi.

Shelumiel stood with his hands on his hips. "This stream should not threaten our camp, but it will make the fruit trees produce. This Garden of Eden will be difficult to leave."

"Moses hints that our departure may be soon," Eliasaph said.

Shelumiel tossed a pebble into the stream. "Yes, to go up to Canaan to fight. I only hope that the enemy will not be large in size and number and their cities poorly protected."

Eliasaph reminded, "He promises victory IF we follow Him. God also says that we *shall not follow other gods … for the* LORD [our] *God in the midst of* [us] *is a jealous God*."[a]

"I'd be surprised if there isn't an idol of some other god or goddess—Anuke, Moloch, Rompha[b]—in most tents," gibed Nahshon, "including ours."

"Our devotion to Him must take preference over our own personal passions," said Pagiel, "like Gamaliel's devotion to improving his athletic abilities, winning almost all physical games we play; Elishama m-m-maintaining his skill as an archer; Abidan pours over his precious scrolls every spare moment he has."

"And Pagiel, how many times a day do you count your money?" countered Nahshon.

"I believe that God sees into every tent. How about my carpentry?" asked Shelumiel.

"Second," said Eliasaph.

"No thanks," said Shelumiel. "Not yet."

*****

Two weeks after Passover, Lashinar walked into Eleazar's tent, leading Coresha along with him. She was the same height as her husband, and her head was slightly bowed. The priest was struck by her astonishing beauty. Lashinar blurted out, "Now, priest, what can I do with my wife who has been unfaithful to me?"

Eleazar responded sternly, "On what grounds do you believe this?"

"Men cannot keep their eyes off of her although, I admit, she does not return their glances. I have seen her talk with the bachelor, our neighbor Meelar, on several occasions," Lashinar spat out. "She keeps me at bay often, and I do not know why. She spends less time preparing meals, and their flavors have waned. She has been away when I come in at night—at least three times in the last month. I believe she is unfaithful—with Meelar."

"When she came home late, where did she say she was?" asked Eleazar.

"At her sister's."

Eleazar looked away for a moment. "And what does her sister say?"

Lashinar glowered. "Of course, she wouldn't tell me the truth; you know how sisters stick together like dye to a cloth."

Eleazar turned to Coresha. "Go home, daughter Coresha. Let me talk with Lashinar alone." She raised her dark eyes to the priest, bowed quickly, turned, and glided away.

*****

Eleazar looked at Lashinar and asked, "Have you talked to Coresha about your concerns, or has she sensed them?"

"We are close friends, do many things together, make love well, but talk about feelings, no. I am a man, I work hard for her, provide for her, do things for her but doubt that I could—absorb—her emotional feelings. I have enough trouble with my own, and she honors that," admitted Lashinar. "It is difficult for me to seek your help, but I-I need it."

Eleazar carefully weighed his words. "If your beliefs are true," he said, "your anger is merited. I suspect that those deeds go on from time to time in our close quarters, although none have been caught in the act, thank goodness. The penalty is severe." He looked off in the distance. "Meelar has always been a trusted worker, but I admit, the ladies are attracted to him. He should be married."

"Trusted by you, maybe, but I would like to kill him."

"Have you lost your love for Coresha?"

Lashinar softened. "No."

"Does Coresha know how much you love her?"

"If I would tell her how much I love her and how important it is that she loves me and is true to me, wouldn't she think me a helpless child? I try to show my love for her by what I do for her." He waited a moment, pondering. "But how I ache in silence at the little attentions she gives to other men. I believe she would be better occupied if only she could have another child. We have been unable to and our only, Zessa, is twelve. But first, I must know if she is but mine—alone."

Sympathy welled up in Eleazar's heart. "God has laid out a ceremony for such an occasion. Tomorrow, bring Coresha to my father Aaron, along with three and a half quarts of barley meal as a grain offering to show your sincerity. God will judge her fairly."

*****

The next day, Lashinar and a compliant Coresha appeared in front of Aaron near the tabernacle with the required grain offering. Aaron said, "Lashinar, you suffer the torments of jealousy and God sympathizes with you, understanding your agony. He has those same pangs when a loved one of His, seemingly devoted to Him, forsakes Him to worship another god.[c] Therefore, to find out the truth for you two, He has given to us His law of jealousy."[d]

She stood before the priest, loosened her hair, and accepted a cupful of grain the priest poured into her hands, the grain offering of jealousy. Aaron brought forth a container of holy water, adding dust from the ground to form a water of bitterness, empowered by God to produce a curse or blessing. Aaron wrote a curse on a small scroll and washed water over it, into the water of bitterness, and then stirred. Over the water, Aaron spoke an oath that Coresha repeated, understanding thereby that if she were guilty of adultery, the water would cause her abdomen to swell permanently and her left thigh to waste away. If innocent, she would be immune from the curse of the water and would not merely be exonerated, but she would be greatly blessed. If previously barren, she would become miraculously fertile. Then she slowly drank a mouthful of the liquid and returned the cup to the priest, who took the grain offering from her hand and burned it on the altar.

"Why don't you punish Meelar also or put him to the test?" asked Lashinar.

Aaron paused, separating his hands before him, "Only God knows," he said, "since the man shares the blame. Is she more in control of the situation, more capable of resisting such a temptation? Might this penalty to her, rather than to him, be more likely to deter others from a similar fate?ᵉ She will be tried, but he must live untested in his guilt."

Coresha's embarrassment hid what little anger she felt toward Lashinar and the priest, and her quiet acceptance of the trial helped her endure it. She thought, "I alone know of my physical innocence; but will I be condemned for my occasional wayward thoughts?"

As she and Lashinar walked from the tabernacle, she felt a deeper love for him. She interpreted his proven jealousy as a sign of his love for her. She had not been sure of that before.

Over the next four weeks, her thigh remained strong, her figure fine, her attention to Lashinar grew, and their marriage flourished.

*****

Lashinar happened upon Sorin, mending the flap of his tent.

"Sorin, my friend, how is your family, your fine son?"

"They are fine, thank you. But Lashinar, you have become a bounding rabbit with a new enthusiasm about you, a joy absent for the last few months. I have been worried about you. But now I am happy to see you at home more."

"I have a secret relief, Sorin; and yes, life is good and I am well. My Coresha, we talk now as we haven't in years. We seem to hear each other better. But tell me about your son."

"He is fine, vigorous, and healthy," Sorin replied. "But lately, he has a restlessness within. Nothing satisfies him. And it is not girls. He is nineteen now and should serve in the army next year. However, he speaks of a different commitment after that. He is drawn to this God and His concern for us, and wishes somehow to serve Him. Several other young men feel the same and have joined together to see what options are open to them."

"That seems strange," puzzled Lashinar. "Would God welcome him? What does the priest say?"

"They have learned of the Nazirite vowᶠ that God told Moses about, a way to draw closer to Him. By it, he may serve God through the Levites for as long as he wishes—months or years—spending each day with them, helping them, and as he puts it, learning of God's revelations."

"With all the work to be done around the camp and all of the pretty girls from whom to choose a wife, that seems a bit unusual," remarked Lashinar.

"I agree, but that is his feeling," said the weaver.

"To get in with the Levites, there must be a price to pay, no?"

"Four shekels, to show sincerity, at the beginning," said Sorin. "Then he cannot shave his hair or beard during his commitment and cannot eat or use any of the products of the grapevine—the juice, the oil, the wine, vinegar, raisins—nothing."

"I hear that grapes are plentiful in Canaan. That will be quite a self-denial. What does Karrinen say?" asked Lashinar.

"She is a loving mother, and whatever Hanniel wants to do is all right with her. She will support him, as I will, and help him to scrape up the shekels."

"You are lucky to have a son, even one with peculiar ideas. Perhaps I will someday be similarly blessed," said Lashinar.

"Oh?" Sorin's eyes brightened mischievously. "Do you know something we do not?"

"We shall see," said Lashinar, as they parted.

*****

Having concluded the orders for the consecration of those on the lower rungs of His holiness ladder—the people, then the Nazirites—God turned His attention to the promoted sons of Levi. He called Moses to the tabernacle's holy of holies and said that the Levites must go through an ordination ceremony,[g] similar to that of the priests, to obtain their consecration as ministers. The details of that ceremony were laid out to Moses, so he gathered the Levites and some of the congregation.

During the service, the Levites shaved their entire bodies, put on fresh clothes, and were sprinkled with water by Moses instead of with oil like the priests. The Levites placed their hands on the heads of two bulls, and past sins were purged from them as the bulls were killed.

In his first twenty-five years, a Levite would live a normal life, doing as he pleased, during which time he could marry and have children.[h] However, for the next twenty-five years, he was to serve God by living with his family near the tabernacle, assisting the priests with its care, and ministering to the people on Aaron's behalf. Prohibited from land ownership by God, he would be given ample land to use for his home, for gardening, and for grazing the few cattle that he was permitted to own. All of his other food and money needs were to be supplied as gifts from the other twelve tribes. At age fifty, he could retire and have his needs still met by the community.

The Levites, forgiven by God, were not, however, imbued with instant perfection. They were to serve their own cousin, Aaron, whose failings were remembered, and his two sons, merely their children's peers. They were allegedly "promoted" from independence to subjection. At least a few resented the arrangement, and they served reluctantly.

Most, however, served dutifully, and they found that most of the people received their teachings well. But it became apparent that many of the Simeonites resented the Levites' presence in their homes and even shunned them out in the village. The Levites soon ceased advising them.

*****

A few days after the Levite ordination, God told Moses that when the cloud ascended out of the tabernacle and moved away, the people were to follow until it stopped, there to set up the tabernacle and their village again.

Moses would need to communicate orders to the camp and, as instructed, he assigned his trusted metalsmith, Bezalel, the task of casting two silver trumpets for that purpose.

*****

Bezalel

Bezalel was underweight at birth. As he grew, he remained short in stature, with a broad nose, large, often protruding tongue, and wide-set eyes. He was always last in foot races because of a lack of energy and soon gave up trying. His mother, Rohja, recognized early that his mind was duller than those of her other three children, so she paid him more attention, encouraging his limited capacity.

She was a frugal housewife and collected the bits of clay that her husband, Uri, brought home in his pockets or on his feet. She learned to make sun-dried pottery from them for her family and often gave finished pieces away to admiring friends. In time, she produced dolls, urns, and figurines from the clay. These were stealthily placed next to bricks in the ovens by Uri's friends. When Bezalel showed interest in trying to mimic his mother's work, Uri—an ox of a man with a tender heart for his family—began to come home with muddier clothing and feet.

The boy found satisfaction in his work and, in time, surprised his parents with beautiful artifacts fashioned by his stubby fingers. Uri once gave one of his son's painted vases to a benevolent Egyptian foreman. Word spread, and soon an Egyptian craftsman and his assistants came to visit the boy. The Egyptian snickered at the unsightly eleven-year-old, but when Bezalel formed a small but perfect running horse out of clay before them, they were impressed. He was eventually sent to artisan's school, primarily so Egypt could make some use of this freakish-looking child.

Through a bull-like perseverance, Bezalel devoted himself to his tasks single-mindedly, mastering the wheel and the kiln, the hammer and chisel soon after, then the forge by age thirteen. His favorite enterprise was sculpting, which often elicited his high-pitched croaks of glee. He flourished under the growing recognition of his accomplishments and was twenty-three when Pharaoh released the slaves. On the journey, he doggedly kept up with the others, in spite of his shuffling gait.

*****

When tapped to supervise the temple construction, Bezalel was in awe at, and gratefully appreciative for, the new skills that God instilled in him. He was beloved by all and now enthusiastically tackled his new assignment.

He drew two nuggets of pure silver from the bag he had brought from Rameses and added them to a silver dish that he melted down, providing enough metal for the trumpets. Traces of other metals hardened the soft silver, and for several days he molded and hammered them into two fore-arm-length trumpets. The instruments had slightly different diameters so that, when blown, they produced different sounds.

Bezalel proudly presented the two lustrous instruments to Moses. "I am unable to blow hard enough to play them," he apologized, "but I have heard my father do so. When blown steadily, their tone is melodious. When a forceful, intermittent breath is applied, the sound of an alarm is produced. I hope God approves of them."

"I am sure that He will," said a pleased Moses. "There will be many occasions for their use. Their blast will summon leaders. They will usher in feast days and days of sacrifice, Bezalel, to remind the people that God is their LORD. God has even told me that should an enemy attack us, Aaron's sons, the trumpeters, are to blow an alarm to alert God and the people, and to assure them that God will go before them. I believe that God's ear is attuned to their distinct sound, just as it is to the tinkling of the bells on Aaron's robe. Thank you, Bezalel."

With that, God's agenda for Sinai was concluded. Much had transpired at that place in a little more than a year. His worship by the priests, the Levites, and the Nazirites was assured. He had provided details of how He would guarantee victory in upcoming battles and had given instructions about consecration at all levels. Now it was time to leave Sinai and put those principles into practice.

To confirm His responsiveness to His priests, God told Aaron that His blessings would be given to the people only after he would publicly pray for them. As they all assembled, ready for the journey to Canaan, Aaron prayed aloud:

"The LORD bless you, and keep you;

The LORD make His face to shine on you and be gracious to you.

The LORD lift up His countenance on you and give you peace." [i]

Section IV
The Journey Resumes

Chapter 15
Dissension Abounds

Once the trumpets were completed, Moses suspected they would be moving out soon. He was familiar with the lands to the east, west, and south through his years of shepherding but knew little of the more rugged valley directly to the north, with its scrubby brush, low trees, and rocky soil, an area poorly fit for grazing. That, however, was the direct path to Canaan, and if God should lead them in that direction, Moses wanted to be prepared. So early one morning, Moses and his son Gershom mounted two donkeys with a supply of food and water, bid good-bye to Zipporah, left the camp, and followed Jethro's path to the northeast. They camped overnight, and the next noon, they arrived at Jethro's home where they were greeted warmly. Moses briefly explained his mission and sought out Hobab, a bachelor and the younger brother of Zipporah.

"Hobab,[1] you are aware of the horde of people that have been thrust into my hands to lead to Canaan?" asked Moses. "It is time for us to depart, and I believe that we will go northward. I know it to be a land of deserts and pits … of drought and of deep darkness.[a] You know the terrain and where we should camp in the wilderness, and you would be as eyes for us.[b] Will you lead us to Canaan?"

Hobab shook his head. "Moses, I have no need to go north now. Besides, I do not believe in your God, and I would feel unwelcome among you."

"I give you my word that whatever good the LORD does for us, we will do for you,"[c] replied Moses. "God will honor you. We are told that Canaan is a wonderland and the opportunities that lie there are limitless."

"So Jethro, now eighty-eight years old, has told me, for he traveled there once with a caravan." Hobab thought for a minute. "I have little holding me here. Jethro has plenty of help to care for his animals. If he will permit me, I will lead you. I will bring two bags with me in case I decide to stay for a while."

"We will need to leave in the morning, if it is agreeable with you," said Moses.

"If Jethro approves, I will be ready."

At sunrise, the party left, traveled all day, camped out, and returned to the Sinai camp the next afternoon.

*****

The next day God spoke to Moses, telling him that it was time to move north and journey from Sinai past Mount Seir and to the town of Kadesh-barnea near the southern border of Canaan. From there, Moses was to launch an invasion northward, first into the hill country where mountains rose 2,500 to 3,000 feet high, then into the lowlands to the seacoast, up to Lebanon all the way to the river Euphrates, *land that* [I] *had sworn to give to your fathers, to Abraham, to Isaac, and to Jacob and their descendants after them.*[d]

*****

Two days later, at dawn, one of the sentries excitedly awakened Ithamar. He arose, followed the sentry out of his tent and, glancing at the tabernacle, ran to Aaron's tent, pushed the flap ajar, and called in, "The cloud is rising from the tabernacle!"

Aaron said, "Then it is time to leave! Tell Moses!"

The sentry took the message to Moses. The brothers left their tents and stood watching as the cloud moved rapidly toward the north and then stopped about thirty miles away. The heartbeat of the people quickened as they made preparations to break camp. There arose a general din of expectant excitement.

While families packed their belongings, Moses and Aaron set out on different missions.

Moses soon found Joshua and told him to alert the leaders of the tribes to prepare to depart. He hurried on to Hobab's tent. "God has indeed set our course to the north," he told his brother-in-law. "Our people are ready to follow you. We will take the morning to prepare, then plan to leave after noon."

"If they are ready for it, so am I," replied Hobab. "We may be in for a few days of difficult travel."

Moses then met with the leaders and went over the final marching orders.

Meanwhile, Aaron sent Ithamar to the Levites' tents. Since the journey to Canaan would require that the tabernacle be relocated often, the tribe of Levi had been assigned to transport it.

"Notify them to meet with us outside of the tabernacle as soon as possible and see that the trumpets are blown," Aaron said to Ithamar.

Aaron walked to the tabernacle, where he met his two sons and many Levitical men. "Let us get moving," he said to the throng.[2] No specific orders were necessary because Aaron had thoroughly trained the men in their respective tasks. As the priests entered the tabernacle, the men of the three Levitical families began their rehearsed work. The family of Merari was in charge of all of the wooden objects, from the wallboards to the pegs, and the family of Gershon, the curtains, the roof, and the screens. They first disassembled the courtyard walls, its gate, and the bronze altar before tackling the tabernacle itself, packing the heavy items onto six carts pulled by twelve oxen, all donated by the other tribes.

Aaron and his sons, who were permitted in the holy of holies for this occasion, worked alone inside. They took the heavy veil that separated the holy room from the holy of holies from its hooks, folded it, and spread it over the ark-mercy seat. Each of the other holy objects was covered with a separate-colored cloth, chosen from a neat pile kept in one corner of the room. Animal skins were carefully fitted over each object to protect it from the weather. Aaron covered the hallowed ark with a pure, blue cloth in order to vividly identify it, per God's instructions, while his sons placed the carrying poles through the handles on each of the other holy items. Once the items were covered, they called the third Levite family, the Kohathites, the clan of Aaron's family, to carry them, for God had said that no one except the Aaronites could see the uncovered holy items even for a moment, lest they die.[e]

"Remember," Aaron cautioned the leader of the Kohathite contingent, "the ark must always be carried by hand. Never put it on a wagon!"[f]

While readying the furniture, the remaining Levites were taking down the tabernacle itself. Each man had an assigned duty, be it the carrying of pegs, the loading of lumber and curtains, separating and loading the layers of the roof, or carrying a holy item from one site to another, there to reassemble it. With such a workforce, all was soon made ready.

✶✶✶✶✶

At midday, the trumpets of Bezalel sounded, and the tribe of Judah, captained by Nahshon, led them out, trailing only Hobab and the ark-carrying Levites. Moses prayed aloud for protection and rallied the people: "Rise up, O LORD! And let Thine enemies be scattered, and let those who hate Thee flee before Thee."[g]

Nethanel and his Issacharites followed, then Eliab's Zebulun.

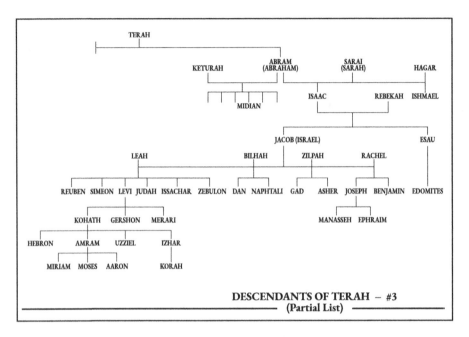

DESCENDANTS OF TERAH – #3
(Partial List)

The fourth group, the Levite families of Gershon and Merari, were protected by the three tribes in front of them. They would arrive at the campsite soon enough to set up the courtyard and the tabernacle so that the holy items could be installed when they arrived.

Two of the men of Merari, traveling together, were talking. "Where are the firstborn males when there is work to be done?" asked one. "I thought God honored them as the first sign of fertility of the womb, so that they would serve Him for life. I am a third-born Levite and honored only in that I am steadying this heavily laden wagon in the hot sun."

"I think God chose them to serve Him in Canaan, not here," said the second. "Besides, how much easier it is for Him to use us, an organized tribe who can serve now, rather than to try to muster up all the firstborn from each tribe? But now look," as he pointed skyward, "a small guide-cloud remains in the distance, but the large cloud has returned overhead to provide shade for us. Seems that your complaints were heard."

*****

The tribes of the south side of the tabernacle walked next, then the Kohathites, carrying the holy items, several hours behind the other Levites. After them were the tribes of the west side of the tabernacle. Then, forming the rear guard, those of the north side.

In three days, the Israelites reached the guide-cloud and made their camp, still in the rugged wilderness. When the ark arrived into the camp, Moses proclaimed, "Return Thou, O Lord, to the myriad thousands of Israel,"[h] a ritual he was to follow at the end of each day's march.

*****

When the early travelers arrived, their weary shoulders and tired hands dropped their belongings. Levites unloaded the wagons and began constructing the tabernacle. As personal tents were put up in the prescribed order, occasional complaints turned into a din of sullen voices growing out of the temporary camp.

"Thirty miles in three days, across that wilderness. What does God expect from us?"

"I thought Hobab knew the best paths. Seems that we skidded off rocks every other step."

"Branches caught my hair."

"My arms were scratched by the shrubs."

"We should have stayed at Sinai. Why did God bring us here? No land can be worth this suffering."

"At this rate, my shoes will wear out in a few days. God better find some new ones for me."

*****

God listened to each murmur against Him and became deeply troubled again. His elaborate preparations had been for naught; after the year at Sinai, their attitudes remained unchanged.

*****

The last of the travelers had wearily finished setting up their camps when suddenly, Moses, who was watching the completion of the tabernacle, heard shouts coming from the camping areas to the south, those of Gad, Reuben, and Simeon. Eliasaph, Elizur, and Shelumiel arrived at the same time. "Moses," Shelumiel panted, "The camp is on fire! Flames began spouting out of several tents, and now they are spreading. It must be the fire of the Lord."

"Some people have been burned and goods destroyed," said Shulemiel. "Even cattle are seared. Pray to God for us, Moses. We are sorry, so sorry, for complaining."[i]

Moses saw smoke rising from the southern edge of the camp. He fell on his knees before them, put his face on the ground, and pleaded, "God, forgive us. Quench the fires, the heat of your anger. We deserve what you have done, but forgive us once again for complaining."

The flames died out, the smoke blew away, and the ground cooled, leaving a perimeter of charred tents and belongings and some minor skin burns.

*****

"What a harsh god," Elishama complained to Abidan the next morning as they stood with Gamaliel and Nethanel, surveying the damage. "He generates His own fire and casts it on us to punish us just because people grouse against Him!"

"It is much more than that," said Abidan. "This is at least the sixth time we have complained that God should have let us stay in Egypt. Each time His punishment escalates."

"God expected us to grow up during the year at Sinai and quit our complaining. We developed no trust," said Gamaliel.

"Don't criticize, Gamaliel," said Nethanel. "You are so often in your prayers. Get your head out of the clouds, and put your tongue on the grimy soil. Taste the tears of our people. They are resentful and afraid."

Gamaliel was undeterred. "Trust God, Nethanel. Look to yourself. Can you part even the stream of water that issues from your bull?"

As Abidan examined a piece of burnt tent cloth, he sought to calm them. "I'm sure God is justified. All He has done for us, only to be needled by complaints."

"More warnings and explanations for our people, correct?" said Nethanel.

"Yes, I'm afraid so," said Abidan.

They named the place "Taberah," which means "burning,"[3] because the LORD's fire was vented there.

*****

After a rest at Taberah, the Hebrew camp followed the cloud north for four more days through a great and terrible wilderness afflicted with fiery serpents and scorpions[j] before breaking out into the desert, where they established another camp.

On the fifth day there, the multitude of non-Israelites who had joined the journey at its inception spoke as pompous guests, asking, "Who will give us meat to eat?" They were joined by a number of hungry Israelites weeping in their chorus: "We remember the fish which we used to eat freely in Egypt, the cucumbers, the melons, the leeks, and the onions and garlic, but now our appetite is gone. There is nothing at all to look at except this manna."[k]

The anger of the LORD was kindled[l] and Moses, the middleman, grew frustrated. The people he represented were murmuring, and the God he served was angry. The embers of Taberah were hardly cool, and he feared greater punishment. He cried out to God, "Why hast Thou been so hard on Thy servant that Thou laid the burden of all this people on me [saying,] *'Carry them in your bosom as a nurse carries a nursing infant, to the land which* [I swore] *to their fathers?'*[m] Where am I to get meat to give to all this people? I alone am not able to carry them." Then, ready to give up, he pleaded, "So, if Thou art going to deal thus with me, please kill me at once—and do not let me see my wretchedness."[n] He had not spoken that way to God since the pharaoh had forced the Israelites to find their own straw.

"Gather for Me seventy men from the elders of Israel," God said, *"and I will take of the Spirit who is upon you and put Him upon them; and they shall bear the burden of the people with you...."*[o]

Moses was anxious. If he yielded some of the precious Spirit to others, would he feel depleted, less powerful, less bound to his Master? "Why must He take it from me?" he wondered. "Doesn't God have a limitless supply of Spirit?" Obediently, Moses handpicked seventy elders, most of whom had accompanied him to the foot of Mount Sinai, and they joined him inside the courtyard near the tabernacle. As the men stood together, God took a portion of the Spirit from Moses and distributed it to the men. The Spirit-guided men then prophesied for a short time, giving witness to God, and a few even foretold future events. Joshua, standing at the gate, was amazed at God's gift.

At the same time, two other men, Eldad and Medad, who had been selected by Moses but who had stayed back in camp, also had the Spirit placed upon them by God. Their families were shocked to hear them unexpectedly, uncontrollably prophesying, and a young man excitedly ran to tell Moses. He first encountered Joshua, who became annoyed when he heard his story.

Believing that the two men were speaking presumptuously without intercession from Moses or from God, Joshua implored Moses, "Restrain them."[p]

"Are you jealous for my sake?" asked Moses. Then he added humbly, "Would that all of the LORD's people were prophets, that the LORD would put His Spirit upon them."[q]

*****

Moses' mind soon returned to the problem facing him: how to satisfy the complainers' tastes. He asked God, "Should flocks and herds be slaughtered—or all the fish in the sea be gathered together—for them to have sufficient food?"[r]

God's answer was withering. *"Is the LORD's power limited? Now you shall see whether My word will come true or not."*[s] Referring to the whining people, He announced they would get so much meat that it would *come out of* [their] *nostrils and become loathsome to* [them], *because* [they] *have rejected the LORD* ... [weeping] *"Why did we ever leave Egypt?"*[t]

*****

"It is an orient wind that blows today," said Cheletra, looking up while she and two other women washed their clothes in a stream, "a gale that suddenly darkens the skies."

In a few moments, Shum pointed upward. "Birds! They are birds. It is a plague of birds."

As they came closer, Ruth cried out, "Now look! They fall like rain!"

"They will engulf us. Get to shelter!" Cheletra shouted.

While many people took cover, the quail fell exhausted, teeming on the earth so that little ground was visible. The people came out, many with bags, and began to gather them. The women built small fires to roast some of them.

"Remember what God ordered," Moses reminded them.

"Who is He to tell us when to stop?" groaned many.

The people did not pick up simply one day's worth, as God had ordered, but ravenously collected for thirty-six continuous hours and began gorging themselves on the longed-for quail meat. Before many could swallow the meat, God's righteous wrath was set fire, unleashing a plague.[u]

*****

Coresha was roasting three quail on a small fire next to a full bag and baking some manna into cakes, when the two men appeared at the doorway of her tent. Before they could say anything, she inquired of them, "Have you seen Lashinar? He has been out with the men all day."

The men went outside and brought the lifeless body into the tent and laid it at her feet. His stilled, cold mouth was full of meat.

"He is only one of many," they said. "We are so sorry."

"Oh, Lashinar, my love, my dear and only love," she cried as she knelt beside him, laying her head on his chest. "Oh, my husband. And I had not even told you that I am with child, perhaps a son for you, the one you wished for, to teach, to hold, to love. Oh, Lashinar …"

Wailing arose from each tribe as grief and remorse seized the victims' families. They were stunned that a plague would be directed against them.

*****

The bodies of those consumed by the plague were buried and the campsite named Kibroth-hattavah, meaning "graves of craving."[4] Moses could only hope that the vulgar gluttony of the people had been removed.

*****

It was time to move again. Trumpets sounded and the march resumed. They journeyed two days farther north to a place named Hazeroth, where the cloud settled, the tabernacle was assembled, God invested Himself within it, and the people camped.

*****

Two days later, Miriam drew Aaron aside as they stood outside their neighboring tents. "God seems annoyed with Moses' leadership. Our brother broke the sacred tablets, we've had to beg for water, then food, and now the plague. He is incompetent."

Aaron sighed. "What do you want?"

"God has gotten so wrapped up in Moses that He has cast me aside. I was His prophetess in Egypt, but He communicates through me no more. Besides that, Moses is indebted to us, Aaron. Where would he have been without me? I saved him. Through the years, while we slogged in mud, he was carried in chariots and spoiled. We kept our promise to keep his birth a secret. But don't you see, Aaron? God has chosen us just as much as he chose Moses."[5]

"You speak sense, Miriam. I have a title and a number of duties to perform now, as high priest" said Aaron, "but still little authority and even less influence.

God still speaks to Moses frequently and meets with him exclusively. He has given him authority over all aspects of the lives of the people: the judging of their sins, the many laws, their relationship with God, even details of tabernacle construction. God has spoken to me with Moses only twice since the calf, and both times it was for simple things, to take a census and to put in place His camping order for the tribes.[v] God even tells Moses how I am to conduct such events as the sacrifices, feasts, and temple rituals. I am just his underling. Besides, I am older and should be leading instead of him."

Miriam smiled. "Of course. See what could be ours, a protected, intimate relationship with God, leaders of these people now and in the promised land of Canaan later. Great honor would be ours. Aaron, I have a plan. We'll use his marriage."

And the LORD heard them.

*****

The two called a meeting of Moses, the tribal leaders, and many of the elders in the courtyard. Miriam began. "You all know of God's statute that we must never marry outside of our own nation, don't you? Moses' wife is a non-Israelite woman, a Cushite, a marriage that makes him a sinner in God's eyes. He does not deserve to lead. Has the LORD indeed spoken only through Moses? Has He not spoken through us as well?"[w]

Moses was surprised, but his meekness silenced his tongue. However, this was not so with God, who appeared as the cloud at the doorway of the tabernacle and called the three to Him. He spoke directly to Miriam and to Aaron, bristling, *"If there is a prophet among you, I, the LORD, shall make Myself known to him in a vision … in a dream. Not so, with My servant, Moses. He is faithful in all My household; with him I speak mouth to mouth…."* Then God questioned them. *"Why then were you not afraid to speak … against Moses?"*[x] In His burning anger, God afflicted Miriam with leprosy, her skin becoming as white as snow.[y]

Aaron anxiously called on his brother, remembering how God had healed Moses' leprous hand. "Oh, my lord, I beg you, do not account this sin to us in which we have acted foolishly…. Do not let her be like one dead, whose flesh is half eaten away."[z]

Moses prayed for healing, and God answered that she must leave the camp for seven days to be cleansed. She gathered some food, donned a shawl, and left in disgrace. The entire camp knew of her deed. At the end of the week she returned, shamed and humbled, but healed. God had answered Moses' prayer. Although Miriam had been the one punished for challenging God's special servant, Aaron's growing envy of his brother had surfaced.

Endnotes

1. For the story of Hobab, Numbers 10:29–32.
2. Moving the tabernacle, Numbers 3:17–28.
3. Taberah means "burning" according to Cheyne and Black, Encyclopedia Biblica. Wikipedia.
4. "Campsite named Kibroth-hattavah, meaning 'graves of craving'" according to the footnote for Numbers 11:34 in the Ryrie Study Bible.
5. The story of Miriam's revolt is told in Numbers 12.

J. Roger Nelson, M.D.

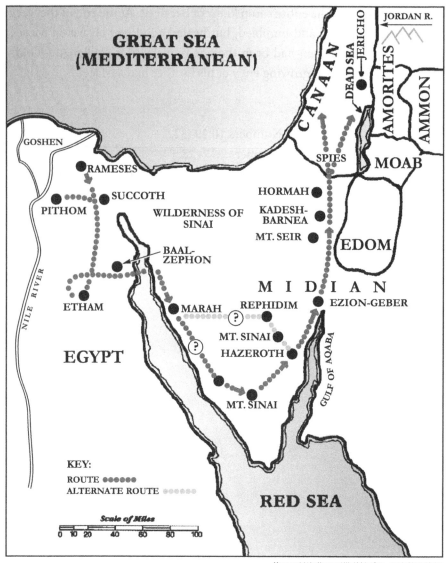

GREAT SEA
(MEDITERRANEAN)

JORDAN R.

CANAAN

DEAD SEA
JERICHO

AMORITES

AMMON

MOAB

GOSHEN

RAMESES

SPIES

PITHOM

SUCCOTH

HORMAH

WILDERNESS OF
SINAI

KADESH-
BARNEA

MT. SEIR

EDOM

BAAL-
ZEPHON

NILE RIVER

ETHAM

MARAH

REPHIDIM

MIDIAN

EZION-GEBER

(?)

MT. SINAI

(?)

HAZEROTH

GULF OF AQABA

EGYPT

MT. SINAI

KEY:
ROUTE ●●●●●●
ALTERNATE ROUTE ○○○○○○

Scale of Miles
0 10 20   40   60   80   100

RED SEA

Map copyright by Hammond World Atlas Corp. —used with permission.

Chapter 16

Attack!

On Miriam's return the congregation broke camp and traveled north from Hazeroth into the desert, following the cloud. They trudged through that dry wilderness for eight more days, finally entering a well-watered valley between rolling hills north of Mount Seir and near the town of Kadesh-barnea, where they camped. Scouts were dispatched and they confirmed, as Hobab had said, that the Israelites were only a one-day's march from Canaan.[1]

After a two-day rest, Moses called the leaders together at the northern boundary of the camp and addressed them. "Tomorrow, you are to instruct your warriors to go north to the hill country and begin the occupation of Canaan, the land which God has given us. Your army will leave at sunrise, and the support will follow immediately."

The leaders responded by fidgeting, looking down at shuffling feet, fingers rubbing dry lips. Ahira spoke up. "Moses, we have been observed by their sentries for the last two days, and word of our presence has certainly reached their captains. We know nothing firsthand about their fortifications or their weaponry—information we need to acquire and carefully evaluate before we act, as any army would."

Gamaliel said, "That is hilly country, Moses, and their troops may be scattered, hiding, ready to ambush us. We had better send men before us to see by which routes we should travel."

"I doubt that is necessary," Moses responded. "God told us that He or His angel would prepare the way for our victory. But if you insist, I shall take this to God."

Moses walked to the tabernacle and entered the holy of holies, saying, "Our people are hesitant to attack."

God granted their wish, repeating, *"Send out for yourself men so that they may spy out the land of Canaan, which I am going to give to the sons of Israel … send a man from each of their fathers' tribes."*[a]

Moses returned to the meeting with God's approval. "Each of you, select a strong, agile spy who is also able to learn dialects easily. Now, who will they be?"

Shelumiel of Simeon spoke first. "I suppose that Shaphat will be ours."

Nahshon of Judah added, "Who would be the most able I have except for Caleb, son of Jephunneh? He is forty years old but strong in body, mind, and trust in God."

After a long pause, Elishama spoke softly. "I am loath to volunteer anyone on such a trip, but the best man from our tribe is Joshua, son of Nun. Moses, he is your assistant. Will you allow him to go?"

"I can get by without him for a while. Yes, he may go for you."

Eliasaph, Pagiel, and Nethanel resisted assigning a man, but in the end, each leader appointed a representative, until there were twelve names.

Early the next morning, well before sunup, Moses spoke to the twelve before sending them out. "Go up beyond the desert into the hill country. Spread out to the Jordan River, to the Sea, even to Lebanon, if possible. Gauge the strength of the defenses of their cities, the might of their men, the quality of their land, and bring back some of the fruit grown there because it is the time of the first ripe grapes.[b] Be back in forty days."

*****

The next day, as the first streaks of dawn lightened the night sky, the twelve men set out to the north with small bags of goods and money, spreading out in pairs. They pulled cowls over their hair and cinched light robes about themselves so they could mingle and observe. They brushed through gates into cities where some took transient jobs to learn about the surroundings and earn money for their food, camouflaging their mission. They learned to converse sparingly in the local language. Among their various destinations, one pair went to the hill country, one reached the land of Lebanon nearly one hundred miles to the north, and another on to the Great Sea.

The spies returned safely to camp at Kadesh-barnea after forty days, bringing with them luxuriant fruits. There were pomegranates and figs; two men brought a single cluster of grapes that was so heavy it had to be carried on a pole between them. They told of a lush land that flows with milk and honey[c] as God had foretold. The people eagerly listened to them. They accepted the report of a land of plenty lying ahead of them as confirmation of another of God's promises.

The spies revealed the whereabouts of the six different nations God had foretold lived there; some by the Great Sea, some in the north, and some by the Jordan river. A new group of people had taken up residence in the nearby southern Canaan hill country west of the Salt Sea: the contentious Amalekites. Toward evening, the spies finished their report by saying that their great and splendid cities were well fortified.

The listeners began to worry.

Moses tried to reassure them by reminding them of God's provision. "Do not be shocked, nor fear them. The LORD your God who goes before you will Himself fight on your behalf, just as He did for you in Egypt before your eyes, and in the wilderness, where you saw how the LORD your God carried you, just as a man carries his son."ᵈ

Joshua and Caleb also spoke up encouragingly. "We should by all means go up and take possession of it, for we shall surely overcome it,"ᵉ said Caleb.

The other spies, however, reported that Canaan was a hostile land, and all the people whom they saw in it were men of great size. "There also we saw the Nephilim,"ᶠ they said ominously, referring to the giant sons of human mothers with fallen gods from heaven as their fathers. "We seemed to ourselves no larger than grasshoppers."ᵍ

Moses heard waves of condemning murmuring from those gathered there. "Because the Lord hates us, He has brought us out of the land of Egypt to deliver us into the hand of the Amalekites to destroy us." ʰ

Moses stepped forward, proclaiming, "If you only knew. The only thing He hates is when He must discipline us—whom He loves. Now, be strong. Let us move out the day after tomorrow in the morning."

The crowd scattered, grumbling against the order.

The next morning, Gamaliel and Eliasaph, among the last leaders to retain a trust in God, conversed outside of Gamaliel's tent. Eliasaph said, "Moses asked us to attack an entrenched giant enemy, a cricket charging into a crocodile. I am feeling lost myself, Gamaliel, afraid and worried for my family."

"Be patient, Eliasaph, and keep strong. We need a plan. Meet me here tonight."

Eliasaph did not appear for the meeting.

*****

Just after the next daybreak, Gamaliel left his tent and, with a sudden sense of relief, blended quietly into the crowd that assembled along with the leaders before Moses.

Ahira spoke first. "Why is the LORD bringing us into this land to fall by the sword? Our wives and our little ones will become plunder! Would that we had died in the land of Egypt or in this wilderness!"[i]

Shouts soon erupted from the crowd. "No, it will not be so! We will not go!"

Fear tore through the crowd and, with it, such anger against Moses and Aaron that many picked up sizable rocks. With wide eyes, they raised their hands. As the first stone was hurled, their leaders ran between the brothers and the crowd, stopping them.

Abidan said in calmer tones, "Moses, even we leaders are withdrawing our support for this senseless attack, hopeless even with the help of the ark and the priests."

"We are uncertain whether God will intercede for us," Ahira added. "And besides, we're not well enough trained or equipped to defeat the Nephilim. No, Moses, God must give us a more concrete guarantee that we can succeed in battle."

Gamaliel hesitantly said, "The people not only refuse to fight, but they wish to go back to Egypt. At least in slavery, we will stay alive. We will retrace our steps using the maps Elishama has made for us."

Nethanel yelled for all to hear, "Let us appoint a leader and return to Egypt—now!"[j] Then, turning to Moses, he added, "Moses, you are on your own. You may come with us if you wish, but not as our leader, for we leave your God here."

Moses was stunned. He could not let the journey end here. As he scanned his leaders, he held out his hands to them and called out, "Will you desert your God? The God who freed you from cruel slavery, prepared you, your nation's hope, for this invasion, even guaranteed your victory? Remember, three times you have vowed to follow God." Becoming more impassioned, he cried out, "Don't you realize that this is the goal for which all Israelites, each man, woman, and child, has suffered for four centuries? The enemy will be delivered, devoured by God."

Nahshon interrupted. "Have we earned that deliverance?" As he turned around, he said over his shoulder, "Your God is hard to please."

Moses tried once more. "You are not abandoning a stone statue. You will tear God's heart out." He paused. Then, his voice rose as he half ordered, half pleaded, "Stay!"

The people grumbled, moving away.

"All right," Moses continued, "but be warned; He cannot, by any means, leave the guilty unpunished."[k]

Then he said softly to himself, "Leave God and go back? Never! I prefer the reproach of God to the riches of Egypt.[l] I stay … with or without the people."

* * * * *

Vexed, Moses and Aaron fell on their faces in front of the crowd. Caleb and Joshua, distraught, passionately tore their clothes in exasperation. Caleb shouted to the people that Canaan was an exceedingly good land. "If the LORD is pleased with us, He will bring us into this land and give it to us. Only do not rebel against the LORD, and do not fear the people of the land, for they shall be our prey! Their protection has been removed from them, and the LORD is with us."[m]

Joshua added, "God did not promise that He would deliver our enemies to us at Rephidim, but here, He does! Just believe Him."

Deep fear and perceived betrayal closed the ears of the congregation. In great anger, many of the men armed themselves again with stones and approached the four, intent on killing them.

Suddenly, the glory of the LORD rose up over the tabernacle for all to see, stopping the would-be assassins where they stood. Moses got up and hurried to it, and God lamented, *"How long will this people spurn Me and not believe in Me, despite all the signs which I performed in their midst?"*[n]

Immediately, God sent a plague that killed the ten spies who spread the bad report, sparing Joshua and Caleb. He also told Moses that He would send pestilence to destroy the others, and He would begin anew with the faithful four and their families, to make a *nation greater and mightier than they,*[o] as He had offered at the golden calf.

Such an improbable offer briefly challenged the struggling, dispirited Moses: to have a fresh start with a small community of believing, trusting families; then, to multiply and thrive in God's garden spot later. But Moses dispelled such thoughts; he was their appointed shepherd. They were still his responsibility. And God was not just allowing them to return to Egypt as they planned. He would kill them all.

He interceded again with God, as he had at Sinai. "If Thou dost slay this people, then the Egyptians will say, 'Because the Lord could not bring this people into the land which He promised them by oath, therefore He slaughtered them in the wilderness.'"p He boldly repeated God's own words: "The Lord is slow to anger and abundant in lovingkindness, forgiving iniquity and transgression."q Moses continued, "Pardon, I pray, the iniquity of this people according to the greatness of Thy lovingkindness, just as Thou hast forgiven them from Egypt even until now."r This time Moses did not offer his own life for the people; his patience with them had run out.

God listened to Moses' pleas, then added, *"I have pardoned them according to your word, but, indeed, as I live, all the earth will be filled with the glory of the* Lord. *Surely, all the men who have seen My glory and My signs ... in Egypt and the wilderness, yet have put Me to the test these ten times and have not listened to My voice, shall by no means see the land which I swore to their fathers."s*

The pardoned nation of Israel would survive. Their sin was forgiven, but not its consequences. God had said that *"He will by no means leave the guilty unpunished."t* All men who were over the age of twenty at the outset of the journey were condemned to die en route to Canaanu except Caleb, *"because he had a different spirit and* [Joshuav who have] *followed Me fully."w*

The journey, originally planned to last only two years, would now be a forty-year ordeal, one year for each day of the ill-fated spying trip. God informed the condemned, *"And your sons shall be shepherds for forty years in the wilderness, and they shall suffer for your unfaithfulness, until your corpses lie in the wilderness ... surely this I will do to all this evil congregation who are gathered together against Me."x*

The irrevocable judgment on the older men was made by a saddened God as He redirected His hopes to the younger men.

He then commanded the people to abandon their camp the next day, turn around, and return southward toward the Red Sea. They were not to encounter the nations of Canaan or the Amalekites for God would not be among them.

*****

Early the next morning, the twelve leaders met outside of the courtyard, some sitting on the ground, most standing. Aaron was occupied with Moses elsewhere.

Shelumiel began: "What a harsh punishment! Thirty-eight more years of this grueling walking and camping! Just because we left Him, knowing that we would be defeated. He won't even let us go back to Egypt. The men of our generation will all suffer and die sometime in the next thirty-eight years. Will it be tomorrow or thirty-eight years from now?"

Nethanel added: "It is not right that God would turn His bitter disappointment upon us. I said that we would never make it to Canaan, but not this way. Our tribe lies in the depth of mourning and anger."

"The dreadful, quick execution of the ten spies put fear and trembling into us," said Elishama. "It reminds me of Aaron's two sons. His wrath is not to be toyed with. Our lives are expendable in this uninvited, risky venture of His."

Pagiel, sadly, "How disappointed God must be. At least our families and c-c-c-children will be spared."

"I was looking forward to the benefits of Canaan. Now what? Death," said a distraught Nahshon. "We need God's mercy on us."

Soldier Ahira offered, "We do have an option as my tribe sees it. We older ones are all doomed unless we act. We have an army, and if we were able to defeat the Amalekites before, we should prevail over them and the Canaanites. Let us go up tomorrow and attack the nations of Canaan. God promised victory once; that offer may still stand. Perhaps He will have pity on us, and we can change His mind and our destiny."

Gamaliel responded, "If you attack them, you will show zeal. But do you think God would prefer contrition—remorse—instead?"

Elishama countered, "We are angry, not contrite. Let us go up and fight. Joshua will lead us again, and God will take notice."

Abidan raised a crooked finger, "I, too, am against direct confrontation. Suppose we just put away, even burn, our hidden idols, humbly kneel in supplication and ask forgiveness from God?"

Eliasaph answered, "A good idea, Abidan. But this camp is seething with anger, disappointment, and remorse. Remember, it was the king of Ninevah who commanded repentance of the people—and they obeyed; it would take Moses to convince this mob, a near-impossible task."

Elishama repeated, "A terrible anxiety has thrown our camp into uncontrolled agitation. Something must be done. I am for fighting."

Ahira, "How many agree with Elishama and me?"

Of the other ten, six hands were raised.

*****

Ahira and Elishama were assigned to meet with Joshua and Caleb. Gamaliel and Eliasaph accompanied them. On the way, Ahira asked the others, "I wonder if Joshua and Caleb will still be willing to help us since the people just sought to kill them. And also, since those two are excluded by God from early death ..."

"... because God said that they have followed the LORD completely[y] and have a different spirit,[z] Moses told us," finished Eliasaph.

Elishama said, "Before our spying venture, they were just as you and I. Was it that 'different spirit' that gave them the courage to defy our stoning?"

"And why did He put the spirit on them" asked Ahira, "as He did on Moses, the seventy elders, and the tabernacle builders, and not the rest of the spies?"

"Perhaps it was because," sparked Gamaliel, "they alone believed in God's incredible promise of victory as He commanded them to go up. God would not command something impossible for us to do."

"Quit complaining and just believe, right, Gamaliel?" said Eliasaph. "Then, hopefully, we receive the spirit that would give us an additional power to obey His difficult commands when we set our minds to it. But until then, we still have the sacrifices."

"Can we change our attitudes?" asked Ahira.

"We must try," said Gamaliel.

*****

The four entered Caleb's tent, where he and Joshua were conferring.

Ahira began. "The leaders have voted to go up. Joshua, are you still willing to lead?"

"I will, if that is your decision, although we go without God's pleasure," submitted Joshua. "Perhaps this action will draw God's mercy. By which route shall we go?"

Caleb said, "God instructed us to go up through the hill country, west of the Salt Sea, although neither Joshua nor I scouted that area as spies. And those who did are now dead. We know nothing about the defenses there."

"We know that the cities in the plains are heavily fortified with high walls," said Ahira. "They have chariots and the Nephilim giants supposedly live there. The Amalekites who live in the mountains of the hill country with the Canaanites had no giants when we defeated them before."

Joshua pointedly affirmed, "There are certainly no chariots in those mountains. We will go up and fight just as the LORD commanded us. It should be easy to go up into the hill country."[aa]

Elishama said confidently, "When we are victorious, we can then proceed northward from there."

In the morning, every soldier armed himself. Moses spoke to the leaders and the army: "You are breaking the command of the LORD. The LORD said to me '[Tell them,] *do not go up nor fight for I am not among you lest you be defeated before your enemies.*'"[bb]

Neither Moses, the priests, nor the ark accompanied them.

*****

What they did not know, with the mountains and deep valleys of the hill country, was that "this region is difficult to get into and out of and thus has its natural protection."[2]

Zuriel watched them depart from a hilltop nearby and penned these lines:
The Amalekites crouch before our ill-advised charge,
wondering why we must again dispense the bane of widowhood,
while Sinai's rills are still scarlet, her ravens sated with dead flesh.

*****

The Israelites' power, however, had remained behind. The Amalekites fought zealously from their entrenched, mountain strongholds, killed many, and routed the rest.

*****

> Zuriel wrote more as he observed the warriors return with the wounded:
> Their flesh-tears profound, foes' blades scarlet, wet;
> thirsty arrows lodged, all senselessly wrought.
> Their wastage He'll mourn.
> Know! His Word, with depths of wisdom, inscrutable,
> once uttered cannot be retrieved,
> but purifies, sears, or saves by its own execution.[cc]

*****

The Amalekites stopped their chase at Hormah. The beaten soldiers bivouacked there with its oasis, where they paused to bandage and succor the wounded before continuing on to Kadesh-barnea.

They received no pity from Moses but only a stern rebuke for their impulsive, costly, defiant attack.

As a result of the battle, the whole earth would soon know that the Israelites attacked without provocation, but that they were not invincible.

Endnote

1. The events of this chapter are based on Numbers, chapters 13 and 14.
2. "protection," *The Hill Country of Judah*; Dr. Carl Rasmussen's blog. Internet.

Chapter 17

Thirty-Eight Wasted Years

At the end of the fifth week at Kadesh-barnea, while the people were resting and beginning to deal with their botched future, a vicious plague of cough, fever, chills, and mental confusion spread throughout the village, attacking the older men. All who fell ill died. Eliasaph was one of the first persons to contract it, coughing uncontrollably from lung congestion, feeling the strength of his mighty arms ebb away. His tribe prayed fervently for his healing, many in gratitude for the prayers he had often offered for them, but to no avail. His self-absorbed wife remained tearless.

Along with the several hundred who also died of the illness was Ahiezar, leader of Dan, a quiet, deep thinker and tactful problem-solver. He died within five days of his first rigor, survived by a wife and three children.

Pagiel and Ahira happened upon Nahshon and Gamaliel at the edge of a large field that was being used as a cemetery. It was depressing watching wagonloads of bodies being deposited there.

"Have we witnessed the first of God's ravaging, or was this just a random disease like He put on the Egyptians?" asked Ahira.

Nahshon said, "God will not murder us all for a little hesitancy to fight. He needs us, as we need Him."

"Perhaps. At any rate, Eliasaph's wisdom will be sorely missed," said Pagiel. "None could m-m-match his faith in God, at least for most of the trip. Ahiezar's quiet, f-f-f-f-firm leadership will be difficult to replace. We must choose new leaders from the tribes of Gad and Dan."

"And young ones too," said Ahira, "those in their teen years when we left Egypt, who will have a chance to survive the trip."

"A trip of attrition. The months ahead will tell," predicted Gamaliel.

*****

On the first day of the seventh month, the sons of Aaron blew Bezalel's trumpets and the people celebrated the civil new year. A bull was sacrificed.

Ten days later, the Day of Atonement was observed. Aaron, his sons, the leaders, and some elders gathered in the courtyard while a number of lay people stayed reverently outside of it. Aaron was dressed in his priestly clothes. With assistance, he sacrificed a bull for himself and one of two goats for the people. He took some of the blood of each animal and entered the holiest room—that singular day of the year—into God's presence and sprinkled it on the mercy seat, purging the tabernacle of any and all accumulated, unconfessed sins of his family and of the people.

Levite assistants took the remains of the animals outside the camp and burned them up at the clean place.

"Now bring me the second of the congregation's goats," he ordered his sons.

As the sons held the goat, Aaron grasped its horns and rapidly confessed all of the known and potential sins of the congregation over it, then sent it alive into the wilderness. "The blood purifies the temple; the scapegoat[a] carries the sins themselves away," he said.

Then Aaron concluded the ceremony by sacrificing his and the congregation's ram as burnt offerings.

Five days later, the week-long Feast of the Ingathering of the Crops began, commemorating the anticipated harvests to come in Canaan. It was a festive week, enjoying Gods favor on them.

*****

God's favor also fell upon Coresha's pregnancy. During the later stages, an uncommon energy filled her, perhaps, she reasoned, because the child was the only part of Lashinar she had been able to cling to. Be it daughter or son, it must look like Lashinar: the soft-lidded eyes, the wide mouth, the large hands. They were not the marks of beauty, as such, but they would bring him back; not in his death pose, but alive, loving, even self-willed. Would she be able to nurture this child's independence while keeping it close by and safe?

After twenty-three hours of labor, the midwife helped Coresha bring forth a normal, healthy, baby boy with a cry heard throughout the community of Manasseh. The cry was greeted with relief, then smiles, by those who heard it, a cry announcing that Lashinar's seed had sprouted, and a warning that the community should prepare to change. Little Machir had arrived.

The first males to see Coresha's jewel were Lashinar's good friend Sorin and his son Hanniel. They made a hesitant visit that first night. "Big cry, big mouth," Hanniel thought when he first saw Machir. On his third daily visit, he was allowed to hold the baby. Hanniel felt an affection unknown before. Thereafter, he treated Machir as a little brother and planned to take him to prayers with the Levites, carry him on hikes into the woods and hills, help with his schooling, and show him the ways of a shepherd.

Machir was six months old when the cloud moved away from Kadesh-barnea in a westerly direction, drawing the camp with it, before settling fifteen miles away. During the year they had been at camp, many Israelites had died of another disease marked by progressive weakness and wasting of the muscles,[b] first of the legs, then the arms, and finally the chest. It had struck the older men, a debilitating illness proving fatal. The people left large graveyards on the northern edge of the old camp as they moved on to a new site with better grass and fruit trees.

After fourteen months at that location, the cloud rose and moved off, this time settling twenty miles to the southwest. Many people had died there from strange accidents. God had not told Moses that the cloud would stay at this new site for five years, so anticipating departure at any moment, the people planted none of the few seeds they had. Without grain, no bread or cakes were baked. The people, sustained by manna, complained less.

In the fourth year there, another plague struck the camp, this one with symptoms of intense, persistent diarrhea and vomiting. It claimed hundreds of older men and women. Nahshon, Elizur, and Elishama were among those affected. Nahshon lost considerable weight with the disease, succumbing after ten days, while his wife Susken ministered to him. He was buried in his white robe. During his illness, he revealed the location of his hidden cache of jewels to her. After his death, troubled by the booty, Susken retrieved the jewels and secretly left them outside Moses' tent one night, with a note to add them to the tabernacle treasury. Caleb was chosen to take Nashon's place, to lead the tribe of Judah. Although older, he had become a popular choice with a promised survival into Canaan.

On the eighth day of his illness, having lost much of his renowned "barley" hair, Elishama died. Though he was industrious and hardworking, his secret mapmaking of the route back to Egypt had showed his lack of confidence in God's mission. When weakened by his condition, he entrusted the maps to Kemuel, his personal choice to succeed him as tribal leader.

Elizur, Reuben's leader, a quiet, humble man, also died.

The dead were buried as quickly as possible as God moved the camp out farther to the south, to a lightly wooded area where the grass was less abundant. The animals would require large supplements of manna to survive.

*****

Not all accepted their dismal fate. Before moving to the next site, twenty-two older men organized themselves and, led by Kemuel, slipped away from the camp one night. Using Elishama's maps, they traveled southward, heading for Egypt. Before they had gone twenty-five miles, four died of snake bites and another two from an acute lung congestion. The remaining ones limped back into camp, humiliated.

*****

A council meeting was called three days later. "Are the rest of you prepared," asked Moses, "to continue this course with God, or will you abandon Him? Will any repeat Kemuel's disastrous escapade?" Kemuel silently bowed his head.

"No," said Kenan, the stonemason from Gad selected to replace Eliasaph. "We new leaders represent tribes who do see, hear, and remember. We may not always understand fully or always be right, but we talk among ourselves of this God often, seeking to please Him. Having a god in our camp is never allowed to be taken for granted."

Moses said, "Although we continue on this march of God-sent attrition, He continues to provide for us. Even though we walk daily in our sandals and shoes, they do not wear out; and your clothes, often washed, show no signs of wear even after thirty years."[t]

"Yes," Pagiel added, "and I hope that the miracle continues because it may be a long time before we leave this mou-mou-mou-mountain, until God sees a different attitude in us."

Nethanel said in a tired voice, "I won't leave, ever. I hate worrying about when I will die."

"Trust Him, Nethanel," Caleb said. "I believe those who die are with God in some way, even the sacrificed animals. But meanwhile, we must mature into holy people and believe in God's promises. Moses knows this, and so does Joshua."

Abidan said as he turned to face Kenan, "We have lost five of our original leaders. The survival of the community rests with you younger ones."

"They know their responsibilities," said Caleb.

"Turn your words into action and all will benefit," said Abidan.

*****

At God's instruction, the congregation moved out to a site fifteen miles to the west, near another wadi, where the tabernacle was set up, and a camp was established.

After six years there, God told Moses that He had altered some requirements of the sacrifices. At Sinai, the limited supply of oil and wine was rationed to the mandatory sacrifice of morning and evening lambs. However, in Canaan, one to two quarts of oil, one to two quarts of wine, and three to six quarts of grain would have to be added to each burnt and peace offering. The oil would be produced by manually beating bushels of gathered olives, the wine processed by trampling troughs of picked grapes, and the grain hand-harvested. The process required countless hours of vigorous labor for sacrifices that were to be simply poured out onto the fire—true sacrifices, not mere donations.

God permitted the foreigners who traveled consistently with the Israelites, the sojourners, to worship and to sacrifice to Him, to be under the same laws, and to be judged just as the Hebrews were.[d]

God instituted material reminders to help His people obey Him. He required each Israelite to wear tassels on the corners of his garments, tied by a cord of blue, *to remember all the commandments of the* LORD *... to do them and not follow after* [their] *own heart and eyes ... and be holy to* [their] *God.*[e] Tassels with blue cords; how could anyone miss them?

*****

But Korah[1] did, a Levite and a member of the privileged family of Kohath who carried the covered, holy tabernacle items. He was jealous of Moses and piqued by the growing numbers of the dead and because of the senseless wandering projected upon them. He was certain that he could do better and, power-hungry, he set out to overthrow Moses. Korah remembered the stories about the two-person threat to Moses' leadership brought by Miriam and Aaron

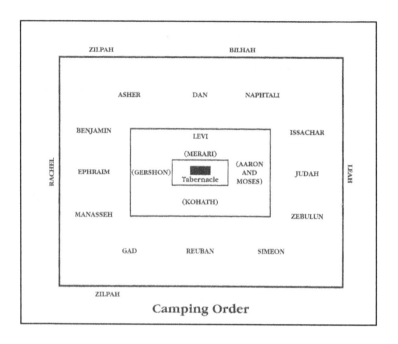

Camping Order

early on the march and her resulting leprosy. So, he sought cohorts. He held secret meetings with three friends of the degraded tribe of Reuben—Dathan, Abiram, and On—who were camped in adjacent tents. They were looking for ways to regain God's approval—their ancestor Reuben had fornicated with his father's concubine—just as the tribe of Levi had achieved by killing at golden calf. Because of widespread dissatisfaction, Korah was able to persuade thirty-five others to join him, some of whom were in his own tribe. God would have to listen to and deal with such a force. However, when this throng finally came to threaten God's two chosen men, the three schemers were absent—Dathan and Abiram cowered in their tents, while On quit the insurrection altogether.

"You have gone far enough, Moses!" shouted Korah, who was half the age of Moses. Pointing to the gathering, he said, "All the congregation is holy, every one of them, and the LORD is in their midst." He raised his fist to Moses and Aaron. "Why do you exalt yourselves above the assembly of the LORD?"ᶠ Then he added, "Any of us, including me, is fit to lead."

The accusations shocked Moses, who fell face down before Korah in humility. Rising, Moses said, "Tomorrow morning, the LORD will show who is His, who is holy."ᵍ He told Korah and his company to take censers, fill them with burning coals and incense, and bring them before God the next day. Aaron was to do the same.[h]

Noting the sizeable contingent of Levites among the rebels, Moses echoed Korah's phrase in parting. "You have gone far enough, you sons of Levi! Hear now! Is it not enough that the God of Israel has separated you from the rest of the congregation of Israel … to do the service of the tabernacle of the LORD, and to stand before the congregation to minister to them? And are you seeking for the priesthood also?"[i] There was no answer.

Moses dispatched an aide to summon the two conspirators, Dathan and Abiram who refused to come up.

Moses became angry, turned toward the tabernacle, and asked God to deal with this unruly mob, pointing out that he himself had done nothing to provoke them.

As they walked back to their tents, Aaron confided to Moses, "I am troubled, Moses. A number of fine men have joined Korah. Since his uprising is against the LORD, if we are confirmed as the holy ones, will they all perish?"

"We will see tomorrow," said Moses.

*****

The next morning, Korah and his co-conspirators appeared before Moses and Aaron in the courtyard near the front of the tabernacle, each with a filled censer, hoping to be chosen. Dutifully, Aaron had his censer also. Dathan and Abiram had summoned up their courage and were present, but On was nowhere to be found. Korah was so confident that God would bless his followers and himself that he had assembled other members of the congregation to observe the event.

The powerful, resplendent light suddenly appeared before the tabernacle, illuminating the skies. Moses and Aaron approached it cautiously as the people withdrew, and God spoke from within it: *"Separate yourselves from among this congregation that I may consume them instantly."*[j]

When Moses relayed the message, Korah became agitated. "God must hear my side of this dispute! We have not joined all these men to us in this cause without just reason. We deserve an advocate and a trial, to argue on our behalf. Ask God to make His decision only after all the evidence has been presented."

There was silence from God. There would be no trial.

Moses sought clemency for the many innocent onlookers, asking God, "When one man sins, wilt Thou be angry with the entire congregation?"[k]

God listened and instructed Moses to have Korah, Dathan, and Abiram return to their tents. The three men and their families reluctantly complied, encouraged to do so by the crowd of curious onlookers who followed them. Moses shouted for all to hear, "Get back lest you be swept away in their sin." As the crowd receded, Moses said, "If these men die the death of all men ... then the LORD has not sent me. But if the LORD brings about an entirely new thing and the ground opens its mouth and swallows them ... then you will understand that these men have spurned the LORD."[l]

A sudden earthquake occurred, the ground split open, and Korah, Dathan, Abiram, and their families were flung screaming, deep into its crevasses. Within minutes, the earth closed[m] back over them to the horror of those who then watched as multiple bursts of fire cremated each of Korah's other schemers. The frightened crowd fell back amid stifled or loud screams from the women who feared that they might be next. Shocked husbands hugged their wives as they hurriedly sought their own tents.

Then God instructed Moses to have Eleazar make a large hammered plate from their censers to serve as a covering for the bronze altar. It also served as a warning to the people that none but a priest should ever burn incense before the LORD, that he might not become like Korah.[n]

*****

It was dusk as Moses and Aaron walked toward the edge of the camp, past groups of stunned and terrified people scrambling aside to let them pass. The brothers left the camp and walked silently into the night alone, still shaken by the ravages of God's swift vengeance.

As they continued, deep in their thoughts, they spoke occasionally. Moses said, "I suggested an earthquake, and God answered with one! What unwavering support He gives me! May I never turn from Him. And yet, for me, it is a fearful responsibility. Had my anger not provoked God to deal with Korah and his followers, the earthquake and fire may not have occurred."

"They rebelled against God, not you," Aaron reassured. "God's growing wrath was justified, although certainly severe."

"Still, I must exercise caution to protect the people," said Moses.

Aaron was silent.

After a while, Moses said, "Many of those burned had been our supposed friends and supporters. What a loss." Then he asked, "Was Korah known to you in Rameses?"

"I hardly knew him," said Aaron, "but he had a reputation as a born leader. Too bad he misused his talent."

As night wore on, the exercise and conversation calmed them. Finally, as the sun rose and they returned to camp, a lingering question remained in Moses' mind: "How to restore their trust in me and to win them to obedience to God?"

With sagging confidence, Moses whispered, "God, you must do that."

*****

During that same night, many of the frightened congregation convened with their leaders. Tensions had grown to the breaking point.

Abidan said, "I thought when we finally left the bulging cemeteries around Mount Seir that God's wrath would have been satisfied. But now He has executed so many more."

"Eleazar said it was partly because they all burned incense in censers before God. And who drew them into that sin but an angry Moses!" blurted Samuel of Reuben, who replaced Elizur.

Nethanel stood with his hands on his hips. "All Korah and the others did was express ideas that many of us share—that Moses and Aaron have too much authority and are too much coddled by God. In Egypt, Moses walked in presenting himself as God's servant. He has no scars on his back, no pieces of his heart torn out, as our fathers had."

Kemuel nodded. "The deaths we suffered when we tried to return to Egypt were too many to just be an accident. I believe Moses has cursed this entire trip."

"We are here because of Moses and Aaron, the people were killed because of Moses, and we will all die because of them," said Samuel.

"You four younger men, bonafide leaders, don't be so hasty," pleaded Gamaliel. "Believe in God's promises of success. But if you persist in your anger and fear, might you evoke more of God's wrath?"

Ignoring old Gamaliel, young Tasun, in place of Ahiezar, said bluntly, "If Moses and Aaron were dead, God would have to deal with us with greater compassion."

"Your arguments hold water," said a resigned Shelumiel.

Most agreed. The spoken convictions of these men found a ready audience in the hearts of the Hebrews, and the word spread, as a flame through dry leaves.

*****

In the morning, a mass of dissatisfied congregants assembled, many in the courtyard and more outside, when the weary Moses and Aaron returned. Zipporah, who had been sleepless and worried by Moses' absence, joined the crowd, hanging back anxiously at its edge.

Tasun and Samuel stepped forward, right into Moses' face, and accused the brothers. "You are the ones who have caused the death of the LORD's people." As the crowd closed in menacingly toward the two, the attention of all was drawn toward the tabernacle, where there appeared again not the cloud, but the brilliant light. *"Get away from among this congregation,"* God again ordered Moses and Aaron, *"that I may consume them instantly."*⁰ The brothers fell prostrate. Moses did not plead for clemency, sensing that God had indeed had His fill of these Israelites, as he himself had.

Lying face down before God, Moses and Aaron heard the wailing as people began to choke, gasp for breath, turn blue, and within minutes, die.

Satisfied at first by God's vindication of him, the plague began to spread indiscriminately. Moses' feelings changed to pity, then to guilt, as so many, he thought, were dying because of him. Drawn once more by responsible duty, he turned to Aaron, saying, "Take your censer and put fire in it from the altar, lay incense on it, and carry it to the congregation, and make atonement for them, for wrath has gone forth from the LORD; the plague has begun!"ᴾ

Aaron felt unbelief! "These were the people who just minutes before hovered over me trying to kill me," he silently winced. "God was doing just what He ought to be doing." Before he said anything, he looked at Moses. Commanding eyes stared back out of a strained face, and he knew he must act. Obediently, but still fearful of the angry mob, he hurried to the tabernacle, filled his censer, and walked toward them. He wove his way between the living and the dying, extending his path outside of the courtyard.

In less than an hour—after Aaron had completely circumscribed and isolated the dead and returned, exhausted, to sit by Moses—God stopped the plague. Tasun and Samuel survived, standing next to Moses.

*****

Zipporah hastily wended her way up through the crowd. When Moses saw her, he grasped her outstretched hand. "The boys?" he asked

"They are safe."

"Walk with me," he requested as they moved through the sorrowful courtyard and continued outside of it to view yet another expanse of carnage and a growing flock of mourners. Moses felt drained. Neither spoke. Finally he said, "The people cannot all be wrong. Perhaps there is one among them who could lead better than I."

Zipporah reassured him, "It was just through these horrors that God endorsed your authority. Persevere, my husband."

"If only they would understand what God is doing and accept that they are being trained for an eternal purpose. Aaron and I are but His hands, hesitant at first but now totally surrendered to His calling."

"No one in their right mind," she said, "the Miriams or the Korahs, should want to trade places with you." They walked toward their tent.

*****

The next morning, Hanniel and eleven-year-old Machir were walking together and ran into Kemuel and Ahira's eldest son, the aggressive but emotional, Jazallun. They stopped.

Hanniel said, "The plague killed so many more than His fire on Korah's conspirators. God continues to ratchet up the severity of His punishments. Their ... our ... resistance must cease."

Machir observed, "Grief, utter despair, has finally replaced the anger of our mourning tribal members, and their fear of God's further wrath has silenced them. They wonder if God hears everything. If they grumble now, it is in whispers."

"Unfortunately," said Kemuel, "the resentment of many of our tribe toward the brothers persists, and their voices, although softer, are far from silent. They feel that they are simply being used as God's puppets in a tragic play, as Tasun and Samuel said."

Jazallun said, "God is bonded to Moses and Aaron; they are His pets. We had better remember that. God doesn't care a shekel for us. We follow Him, but grudgingly."

Machir answered, "Come on, Jazallun. You think it is easy for Him to discipline, even kill, His people? Of course He protects Moses, His steadfastly loyal servant. As to being puppets, remember the rich, fulfilling life you will lead in Canaan and the blessings of your service to others. You are highly honored, the only force God has to carry out His goals. At least now there will be no more threats to kill the brothers."

"I wouldn't count on that," mumbled Jazallun.

Hanniel added, "How disappointed God must be. We must reassure our tribal members of His concern for us."

Their meeting ended.

*****

During subsequent years, the company would follow the cloud from sites near villages Rithmah to Rimmon-perez to Libnah to Rissah to Kehelathah,[q] each of the campsites being about five to fifteen miles apart and arranged in a great meandering circle. They kept Mount Seir[r] in the center and stayed in each place for an average of three years.

The years of freedom passed faster than those of slavery and were met with varying results. A mist of sympathy for the older men sentenced to die hung over the camp as they struggled with their apprehensions.

Those born along the way, by and large, accepted the lengthy journeys as their fathers' due and became accustomed to it. A slowly growing sense of safety filled the younger men who found some peace, and even a smoldering joy, in their traditional community. Creativity returned in the form of plays, songfests, and small orchestras. Occasionally, a comedian, a younger version of Pagiel, arose to interject slices of laughter to lighten their lives.

In the fifteenth year, a heavy board fell on the carpenter Shelumiel's leg. The bone fragments broke through the skin. Although it was bandaged and splinted, it became red, swollen, and pustular. Poultices were applied, but it gradually turned black. Shelumiel grew confused, shouting incoherently, until he finally fell into a coma and died with Abidan at his bedside.

*****

Abidan's trust in God's plan had grown during the trip from Egypt to Sinai. However, fearful and distrusting after the spies' report, he had sided with the deserters. Since then, however, his faith had been restored and he became, again, a steadying influence on his Benjaminites. When another plague of the dreaded lung disease, with coughing, fevers, bloody sputum, and chest pain, swept through the camp, he visited and ministered to the sick until he finally contracted the illness himself. Moses visited and comforted him often until his laborious breathing ceased.

The rekindled loyalty of several of the leaders, including Abidan and Gamaliel, had been a source of welcomed encouragement to Moses, while the people blamed him for the plagues, the growing list of wailing widows and orphans, and their nomadic existence, all the while pointlessly following the cloud. Their belligerence gave Moses occasional concern for his own safety. He also knew that his prayers to God for the plagues to cease, repeated by rote at the leaders' urging, could not be met. In spite of all these challenges, he doggedly maintained a civil, deeply caring, encouraging attitude toward the individual problems of his people.

Through the difficult years, he clung to the promises of conquest and of the plenteous, even possibly altruistic, life they would live in Canaan; once there, contention with his people would end and his family could thrive, with God at its center.

*****

For the most part, Moses also had pleasure in his own family. In his earlier years, he enjoyed fatherhood, sharing his beliefs and ancestral tales with his growing sons and teaching them the skills of shepherding. Now that they were married and had their own families, he enjoyed grandfathering. His chronic concern was for his son Gershom; an Israelite? Although not living in Egypt, he was twenty-one years old at the beginning of the exodus. Was he also doomed to die?

Moses appreciated Zipporah's growing trust in God and the gradual softening of her headstrong obstinacy, taking a shred of credit for his own patient, understanding way with her. She satisfied him and grew to be a valuable, trusted supporter, providing the glue of their mellowing marriage.

*****

Eliab, Zebulun's leader, died two short days after contracting the same illness that claimed Abidan. A quiet, reserved person, he had retained leadership because of his steadfast support for all of his tribal members.

*****

Nethanel's depression worsened over the next year. Nara often stayed up with him during his sleepless nights, listening to his ravings, trying to calm and reassure him. Occasional visits by his son and daughter did not help. He slowly descended into himself, becoming quieter. Pagiel spent seemingly useless hours talking and listening to him. Then one morning, Nethanel's joy returned. He spoke freely and pleasantly to Nara, even straightened up his sleeping area and changed his clothes. Nara arose the next morning to find him lying on his side in a pool of blood near to the door, the handle of his knife protruding from the left side of his chest.

*****

Hanniel was chosen to speak at Nethanel's memorial gathering. He had concluded his voluntary, five-year service as a Nazirite by shaving his long hair and beard, throwing them on the altar fire, and sacrificing his appointed animals. He marked his return to secular life by drinking wine made from the previously forbidden grapes. His resolve to serve God persisted, and he accepted a role with the Levites. His father, Sorin, had died of the stomach disease, but Hanniel perpetuated his father's humility and honesty. His friendship with Machir had remained strong.

"In Nethanel, we have buried another courageous leader," said Hanniel. "Often outspoken, independent, and protesting, he challenged us, made us think, and better decisions resulted. Recently, he sorrowed for any obstruction he may have caused to God's agenda. Finally, his impatience for the peace of his appointed death was more than he could endure. How deeply he loved his family; it was clear to all who knew him that the steadying rock, the beacon of his life, was Nara. He will be missed."

Nara and her two children embraced in silent tears next to his grave.

The camp was disassembled, and the congregation was led from campsites at Mount Shepher and Haradah, to Makheloth, on their way to Tahath, to Terah, and to Mithkah.⁵ Local villagers were astounded to see this large body of people seemingly following aimlessly after the strange white cloud. The Hebrews often told them about the God who led them and of their eventual goal of Canaan, while avoiding mentioning their own desertion. They carried on a limited trade, and when the Israelites moved on, they left the villagers largely undisturbed.

God tested the Israelites from time to time with thirst, hunger, even temptations to worship other gods, including their revered Moloch and Rompha. When they erred, He disciplined them, but afterward, always came to their rescue. Their murmuring slowly changed to gossiping, to soft grousing, and then, for some, to resigned silence as their anticipation of promised deliverance grew.

*****

In the thirty-first year on a particularly hot, dry day, swarms of flying insects attacked the camp from the east, stinging and biting both man and beast; there seemed to be no escape from them. On the fourth and fifth day, large numbers of older men began to fall ill with fever, headache, and lethargy, each finally drifting into a coma. Death uniformly followed. After a week, the insects mercifully left, leaving a scattering of dead animals also in their wake.

Ahira had set up and supervised the many pots of animal dung that smoked over fires surrounding the village. He exposed himself to the insects, almost recklessly, trying to drive them away before finally falling ill on the fifth day. He died seven days later and was replaced as leader of his tribe by his son Jazallun.

Gamaliel also contracted the illness. On Gamaliel's last day, a small, respectful crowd gathered outside of his tent while inside, Hanniel and Moses stood near his bed. A grieving Pagiel was holding his hand when he died.

Hanniel was invited to replace Gamaliel as leader of Manasseh. He hesitated, realizing that he would have to relinquish some of his cherished duties assisting the Levites if he accepted the offer. He consulted long with Pagiel and Machir and only said yes after Machir agreed to be his advisor. And a good advisor he would be, for Machir had grown to be the independent thinker and actor his mother Coresha had envisioned, devoted to God and standing up repeatedly for Him.

*****

The deaths of Ahira and Gamaliel left Pagiel as the lone survivor of the original leaders. He appreciated the fellowship of the younger men and of their council meetings. Although he was referred to as "the relic," his opinions, occasionally with some humor, were given great weight by the councilmembers. He rued his generation's desertion and recommended a direct strike to the northwest to Canaan, toward the Jordan, should they be given the opportunity again. His support for God and Moses had persisted.

*****

It was in the thirty-second year of the march that Kemuel called a meeting of the leaders in the big tent, excluding Moses.

After greetings and the usual small talk, they sat on the ground, and Kemuel began. "Eleven of us leaders are new as God culls out the older men. We simply labor and march on without recognition. What can we do? The deadly lesson from Korah is clear: leave Moses alone. But how about Aaron? He, Moses, and God are thick with one another. After their meetings, Moses just brings God's messages to us, and we are to obey. We have no representation."

"What a great position Aaron has,"[2] said Kenan. "Wouldn't it be nice to live his life? He has access to the holiest room and to God Himself. If we cannot have the authority of Moses, how about Aaron's? He was just a leader like you, Pagiel, until Moses made him high priest. None of us new men were around when he was appointed. All we have for it is Moses' word from the mountain. It could have been a cooked-up scheme as payback for Aaron's keeping his birth a secret for all those years, allowing him the luxury of the palace."

Samuel said, "He hasn't measured up to what I believe a priest should be. He made the golden calf, he and Miriam tried to usurp Moses' power with God, and circumcisions have stopped.[1] He didn't train his sons well as they tried to get into the holiest room. He did seem to stop the plague, but he acted only under Moses' direction."

"Was the whole ordination ceremony just a sham?" questioned Kenan.

Caleb said, "You are all good, young leaders, and I am proud to serve with you. But Aaron's is a revered role which serves God directly. God guides him and tolerates his missteps. He would remove him if need be. Besides, if he did step down, his son Eleazar would replace him."

Samuel said, "We mean to clean house, Caleb, a whole new family with the high priest."

"I agree with you," said Kemuel. "How about you, Hanniel?

Hanniel said, "Your view is reasonable. I can tell Moses that we have grave, lingering doubts concerning his appointment, you being his brother. With Aaron's faults, might God admit that He may have made a mistake? Many of our leaders resent him and feel qualified to replace him. Would Moses talk to God and voice our concerns?"

Hanniel informed Moses of their worries.

Moses defended his brother, saying, "Hanniel, Aaron has made some mistakes on the march. But he and his sons have done all of the work of the most holy place and to make atonement for Israel, according to all that I have commanded." Please let it be."

"If you don't take it to Him, that will just confirm the doubts we all have."

*****

Moses did take their petition to God, who decided it was time to settle, once and for all, who was to serve as His high priest.

Moses returned and told them that God would allow them to participate in the decision. Following divine directions, Moses instructed each tribal leader to bring him a dead branch. He would write the name of its leader on each and deposit them in the tabernacle that night. A thirteenth rod was to be added for the tribe of Levi, with Aaron's name inscribed on it. *"The rod of the man whom I choose will sprout,"* said God.

*****

Moses brought God's answer to the leaders.

Hanniel began enthusiastically, "I am surprised that God would answer our doubts like this. Maybe He is indeed unhappy with Aaron. Has He seen something in one of us that he wants to reward? Moses, something we did not think of; if one of us wins, what compensations would we receive?"

Moses answered, "Once in Canaan, the animals, flocks, fruit, grain, and money owned by the twelve tribes must be tithed to the tribe of the Levites every third year. Of these, the Levites must give one-tenth in thanksgiving to Aaron and his family, who also receive part of the most holy sacrifices that are kept from the fire and, after entry into Canaan, Aaron's family will receive the first fruits of the harvest, the oil, the grain, and wine."

Moses continued, "The Levites and priests were both told by God, *'You shall have no inheritance in their land. I am your portion and inheritance among the people of Israel.'"* Unencumbered by concerns of property ownership, Aaron and his sons were to lead lives of service to God with the Levites serving them and the people. Their only associations would be with their families, Moses, and the Levites. *"An outsider may not come near you,"* declared God.

"That is good enough for me. I'm in!" said an enthusiastic Samuel.

"We, too," said the rest, as each left to find a large twig.

*****

Aaron felt unsure, while the leaders were hopeful, as they offered their branches to Moses. Under the eyes of all leaders, Moses signed each, placed the rods in the tabernacle, and departed. Kenan and Pagiel volunteered to stay up all night to guard the entrance.

The next morning, Moses left the leaders outside as he entered the tabernacle. He found the thirteen sticks still on the floor. All remained dry and dead except for Aaron's. As he picked it up, he was amazed; it was green, supple, and the end had even budded. Beneath blossoms, Moses saw ripe almonds! Moses exited the tabernacle with all of the branches in his arms and showed them to the shocked, but disappointed, leaders. Each one, including a relieved Aaron, examined the live branch to confirm that it was Aaron's.

The tribal leaders bargained with Moses saying that they finally and reluctantly would accept Aaron's priesthood if Moses would help to protect them. Kenan said, "According to God's law, if anyone but a Levite walks next to the tabernacle of the Lord, except by invitation or to sacrifice, they shall be put to death.[y] The toll of our careless intruders is mounting. Are we to perish completely?"[z]

Moses consulted with God, who first told Moses, *"Put back the rod of Aaron* [into the ark] *to be kept as a sign against the rebels, that you may put an end to their grumbling against Me, so that they should not die."*[aa] Thereafter, the rod was Moses' own responsibility.

To solve the other problem, God held the Levites responsible to prevent any common person from accidentally approaching the tabernacle, except to make a sacrifice. If they failed, the Levites were to take the trespasser's punishment, becoming their brothers' keepers.

The satisfied leaders departed.

Moses placed the branch in the ark.

*****

At the end of the fortieth year, God put them on the move again, bringing them all back toward Kadesh-barnea,[bb] where the wandering years had begun. Most of the men who were over twenty years of age at the beginning of the march had perished during those years as God had warned: *"Surely this I will do to all this evil congregation."*[cc] Children and grandchildren had grown to adulthood, some to assume leadership. Among the latter were Samuel of Reuben, replacing Elizur; Tasun of Dan for Ahiezur; and Kemuel, Kenan, and Jazallun for Ahira.

As Moses viewed the congregation, he thought, "Perhaps the younger generation can become the priests that God needs. He hasn't given up on them. These forty years the LORD has been with them they have not lacked a thing.[dd] Now, prove yourselves worthy of His faith in you."

*****

When they were still one day away from Kadesh-barnea, Miriam developed a fever and cough and the next morning was found dead in bed, ending two weeks of suffering from the wasting disease. She had lived thirty-seven years since her leprosy. Although God had burned with anger at Aaron and her, His love had preserved her life. She lived forgiven and Aaron had been spared.

After God's healing, she had kept largely to herself. Later, humbled and self-accepting, she mingled more and became a valuable help to Moses in matters dealing with women.

During her recent illness, women had visited her often, bringing gifts of food and drink. Aaron had spent many comforting hours with her. Moses had long since forgiven her and their visits had afforded him the opportunity to repay her for her courageous, early care of him.

When they reached the village, her burial was a simple, private affair attended by Moses, Aaron, Hur, and a few of her close female friends.

Endnotes

1. The story of Korah is told in chapter 16 of Numbers.
2. The story of Aaron's rod is told in chapter 17 of Numbers.

Chapter 18

Moses Fails

As they approached Kadesh-barnea, baking in the searing sun that reflected off the rocks, the people's water bags were empty, their lips shriveled. The new, younger leaders accosted Moses. "You and your God find us water to drink!" they demanded.

"The oasis is but a short distance ahead," Moses replied.

"There had better be water there."

When they reached Kadesh-barnea, the formerly lush oasis was dry. The leaders complained just as their fathers had, "If only we had perished when our brothers perished before the LORD! Why have you made us come up from Egypt, to bring us to this wretched place? It is not a place of grain or figs or vines or pomegranates as you had promised, nor is there water to drink."[a]

Moses knew that God was listening and he thought, "Let God deal with them." He walked with Aaron, whose frustration exceeded even that of his brother, to the tabernacle. They fell down on their faces, expecting that the worst would befall the crowd.

"God," Moses railed, "listen to their complaining. Do not pity them. You gave me Aaron's branch to prevent this, but I chose not to use it. Deal with them."

But God did not punish the people. *"Take [your] rod and you and your brother Aaron assemble the congregation and speak to the rock before their eyes, that it may yield its water,"*[b] God directed.

The cloud hovered over a huge boulder at the foot of a cliff. *"You shall thus bring forth water for them out of the rock and let the congregation and their beasts drink."*[c]

Moses said to Aaron as they walked a few steps away, "God wants me to just talk to the rock! What if I stand there, speaking to the rock, and nothing happens? I believe that this belligerent crowd would rather see me fail than to get the water. No, that is too big a miracle."

Moses' face flushed as he grabbed Aaron by the forearm and instructed Joshua to "Bring the people together before that rock," as he pointed to the boulder.

The people shuffled slowly to the rock, where Moses shouted, "Listen now, you rebels: shall we bring forth water for you out of this rock?"[d]

"Yes!" yelled the doubting crowd, bristling at his moniker, "let's see you do that!"

Moses approached the rock. For a brief moment, he considered standing back from the rock and speaking to it, as God had commanded. Instead, he raised his staff over his head for all to see. Aaron encouraged him with a whispered, "Go ahead, hit it."

Crack! Nothing happened! The crowd tittered. "Your tricks aren't working," someone called. "Come on, Moses, we thirst," demanded another. Moses felt the hairs on his neck standing up. He dared not face the crowd. He approached the rock again, raised the staff, and struck it harder. To his great relief, the rock split, water gushed forth, and the people and their animals drank their fill. "Thank you, Moses," was heard from a few.

"It's about time," said Kenan.

From the cloud, God said in a grieving voice, *"Because you have not believed Me, to treat Me as holy in the sight of the sons of Israel, therefore you shall not bring this assembly into the land which I have given them."*[e] It had taken two whacks to break the rock—and God's heart.

"No, God!" cried Moses. "Have I not served Thee well on this trip, only to lose all for this simple act? Does it deserve death?" Then, looking at his hand, he argued, "Why did Thee tell me to bring this rod if not to use it?"

Aaron asked of the cloud, "Am I condemned also, LORD?"

God's silence swallowed their hopes.

Devastated, the brothers walked away from the crowd. After some minutes, Aaron said, "Moses, how much one mistake cost us!"

"I didn't trust Him enough." admitted Moses.

*****

Aaron entered Moses' tent the next day and said, "All night I was trying to understand God. At Rephidim, He wanted you to strike the rock so that the people's trust in us would grow. Here, it was time to give Him all the glory.

"But later, I understood more. What has happened in the last weeks? A series of miracles to demonstrate God's commitment to us. He defended you by killing Korah's families by the earthquake you asked for, then more by fire. Many more died when He protected you by the plague when you were threatened. He empowered me to stop the plague; He confirmed me as priest; He offered you to protect the people through my fruit-bearing branch. Perhaps God was readying us for another, greater role. Then He told us to speak to the rock and we—we, Moses, would bring forth water. God offered us His very word to use, the word by which He created all things. A wondrous, unique gift—and we wasted it."

Moses nodded his head and said, "You speak well, Aaron. We share the same understandings. It was also the grace of God that saved me from embarrassment at the rock. While God was promoting us, He knew that I was wearied by the people, concerned more with myself and growing less dependent on Him. It was time to quit testing the people and to try me. And I failed Him."

Aaron added, "We both failed. I think God was more deeply disappointed in us than angry. We were the last to believe, and we betrayed Him."

✳✳✳✳✳

At a leaders' meeting four days later, Moses censured them, "You provoked me. The LORD was angry with me on your account and swore to me that I should not cross the Jordan."*

"We are sorry about that, Moses," they shrugged.

Chapter 19

A New Journey; A New High Priest; A New Faith?

God did not permit the brothers time to mourn their loss before He soon instructed them, *"You have circled this mountain* [Seir] *long enough. Now turn north … through the territory of* [Edom] *… do not provoke them, for I will not give you any of their land, even as little as a footstep because I have given* [Edom] *to Esau as a possession."*[a]

Although God had originally planned for the Israelites to invade due north from Kadesh-barnea, where the spying trip had originated, He altered His tactics and opted to make the assault from east of the Jordan River. Moving the Israelites there required travel through Edom, whose border was nearby. The land of Edom, south of the Salt—or the Dead—Sea, was composed mainly of rolling hills interspersed with many deep ravines. God intended His people to go quickly through this infertile land, using it merely as a thoroughfare. *You shall buy food from them with money so that you may eat, and you shall also purchase water from them with money so that you may drink. For the LORD your God has blessed you.*[b]

Moses sent messengers, Caleb, Hanniel, and Machir, to Edom's king to request passage through his land. On the first night, after their donkeys were watered, they sat around a small fire, eating.

Machir asked, "Caleb, Moses says that we are not to go straight north as Pagiel had predicted, but to begin by going northeast. What do you know of that land of Edom?"

Caleb said, "Abidan told us that it is populated by the descendants of Jacob's twin brother, Esau. After Jacob had cheated Esau out of the family's inheritance in Canaan, he fled eastward from him to live with his uncle Laban, where he sired twelve sons by Laban's daughters and their maids. Meanwhile, Esau incurred his mother's displeasure by marrying outside of the tribe and so moved to this land under the protection of God, where his descendants multiplied greatly.

"On his way back from Laban's, Jacob had a spectacular dream wherein God changed his name to Israel.^c Esau heard of his returning, went out to meet him, and forgave Israel in a highly-emotional reunion north and east of here. When Israel and his family proceeded to Canaan, Esau returned here. God has blessed and protected Edom."

Hanniel asked, "Is it blessed because Esau forgave his conniving brother?"

Caleb continued, "Perhaps; it was God's decision. We, the descendants of Jacob, should be welcomed."

*****

Late the next afternoon, when the three reached the palace, the king granted them an interview. Caleb used the words that Moses had given him: "You know all the hardship that has befallen us, the many descendants of your brother, Israel, since you last saw him. Israel and his family went down to Egypt where they were terribly mistreated by the Egyptians as they multiplied over the centuries. Finally, they—we—cried out to the LORD, and He brought us out from Egypt. We are now at Kadesh-barnea. Please let us pass through your land,"^d they asked.

"You shall not pass through us lest I come out with a sword against you!"^e said the king.

"Hanniel pleaded, "We have long walked over difficult terrain. Please let us walk up north by your King's Highway. If I or my livestock do drink any of your water, then I shall pay its price."^f

The king ordered, "You shall not pass through. Now go."

On their way back, Machir said, "Apparently Esau's descendants are not as kind and forgiving as he was. Or perhaps our great numbers frightened him."

To assure their compliance, the king's army followed them to the border, foiling God's plans.

*****

Two days later, God called Moses to Him at the tabernacle.

He informed Moses that because entry into Edom was blocked, the only other, less-favorable, option was to lead the people south and then east beyond the land of Edom, and finally north, through the land of the Midianites, across the corner of Moab to the land of the Amorites, then north to Bashan. God informed Moses that the Midianites would be peaceful, but not the Amorites and Bashanites.

During the forty years living with Jethro, Moses had learned of those countries from caravanners and had a rough mental picture of their locations.

*****

Moses drew the leaders together to give them God's new plans.

After outlining the journey, Moses asked for questions.

Samuel said, "Moses, our people have all grown tired of this trip. They are afraid to openly complain. But what you describe adds over one hundred miles to it, several weeks at least. I wonder how many will survive."

Moses responded, "You have all grown physically and mentally tough during these years. You are survivors. God says that we will find plenty of water at the wadi and oases, and the manna suffices."

Kenan observed, "This will delay our battles, which is good. However, instead of just having to make war against the Canaanites, we will also have to fight the Amorites, then the Bashanites. We will wear out."

Moses said, "Remember, God has promised us victory. The battles should not be too difficult."

Kemuel interjected, "But weren't those victories dependent upon our trusting Him?"

"Yes, Kemuel, and we might have more tests ahead of us to prove our trust," said Moses.

*****

The people broke camp and headed south from Kadesh-barnea in a valley along the western border of Edom. They soon arrived at the base of a small mountain, Mount Hor.

There, God told Moses that Aaron must now die. *"Because you* [and he] *rebelled against My command at the waters of Meribah."*⁸

Following God's instruction, Moses helped Aaron don his full priestly regalia, and they began to climb up the mountain, accompanied by Eleazar. As they walked, Moses said, "Brother, what we are about now is God's doing, you know; I only act as His intermediary."

"I understand," said Aaron.

Once when they paused, Moses said, "We have been through a difficult march together. I had the advantage of being alone with Him for eighty days, but you have believed all of the information I brought down and helped me to apply it. You have kept the laws that God gave you[h] and faithfully performed the burnt offerings and Atonement according to all that I have commanded,[i] but now you must die, though it was I who struck the rock."

"I encouraged you to do it." Aaron touched Moses' arm. "God has apparently forgiven me my human failings; my envy that prompted Miriam and I to challenge your authority and also my fears, caving in to the pressure to make the golden calf. But He could not forgive our defiance of His crucial commandment at Meribah. Miriam is gone now, and apparently God has had His fill of me."

"God has great love for you, brother. Remember, it was your rod that budded, and you stopped the plague."

"It's no use," Aaron answered as they walked on. "God's decisions are irrevocable. Do what you must. At least Eleazar will come into the priesthood with clean hands."

"Take hope for what is ahead for you," said Moses. "Remember that at the burning bush, God told me that He *is*, not *was*, the God of Abraham, Isaac, and Jacob. Although physically dead, they must live with Him[j] as, I believe, you will also in some way. God said *you will be gathered to your people.*[k] There may be quite a reception awaiting you."

On reaching the summit, they embraced. "We shall look after Elisheba," promised Moses. "Be strong."

There, Aaron, a recluse by decree, stood in full view of the congregation while Moses performed his difficult assignment. He stripped his brother of his cherished priestly garments, leaving him only in his breeches, and methodically put the holy raiment on a hesitant, tearful Eleazar who, thereafter, would be recognized as the high priest. Then God took Aaron's life from him, and Moses buried him. He was one hundred and twenty-three years old. Moses and Eleazar climbed down the mountain.

Out of respect and to honor him, the congregation wept for Aaron[l] there a full month.

*****

At Aaron's memorial, Moses' prayer concluded: "As God turns all men soon back into the grave, into mere dust, with each death He cries out to the living, *'Return, O children of men,* [to Me].'[m] O LORD, as we do, make us glad; satisfy us with Your lovingkindness; teach us to number all our days that we may present to you a heart of wisdom."[1]

*****

Near the end of the time at Hor, Hebrew sentries reported to Moses and Joshua that they had seen two towns to the east. On closer inspection, they had found a stable of horses and donkeys near one town, but the inhabitants of the cities seemed peaceful.

Two days later, at dawn under clear skies, a cavalry and many foot soldiers brandishing swords swept down from the northern hills, butchering many Israelites as they advanced toward the tabernacle.[n] Sentries blew the alarm, but the Israelite soldiers responded haphazardly, unlike the Levites, who quickly surrounded their tabernacle.

Bezalel was polishing a handcrafted chair in his tent, not far from the courtyard and close to the path of the advancing army, when he heard their shouts. Fearing for his beloved tabernacle, he hobbled over and impulsively ran headlong in front of the lead horse with outstretched arms, shrieking, "No, no! Away!" The horse reared when startled by the odd man, and a hoof struck him in the head. The rider leaned over, and in a quick jabbing motion, thrust his sword in and out of the tottering Bezalel's neck, tumbling him beneath the trampling hoofs.

Heavy, dark clouds suddenly covered the camp and increasing numbers of armed Hebrews slowed the advance of the attacking army. The invaders, surprised by the darkness, retreated with small losses, carrying off choice items from the tents and a number of female captives.

Moses picked up the dying Bezalel and carried him up to the tabernacle, followed by Joshua and an apprehensive crowd. As his breathing faltered, Moses placed him before the doorway where another small cloud hovered over him until he died. He would be buried in a plain grave the next day, as he would have liked; that grave would be moistened with the tears of many mourners and lovingly strewn with flowers.

*****

As the Hebrews tried to regroup, Moses interviewed several wounded attackers. The enemy's leader, he learned, was the king of Arad, a small nation of Canaanite descendants nearby in the Negev Desert.

"Who are you and why have you attacked us?" Moses asked.

One blurted out, "Our king became enraged at the prospect of your army of people coming toward his domain—unannounced, uninvited, and without his permission—threatening us."

On questioning, another said, "He had learned that a powerful, foreign god, antagonistic to our god, leads you and wants to destroy both us and our god."

Another added, "He decided to strike first, hoping to stop your advance and drive you into another direction. Beware, our army is larger and mightier than yours."

*****

Aware of this information, the leaders hastily gathered with Moses.

Hanniel began, "This unprovoked attack cost us the lives of many of our people, and our women were carried off. What do you say that we should do?"

Tasun said, "My wife and children were taken as were many others. We must rescue them. Our soldiers are eager for revenge, but are we strong enough?"

Hanniel said, "Machir and I see this as an opportunity, the first battle for our generation. We may be able to wipe away the shame of the desertion. But we must have God's help and He is silent, perhaps waiting for us this time?"

Caleb said, "Moses, didn't God tell you that when we encounter the Canaanites, the entire culture has such an evil lifestyle that He would deliver them to us? And the Aradites are mainly Canaanites."

Moses said, "Yes, and God has commanded you that *'In the cities I give to you, do not leave anything alive in order that they may not teach you to do according to all their detestable things which they have done for their gods, so that you would sin against the LORD your God.'*⁶

Samuel said, "Slaughter them all? Not me. I would have to be convinced that I was doing the right thing, like killing a snake, and that God would reward me."

"Samuel, that is our … merciless end of the bargain with God," said Hanniel. "We must attract Him. I say let us make a new, binding commitment to the LORD, what we promise to do. Then He may help us. But this time without Moses' intercession, for it was our people who failed, who deserted, not Moses."

Machir surveyed the room. "Are we in one accord?" Most said "yes," while others nodded in agreement.

Caleb raised a hand toward the tabernacle and vowed, "If You, God, will indeed deliver this people into our hands, then we will, as You ask, utterly destroy their cities."ᵖ

"We must prepare our soldiers," said Ahira.

*****

In the morning, two days later, Joshua and the mobilized army advanced on the two towns. When the Aradite army came out to battle, they met Hebrew soldiers who fought with new conviction as the LORD heard the voice of Israel and delivered up the Canaanites.ۥ

They entered their cities, freed the hostages, destroyed the cities, and slaughtered every inhabitant.

God did not prevent His people from being attacked, but the word spread that the Hebrews' ferocity had returned. The soldiers were smugly proud of their victory, but a few of them saw the hand of the LORD and gave Him praise. This was the first time that the people prayed to the LORD before a need or a conflict arose—and He answered!

*****

God told Moses to abandon the Aradic ruins and journey southward toward Ezion-geber on the Gulf of Aqaba. From there, they would turn east to skirt Edom. After eight days on that route, the Hebrews made camp. Hot, dry, thirsty, and bored with living on manna, this younger generation complained again with the same old accusations, learned from their parents, "Why have you brought us up out of Egypt to die in the wilderness? For there is no food and no water, and we loathe this miserable food."ʳ The tassels on robes did not remind them of God's provisions, and Moses again ignored Aaron's rod.

The complaining grew in intensity until it reached Joshua's ears. "Moses," he said, "you know that God hears the prattle of this people. Has He talked to you?"

J. Roger Nelson, M.D.

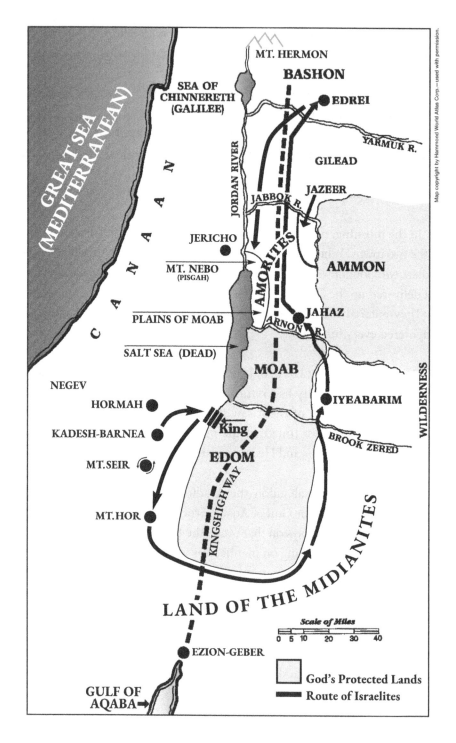

264

"No, and that is worrisome," answered Moses. "He must know that I have asked the leaders to control their people. Some have earnestly tried, but the mood of the village has become rebellious again."

"Will He punish with fire or another plague?" Joshua asked.

"He might. Zipporah worries even now for our own safety." Moses spread out his hands. "Perhaps I may have a new chance to speak to a rock."

*****

God was angered by their demeaning of His miraculous food and His purpose in bringing them there. Their eleventh complaint! Before dawn the next day, nests of fiery poisonous snakes slithered out of rocks and into their camp.

"Snakes!" they shouted. "Kill them or avoid them." But the snakes were too fast for them. Many were bitten and people began to die. Terror reigned. They saw God's hand in this. "How can God do this to us, Abraham's children?" Others realized that He had said, *"I will not leave the guilty unpunished."* Find Moses! "Moses, we have sinned because we have spoken against the LORD and you. Intercede with the LORD that He may remove the serpents from us." (Ah, a confession.) Moses listened and interceded, "Remove the snakes, I pray." (God listened. Are their words but spoken in transient fear?) He tested them. He refused Moses' request. The snakes stayed. God told Moses to *"Make a fiery serpent and set in on a standard; and it shall come about that, everyone who is bitten, when he looks at it, he shall live."*

Two of Bezalel's assistants quickly fashioned the serpent. To make it "fiery," they made it of bronze, mouth open, fangs threatening. They erected it on a tall post near the center of the camp. Their savior would be God's transformed agent, the now-enfeebled, yet dreaded snake; the agent of death will be the agent of life. Will those bitten trust, will they walk or run to it?

*****

Chaletra, Ruth, and Shum were each trying to gather a skin of water from the scattered puddles of a wadi bed near the camp. As they knelt, intent on their tasks, four crimson snakes shot out from the midafternoon shadows of the creek-bed wall. One struck Ruth on the thigh, and another bit Shum on the ankle. Chaletra grabbed a crook, killed one snake, and drove the others back into the shadows. The paired teeth marks of each wound caused searing pain, and Shum cried out. To keep from sobbing, Ruth bit into her fleshy thumb.

Chaletra shouted, "Don't move; I'll go for help!"

Still shaking, Ruth relaxed her jaws enough to say, "The poisonous serpents of God! Let's hurry to the bronze snake."

Shum was immobilized with fear and pain. Between sobs, she cried, "I will wait for a physician. Chaletra, get a doctor for me!" Chaletra ran to the tents, calling for help. Her brother responded quickly and soon arrived at the wadi with a village doctor. Ruth rose and hobbled toward the brother. The doctor warned, "If you walk, the venom will spread faster."

Ruth replied, "Come with me, Shum; it is your only chance. The doctor cannot cure you."

"You and your superstitions," said Shum. "I'll trust the physician." Ruth left, assisted by Chaletra's brother, while the doctor applied poultices to Shum's wound.

As Ruth stumbled along, supported by the brother, she began to vomit and felt weak as the burning pain from the bite persisted. Her mind whirled, and soon she was delirious. However, as soon as she reached and gazed upon the bronze snake, the confusion began to clear, the pain subsided, and during the next half hour, her strength returned. She and the brother ran back to the wadi and found Shum dead in the arms of the physician.

Some others died, including the unbelieving leader of Dan, Tasun. But a few, then more, walked or ran to the serpent after being bitten and, on looking on it, were healed. Others saw the miracle and followed. Healed, forgiven, in gratitude, their complaining finally stopped.

*****

The Hebrews continued eastward along the southern border of Edom through the hilly land of Midian. Then after two weeks, they turned north. In order to reach the land of the Amorites, at God's direction, they crossed the Brook Zered, camped at Iyeabarim, opposite Moab, and then entered the extreme northeast corner of Moab. But God warned His people, *"Do not harass Moab, nor provoke them to war, for I will not give you any of their land ... because I have given it to the sons of Lot as a possession."*[u]

"What do you know of Moab?" Machir asked Caleb.

"This information came from Abidan again," said Caleb. "When God's fire from heaven leveled the evil cities of Sodom and Gomorrah, Abraham's nephew Lot escaped with his two daughters. In order to preserve the family,

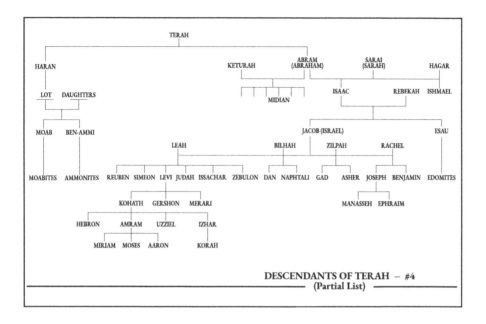

DESCENDANTS OF TERAH – #4
(Partial List)

each daughter conceived through contrived incest with a drunken Lot.[2] Two sons, Moab and (Ben) Ammon, were born and blessed by God, who accepted the dire circumstances of their births. Subsequent generations populated the lands bearing their names, lands blessed and protected by God."[v]

When Caleb, Hanniel, and Machir were sent to Balak, the king of Moab, he likewise refused them permission to traverse his land. When the three returned to Moses with the negative report, Moses was surprised. "God had arranged our safe travel across both Edom and Moab. Why did we not receive such permission?"

Machir said, "It was not just a refusal, but our request seemed to provoke anger in the kings. Their faces and voices showed fear."

"That is it!" said Moses. "Most of you were very young at the time, but I remember the words of the Song of Victory we sang after the Red Sea crossing. I have considered them often since, words of prophesy given to us by God that we didn't understand then. God's drowning of the pharaoh's army caused fear in the people elsewhere. The words of the song were, 'the chiefs of Edom were dismayed; the leaders of Moab, trembling grips them; all the inhabitants of Canaan have melted away. Terror and dread fell upon them.'"[w]

Caleb added, "I see now, Moses. It is because of the God-generated fear of us that they refused us."

"A dreadful fear that has persisted and grown over these thirty-eight years," Moses proposed, "a fear so deep-seated that it has overcome God's intention. We experienced human fear at the calf, at the Red Sea, and at desertion. But when God casts His fear, it must be far worse."

"Had we succeeded in our original attack on Canaan, we would not have encountered Edom, Moab, or the lands closer to Canaan," said Machir. "God knew we would desert Him, even back at the Red Sea. He knows the future, perhaps projecting it from our sour attitudes."

*****

Although the Moabites were committed to other gods, God tried to influence them through visions and revelations to provide for the hungry and thirsty Israelites whose supplies were low[x] as they entered the far northwest corner of Moab to reach the land of the Amorites. The Moabite king, whose fear of them had been heightened by news of the recent slaughter at Arad, refused God's request for supplies, hindering His plans again. The king did, however, permit the Hebrews their limited passage.

God did not leave his tired people to suffer from thirst. When they arrived at a place named Beer, He did not instruct Moses to strike a rock or to speak to one, but simply told him to assemble the people and that *He* would give them water. Another marvel occurred when the leaders easily dug a well without shovels, and the people sang: "Spring up, O well! Sing to it! The well, which the leaders sank, which the nobles of the people dug, with the scepter and with their staffs."[y] Moses understood that his role as an intermediary in miracle production was ended.

*****

The Israelites made the short trip across the corner of Moab, again forded the Arnon River that had turned ninety degrees to the west, and entered the land of the Amorites. To the east was the land of Ammon, populated by the descendants of another of Lot's sons. God had said to Moses, *"Do not harass the* [Ammonites] *nor provoke them … because I have given* [their land] *to the sons of Lot as a possession,"* a third protected land.[z]

Determined to gain access to a better road, Moses sent a message to Sihon, king of the Amorites, requesting permission to travel north through his country on the King's Highway. He promised to disturb nothing.

Sihon not only refused but gathered his entire army and marched toward the Israelites to attack them.

God had long hated the evil deeds of the Amorites, deeds including child sacrifice, sorcery, witchcraft, worshipping other gods, and engaging freely in adultery, incest, and sodomy, like their Canaanite neighbors. Their iniquity had reached the fruition God had predicted in Abraham's time.[aa] This was God's opportunity, and He said to Moses, *"I have given Sihon … into your hand…. This day I will begin to put the dread and fear of you upon the peoples everywhere."*[bb] Buoyed by their victory over the Aradites and encouraged by God, this sword-slashing force won a resounding victory in the Battle of Jahaz in southern Amorite country.

*****

The Israelites moved north, occupying the Amorite land, carrying out God's mandate to kill her inhabitants on the way, again leaving *no survivor.*[cc] Their spoils included the excellent grazing land of Jazeer to the northeast, and the arid Arabah Desert to the west that encompassed the Plains of Moab across the Jordan River from the city of Jericho. Under God's direction, they later moved north and crossed the Jabbok River, which lay at the bottom of a deep valley,[3] entering the lush grazing land of Gilead. They conquered part of it with relative ease and advanced northward to the Yarmuk River, which bordered the land of Bashan.

Og, the king of Bashan, reputed to be twelve feet tall, had learned of the Hebrew advance. He mobilized his army, stationing them around the city of Edrei, located on a northern bluff of the Yarmuk River. The Israelites forded the river, climbed the hills, and engaged in a fierce battle. God had said to Moses, *"I have delivered him and all his people … into your hand. Do to him just as you did to … the Amorites."*[dd]

*****

After the victorious campaign, Moses and Caleb stood, overlooking the gruesome site. Caleb spoke: "Another battlefield strewn with dead soldiers,

twenty of theirs for every one of ours. There is no living remnant left of them.[ee]
He keeps His promises."

Moses said, "Even though we remain a disobedient people, He is determined
to use us to destroy their vile cultures and move us," as he pointed west, "on to
Canaan. Let us hope that we have no further troubles."

*****

Despite the victory, the sweetness was tragically marred for Moses and
Zipporah. While leading a charge, their son, Gershom, sustained a fatal blow
from a thrown spear. His death—coincidental or decreed?—answered their
long-held fears, although they had prayed otherwise.

The Israelite army captured the sixty cities of Bashan, many high-walled
and well-fortified, before returning over the Yarmuk to conquer the remainder
of Gilead. Several tribes settled in Bashan and on the fertile, grassy slopes of
Gilead, while the main body of the Israelites moved southward. They retraced
their steps for sixty miles, finally erecting the tabernacle in the valley on the
east bank of the Jordan, across from Jericho.

Endnote

1. Psalm 90, paraphrased.
2. Lot's sons, Moab and Ben-Ammon, conceived through incest under
   extraordinary circumstances, had been blessed; their lands were
   protected. Genesis 19:30f.
3. "bottom of a deep valley" Merill Tenney. *The Zondervan Pictorial Ency-clopedia of the Bible.* 1975, p 381.

Section V
Plains of Moab

Chapter 20
Parching the Jordan Valley

Many scattered rivulets, born of the melting snow and enlarged by rains, ran down from the summit of nine-thousand-foot Mount Hermon, high in the north of Canaan, finally merging to form a river that raced southward away from the mountain base. Its course was studded with rapids and cataracts as it progressively fell eight hundred feet before flowing into the Sea of Chinnereth fifteen miles away. This fourteen-mile-long, freshwater lake, teeming with fish, drained southward as the snakelike Jordan River.

Several miles down the Jordan River Valley, a sizable tributary emptied into it from the east, the Yarmuk River, whose waters in springtime equaled or exceeded the upper Jordan's. Other rivers drained into the Jordan as it wound sixty-five miles[1] south into the Salt Sea.

This is the valley where, five hundred years earlier, Lot chose to live when he and Abraham parted ways. The valley of the Jordan was well watered everywhere like the garden of the LORD,[a] Lot had observed. In the adjoining hills were several cities, including Sodom, where Lot had lived, and Gomorrah. However, the valley's fertility had been ruined—becoming a burning waste and no grass grew on it—when God destroyed those wicked cities by pelting them with fire and sulfur from heaven in His anger and His wrath.[b]

✶✶✶✶✶

It was on the parched lowlands north and east of the Salt Sea, just north of the land of Moab, with mountains to the east, where Moses established the Israelite camp. To the west, dense thickets, the little remaining greenery, guarded each bank of the Jordan.

Endnote

1. "sixty-five miles": Harold Brodsky, "The Jordan, Symbol of Spiritual Transition." *Bible Review,* June 1992. p. 42.

Chapter 21

The Seer[1]

Balak, king of the nation of Moab, met with his advisors. "This aggressive people, the fierce Israelites, are camped on our northern border, having overwhelmed our neighbors, the Amorites, and also the Bashanites. They will probably invade us next, driven by their alive, warlike god who must carry deep resentments for us since we did not provide for them when they came up from the south. Also, we respect the supernatural catastrophe he caused at the Red Sea, and we want none of that here."

Balak had forgotten God's promised protection of his country through their patriarch, Lot.[a] He said, "I feel that our strong army will be no match for them. My emissaries returned yesterday from meeting with the kings of Midian and reported success in the finalization of a military alliance with them. But I need a supernatural power to deal with their god."

"I have heard of Balaam, a seer from the land of Mesopotamia, far to the northeast," offered one. "It is said that he has influence over their same god, and through him, everyone Balaam blesses is blessed and those whom he curses are cursed."

Another advisor concurred with the first.

"If this Balaam has favor with their same god, perhaps we can entice him to have their god leave us alone," said the first.

"I know of Balaam's deeds," said Balak. "He might be just the one we need. I shall send emissaries to bribe him to help us."

Balak sent messengers from Moab and Midian to Balaam, offering to pay his usual fee and saying, "Behold, a horde of people came out of Egypt, and they are living opposite me. Please curse this people for me, since they are too mighty for me; perhaps I may be able to drive them out of the land."[b]

*****

Balaam, although not an Isrealite, enjoyed a cherished relationship with God. He invited the messengers to spend the night while he humbly sought God's advice. God indeed answered the invitation and replied, *Do not go with them; you shall not curse the people, for they are blessed.*[c] Balaam sent the messengers home with a curt response: "The LORD has refused to let me go with you."[d]

Other distinguished leaders soon came, urging Balaam to reconsider and promising him great honors, riches, and a prized position in the king's court. Balaam stood firm. "Though Balak were to give me his house full of silver and gold, I could not do anything, either small or great, contrary to the command of the LORD, my God."[e] But then he made a costly error. "And now, please, you also stay here tonight," he said to the messengers, "and I will find out what else the LORD will speak to me."[f] "Perhaps," he thought, "God will reconsider." God did return that night, and sensing that Balaam's feelings and desires were at odds with His, He approved of the trip but cautioned, *"Only the word which I speak to you shall you do."*[g] God could use Balaam's trip to His advantage.

Overnight, Balaam's heart became filled with thoughts of riches.[h] In the morning, he saddled his donkey, and while he rode with the leaders, his daydreams were read angrily by God, who stationed an armed angel, visible only to the donkey, in Balaam's way. As the angel repeatedly thrust its sword, the donkey protected its master by dodging off the road and then leaning against a wall, trapping Balaam's foot. Finally, the donkey backed up and fell into a crevice. Balaam beat the donkey each time it jostled him until, in anger, he dismounted the beast.

"What have I done to you that you have struck me these three times?"[i] wailed the donkey. As a wonder-worker himself, Balaam had grown accustomed to hearing God speak to him out of nothingness, but not out of a donkey! And this was not God's voice!

Balaam looked around at the other men and finding none near, walked up close to the donkey, frowned, and stared into the beast's left eye. "You have made a mockery of me," he raged. "If there had been a sword in my hand, I would have killed you by now!"[j]

The donkey answered, "You've ridden me all my life. Did I ever injure you?"[k]

Balaam forced himself to consider the unique question. "No, I suppose you haven't,"[l] he said.

With that, God opened Balaam's eyes to see the sword-bearing angel dressed in white, standing next to the donkey. Balaam's bewilderment changed to fear. Believing the angel knew about his greed, he fell to his knees and admitted, "I have sinned." The angel said nothing. "I will turn back if you wish,"[m] he added.

"*Go with the men,*" admonished the angel, who repeated God's warning. "*But speak only the words which I shall tell you.*"[n]

Balaam felt relieved as he mounted his donkey and rode on. Fording the Arnon River, he entered Moab, where an impatient Balak scolded him for the delay. "Only the word that God puts in my mouth, that I shall speak,"[o] Balaam said to him.

Balaam

Balaam was born in southern Midian, the fourth son and the seventh and youngest child in his family. His father, Beor, was the chief diviner for the king. Balaam was drilled in his father's craft on the use of divination tools: reading thrown dice; the reaction of a suspended, severed tail of a pregnant, two-year-old cow to the winds at dawn; the random draw of his picture cards; and the layering of ashes after being swirled in a beaker of water. However, Balaam proved useless in their deliberate manipulation, whereas his oldest brother, Bela, became proficient and was appreciated in the court.

One day, at age seven, beaten and bloodied by a local bully, Balaam cursed the boy in anger before a group of his peers. Four days later, the bully drowned in a swimming accident. Thereafter, Balaam was treated with wary courtesy. A year later, a dying uncle, blessed by the prayers of Balaam, surprisingly recovered in a week. The young boy began to realize that his powers exceeded the family's secret potions and objects.

As Bela rose in the king's sight, he felt threatened by his younger brother's budding powers. Two years after their father's death, when Balaam was thirteen, Bela drove him away, supplying him with donkeys, three manservants, and bags of supplies.

Balaam traveled north and east to the land of Mesopotamia, the city of Pethor, to the house of an aunt. God appeared to him one night in a vision and warned him of a planned attack on the life of the king of Mesopotamia. He informed the king, who foiled the plot and offered a great reward for his warning. But Balaam refused it, crediting God with the revelation.

God appeared to him many times over the years, to advise and empower him. Occasionally, God even came at Balaam's invitation, an invitation frequently fortified by animal sacrifices. Balaam's reputation for magical powers spread widely.

He married and reared a family in modest surroundings, appearing humble before God. He made a satisfactory living as a diviner. As the years went by, however, he often secretly rued his rejection of wealth from the king, hoping always for a second chance at riches.

*****

Early the next morning, Balak took Balaam to a site where the Moabites worshipped their god, Baal—a hill overlooking a portion of the Israelite camp. As was his habit, Balaam required the construction of seven large altars and the sacrifice of seven bulls and seven rams, to curry God's favor before he would speak.

Balaam was nervous, feeling that he was not in control himself. He delayed, saying, "Balak, you know them, Jacob, Israel, relatives of your ancestor, Lot. You all have descended from Abraham and once worshipped his God, Yahweh. Now, after several conquests, they and He are here, at your border.

"I know that you have gone to great effort and promised me great riches to curse these people—and how I hope that I can! However, under threat of death, I have promised God to be but His spokesman in our arrangement. He has chosen me, a simple man, to bring His message to you. At this time, I do not know what He will command me."

"Curse them!" urged Balak.

*****

Then Balaam climbed a small rise alone, where he received God's words.

He returned to Balak, who was standing with many of his leaders, eagerly anticipating the curse of the Israelites. However, a reluctant Balaam pronounced, "These are God's own words. Balak, you have your own gods of wood, clay, and metal, but this God is alive, conversant, powerful, even controlling nature. He is not a man that He should lie or the son of man that he should repent.[p] He can be counted on to do exactly what He says He will do.

"As you can see, the Israelites are numerous beyond counting. They are not aware of all of the many good things that God has done for them or that He plans to do. God does not curse the Israelites, and since He does not, I cannot. He has brought this people out of Egypt and prods them with the horns of a wild ox.[q] Let me die the death of the upright and let my end be like his."[r]

Stunned, Balak said, "What have you done to me?! I took you to curse my enemies, but you have actually blessed them!"[s]

"Must I not be careful to speak what the LORD puts in my mouth?"[t] a resigned Balaam said.

*****

In the afternoon, the furious Balak led Balaam to the top of the tall Mount Pisgah, overlooking another section of the Israelite camp, and demanded that Balaam curse them. After the ritual of sacrifices, Balaam went off to inquire of the LORD. More words were given to him and he returned to Balak.

"What has the LORD spoken?"[u] Balak asked.

Balaam spoke hesitantly, apologetically, "They are a people who live alone and are not like other nations. I must bless all of these people because this God has just informed me that He is not just their prodder but that He is their own special God! A living God devoted to just one nation! Blessed is everyone who blesses Israel, and cursed is everyone who curses her."[v]

Balak, feeling betrayed, shook with anger. "Do not curse them or bless them at all."[w] He took several deep breaths to calm himself, glared at Balaam, and led the way back to their nearby encampment for the night.

Balaam spent a restless, perspiring night alone on his mat wrestling with conflicting urges. "I dare not endanger my relationship with God by disobeying His compelling hand. Yet how can I escape from it and gratify this ravenous hunger to fill my bags with Balak's gold? This is not what I had planned," he writhed.

Balak also arose from a fitful sleep. He thought, "This man who sold himself to save us, is but a farce, just another enemy. He uses the excuse that his mind is being constrained by forces he dared not deny. I would send him home except that the Israelites would surely overrun us unless he acts. I must try him one more time."

The next morning, Balak led Balaam to the top of Mount Peor, overlooking another wasteland where additional Israelite tribes camped. "Perhaps," Balak said brusquely, "it will be agreeable with God that you curse them for me from here."ˣ He ordered the same sacrifices. As Balaam looked down over the wilderness, God did not just speak to him but poured out His Spirit upon him.ʸ

Balaam, thus further inspired, told the king what he foresaw. The Israelites would dwell in security and flourish. They would become like medicinal aloe plants, planted in beautiful valleys, near a river beside which are lovely gardens and rooted, strong cedars.ᶻ They would establish an exalted kingdom. Their king would become great. "But do not become their enemies because, as a lion, it lifts itself and it shall not lie down until it devours its prey,"ᵃᵃ Balaam added.

Balak could stand it no longer. He told Balaam to return home without the riches he had promised. "The LORD has held you back from honor."ᵇᵇ

But Balaam stood firm, no longer defensive, saying, "What the LORD speaks, that I will speak. I'll tell you what this people will do to your people in the days to come.ᶜᶜ He told of the later coming of a great king, descended from Jacob, who would crush Moab and also Edom to the south. Moab would be allowed to exist until that time—a small consolation for you, Balak. Also, the Amalekites would finally be destroyed.ᵈᵈ Alas, who can live except God has ordained it?"ᵉᵉ

Balaam thought, "I hope that God is satisfied. What to do? My one chance at riches!"

With these words, Balaam and a disappointed Balak parted company, each going his own way.ᶠᶠ Balak's military forces would have to suffice.

*****

Unaware of God's dealings with Balaam in the overlooking hills, the Israelite soldiers who were patrolling the southern outskirts of the camp, near the border of Moab, were flush with pride from their recent military victories. This was a time of rest before their war with Canaan. They and God had no desires for the lands of Moab or Midian.

*****

Soon, young Midianite women, trained to please men, were joined by Moabite accomplices, as they crossed the border from the land of Moab.[2] They walked among the Israelite soldiers, coyly displaying ankles and legs, and inviting with their dark eyes. Offering silks, aromatic spices, samples of delicious foods, and gums that, when chewed, invigorated, they enticed many battle-fatigued young men to cross over into Moab and into their bedrooms.

There the women indulged the men, satisfying their sexual desires, fulfilling their fantasies as Baal's representatives while listening to often-skewed stories about the men's strict, austere Israelite God. The women described their own god, their god of fertility, as a more lenient god who fertilized the soil with his rains and fulfilled the lusts of his followers. Overcome by unexpected delights, the men's loyalty to their own God vanished, and they began to believe in Baal, to bow down to him, and to make sacrifices to him.

*****

As word of this garden of lasciviousness filtered back to the Israelite camp, more young men volunteered for patrols, eagerly trading the God of Abraham for this god of vibrant, sexual pleasures offered by enchanting women.

Some of the Israelite leaders looked the other way. "Harmless," they said. Moses, along with Caleb, Hanniel, and Machir, condemned this behavior and reminded the men that God had told them to have no other gods before Him. What was more, God had specifically said in the covenant of Sinai, *"Watch yourself … lest you make a covenant with the inhabitants of the land … and play the harlot with their gods, and sacrifice to their gods."*[gg]

But the men ignored the warnings, as did Zimri, the handsome son of a Simeonite leader, recently assigned to an evening shift on the patrol.[3] He was quickly singled out by Cozbi, the short, dark, youngest daughter of a chieftain of a northern Midianite nation. Her older sisters were all taller and more willowy, so she had to work to attract the young men. She became proficient at her craft, and when she saw Zimri, she cast her net for him. She flounced in front of him and soon captured his interest. One day, arousing him with kissing, she coyly asked, "How much do you love me?"

"More than anything," he said.

"Prove it to me, Zimri. Make love to me for the first time in your tabernacle."

"No! God forbids us from even walking into that building," he said.

"Do you believe that, silly one? He wouldn't hurt a man as brave as you. You just don't really love me enough."

Zimri had never cared much for God's overpowering restrictions. Overcome with emotion, he said, "Cozbi, I do, I do. And I want you so much. I have a day off again in three days."

*****

When God realized that the tribal chiefs would not intercede and punish their own licentious soldiers, His anger erupted. *"Take all the* [guilty] *leaders of the people and execute them in broad daylight before the LORD, so that the fierce anger of the LORD may turn away from Israel,"*[hh] He commanded Moses.

The next day, an irate Caleb opened the council meeting. "We have permitted these orgies, this flagrant contempt of our faithful God! At least three times we swore all the words which the LORD has spoken, we would do, and we would be obedient[ii] and not become involved with their women.

"Ha! Our betrayal has provoked God's righteous jealousy. Don't you know how much He cares for us? He knows that unpunished, flagrant lust and the sacrifices to demons must be punished before it infects and destroys us all. We all deserve to die. However, God begins by selecting only our guilty elders; our leader Jazallun, the respected son of Ahira, is one of them! Have our judges prepare them to die tomorrow."

Hanniel added, "This is only the second time that we have been called on to execute our own, the first time since the golden calf. God refuses to even touch such sinners! We are to know just how sickening it is for Him to kill."

"When will we learn?" groaned Machir. "If God doesn't provide a miracle today, we shun Him tomorrow and reject Him the next day. We paint our lintels with grape juice, and self-discipline departs by noon."

Moses and a number of spectators gathered at the foot of a high cliff, waiting as Jazallun and eight of the guilty elders were paraded by a squad of soldiers up ascending paths to appear at the peak of its overhang. Hoods were placed over the heads of the convicted men, and they were placed at the summit's edge. After a short pause and some words by the soldier's captain, the men were thrown off the cliff, to be left unburied.[4]

*****

After the executions, God began to complete the penalty by sending a plague that killed the other guilty soldiers, and it began to spread to other sons of Israel.

Many of the unaffected, weeping in fear, followed Moses and the priests as they hurried into the courtyard, praying that God would stop the plague.

At that moment, Zimri nervously walked into the crowded courtyard, arm in arm with Cozbi. The skies darkened as Cozbi and Zimri proceeded all the way up to the entrance of the tabernacle. What little respect he retained for the tabernacle crumbled under Cozbi's coaxing. They slipped through its doorway. Once inside the tabernacle's holy room, Cozbi quickly disrobed, giggled, and squirmed to the floor, pulling Zimri after her.

While Moses and Eleazar rose in disbelief, Phinehas,[ji]—one of the sons of the priest, Eleazar—wrenched a spear from the hand of a soldier. Acting on his fiery devotion to the tabernacle, he raced after them—although without the protective attire of a priest—into the tabernacle. There, he raised his spear and pierced both of them through their chests with one stroke. They died instantly. Phinehas pulled the spear out and walked to the door, surprised that he himself was unharmed. When he emerged, holding his bloody spear, the sun broke out from the clouds, and suddenly the plague was checked. News of his feat spread quickly, even to neighboring nations.

*****

Later that day, God's cloud appeared to Phinehas and praised him for his courage. As a reward, he and his descendants after him would inherit the perpetual priesthood from his father, Eleazar, because he was jealous for his God and made atonement for the sons of Israel. But Phinehas' mind could not rest. The incursion of the harlots had been too orderly, too orchestrated, to have happened without some master plan.

The following morning, he entered the land of Moab with two armed men to seek answers. Because he was now feared and respected by all, he found a few women willing to cooperate with him. In just three days, the trail of information led to the higher echelons, and the orders for the deeds were finally traced back to Balak himself.

Phinehas used money he had taken from the treasury to bribe one of Balak's aides who had overheard several private conversations. It had been

Balaam—the God-fearing, God-guided Balaam—who advised the Moabites and Midianites to seduce the Israelites. After his extraordinary stand before Balak, Baalam had been left alone with his avarice and sought to profit from Balak's power and wealth. He had been prohibited by God from directly cursing the Israelites so, freed from the influence of God and his mountaintop experience, he cleverly suggested to Balak the harlotry plot, knowing that God would severely punish His own prurient, traitorous people.

Despite an intensive search, Phinehas returned empty-handed to Moses. The seer remained at large.

Endnotes

1. The contents of this chapter, widely quoted and paraphrased, are based on chapters 22 through 24 of Numbers.
2. The story of Baal worship is recorded in Numbers, chapter 25.
3. The story of Zimri and Cozbi, Numbers 25:6–15.
4. "Thrown off a cliff ..." *Numbers, The Daily Study Bible,* Walter Riggans, The Westminster Press, pg. 191.

Chapter 22

An Army at the Ready

"Six hundred[1] men died as victims of the plague," grumbled Kemuel. "I thought we were through with mass killings of our own people. He remains too harsh for me and for our tribe of Gad. How can He justify His violence?"

Hanniel responded, "Good grief, Kemuel! Worshipping a calf idol, insurrections, child sacrifices to an evil god, and desertion! What do you expect; just a slap on the wrist? We are to Him like pagans when disobedient. Fear Him and obey."

"I am afraid that fear is not enough," said Machir. "As we have seen, flaming lusts overcome fear."

"And our meager gratitude doesn't keep us right. I suspect that further violence lies before us unless we change," predicted Hanniel.

*****

After the mass burials, God ordered an attack on the Midianite nation in retaliation for the seductions and for Cozbi's sacrilege. But first, Moses would need to organize his troops, beginning with a new census.[2] Like the one taken at Sinai, the census would enroll all men over twenty years of age who could go to war, establish the size and military strength of each tribe, and provide data by which to allot present and future conquered lands.

Moses dispatched the tribal leaders and in two weeks they returned with their census tabulations. Judah's tribe was the largest, whereas the chastised Simeon's had dwindled to be the smallest. The total count of the men was 15,000,[3] a total population of 39,800. About 30,000 people had died during the 40-year march.[4]

The figures also confirmed that only six men survived who had been over twenty years of age when they left Egypt: Moses, Joshua, Caleb, Pagiel, and Aaron's sons, Eleazar and Ithamar. Many had died in the battles, but for most, as Moses said, "The hand of the LORD was against them, to destroy them from within the camp, until they all perished."[a]

*****

With the census completed, Moses' thoughts turned to himself and his own desire to stay alive.

That night he returned to the tabernacle to plead for himself. "I am broken, my God. When miracles are needed, mine are no longer the hands, the feet, the tongue for their accomplishment. You speak to me still, but as to one condemned. The love I have for You seems one-sided, not as a glass, but as a mirror. Did one mistake doom me?

"You had warned me, '*You shall not turn aside to the right or to the left … that it may be well with you, and that you may prolong your days in the land which you shall possess.*'[b] And although I rebelled, is the blame mine alone? From a glob of clay, You molded and baked me. Am I too hardened to be reshaped by You? I would pay a ransom or sacrifice twenty prized, unblemished animals, but You seem inflexible. I would even march as an underling in Your army to enter the glorious land of Canaan. If You will but yield."

God responded, "*Speak to Me no more of this matter.*"[c] Moses recalled God's words, "*I will be gracious to whom I will be gracious and will show compassion on whom I will show compassion,*"[d] Moses moaned.

God mercifully said, "*Go up to this mountain of Abarim* [Nebo], *and see the lands which I have given to the sons of Israel…. When you have seen it, you too shall be gathered to your people as Aaron your brother was.*"[e] After years of leading, Moses was to be denied the final conquest of Canaan. The glory of victory would rightfully go to God.

Moses would still be allowed to be the people's guardian for a while longer. He knew they needed a strong leader to succeed him, and he asked God to appoint a responsible man so that the congregation may not be like sheep which have no shepherd.[f]

There were two obvious candidates. Although God had spoken of both Caleb and Joshua as having *followed Him fully*,[g] He selected Joshua to be His captain. God told Moses to bring him before Eleazar, the high priest, and the congregation. When he did so, Moses placed his hand on Joshua and publicly commissioned him, ensuring that the congregation would follow him after Moses died.

*****

The strength of the army was now catalogued for the invasion. God promised Moses and Joshua that He would plan all of the strategies, send the ark and priests to lead, and provide the victories, if the Israelites devoted the time before they invaded Canaan in worship to Him. God said, *"Command the sons of Israel and say to them: 'You shall be careful to present ... My food for My offerings by fire ... at their appointed time.'"*[h] The priests must no longer omit any ritual.

The appointed times included all daily, weekly, and monthly sacrifices, and the specified feasts. Feasts would be joyful times, except for the solemn Atonement and the upcoming Passover.

God surprised Moses by announcing that the Israelites would observe the Passover in Canaan because they were to cross the Jordan and invade just before that celebration.

But even before that, God had unfinished business.

Endnotes

1. "six hundred" died from the plague = Bible numbers of 24,000/40=600.
2. "Census," Numbers, chapter 26.
3. Bible numbers of the men 601,730/40 = 15,000.
4. "... 30,000 died." Bible figures: one million two hundred thousand died/40=30,000. This information is found in the footnote for Numbers 26:5–51 in the Ryrie Bible.

Chapter 23

A Stain Stamped Out by Grace

"It's time to go to war against the Midianites!"[1] Moses announced to Joshua and the leaders. "This will be a different kind of war—a holy war. God is sending us to administer His vengeance, not to conquer their land. I will need two hundred warriors from each tribe to attack their army—one that is larger than ours. We shall have a distinct advantage; Phinehas, as the priestly representative, will lead the soldiers with the ark."

Joshua spoke to the leaders, "Advise your men. At sunup in two days, we will march south and east, back through the corner of Moab to Midian. Our scouts say that their cities lie east of the path we took coming up when we hugged the borders of Moab and Edom."

Moses said, "Remind the men that God has promised, *'Before all your people I will perform miracles which have not been produced in all the earth … for it is a fearful thing that I am going to perform with you.'*[a] Therefore, encourage the men to fight with assurance and kill every man."[b]

*****

Balaam did not return to Mesopotamia after being rewarded for making his cunning recommendation to Balak, but settled in a northern province of the land of Midian; he lived in the luxurious style aided by Balak's gifts. He felt secure under the protection of Reba, one of the kings of Midian, and was unaware that knowledge of his deceit had been circulated among the Hebrews. He had broken his bonds with God by his betrayal, and dialogues between them had ceased.

*****

As the Israelites approached the first Midianite city, surrounded by a four-foot-high wall, they saw the tops of flag-bearing standards in the midst of a group of milling soldiers. They stormed the city gates, climbed the walls, and engaged the enemy. They routed them with ease, killing every man. Scattered, dead hornets speckled the dust about the victims. The victorious army advanced to the next town, finding its defenders disorganized, weak, and an easy prey.

One Hebrew officer, moving from street to street, encountered a fleeing Balaam dressed in fine robes. The officer pursued and soon overtook him. Balaam desperately proffered a handful of gleaming jewels. "I am Balaam," he panted. "Do you not know me?" The officer thrust his sharp sword deep into Balaam's upper abdomen, severing the aorta.

As he withdrew his blade out of the slumping body, the wise soldier flared his nostrils in disgust. "How many hundreds of lives would have been spared had you just stayed home in Mesopotamia!"

*****

In two weeks, the army easily conquered the entire northern kingdom of the Midianites and slew the five kings of their tribes, including King Reba.

Moses went out to greet the victorious army but, observing the captives, was instantly angered. He turned on the captains: "Have you spared all the women? Behold, these caused the sons of Israel to trespass against the LORD so the plague was among the congregation. Now, therefore, kill every male among the little ones, and kill every woman who has known a man intimately. But all the girls who have not known a man intimately, spare for yourselves."[c]

Four nights later, while the captives were sleeping in their tents, the soldiers obediently carried out Moses' order, killing all male babies and non-virgins. Many short, muffled cries arose from the compound.

*****

The next morning, the slaughter of the night was revealed as the many bodies were heaped up for burial by civilians.

Hanniel, Machir, Kemuel, and Kenan walked out together among the bodies.

"How could Moses have ordered our soldiers to kill all those male babies?" snapped Kenan.

"Males must represent a future threat to our still-fragile faith," replied Machir. "If only we'd shown greater loyalty, God might have been more lenient toward our enemies."

"But don't kill all of those pretty, defenseless women," Kemuel said angrily. "God gave us a law that said that if a soldier in a foreign land [shall] *see among the captives a beautiful woman,* [he could] ... *take her as a wife.*[d] Moses overstepped God's law in ordering their massacre."

"Some of those were the same women who enticed our soldiers," said Hanniel. "All had to suffer for what a few did."

"But, Kemuel, God did spare the young girls," said Kenan.

"Don't fault Moses too much," Machir defended. "Didn't God tell him to *take full vengeance for the sons of Israel on the Midianites* [after which he] *will be gathered to* [his] *people?*[e] As Moses ordered the war, so he also ordered his own death."

"I was told that Moses did not sleep last night," Hanniel added. "Others heard him weeping and heard Zipporah's words of comfort from their tent. I would not wish that man's office on any other."

*****

Soon the time came to divide up the live booty. There were large numbers of sheep, cows, and donkeys, and also many virgins. God instructed Moses to divide them equally among the warriors and the remainder of the congregation, a practice that rewarded those who had stayed behind to provision the army and maintain the camp.

Then the captains approached Moses and Eleazar and told them that, in the Midian war, not one of their soldiers were killed. "In thanksgiving for God's protection … each soldier has brought all of the articles of gold he found: armlets and bracelets, signet rings, earrings, and necklaces[f] to you, worth over a thousand shekels of gold. Please accept them for God."

Moses looked at Eleazar, deeply moved. "Evidence of God's trustworthiness mounts before them." They took the gift and put it in the tabernacle's holy room as a memorial for the sons of Israel.[g]

*****

The soldiers' courage and generosity contrasted with the selfishness of the tribes of Reuben and Gad—cattlemen who had accumulated moderately large herds—and their attitude threatened the long-awaited invasion of Canaan.

One day, Samuel of Reuben and Kenan of Gad asked Moses if their cattle might remain in the lush pasturelands of Jazeer and Gilead, freeing their owners from the obligation of crossing the Jordan River and fighting the Canaanites. Moses was stunned by their proposal, counting on each of the twelve tribes to provide manpower for the invasion.[2]

"Shall your brothers go to war while you yourselves sit here?" Moses censured them. "Remember that your fathers turned away from following God when they discouraged the sons of Israel from going up against the Canaanites. In anger, God caused them to wander until that generation was consumed. Now, if you turn away, are you not concerned that He may again abandon us in the wilderness … and destroy all this people?"[h]

The two chagrined leaders countered with a compromise. They would begin to build up cities for their families and fenced areas for their cattle in Jazeer and Gilead, and then accompany their brothers across the Jordan into battle. "We will not return to our homes until every one of the sons of Israel has possessed his inheritance,"[i] promised Samuel.

Moses accepted, but changed the conditions; they must arm themselves and cross over the Jordan before their brothers, spearheading the invasion, or their inheritance would be denied them.[j] Hesitantly, they accepted this agreement.

The following day, Moses returned to Samuel and Kenan to assign them their specific lands east of the Jordan for their inheritance. Moses also gave some of the land east of the Jordan to half of the tribe of Hanniel's Manasseh because of their cattle holdings. Each tribe soon began to make plans to build more fortified cities and enlarge the existing ones on their land.

Endnotes

1. Midianite war: Numbers, chapter 31.
2. The request of Gad and Reuben to be excused from the attack is based on chapter 32 of Numbers.

Chapter 24

God's Command: Destroy Their Gods

Four weeks later, as the people continued their preparations, God called Moses to His tabernacle and gave a message for the people. "*The LORD, your God, is bringing you into a good land, a land of brooks of water, of fountains and springs, flowing forth in valleys and hills, a land of wheat and barley, of vines and fig trees and pomegranates, a land of olive oil and honey, a land where you shall eat food without scarcity, in which you shall not lack anything, a land whose stones are iron, and out of whose hills you can dig copper. When you have eaten and are satisfied, you shall bless the LORD, your God, for the good land He has given you.*"ᵃ

*****

When Moses informed his leaders of this, Joshua said, "As a spy, I walked north, west of the hill country. I almost reached the Sea of Chinnereth. The land was just as God relates to Moses. It will be quite a treasure for us to conquer. The people will realize that their struggles were worth it."

Caleb agreed.

Moses added, "Our conquest may be slow because God said, "*I will not drive them out before you in a single year, that the land may not become desolate, and the beasts of the field become too numerous for you.*ᶜ Once victorious, each Israelite, except for the Levites, will have his own parcel of land to own and use as he sees fit, and he will have freedom to choose his spouse and leisure activities. The people will govern their own cities. But as they enjoy His blessings, they should recognize Him as Provider and obey the unique laws made for their own good to assure their safety, peace, and joy. It will be another chance—almost another Garden of Eden."

*****

The next day Moses reminded them that although the land of Canaan was good, its occupants were not. He repeated God's warning first made at Sinai: *When the LORD your God shall bring you into* [Canaan] *… and deliver them before you … you shall utterly destroy them.*ᵈ [If not,] *then it shall come about that those whom you let remain of them will become as pricks in your eyes and* *thorns in your sides, and they shall trouble you in the land in which you live.ᵉ You shall utterly destroy all the places where the nations that you shall dispossess serve their gods, on the high mountains, and on the hills and under every green tree. And you shall tear down their altars and smash their sacred pillars and burn their Asherim with fire ... and you shall obliterate their [god's] name from that place."ᶠ*

*****

"We must not leave alive anything that breathes.ᵍ That is a tall order for our troops," said Kenan with a sigh.

Kemuel responded, "Killing people is one thing, but destroying their gods is another. Those gods might bring frightening revenge on us for our sacrilege."

Samuel said, "At Sinai, when God said that we should destroy their sacred images, I am told that our leaders voiced concern about doing so, fearing retribution from their gods. But Abidan quieted their fears by saying that when that time came, we can 'let God do the dirty work.'

"Now, we are at their doorstep and God plans no 'dirty work' Himself. We must do it ourselves. The axe is in our hands."

Hanniel added, "We must continue to impress on our soldiers that their gods are evil, competing gods that threaten our future."

Kemuel said, "I have talked with many of the soldiers of our tribe and some are becoming tired of war. Their motivation is dwindling."

"Some of the men who married the Midianite virgins are listening to them and are being softened by their female compassion. We must strike soon," said Samuel.

Then Moses added, "I will not be here for the invasion. That will be Joshua's task. Now, prepare your soldiers. If they are to destroy these places of worship, they must first discard their own idols, idols that many still cherish and worship."ʰ

Moses reminded them that God was bringing the Israelites to the land of Canaan to fulfill a longstanding promise. He quoted God, *"It is not for your righteousness or for the uprightness of your heart that you are going to possess their land; but it is because of the wickedness of these nations that the LORD your God is driving them out before you, in order to confirm the oath which the LORD swore to your fathers, to Abraham, Isaac, and Jacobⁱ... you are a stubborn people."ʲ*

The leaders silently filed out of the meeting. Their proud feelings of promised victory over the Canaanites had been tempered by God's personal rebuke—issued by Moses. Having also been called rebels, stiff-necked, obstinate, and now stubborn did not help as they continued to distance themselves from Moses.

*****

Moses and Joshua walked outside of the camping village to talk. As they walked, they came upon Samuel and Kenan, engaged in conversation.

Samuel asked Moses, "Should we become successful in the conquest of Canaan and, less likely, become His kingdom of priests, what do you think God will want us to do next?"

"God has never told me," answered Moses. "Abidan once related that God told Abraham that *in your* [descendants] *all the nations of the earth shall be blessed, because you obeyed My voice.*[k] God repeated to Jacob that *in* [his] *descendants shall all of the families of the earth be blessed.*[l] It seems that God's far-reaching blessings on others are dependent on our obedience and the example we set; quite a responsibility!"

"Moses, we have many good men among us, but for our nation to become what you suggest, we will need a different way, a special power in each of us— like the power that Caleb has … and that you have—to enable us," said Machir.

"But if we could change, Moses, how might we influence nearby nations— nations like Edom, Moab, and Ammon—who have been hostile toward us?" asked Kenan.

Moses said, "If we would prosper in peace, other nations may say of us, 'Surely this great nation is a wise and understanding people.' For what great nation is there that has a god so near to it as the Lord our God whenever we call on Him? Or what great nation is there that has statutes and judgments as righteous as this whole law, which I am setting before you today?[m] They might want what we have."

Moses paused, then said, "Our obedience may also usher in the awaited 'prophet like me, through whom God will speak'[n] as He promised to me years ago."

"That is quite a leap from here to what you foresee," said Joshua. "I will have a heavy burden. We must live lives different from our neighbors."

"Absolutely. Be strong and courageous, Joshua,"[b] ended Moses.

Chapter 25

Crucial Decision Time

Kemuel, Samuel, Machir, and Hanniel sat together a week later in the midafternoon. "God told Moses that there are witches and sorcerers living in Canaan," said Samuel, "casting spells in concert with the devil, even spiritualists who call up the dead and who divine the future."[a]

"I have dealt with one of them before. They frighten me," said Kemuel.

Hanniel said, "God said that He will drive out those peddlers of evil before us, protecting us."

"That is reassuring," said Machir. "In remembering some of God's promises, one is that someday He will send us a special man, one of our own countrymen, through whom He will speak His truths. And we must listen."

"We already have two men, Moses and now Joshua, through whom God sends us messages," said Kemuel.

"This man will be more than a leader," said Machir, "God refers to him as *a prophet*."[b]

Samuel nodded in assent. "I wonder if we will fear the prophet as we sometimes do God?"

"God said that we will be able to listen to him without fear," said Hanniel.

"How do you think he will be recognized?" asked Samuel.

"I guess that God will arrange that," said Hanniel. As he peered outside, Hanniel noticed a change in the weather.

*****

Moses also was watching from his tent as a barely visible darkness gathered over the northern horizon. Although the clouds probably would not reach them, rains upstream would raise the Jordan beyond the reported current flood stage. He summoned a driver and a captured chariot and set off to inspect the river.

While crossing the plains, they passed a group of Hebrew archers on the right, target shooting at a wooden figure mounted on a small, three-wheeled platform pulled by a galloping horse. Farther on, to their left, an officer was drilling a formation of soldiers.

Upon reaching the river's edge, Moses looked out at the swift current swirling past largely submerged but well-anchored thickets. "The flood waters are higher than the scouts reported," he observed. "Crossing will be difficult."

Nearby were two groups of men who were binding logs and small trees with dried reeds and hemp ropes. "What are you doing?" Moses asked.

"We have retrieved these logs from the river and are building rafts," replied one man. "It will be the only way for us to get across."

Moses became angry. "I do not know how God will arrange our crossing, but if He wanted us to build rafts, He would have ordered it. Cease your labors!"

"We will complete these two but build no more."

Moses sighed and turned toward home.

*****

On returning to camp he found Joshua, and the two men entered the tabernacle to present the flood problem to God. To their surprise, God's concerns focused mainly on assuring the people's worship in Canaan. He gave Moses words for the people.

*****

The next morning, Moses and Joshua called a meeting of Levites, selected soldiers and elders, tribal leaders, and a number of common people to share God's message. "Unlike the war against the Midianites, you men had some difficulty fighting your way into the lands of the Amorites and the Bashanites," said Moses. "This time, however, you will not be met by such an expectant army in Canaan. God has planted a great fear of you in them.

"Two weeks before Passover you are to cross over the river. The priests, carrying the ark, will lead you, followed by the soldiers, and then the people. As you cross, God says that somehow you must pick up a number of large stones from the riverbed and carry them with you, then move northwestward and climb into the hills until you reach two adjacent mountains, Gerizim and Ebal. At Mount Ebal, you should place the stones together in a row, coat them with lime, and the priests will copy all the words of God's new laws upon them. You will fit other stones together to form an altar, without cutting or shaping them with tools, and there we will perform peace and thanksgiving sacrifices."

Kemuel suggested, "We are craftsmen and can shape the stones to make a perfect altar."

"God says, '*if you wield your tool on* [the stones], *you will profane* [them],'"c said Moses. "These are temporary altars only."

He added, "You are to spend the first two weeks in concentrated worship of God, strengthening your faith, because He knows that the temptations ahead of you will be powerful."

The bachelor Kenan, spoke up, "Powerful indeed, Moses. I doubt that I can do all that God asks: killing or expelling the Canaanites, taking an axe to their gods, avoiding sexual temptations, worshiping only Him! We are fallible men, yet we are to be God's dispatched legions. If we should succeed, what do we get out of it?"

Moses answered, "God cares deeply for each of you and bountifully wants to bless you. If you honor His holiness[1] by faithfully maintaining your obedience, contritely practice forgiveness of sins by the surrogate animal sacrifices and honoring the Day of Atonement, that would assure the Lord's continued presence with you and endless blessings from Him.[d] You will receive rains in season, fruitful trees, and an abundance of food; protection from harmful beasts; the offspring of your body, of animals and herds will be blessed; enemies shall flee from you; you will lend and never have to borrow; He shall set you high above all other nations which He has made, and you shall be a consecrated people to the Lord, your God."[e]

"Moses," Kenan said, "since love is God's nature,[f] those blessings for our obedience flow freely from Him. But we often fail obedience. Although He is slow to anger, when we commit grave sins, we incur His righteous justice, His wrath. Our camp has experienced His wrath for golden calf; for Aaron's sons, desertion, threatening Moses and Aaron; for Cozbi's temple desecration, worshipping other gods, and persistent rebelliousness. Those are not simply lying, stealing, or gossiping that are covered over by our animal sacrifices. What will happen if we persist in disobedience?"

"Because He is jealous for you, God holds nothing back; His mission must succeed. If the people as a whole continue to disobey, [they will] suffer progressively in untold hardships; supernatural blessings would be exchanged for progressively severe curses," answered Moses. "All of the things He blesses He will curse.[2] In addition, unless you turn to Him, God will increasingly send disease, then consumption, drought, defeat, terror, and blindness on you; you would flee at the sound of a driven leaf;[g] your enemy will besiege you in all of your towns; …you and your sons and daughters will go into captivity, scattered from one end of the earth to the other, as He ultimately banishes them from Him into the hands of their enemies. But while you are gone, at least the land would enjoy its Sabbaths."[h]

Moses wiped the perspiration from his forehead. Replaying God's litany of curses for his wards was difficult.

"I want out of this horrible journey! I didn't ask for this!" said Kemuel.

"What an abhorrent future!" said Samuel. "I'll take Egypt again."

"Our choice is not 'follow God or leave'," said Machir. "The choice is 'be faithful to Him or suffer,' for we are eternally adopted."

"It seems that way," Moses said. "Today I have set before you life and death; choose life."[i]

"Is there no way out of this?" asked Kenan.

"There surely is, Kenan, and it is not difficult. God offered that [if] *you return to the* LORD *your God and obey Him with all your heart and soul … then the* LORD *your God will restore you from captivity, and have compassion on you, and will gather you again from all the peoples where the* LORD *your God has scattered you."[j]*

Hanniel said, "We must do whatever we can to prevent this censure."

Moses said to all, "Consider this covenant thoroughly before you agree. It is decision time for you, individually and collectively!"

Although a small, silent chorus mocked in unison, "I know what is right and wrong. He doesn't have to tell me."—the assembly finally pledged, on behalf of themselves and their tribes, obedience to all of God's conditions.

*****

Moses wrote the words of the covenant in his book, and he gave it to the high priest who would give it to the Levites to copy it on the stones. The priest would read it to the people every seventh year so that those who have not known would hear and learn to fear their God.

*****

In his tent later that day, Moses heard God telling him that the time for his death was approaching, and he should bring Joshua to Him.

Moses found Joshua inspecting a makeshift armory with Hanniel and Kemuel. "Come, Joshua, God wants to see you," Moses said. "And you two accompany us."

Moses said as they walked, "God knows that our men are more committed than their fathers were. However, He sees that future prosperity after the war will cause them to defect to other gods. Should that happen, God will finally *hide* [His] *face from them.*[k] The curses will begin."

"Moses, would God really do all of that?" Hanniel asked.

"That and more, Hanniel," Moses assured him. "God says that He would turn the land of Israel into *a burning waste, unsown, and unproductive … like the overthrow of Sodom and Gomorrah.*[l] Only God can see the horrible state to which mankind might sink, and He will do whatever He can to prevent that."

"What can we do?" asked Kemuel.

Moses said, "God's answer, '*Return to the* LORD *your God and obey Him with all your heart and soul.*'"[m]

Joshua added quickly, "I wish that God would, for once, impose obedience on us."

Hanniel said, "If God projects the future from our current thoughts and actions, can't we change? Joshua, you must keep us vigilant."

*****

They reached the gate, and only Moses and Joshua entered the courtyard.

God appeared before them as the cloud. "Joshua!" His name rolled out of the cloud, and Joshua's eyes widened. *"Be strong and courageous, for you shall give this people possession of the land, which I swore to their fathers to give them."*[n]

Joshua shivered when God pronounced his name. He thought, "I will be what he wants; I must succeed." As Joshua's doubts diminished and his spirit was lifted by God's words, Moses' shoulders sagged under the morsel of envy he harbored and of the finality of God's censure.

God had more for Moses to do. As a lasting legacy, God commissioned Moses to compose a song based on his understanding of this people and on insights given him by God. It would describe a future in which the Israelites would renounce Him. Memorized by the people as a rote melody, they and their descendants would sing it in years to come during times of discipline, so they might understand the cause of their plight and its only remedy.

*****

The Song of Moses.

"Give ear, O heavens, and let me speak," wrote Moses.

"Ascribe greatness of our God, righteous and upright is He.

"The Rock! His work is perfect.

"They have acted corruptly toward Him; they are not his children, but a perverse and crooked generation.

"Remember the days of old; ask your father and he will inform you when the Most High gave the nations their inheritance; the LORD's portion is His people, Jacob, His allowed inheritance.

"He found him in a desert land; the LORD alone guided him and there was no foreign god with him.

"He provided the best produce of the field; they would suck honey from the rocks, curds of cows, milk from the flock, fat of lambs and rams, the finest of the wheat, and the blood of grapes.

"But the people have acted corruptly toward God, even though He had greatly blessed them.

"They had made Him feel forsaken, jealous, provoked, and forgotten as they sacrificed to demons.

"A fire was kindled in His anger that burned to the bottom of the earth.

"He would destroy them and remove the memory of them except that their enemies would take credit for it saying, 'Our hand is triumphant, and the LORD has not done all of this.'

"His Israelites are a nation without sense; there is no understanding in them. How could one thousand of our soldiers be chased by one of their soldiers unless their Rock had sold them—given up on them?

"But after awhile, God will take vengeance on their enemies. '*Vengeance is Mine,*' He says.

"Finally, He will come to the Hebrews' aid. The LORD will have compassion on His servants, only when their strength is all gone.

"There is no god besides Me; it is I who put to death and give life.

"Rejoice, O nations, with His people because God Himself *will (ultimately) make the atonement for their land and His people.*"ᵇ

＊＊＊＊＊

When Moses shared the song with him, Joshua said, "That means that I and future leaders will have failed to become what God wanted His people to be. We will have squandered our divine mission."

Moses emphasized the last line with its surprising revelation, "Yes, but finally, in spite of their lack of repentance, God will still preserve His people, making the necessary payment for their sins Himself."

＊＊＊＊＊

Moses and Joshua came before the people the next morning to teach them the words to the song. "Take to your heart all you have heard today." Moses pleaded. "It is not an idle word for you; indeed, it is your life."ᴾ

After the song was concluded, Joshua led Moses away from the crowd. When they were alone, Joshua said, "Moses, how can we convince others that God is not a cruel tyrant, but a wise, forgiving, and, indeed, a loving God?"

"Soon that will be one of your most important tasks—and yours alone," said Moses. Then he added, "Do not let the people undermine your relationship with God as they have mine. Be strong and courageous in your trials and leadership. As for me, I am ready to die. My son is independent and can take care of Zipporah."

After dinner that night, Moses, Hanniel, and Machir visited Pagiel, who was weakened by a month-long illness. They sat around his bed, sharing stories and reminiscing. After a while, Moses looked at his friends affectionately and said, "God has told me that I must die soon, probably long before you, Pagiel. Death is still an unknown to me, even after watching many die. I wonder if we will become merely corpses in a grave, or will we be gathered to our people as Aaron was, perhaps deemed worthy to live with Him as Abraham does?"

Hanniel, turning to Moses, said, "You are worthy to live with God, Moses. As to why you must die and not be permitted even a sacrifice, the way I see it, God invested too much of Himself into you. You became almost a part of Him, and He could not tolerate even your brief defiance. Even by His great mercy, He could not let you live."

"You have been loyal to God all along," said Machir. "God even said that you were the most *faithful in all of* [His] *household.*[4] I believe He saw that the frustrations, failures, and perhaps a re-awakening pride, were allowing the devil[r] to draw your loyalties away. To save you, His great love will jealously and mercifully take you to Himself and away from evil."[5]

Pagiel said, "I share your concerns, Moses, but the hour fatigues me. Good night, all of you, and thank you for your visit."

Two days later, Pagiel died.

Endnotes

1. "His holiness," *Heaven*, Robert A. Petersen, Crossway, Wheaton IL, pg.176, (paraphrased)
2. "curses," Lev. 26, Deut. 28:15–68. These curses did occur in subsequent years during the reign of many evil Hebrew kings, the invasions of the Assyrians and Babylonians as depicted "in Joshua, Judges, Samuel and Kings" because they did not obey …" ending in total disaster." (Deuteronomy, Daily Study Bible Series, David Payne, Westminster Press, Philadelphia, pg. 155-157.)

Chapter 26

A Call from God

After Pagiel's funeral, Moses called the congregation together, unwilling to leave them with only dire prophecies, and gave them blessings[1] like those given by Isaac to Jacob[2] and by Jacob to his sons.[3]

Moses addressed each tribe individually, and it would be for the last time. He foresaw a different occupation and blessing for each tribe; there would be tribes of seamen and farmers, vintners and warriors, gardeners and judges, priests and miners; and he pictured one tribe, in particular, the Benjaminites, who would simply walk closely with God. The greatest blessings were given to the descendants of Joseph and Levi.

Moses ended his blessings with his arms stretched toward his people. "God rides the heavens to your help, and through the skies in His majesty. He drove out the enemy from before you. Blessed are you, O Israel; who is like you, a people saved by the LORD?"[a]

*****

Later that night, Moses drew his family around him. They knew God would call him in the morning. They spent the evening reminiscing about family activities, a few of Moses' challenges and successes, and God's graciousness toward him, while receiving Moses' blessings and hopes for their future. They found comfort in God's promises while some still prayed that He would rescind His judgment. Laughter mingled with tears.

In the morning, there were warm hugs and soft, tearful goodbyes. Moses' hand lingered in Zipporah's as their eyes held each other until the final moment.

The time came. At God's bidding, Moses left the plains of Moab and climbed Mount Nebo to the peak called Pisgah. His energy and vision were good despite his one hundred and twenty years. He had served God and the people well, seeking as his only reward to see his task through to the end. He had asked little for himself.

God met him on the mountain and showed him all of the land that was to become Israelite territory—from the northern border to the southern border, and all the way to the Great Sea. *"This is the land which I swore to Abraham,*

Isaac, and Jacob, saying, 'I will give it to your descendants,' God said to him. *"I have let you see it with your eyes, but you shall not go over there."*[b] The lingering waves of disappointment that had lapped at Moses were suddenly replaced by a surprising peace, a confident calm.

Moses died there, and after a struggle for his body between the devil and God's angel, Michael,[c] God Himself buried the body.[d] His family and the other Israelites searched but found no grave or body; there would be no gravestone to visit and revere. Moses was God's alone. The people grieved for Moses, weeping for him for thirty days. Then they turned to Joshua, listened to him, and obeyed his word.

Endnotes

1. "blessings," Deut. 33.
2. Isaac to Jacob, Gen. 27:27–29.
3. Jacob to his sons, Gen. 49.

Chapter 27

The Invasion

On the day following the end of the mourning period for Moses, God called Joshua to the tabernacle and said, *"Cross this Jordan, you and all this people, to the land which I am giving to them … No man will be able to stand before you, all the days of your life. Just as I have been with Moses, I will be with you; I will not fail you or forsake you.*

"Be strong and very courageous; be careful to do according to all the law which Moses My servant commanded you; do not turn from it to the right or to the left, so that you may have success wherever you go. This book of the law shall not depart from your mouth, but you shall meditate on it day and night, so that you may be careful to do according to all that is written in it; for then you will make your way prosperous, and then you will have success.

"Have I not commanded you? Be strong and courageous! Do not tremble or be dismayed, for the LORD *your God is with you wherever you go."*[a]

*****

As Joshua left the tabernacle, whatever self-doubts he had were ebbing away under God's encouragement and reassurance. Reading the book, thanks to Moses' tutelage, would keep those convictions going in him.

He dutifully assembled his leaders. "Tell all the people that we will cross the Jordan River in three days. Make your preparations, and you leaders of Reuben, Gad, and Manasseh will lead us over."[b]

The leaders of the three tribes responded as one, "We are ready." Then, to his surprise, they added, "Anyone who rebels against your command and does not obey your words shall be put to death."[c]

The people departed the plains of Moab and traveled to the vicinity of the raging Jordan, where they settled temporarily.

*****

On the morning of the second day, Ithamar entered the tent of his brother, Eleazar, the high priest, and his son, Phinehas. "The Levites grumble that we prepared no rafts to get them over this swollen river," Ithamar said. "They fear for their lives. You have assigned several of them to carry the ark into the water, but the torrents will carry them away!"

"*They* are concerned!" scoffed Eleazar. "It is I who must lead the whole procession, I who cannot swim, who must enter those swift currents first. I am fearful for my life! Let us go talk to Joshua."

They walked the twenty paces to Joshua's tent, where he was sitting on the floor reading the Book. "Come in," he said.

"Is this foolishness?" Eleazar asked Joshua. "We are supposed to try to wade across those strong waters. We might as well tiptoe into a crocodile's mouth. Even Moses would not have asked this of us. And besides, we no longer have Moses' miracle-working staff. It disappeared along with him."

"I also wish that we had his staff, but we don't," Joshua said. "God said that you, Eleazar, must lead with the ark, followed by the soldiers, then the people. God said that you are to walk into the water and that is all."

Phinehas cleared his throat. "Joshua, would it be all right if I tie a rope around my father's waist, to pull him to safety if things do not go well?"

"I suppose so," said Joshua. "God has told me to be courageous, and so must you be. This time we cannot fail Him."

At dawn on the third day, Joshua shouted the command, "Cross the Jordan!" Only after the Levites had taken up the ark and followed the priests toward the water's edge, with the mass of people following the specified distance behind them, did God speak to Joshua again. "*This day I will begin to exalt you in the sight of all Israel, that they may know that just as I* [was] *with Moses, I will be with you. You shall, moreover, command the priests who are carrying the ark of the covenant, saying, 'When you come to the edge of the waters of the Jordan, you shall stand still in the Jordan.'*"[d]

Joshua walked up to the priests and the Levites carrying the ark and pronounced God's message, adding that, "*When the soles of the feet of the priests who carry the ark of the LORD ... shall rest in the waters of the Jordan ...* [those waters] *shall be cut off, and the waters which are flowing down from above shall stand in one heap.*"[e]

Hesitantly, but obediently, Eleazar approached the lapping waters. He forced himself to place one foot into the water—and the waters above stopped! Those below flowed out toward the Salt Sea, leaving an empty riverbed that

God dried up with a fierce wind. The awe-stricken, yet relieved, priests and the Levites who carried the ark cautiously entered the riverbed. Following God's instructions, the priests stopped in the middle of the Jordan with the ark. Next walked an incredulous Kenan, looking upstream, then expectantly ahead as he led his armed tribe of Gad past the priests. He was encouraged as he saw no Canaanite soldiers on the far shore. Samuel, then Hanniel, followed with their tribes. Soon the remainder of the wary nation crossed over safely before them with their animals.

On the way through, one strong man from each tribe picked up a large stone from the river bottom and carried it out. Others collected smaller stones. When the last person had crossed and the priests joined them on the riverbank, the waters burst back into their accustomed channel.

The men carried the stones inland to their first camping spot at Gilgal, just east of Jericho, and near the mounts, Gerazim and Ebal, where they arranged them for the priests to write upon them.

On that day, the LORD exalted Joshua in the sight of all Israel so that they revered him, just as they had revered Moses all the days of his life.[f]

The next morning, the sentries announced to the camp that no enemy had moved against them. God indeed must have melted their resolve.

Three days later, God ordered Joshua to take flint knives and circumcise those males who had been born along the journey, for none had been circumcised since they left Egypt.[g] So Joshua and the priests did so, marking them irrevocably as God's covenant people.

Six days later, lambs were selected for Passover. In four more days, at a time when the men were also healed from the operations,[h] the lambs were to be killed and Passover celebrated.

The following day, the people ate the grains from the captured fields and made cakes of them, and God stopped the production of manna.

After the Feast of Unleavened Bread, the invasion began. Would they be able to conquer the Canaanites as they did the Aradites, the Amorites, and the Bashanites? The first objective was the high-walled, seemingly insurmountable city of Jericho.

*****

J. Roger Nelson, M.D.

Scripture References

CHAPTER 1

a. Ex. 1:10
b. Gen. 15:13
c. Ex. 12:40
d. Gen. 41:12
e. Gen. 22:17–18
f. Heb. 11:26
g. Deut. 3:11
h. Heb. 11:25
i. Ex. 2:12
j. Ex. 2:12
k. Ex. 2:15
l. Ex. 2:14
m. Heb. 11:27
n. Gen. 46:34
o. Gen. 25:1–2
p. Gen. 25:5–6
q. Ex. 15:26
r. Ex. 2:22, footnote
s. Ex. 18:4
t. Num. 12:3

CHAPTER 2

a. Ex. 1:22
b. Gen. 45:10
c. Gen. 14:19, 22

CHAPTER 3

a. Ex. 3:4
b. Ex. 3:4
c. Ex. 3:5
d. Ex. 3:6

e. Ex. 3:7–8
f. Ex. 3:10
g. Ex. 3:11
h. Ex. 3:12
i. Ex. 3:14
j. Ex. 3:16–17
k. Ex. 3:18
l. Ex. 3:20
m. Ex. 3:22
n. Ex. 4:3
o. Ex. 4:4
p. Ex. 4:6
q. Ex. 4:6
r. Ex. 4:9
s. Ex. 4:10
t. Ex. 4:11–12
u. Ex. 4:14–16
v. Ex. 4:18
w. Ex. 4:18
x. Ex. 4:22–23
y. Ex. 4:24
z. Ex. 4:25
aa. Ex. 4:27
bb. Ex. 15:20
cc. Ex. 3:14–15

CHAPTER 4

a. Ex. 5:1
b. Ex. 5:2
c. Ex. 5:3
d. Ex. 5:21
e. Ex. 5:22–23

J. Roger Nelson, M.D.

f. Ex. 6:1
g. Ex. 6:6–8
h. Ex. 6:12
i. Ex. 7:1
j. Ex. 7:3–5
k. Ex. 7:12
l. Ex. 7:22
m. Ex. 8:7
n. Ex. 8:8
o. Ex. 8:9
p. Ex. 8:10
q. Ex. 8:14
r. Ex. 2:2
s. Acts.7:20
t. Ex. 8:16
u. Ex. 8:19
v. Ex. 8:20–23
w. Ex. 8:27
x. Ex. 9:12
y. Ex. 9:25
z. Ex. 10:3–6
aa. Ex. 10:7
bb. Ex. 10:12
cc. Ex. 10:16–17
dd. Ex. 10:21
ee. Ex. 10:21
ff. Ex. 10:26
gg. Ex. 3:22; 12:35–36
hh. Ex. 11:3
ii. Ex. 4:22–23
jj. Ex. 12:8
kk. Ex. 12:17
ll. Ex. 12:15
mm. Ex. 11:6

nn. Ex. 11:7
oo. Ps. 78:49
pp. Ex. 12:30
qq. Ex. 12:12
rr. Ex. 12:32
ss. Ex. 14:8, (RSV)
tt. Gen. 15:14
uu. Ex. 12:40–41
vv. Ex. 12:38
ww. Ex. 13:2ff
xx. Lev. 5:11

CHAPTER 5
a. Deut. 1:10
b. Ex. 13:21
c. Ex. 13:21
d. Gen. 9:20–27
e. Gen. 9:25
f. Ex. 14:4
g. Ex. 14:2
h. Ex. 14:5
i. Ex. 14:11
j. Ex. 14:12
k. Ex. 14:13–14
l. Ex. 14:18
m. Ex. 14:15–16
n. Ex. 14:26
o. Ex. 14:28
p. Isa.19:18–25
q. Ex. 14:31
r. Ex. 15:10
s. Ex. 15:9
t. Ex. 15:2
u. Ex. 15:21

CHAPTER 6

a. Ex. 15:24
b. Ex. 15:26
c. Ex. 16:3
d. Ex. 16:4
d. Ex. 16:12
e. Ex. 16:4–5
f. Ex. 16:31
g. Ex. 16:28–29
h. Ex. 17:3
i. Ex. 17:2
j. Lev. 17:2
k. Lev. 17:7
l. Ex. 17:4
m. Ex. 17:5–6

CHAPTER 7

a. Ex. 17:15
b. Ex. 17:14, 16

CHAPTER 8

a. Deut. 1:2
b. Ex. 19:4–6
c. Ex. 19:8
d. Ex. 19:10–11
e. Ex. 19:13
f. Ex. 19:21
g. Ex. 20:1–17
h. Ex. 20:20
i. Ex. 20:23
j. Lev. 25:21
k. Ex. 23:17
l. Ex. 34:24

m. Ex. 23:22
n. Ezek.18:4
o. Ex. 24:7
p. Ex. 24:7
q. Ex. 24:8
r. Ex. 19:6
s. Ex. 24:10

CHAPTER 9

a. Ex. 24:12
b. Ex. 25:9; Heb. 8:5
c. Ex. 6:13, 26
d. Ex. 31:13–14
e. Ex. 31:18
f. Ex. 32:1
g. Ex. 32:2
h. Ex. 32:4
i. Ex. 32:5
j. Ex: 32:6, (TLB)
k. Ex. 32:7–8
l. Ex. 32:10
m. Ex. 32:12
n. Ex. 32:13, Gen. 12:7
o. Ex. 32:17
p. Ex. 32:18
q. Ex. 32:21
r. Ex. 32:24
s. Deut. 9:19–20
t. Ex. 32:19–20
t. Ex. 34:7
u. Ex. 32:26
v. Ex. 32:27
w. Ex. 20:3
y. Ex. 32:29

z. Ex. 32:30
aa. Ex. 33:5
bb. Ex. 33:15
cc. Ex. 33:17
dd. Ex. 33:13
ee. Ex. 33:18
ff. Ex. 33:19
gg. Ex. 33:19
hh. Ex. 33:23
ii. Deut. 9:18, (NIV)
jj. Ex. 34:6–7
kk. Ex. 34:9
ll. Ex. 34:10
mm. Ex. 34:10–14
nn. Ex. 34:27
oo. Ex. 34:30
pp. Ex. 34:6–7, paraphrased
qq. Ex. 34:6–7
rr. Deut. 32:15–18
ss. Deut. 4:24
tt. Deut. 6:15
uu. Ex. 23:28
vv. Ex. 19:5–6
ww. 2 Cor.3:13
xx. Num. 16:4

CHAPTER 10
a. Ex. 18:11
b. Ex. 18:18–23
c. Ex. 25:17
d. Ex. Chapter 28
e. Ex. 28:3
f. Ex. 28:35
g. Deut. 33:26

h. Ex. 40:34
i. Ex. 20:3
j. Lev. 1:1ff
k. Lev. 3:1ff
l. Lev. 4:1ff
m. Lev. 5:13
n. Lev. 17:11–14
o. Lev. 2:1ff

CHAPTER 11
a. Lev. 8:33
b. Ex. 29:36
c. Num. 7:10ff
d. Gen. 35:22
e. Gen. 34:1–31
f. Ex. 30:9
g. Lev. 10:4
h. Lev. 10:3
i. Lev. 10:6
j. Lev. 10:9
k. Num. 9:2
l. Ex. 12:8

CHAPTER 12
a. Lev. 25:23
b. Deut. 1:27

CHAPTER 13
a. Num. 1:1–46

CHAPTER 14

a. Deut. 6:14–15
b. Acts 7:43
c. Deut. 32:16
d. Num. 5:12–29
e. Deut. 17:13
f. Num. 6:1–21
g. Num. 8:5–22
h. Num. 8:23–26
i. Num. 6:24–25

CHAPTER 15

a. Jer. 2:6; Deut. 1:19
b. Num. 10:31
c. Num. 10:32
d. Deut. 1:6–8
e. Num. 4:20
f. Num. 4:15
g. Num. 10:35
h. Num. 10:36
i. Num. 11:1–3
j. Deut. 8:15
k. Num. 11:5–6
l. Num. 11:10
m. Num. 11:12
n. Num. 11:11–15
o. Num. 11:16–17
p. Num. 11:28
q. Num. 11:29
r. Num. 11:22
s. Num. 11:23
t. Num. 11:20
u. Num. 11:31–35
v. Num. 2:1; 4:1

w. Num. 12:2
x. Num. 12:6–8
y. Num. 12:9–10
z. Num. 12:12

CHAPTER 16

a. Num. 13:1
b. Num. 13:20
c. Num. 13:27
d. Deut. 1:29–31
e. Num. 13:30
f. Num. 13:33; Gen. 6:4
g. Num. 13:33
h. Deut. 1:27
i. Num. 14:3
j. Num. 14:4
k. Ex. 34:6–7
l. Heb. 11:26
m. Num. 14:7–9
n. Num. 14:11
o. Num. 14:12
p. Num. 14:15–16
q. Num. 14:18
r. Num. 14:19
s. Num. 14:20–23
s. Ex. 34:7
t. Num. 14:22
v. Num. 32:12
w. Num. 14:24
x. Num. 14:33, 35
y. Num. 32:12
z. Num. 14:24
aa. Deut. 1:41
bb. Deut. 1:42
cc. Is. 55:11, paraphrased

CHAPTER 17

a. Lev. 16:10
b. Ps. 106:15
c. Deut. 29:5
d. Num. 9:14
e. Num. 15:38–40
f. Num. 16:3
g. Num. 16:5-7
h. Num. 16:17
i. Num. 16:8-10
j. Num. 16:21
k. Num. 16:22
l. Num. 16:29–30
m. Num. 16:32
n. Num. 16:40
o. Num. 16:45
p. Num. 16:46
q. Num. 33:18–22
r. Deut. 2:1–3
s. Num. 33:25–28
t. Josh. 5:7
u. 1 Chron. 6:49
v. Num. 17:5
w. Num. 18:20
x. Num. 18:4
y. Num. 1:51; 18:7
z. Num. 17:13
aa. Num. 17:10
bb. Num. 21:1
cc. Num. 14:33, 35
dd. Deut. 2:7

CHAPTER 18

a. Num. 20:3–5
b. Num. 20:8
c. Num. 20:8
d. Num. 20:10
e. Num. 20:12
f. Deut. 4:21

CHAPTER 19

a. Deut. 2:3–5
b. Deut. 2:6–7
c. Gen. 35:10
d. Num. 20:14–17
e. Num. 20:18
f. Num. 20:19
g. Num. 20:24
h. Ps. 99:7
i. 1 Chron. 6:49
j. Mk.12:26–27
k. Num. 20:24
l. Num. 20:29
m. Ps. 90:3
n. Num. 21:1–3
o. Deut. 20:16–18
p. Deut. 7:2
q. Num. 21:3
r. Num. 21:5
s. Ex. 34:7
t. Num: 21:8
u. Deut. 2:9
v. Deut. 2:9 [Moab]; Deut. 2:19 [Ammon]
w. Ex. 15:14–16
x. Deut. 23:4
y. Num. 21:17–18
z. Deut. 2:19
aa. Gen. 15:16
bb. Deut. 2:24–25

cc. Deut. 2:34

dd. Deut. 3:2–3

ee. Num. 21:35

CHAPTER 20

a. Gen. 13:10

b. Gen. 19:24; Deut. 29:23

CHAPTER 21

a. Deut. 2:19

b. Num. 22:5–6

c. Num. 22:12

d. Num. 22:13

e. Num. 22:18

f. Num. 22:19

g. Num. 22:20

h. Jude v.11

i. Num. 22:28

j. Num. 22:29

k. Num. 22:30

l. Num. 22:30

m. Num. 22:34

n. Num. 22:35

o. Num. 22:38

p. Num. 23:19

q. Num. 23:22

r. Num. 23:10

s. Num. 23:11

t. Num. 23:12

u. Num. 23:17

v. Num. 24:9

w. Num. 23:25

x. Num. 23:27

y. Num. 24:2

z. Num. 24:6, paraphrase

aa. Num. 32:23–24

bb. Num. 24:11

cc. Num. 24:14

dd. Num. 24:17–20

ee. Num. 24:23

ff. Num. 24:25

gg. Ex. 34:12; 15–16

hh. Num. 25:4

ii. Ex. 24:7

jj. Num. 25:7f

CHAPTER 22

a. Deut. 2:15

b. Deut. 5:32–33

c. Deut. 3:26

d. Ex. 33:19

e. Num. 27:12–13

f. Num. 27:17

g. Num. 14:24

h. Num. 28:2

CHAPTER 23

a. Ex. 34:10

b. Deut. 20:13

c. Num. 31:17

d. Deut. 21:11

e. Num. 31:2

f. Num. 31:50

g. Num. 31:54

h. Num. 32:8–15

i. Num. 32:18

j. Josh. 4:12

CHAPTER 24
a. Deut. 8:7–10
b. Deut. 9:1
c. Ex. 23:29–30
d. Deut. 7:1–2
e. Num. 33:52–55
f. Deut. 12:2–3
g. Deut. 20:16
h. Amos 5:26; Acts 7:43
i. Deut. 9:4-5
j. Deut. 9:6
k. Gen. 22:18
l. Gen. 28:14
m. Deut. 4:6-8
n. Deut. 18:15-19
o. Josh. 1:6

CHAPTER 25
a. Deut. 18:9–14; Lev. 19:31
b. Deut. 18:15–19
c. Ex. 20:25
d. Deut. 28:1–14
e. Deut. 26:19
f. Deut. 7:7–14
g. Lev. 26:36
h. Lev. 26:34
i. Deut. 30:19
j. Deut. 30:1–3
k. Deut. 32:20
l. Deut. 29:23
m. Deut. 30:2
n. Josh. 1:6
o. Deut. 32:1–43; italics mine; abridged; a few of the phrases paraphrased

p. Deut. 32:47
q. Num. 12:7; Heb. 3:5
r. Jude v.9
s. Isa. 57:1–2

CHAPTER 26
a. Deut. 33:26–29
b. Deut. 34:4
c. Jude v.9
d. Deut. 34:6

CHAPTER 27
a. Josh. 1:2–9
b. Josh. 1:12–18
c. Josh. 1:17–18
d. Josh. 3:7–8
e. Josh. 3:9–13
f. Josh. 4:14
g. Josh. 5:2–5
h. Josh. 5:8

POSTSCRIPT
a. Hosea 6:4–11:11, rearranged—God speaking, 700 years later

Bibliography

Brodsky, Harold. "The Jordan, Symbol of Spiritual Transition." *Bible Review,* June 1992. Cheyne and Black, Encyclopedia Biblica. Wikipedia.

Crim, Keith ed., *Interpreter's Dictionary of the Bible, Supplementary Volume,* "Atonement," Nashville, Abingdon Press, 1991.

Crim, Keith ed., *Interpreter's Dictionary of the Bible, Supplementary Volume,* "Philistines," Nashville, Abingdon Press, 1991.

Daiches, David. *Moses: Man and His Vision.* Praeger Publishers, New York, 1975.

Edersheim, Alfred. *Bible History: Old Testament,* "Wanderings in the Wilderness," William B. Eerdmans Publishing Co., Grand Rapids, MI, 1949.

Edersheim, Alfred. *Bible History: Old Testament,* "The Exodus," William B. Eerdmans Publishing Co., Grand Rapids, MI, 1949.

Egypt: Gods of Ancient Egypt—*Egyptian Mythology* http://www.touregypt.net/gods1.htm

Gods and Mythology of Ancient Egypt http://www.touregypt.net/godsofegypt/

Horowitz, Edward MA., DRE. *How the Hebrew Language Grew,* KTAV Publishing House, 1960.

Josephus, Flavius. *The Antiquities of the Jews*, translated by William Whiston, A. M., Hendrickson Publishers, Peabody, Massachusetts, 1987, book 2, chapter 10.

Keller, Dr. Werner. *The Bible as History: A Confirmation of the Book of Books.* Translated by Dr. William Neil. New York. William Morrow, 1964.

Kurtz, J. H. *Offerings, Sacrifices and Worship in the Old Testament,* Hendrickson, Peabody, Mass., 1998.

Meyer, F.B. *Moses, The Servant of God.* London: Marshall, Morgan and Scott: 1960.

Neuser, Jacob. *The Mishnah, A New Translation.* "Pesahin 2:1, 2, 3" New Haven. Yale Univ. Press, 1988.

Packer, J.I. *Knowing God,* Intervarsity Press, Downer's Grove, IL 1973.

Palmer, Edward Henry. *Desert of the Exodus*, Vol. 1, Harper and Bros., New York, 1872.

Peck, M. Scott. *The Road Less Traveled, A New Psychology of Love. Traditional Values and Spiritual Growth.* New York, Simon and Schuster, 1978.

Raban, Avnr and Stieglitz, Tobert R. "The Sea Peoples and Their Contributions to Civilization." *Biblical Archeology Review,* Nov.-Dec. 1991.

Rawlinson, George. *Moses, His Life and Times,* Anson D.F. Randolph and Company, 1887, New York.

Reeves, Nicholas. "Pithom" and "Rameses," *Ancient Egypt: The Great Discoveries,* Thames and Hudson, New York, 2000.

Robertson, Reverend George W. Ph.D., senior minister, First Presbyterian Church (PCA), Augusta, Georgia.

Saenz-Badillos, Angel. "New Hebrew alphabet" *A History of the Hebrew Language*, Cambridge University Press, 1993.

Tenney, Merill. *The Zondervan Pictorial Encyclopedia of the Bible.* Grand Rapids, Michigan: Zondervan, 1975.

Velikovsky, Immanuel. *Ages in Chaos,* Vol. I., Garden City, NY, Doubleday, 1952.

Wood, Bryant G. "The Philistines Enter Canaan: Were They Egyptian Lackeys or Invading Conquerors?" *Biblical Archeology Review,* Nov.-Dec. 1991.

Made in the USA
Monee, IL
11 March 2024

54309710R00184